Alan Sillitoe

was born in 1928, and left school at fourteen to work in various factories until becoming an air traffic control assistant with the Ministry of Aircraft Production in 1945.

He enlisted in May 1946 into the RAFVR, and spent two years on active service in Malaya as a wireless operator. At the end of 1949 he was invalided out of the service with a hundred per cent disability pension.

He began writing, and lived for six years in France and Spain. His first stories were printed in the *Nottinghamshire Weekly Guardian*. In 1958 *Saturday Night and Sunday Morning* was published, and *The Loneliness of the Long Distance Runner*, which won the Hawthornden Prize for literature, came out the following year. Both these books were made into films.

Further works include *Key to the Door*, *The Ragman's Daughter* and *The General* (both also filmed), the *William Posters* trilogy, *A Start in Life*, *Raw Material*, *The Widower's Son* – as well as eight volumes of poetry, and *Nottinghamshire*, for which his son David took the photographs. His latest novels are *Her Victory*, *The Lost Flying Boat*, *Down from the Hill*, *Life Goes On*, *The Open Door*, *Last Loves* and *Leonard's War*. With his wife, Ruth Fainlight, he divides his time between London and a house in France.

Fiction
Saturday Night and
    Sunday Morning
The Loneliness of
    the Long Distance Runner
The General
Key to the Door
The Ragman's Daughter
The Death of William Posters
A Tree on Fire
Guzman, Go Home
A Start in Life
Travels in Nihilon
Raw Material
Men, Women and Children
The Flame of Life
The Widower's Son
The Storyteller
The Second Chance
    and Other Stories
Her Victory
The Lost Flying Boat
Down From the Hill
Life Goes On
Out of the Whirlpool
The Open Door
Last Loves
Leonard's War

Poetry
The Rats and Other Poems
A Falling Out of Love
    and Other Poems
Love in the Environs of
    Voronezh and Other Poems
Storm and Other Poems
Snow on the North Side
    of Lucifer
Sun Before Departure
Tides and Stone Walls
Collected Poems

Plays
All Citizens are Soldiers
    (with Ruth Fainlight)
Three Plays

Essays
Mountains and Caverns

For Children
The City Adventures of
    Marmalade Jim
Big John and the Stars
The Incredible Fencing Fleas
Marmalade Jim on the Farm
Marmalade Jim and the Fox

ALAN SILLITOE

Snowstop

Flamingo
An Imprint of HarperCollinsPublishers

Flamingo
An Imprint of HarperCollins*Publishers*
77–85 Fulham Palace Road,
Hammersmith, London W6 8JB

Published by Flamingo 1994
9 8 7 6 5 4 3 2 1

First published in Great Britain by
HarperCollins*Publishers* 1993

Author photograph by Brett Hambling 1992

ISBN 0 00 654717 6

Set in Lintron Sabon by
Rowland Phototypesetting Ltd
Bury St Edmunds, Suffolk

Printed in Great Britain by
HarperCollinsManufacturing Glasgow

For Roy Davids

O eloquent, just, and mighty death! Whom none could advise, thou hast persuaded; what none hath dared, thou hast done; and whom all the world hath flattered, thou hast cast out of the world and despised: thou hast drawn together all the far stretched greatness, all the pride, all the cruelty, and ambition of man, and covered it all over with these two narrow words, *Hic jacet*.

Sir Walter Raleigh

Part 1

ONE

One skid of the boot and he would be down, clutching at weak or non-existent straws. Well, Keith Blackwell didn't want to go down, so he would take care not to, but there was snowy ground ahead and a precipice to the right, and no other way to reach Beagle Tarn except twelve hundred feet up and four miles from Ullsridding.

Rohan jacket zipped against the wind, boots oiled and laced, he carried a small rucksack with an extra shirt, and changes of under-wear to be sparingly used, like the soldier he'd briefly been. In one sidepocket were packs of Kendal mint cake, plus a sportsman's flask of four-star brandy — more for show than sustenance, because you didn't booze while on the run. In the other compartment was a sheathed survival knife which could skin a rabbit or sharpen a pencil. Four crisp fifties folded into his wallet were equal to the pre-War five-pound note his father had said you should always carry on your person.

Keith was fed up with wheeler-dealing on the telephone, and semaphoring across halls of money. Sooner or later the eyes began to swizzle at dancing firefly figures, fingers numb from tapping keys yet loving the changing cash register screen as if the Mona Lisa was stripping off and getting dressed and stripping off again.

He had BMW'd three hundred miles up a motorway more perilous than the rocky gradient to starboard, threaded the needle of wall-like pantechnicons and the fragile mid-road barrier in a welter of oil and grey rain, all lights on and systems go but blinded each time by enveloping slush.

The stream ran dark green where he set up his tent, pegs into the black butter of the turf to hit rock after a few inches. When the night wind threw its weight, the dank covering came in on him, a swathe of stars clearer than ever above London winking on his effort to get it upright. He was surprised at such good temper because far less disturbance at home would have sent the blood racing with venom. The seemingly sackcloth roof dropped again at five but he ignored it and went healthily back to sleep, head near a gap by which to breathe the sweet air of the Lakes.

Unperturbed at the wreck of his billet, in spite of bruised fingers where the mallet had missed, he pulled his primus from the boot at dawn to boil water and fry eggs, starving hungry and shivering through the coat covering his pyjamas. Using the wing mirror, he shaved with his cut-throat, and took time to dress.

Next night the tent couldn't even fight back – no way. Forsaking lukewarm mush he ate at a hotel, and stayed, the room unheated, window frames rattling like dried bones. Less comforting to his spirit than the tent, dreams unrolled with a phantasmagoric idiocy matching the final mayhem at home.

Lacing his hood against cutting air that blew bad dreams clear, he went on slowly, boots leaving a trail of grey footprints in shallow snow. Sheep scrounged at tufted grass, no human near as he looked at the map because white had untraced the path. His lungs ached from cigarettes, ankles hard and burning from too many sedentary hours. At thirty-seven he needed a few days to get his wind, humping his pack into the hills to set up camp and daring man or beast to dislodge him. He drew a vector on the map and, adding a few degrees of variation, followed a course between low hills, knowing there would be water at the tarn, maybe rabbits to trap and birds to snare.

Summer or winter he would leave London, alone because you could trust no one but yourself, nor want better company, a joy to navigate up hill and over moors, treading blisters down and camping under the lee side of wall or hedge. The desolating question always came: What the hell am I doing here? Did I leave my cushy home for this? But by day three the sky was his roof, down to head level, or lifting so high that the space inspired him to move away from legal footpaths, going stealthily through all obstacles to break the carapace of office and home.

Beagle Tarn reflected the surrounding slopes, no smudge of cloud as he trained his Zeiss on a man wearing a checked shirt, crouching to place white fuel cakes under a kettle. A young woman hung a towel over the rear rope of the tent, then put on a khaki jacket as Keith came near. 'You're just in time for coffee. But you'll have to share my mug, because we've only got two.'

'No, thank you. I had buckets at breakfast.' Their openness

4

annoyed him, but he let down his pack and offered the flask.

Freckles dotted her pale skin when she smiled, her mug ready. 'Yes, please.'

He splashed some in. 'I came for the birdwatching' – but it didn't sound right, because what could you see in such a season?

'Gulls and ravens.' The man's face was gaunt above a reddish beard. 'Not much else at the moment. You might be lucky, though.'

'Cheers!' She swigged. 'Would you like a biscuit?'

The packet was under his nose, but he was tempted to destroy such amiable figures in the landscape, cut them up and feed the wildlife. What a treat for the newspapers. Another, after Gwen was found. But the headlines would be forgotten in a week. You had to kill by the score to be remembered. In any case, he liked the woman's smile, and the way loose breasts moved under her jacket. 'It's nice to see someone else in the wilderness.'

Her weedy boyfriend – though no doubt hardier than he looked – put powdered coffee into a mug. 'We love it up here in winter.'

The spoon was tiny, and Keith asked if he was a chemist.

'I'd earn a lot more if I was. We're teachers, up from Manchester.'

He wondered what they knew between them. His daughter was at boarding school, though he couldn't say the teachers were much better. In the old days you got what you paid for, but now you paid for what you got whether you liked it or not. 'I must be going. I have to be back in London by this evening.'

'Look after yourself,' the man said.

'You too. Take care.' He followed the same way down, fingers sliding icily over tufts of grass, which held him at boot length. Stupid to slip, but that would be one solution, unless he survived as a basket case. He brushed snow clear, laughter at being sent home in a plastic bag to Gwen who, before, would have had to care for him, no time then for her lover. 'You did it on purpose,' she would have ranted. 'You bastard. But it won't work. I'll go on doing just as I like.'

Oh, she would have shouted all right, knowing he wouldn't depart while Laura was young. But why had she let him find out? To leave a letter on the hall table, or an edge showing under her handbag, to have the telephone make its hungry canary call and whoever it was click off on hearing his man's voice, to call her from work and get no reply when she afterwards swore she had been in all day – such clues dropped in order to wake him to the fact that she was still alive. He did not appreciate it, as she knew he wouldn't, and when he asked who it was, as she knew he had to, she acted the caught-out wife and told him. She couldn't bear the pain of deception, wanted the luxury of an affair but also the comfort of his permission.

You weren't supposed to care these days, though she had told him knowing that the torment would send him to the wilderness for solace, leaving her a few days with her boy friend who was going to Australia for three weeks. When the man had gone she would be pleasant again, and say it was all over anyway, and she was sorry, so let's carry on where we left off, because it was undignified to let it bother you.

He recalled the affairs he had had since they were married, none of which he let her know about, mouth shut for ever on that score, for her sake, though she would never know it, and for his own sake because silence was more dignified, and also for the sake of any girl friend who, if she wasn't married, would be sooner or later. Not that it was such a long list, but by the time he had come to the end he found himself back at the car.

Laying his rucksack in the boot, he noted a feather of cloud, distant banks marshalled by a smart northeasterly. Perhaps she had always wished him dead when he went on such expeditions, abominating the stomach gripes he complained of if he didn't go. She couldn't understand the uncontrollable panic to escape the City, his work, even himself – not only her.

At the edge of the lake his boots sank into the sedge, and he did not know how long he stared, but looked at his watch on feeling hungry. The mottled water turned green, rags of cloud edging in, humidity weighty with the promised snow that he could smell in the half-gone afternoon.

The wind chewed his tousled, already greying hair, snapping at his ears that had always been too big, as if to make up in power for what his other senses lacked. The weather would be foul for days, all roads blocked if snow came down, which it surely would. A hole in the cloud was so fiercely ragged it seemed to have been made by an exploding shell. He wanted to reach home as quickly as it took to zip himself up, but the inside of the car was the nearest he could get, snug enough as he stared at a dashboard more complicated, he supposed, than that of a Spitfire. He could never go home again, anyway, and the chances of fixing up a tent in such a wind were zilch. Pegs into holes always went, square or round, you hammered them in regardless, trouble only if they wouldn't go in far enough.

He cruised the motorway on the middle lane, nothing at the moment to overtake, four o'clock and dark already, mint cake gluing to his palate. Below Stoke he might cut southeast through Burton and Leicester, then toss a pound for the Broads or the New Forest. A secretary he'd had fun with after office hours was married and lived near Bournemouth. 'If you're ever in the area,' she had said, 'here's my number,' which he thought only right after the Mappin & Webb gewgaw he had handed over at the wedding, the husband as dim as they came in thinking what a generous boss she had.

Two years had gone by, and he saw himself in a phone box that yobbos hadn't paralysed with boot and fist, rain as horizontal as in one of those Japanese prints framed in the hall at home, and hearing her say she didn't remember him or, hubby hovering, that they already had enough insurance. Or, on the other hand, that she was so happy he had thought of her, and would love to see him, but he would hear a baby screaming from some cosy alcove and say: 'I'm too far away, otherwise I would pop in for old times' sake. I just wanted to know how things stood.'

He veered off the motorway towards Macclesfield, and then beyond on one of England's high-up arterial lanes, lights twitching from farms away to left and right. The road to himself, he couldn't see the sky but felt it moiling overhead; killed the radio because unable to tolerate the senseless yacker of the disc jockey; better the silence his own brain concocted, which these days was more likely to surprise him than chitchat from the ether.

Blips of snow came into the zone of the headlamps, stuff already fallen shouldering the roadside. Speed made bends and crookbacks, but he took care, oh yes, care not to die or get mangled. He wondered how long he would survive if he holed himself up in the huge forest to the south, a wild man of the woods lost to the world, all ropes cut and nevermore for home.

In his seat of familiar calm, hands lightly at the wheel, he bombed up to seventy on straight bits while brakes shuddered at bends and

7

corners, more bash than on the motorway, a ballet of manoeuvring but always within the forward throw of main beams. Other cars were visible for miles, dip-flash-dip-flash, a corps of signals passing to the west but no one overtaking.

A grey piece detached itself from the snowy verge and hobbled into his track. The car swerved, bumper glancing the bank. Treadling the brakes he went bang, hit a sheep, left it dying behind, and what was worse there was maybe a scratch on his precious car. He fucking-helled, crunching over whitened gravel into a lay-by.

The beam of his heavy-duty Maglite went up and down the paint-work: a feather of wool stuck on the fender turned out not to be when he rubbed back to green with a rag. The cigarette shook at his lips, but it was hunger that unnerved, not fear, as he set a box on the bonnet, pulled out a stove, a pan, a packet of bacon and some bread.

The smell of a common fry-up dispelled the icy cold and, door open, sitting on the step, he looked for stars but saw none, overcast complete, heaven's roof poised to unleash its burden: I should have continued south on the M6, but here I am, instead of heading for Hampshire, set to steer across the ominous High Peak towards milder pastures in Norfolk.

A car some way behind stopped, turned on a descent to the left. The kettle steamed. Never at a loss for a brew, he looked for a teabag. Another car passed, then one from the opposite direction: the Peak District rush hour. What would he find at those mythical fields of ease, supposing they existed? Not knowing seemed the ulti-mate comfort, a state he had deserted home and London to attain. On the other hand, snowbound in Buxton or Bakewell on Saturday night was not his idea of adventure, and hellfire scalded his wrist as the kettle fell. A panic button of warning said he wouldn't be able to drive, but he filled his mug, regretting he couldn't hold his injured skin under a cold tap, and while the tea cooled walked ten yards to bury the hand under snow till the whole arm ached.

'Where are you going?'

He stayed calm at the disembodied voice.

'I'm only asking where you're going.'

'Why do you want to know?'

A girl came into the light. 'That old cow dropped me off in the

8

middle of nowhere after she told me she was going all the way to Buxton. I got frightened when she put a hand up my skirt. I told her what I thought of her, though, and now I'm stranded, unless I walk my bleeding feet off.'

TWO

The dubious gift of confetti across the windscreen did not promise a happy marriage to the weather, but rather reminded Aaron Jones that being caught driving in it must prove that earning a living was the most important activity of life. He spun the roundabout of London's Orbital and steered northerly, twigs from black branches standing out in sulphurous light. The elements had been anybody's guess, but such behaviour proved that guessing was, even at the best of times, a no-win game.

Solid trunks spaced along patches of January grass stood behind a mourning verge of mud splashed up by passing traffic. Toothache had gnawed since breakfast, top-left on a bed of infection making the rest feel rotten as well. He would have to endure till he got to the dentist, meanwhile recollecting that according to Napoleon the only two things certain in life were death and taxes, though Aaron could add a third which was toothache.

Similar pangs six months ago had receded when his cold got better, and he had gambled on it not coming back, hoping that mortality would cease its inch-like advance yet knowing that it could not. Life was hope, and hope nothing but ignorant optimism, though without hope existence would be untenable.

Last night a floorcloth around the moon prophesied rain, but he hoped to beat the two hundred miles home before wet or worse descended. Plastic rags in a tree waved white and purple to the east: the remains of daylight would clear him of London, and from then on he would set the compass, put the mind into overdrive, and let deca-miles pass while he dreamed of better climates.

The back seat and large boot were packed with books: books in boxes, books in plastic bags, books laid out on an old sleeping bag and on newspapers. With a Schimmelpenninck comfortably lit he gloated over a haul netted on his three-day trip through shops on the south coast. People from the north or abroad retired with their books. When they were unable to make their last shuffle along the promenade and died, the family threw them out as lumber for next to nothing.

A man stood by the roadside, thumb up for a lift, and Aaron stopped all thought till he got by: a young bloke with long hair and a rucksack at his feet, as if he had been there half the day. Can't do it. Want to be alone with my maunderings. Sorry, very sorry. He had given lots of lifts in his time, so maybe he had done his share.

Still, he felt vile for a couple of miles, then went back to the bargains he often brought home which more than paid for petrol and overnight bed and breakfast. As for his time, if you dealt in books there was no such measurement. Books glutted the second-hand shops, shelves and even tenpenny boxes spilling treasures, though the finds were less good than ten years ago because assiduous hunters nearer to the sources went fine-tooth combing for what seemed better to have than money, and could be traded if you knew the right place to pass them on to. Prices had gone up, but he could still find what he wanted, and looked forward to showing Baring-Gould's work on the Cévennes for a pound, which he'd put in the next catalogue for ten and have no bother to sell.

Such care and industry made a living, after dropping his laboratory job to earn money out of his lifelong enthusiasm for books. Early retirement pay had bought two houses knocked into one, at the end of a row in a mining village crumbling under Thatcher's fist, with a fine view of emerald hills from the front bedrooms. Change jobs in middle age and you end up with two lives for the price of one, because after his wife went away to train as a social worker and didn't come back, his sister Beryl moved in as a partner to his industrious dealings.

A juggernaut overtook on the dual carriageway, the splash at his windscreen swept aside by clean jets and chasing wipers. Ahead lay high flying galleons of cloud, while his rear-looking mirror showed menacing gaps of steely blue. Living from one bank statement to the next, he no longer worried about the significance of life, as he had to a tormenting degree when working for a salary. Existence had become too real to question why he was on earth. All he needed was faith in the engine which carried him from place to place, and trust in the knowledge that bookselling hurt no one. He kept Beryl and himself in moderate comfort, while anxiety and striving shut out self-indulgent doubts.

The car was a cocoon of odours: the whiff of cigar smoke, a damp overcoat, and the reek of books that had been too long in cellars, garden sheds, Wendy houses, garages or attics. Some nights he dreamed of going into the sort of Nissen barrack he had done national service in, full of such tomes he had never hoped to find, dusty from motes continually shed by cobwebs and age. Eyes bedazzled, hands clasped with uncertainty as to what shelf he would go to first. He opened a nineteenth-century volume of travels to find coloured plates botched beyond definition, and maps – of no country ever heard of – falling to pieces while unfolding.

Headlights made little difference to the road. A grey Cortina shot into the dimness, twin brakes reddening at an unexpected bend, so far out that a car from the other direction flashed him rabidly because it almost went into the hedge.

Aaron felt a tremor at the stomach. The road was a linear battle-field, every month the same number of people killed and maimed as in the Falklands War. All you could do was take advantage of your age and, like an old soldier, never die, treating each journey as the first, and whatever route you chose as *terra incognita*.

Before he left on any trip Beryl was as shaky as if he was going off to the underworld and might never come back, not strange for the kind of person she was. No husband had been good enough for her, and he had been good enough for no wife. Village people had taken it that they were married, not brother and sister – as well they might, because on their walks she held his hand, would kiss him on his return even before he got through the door. Well, she was always anxious. Why do women worry so much? Beryl did because he couldn't, so someone had to. The perfect couple, you might say. He would telephone in an hour when he turned off the main road, knowing she would be glad of that.

Stopped at a lay-by, he smelt snow in the air, a peculiar damp wind caressing the back of his head as he stood by the hedge hoping he was wrong. Beyond LBC range and the soothing rasp of Brian Hayes he buttoned onto long wave for a weather forecast whose threatening prognostications he hoped to foil.

Driving in the dark was a chore, but in winter you had no choice.

He envied those in their safe houses, lights glowing, homely smoke from the chimneys. Half-past four seemed like midnight, but he would call at one last shop, branching fifteen miles off the trunk road to Morford, where the woman who ran the place didn't pull down the shutters till six. He would be in plenty of time, but knew that whenever he made a special deviation he rarely found anything.

Every rule had its exception, and he could not afford to turn any chance down, uneasy when the turning came and he forked off like a somnambulist. He had no say in the matter, never had in anything of importance in his life. He had always liked it that way, because that was how things worked best and, reasoning in the process of an unreasonable act, he knew that what he had done must, happen what might, turn out to be right after all. Having come to the end of such zigzag cogitation, the toothache reasserted itself.

THREE

'Do you always curse like that?'

She came into the light, a young girl wearing a bomber jacket and carrying a portable radio, with dark bubbly hair and a snub-nose, haversack hanging loose. She laughed at the tall, slightly stooped man looking at her, a rare specimen with his short-back-and-sides haircut. Some blokes are born that way – though he seemed a bit harassed. 'You mean how *you* swore? I heard you effing and blinding like a trooper. "What a dirty-mouthed bastard," I said to myself. You went on so long I thought you'd never stop.'

'I suppose I did.'

She nodded at the handkerchief over his wrist. 'Did you trap your hand in the door?'

He wasn't happy at having her crash his privacy, damned if he would give her a lift. The only paradise in the world was to be on your own, encapsulated in a motor car and floating from point to point. Contact with people, even at parties and meetings, was hectic, nothing calm anywhere, the constant clatter of noise, pounding of torment. Yet he was known as being sociable, so had a right to claim at least that for himself.

He packed mug and stove into their wooden box, all things fitting neatly, and she was too interested in his painstaking movements to broach a request for help. 'Are you a sales rep?'

'Certainly not.' He pushed by her, carrying the box to the boot. When he started the car she banged on the window, as he had known she would, and he smiled at her disappointed face and shouted message of abuse coming through the Plexiglas. He got out intending to pound her head into a pulp of turnip and blood, leave her dying under a drift of snow. No one would pester him from then on, except his conscience which, belonging to him alone, would also take a long time to discover. Spread fingers patted the side of his trousers, then opened a door to the rear seats. 'Why didn't you ask properly?'

She was surprised as much as he at his change of mind. 'It's perishing out there.'

His expensive jacket and sweater had been like paper near Beagle Tarn. 'For a few miles, then.'

'My boy friend chucked me out.' She sniffed, hugging her slimline knickerpink trannie. 'He's earning two hundred quid a week as a chippie, and thought I was too expensive because I asked for a gin. Some people are born rotten. I winked at one of his mates, as well, but it didn't mean anything. Just a bit of fun. Anyway, you've got to show you're alive now and again, haven't you?' She patted the seat and looked around. 'It's a lovely car, though.'

Wheels crunched onto the road, tarmac buttered with light. 'Why didn't you go back home?'

Her laugh ended as a squeal. 'Home? What's one o' them? Oh yes, I used to hear people talking about such things. I wrote to Santa Claus asking for one at Christmas. I even saw one on telly once. It looked ever so funny.'

He drove as carefully with a hitchhiker in the car as he always had with Gwen and Laura. She didn't know how lucky she was, finding someone who also had no home.

'He didn't even like me to talk. Whenever I said anything he told me to shut up. *He* talked, though. It was all right for him to open his mouth. But I like to talk as well, and when I said so he told me to wrap up or he would belt me one. I can't think why I stuck him for so long. Three whole months, or near enough, but it felt like all my life. I would have left even if he hadn't chucked me out. He'd got no consideration.'

He thought she was being sick, but she was retching out tears, the indigestible food of her spirit, hands gripping the back of his seat. The words, harsh as ice, were in his throat to tell her to shut up as well, but he crushed such resemblance to her loutish boy friend, and passed a clutch of Kleenex from the glove box.

Why am I crying? she wondered, at the shock of getting a lift when she thought she had been left to die, a change for the better that would break any heart. Getting into such a car was like climbing into heaven: two soft seats to herself, a smell of fags and leather, and a stranger's breath.

Since he felt so superior to the poor waif he thought he was obliged to say something. 'Are you hungry?'

She wiped her face, and passed the remaining Kleenex as if they were too precious not to be used again.

'It's all right,' he said. 'I don't need them.'

She stuffed them in her pocket, and smiled. 'I'm starving, if you want to know.'

'You'll find some biscuits and a bar of chocolate in that box on the floor.' Her presence was disturbing, and he took a bend too sharply, treadling his way back onto a straight course. A rustle of paper as she burrowed around as if a hamster had got loose, her face in the rear mirror pale and oval, with regular features and dark untidy hair — nothing that a comb and a bar of soap wouldn't improve. He wondered what her body was like under the baggy clothes.

'I feel a bit sick, sitting in the back. That woman had me in front. We nearly hit a dead sheep on the road. But I'll be all right in a bit. Have you got a wireless in your car?'

He wanted to stop, throw her out for being such trouble. 'I have, but I won't put it on, if you don't mind. And don't you put yours on, either.'

'I can't. The batteries are dead. It costs about a fiver to buy new ones.'

'I like to concentrate on the road.' Seeing a space by a gate he drew in so that she could sit beside him. Her smell of sweat was not unpleasant. He sweated too when he walked. 'Is that better?'

'Thanks. I had to traipse bloody miles before I got a lift.'

He slipped into first and eased out. She ate the biscuits. 'I'll try not to get crumbs in your nice car.'

He stopped by the theatre in Buxton. 'Is this where you wanted to get to?'

'I suppose so.' She stared unmoving at the windscreen, while he lit a cigarette, seconds turning into minutes. 'What's your name?' he asked.

Shall I tell him? 'Eileen Chettle.'

A man wore a Russian-style fur hat, bundled up against the wind. When a bull terrier (though it had floppy ears) sniffed the wheel, a woman carrying a chain-lead called it away in a tone that threatened butchery if it didn't obey. After the mistake of picking her up he wanted to be on his own and get to where he didn't know where. 'I think you'd better go, then.'

Every time she swore she knew she shouldn't, but it just came out, and he looked the sort who didn't like women – or men, for that matter – who swore, which was why he was going to ditch her. 'The weather's bitter.'

'Is it?'

She wiped crumbs from her face. 'Don't you know?'

Make yourself at home, he ought to say, but resisted: an Englishman's car was his castle. 'Won't your parents be worried?'

'Parents?' He might as well have stuck a pin in her. 'Aren't they the funny people who live in homes? The man smokes a pipe, and the woman cooks cakes and boils eggs. They lean arm in arm at a window, looking at kids in the garden getting their clothes dirty? I've seen them on telly, as well.'

No wonder they threw her out.

'I never wanted to come here. Fucking Buxton! What a dump. The rubbish men must be on strike or they'd have taken it away. You should have left me on the moors, then death would have come quicker. Or I could have had breast o' mutton for breakfast.'

Open the door and prise her loose. 'Where do you want to go? Don't you have any idea?'

She couldn't move because her feet ached, only chilblains warming them, which hurt. 'I've got a sister in Norwich. She's married, but I expect she'll put me up for a night. I'll get a living-in job at a hotel if I can.'

'They're all closed in the winter. Do you know where Norwich is?'

'It's about a hundred miles away, isn't it? East, I suppose. I did geography for O Levels, but failed, didn't I? I liked it, though. I learned a lot. I'm just no good at passing exams. I know where Norwich is because Trevor, my boy friend, was in Borstal that way. Porridge in Norwich. He'd say it every day, the fat rat. Porridge makes you a rat, though, don't it?'

He wouldn't know. A scrap of fire ash flowed across the windscreen as if it had wings. The weather was about to deteriorate – or deter'iate, as he'd heard Kinnock say before the elocution mob got onto him. Eight o'clock, and a deadly night wind, two snowflakes hurrying after the first, a perfect time to put her out, though it was clearly impossible to do so in the middle of Buxton. In any case, whenever there was a time for something, that time was not yet. The engine went like a clock, wheels and steering, lights and wipers in unison. 'On your own head be it. I'm going in that direction for a while. But as soon as I alter course you'll have to get another lift, whatever the weather.'

She felt the big laugh inside her, then let it out as a sigh of relief. He noticed how much stronger her hands looked than Gwen's. She must have worked in a factory – or mill, where she came from.

'Fair enough.' She seemed even more lost than he was, but that was impossible. All he had for the moment was the familiar cocoon of the car to stop his spirit spreading so extensively into nothingness that he would lose all idea of himself. She had had no such glove around her on the moors, and for most of her life it had no doubt been the same, a sense of camping, nothing permanent, no certainty from one day or even hour to the next, her perceptions so dulled that she would live quite cheerfully within other people's limits as long as she had food, a roof, a coat. Being put out in the middle of Buxton hadn't really alarmed her, which was maybe why he had changed his mind and let her stay.

FOUR

We do not know what we look like till someone tells us, Sally thought. If they tell us what they see – which they won't, for fear of offending us, unless they want to offend, in which case what they say may be only half true – then so much the better, though even in friendship how can we know if it's true? We still have to match it with what we see in the mirror, and with what we already know of ourselves, which is just as likely to be distorted. Then again, does it matter what we – or I, anyway – look like? unless it has some connection to the inner temperament, then of course it matters a lot.

Now what made me think funny things like that? Driving at night, she supposed, and an ominous clarity in the decreasing light, hedges and walls in sharp detail, as if someone she very much would *not* like to see lurked behind each.

She changed gear to get uphill, flicking mainbeams in case some idiot came shearing round the elbow bend. Stanley had been away a fortnight, and being on your own disorientated the senses, till you got used to it, which she almost had, but driving to the airport to meet him brought a little of the feeling back.

The funniest of all was the notion that she wouldn't recognize him as he came out of the Customs, though they had been married eighteen years. She laughed, knowing she would spot the Antler luggage pulling at each arm, though the suit he would be wearing wouldn't much differentiate him from other Identikit businessmen. At one time he had tried to dress as much as he could in the young fogey style because he thought it impressed the men overseas, but she put a stop to that. When it came to the finer harmonies of dressing he hadn't much sense at all, so it was always she who packed his case and kitted him out for his trips, and even for their sojourns at the house in France, choosing ties and shirts and shoes and hoping he would remember which to wear with each. Her 'action man', she smiled, whenever he tried to object.

Yet what if she didn't in fact recognize him, and picked up someone who wasn't Stanley at all? A personable man so quick in understanding he would play up to it, and off they would blithely go to have fuck after fuck in an anonymous hotel room, so well matched as never to part. And Stanley would be greeted by the wife of the man *she* had gone with, so that their future would change as well.

She played the game for a while, working out even shadier permutations, certain areas so exciting she wobbled the steering and burred a hedge. Such luggage wasn't so uncommon but neither was Stanley. Nor, come to that, was she. He made the trip twice a year to inspect the firm's factories in the Far East, though thoughts like these hadn't popped into her mind before. They had been married so long that maybe similar thoughts, as he stared up the long sardine box of the aeroplane, bothered him as well, and he wondered whether or not he would know her as he strolled out of the Customs.

Life was funny when it wasn't boring. He had said: 'Don't meet me at the airport,' and she answered: 'All right, I won't,' knowing he expected her to be there nevertheless. 'I can get a train,' he said, 'and then the bus,' but the pathetic vision of him shifting two cases, raincoat and sundry bits from point to point burdened her heart, if only because he had met her when she flew back from Nice after her brother's accident.

Anyway, he earned enough to be brought home in style, deserved it after his nonstop nerve-racking wining and dining which was even more exhausting, he said, than the technical discussions. She once teased him about the 'bedding' as well, but he put on his especially hurt look (no less genuine for that, she hoped) saying that even if he was inclined that way there was neither time nor energy to indulge.

Nor, in any case, was it offered, everyone was so scared of Aids, condoms or not, apart from which he supposed that the managerial element he mixed with, well accustomed to reading character, and taking hints in response to theirs, did not, he went on, push matters onto that particular stage, and this was proved by his extreme randiness the minute they got into the house, which induced her, always before leaving to meet him at the airport, to put the tube of K-Y Jelly on the shelf above the Aga so that it would not be so icy, because though the house was blessed with full central heating the odd tucked-away corner could nevertheless be bracing. Another vital item was a bottle of Moët et Chandon in the fridge. Absence made the heart grow fonder, but after a fortnight hers had to be cosseted back into life for the reunion.

Sleet came against the windscreen as if a bag of sago had burst somewhere above the car. Cleared, it rattled again, changed to grated coconut, then settled to a steady veil of wet and grainy white. Hell! There were twenty miles to the motorway, and then, she supposed, an open run. Would the car cope? Chains for the wheels were rusting in the garage, and in any case they clattered so bothersomely when the roads were unexpectedly free.

Snow played hide-and-seek, here one mile and gone the next, which made her nervous, a bad sign. Luckily, she had taken the green Volvo, instead of her dented Mini, from the driveway. Except for a bit of rust around the left headlamp the Mini was the best little run-about she'd ever had, but on a night like this the Volvo was more the job, though Stanley was always fidgety when she drove it, and might even use his god-given right to get at the wheel in the airport car park.

She recalled their first meeting at a Youth Hostel in the Lakes, campers in the common room going over the day's walk with maps and Wainwright. Afterwards they played guessing each other's sign of the zodiac, and she tried eleven times with Stanley, till it was obvious he was her own.

'Brilliant,' he called. 'Sally's rumbled me at last.'

She was uneasy. 'What date, though?'

'The twentieth.' His face had caught the sun and the wind.

'You're joking.' He had to be. Or it was uncanny. But the chances weren't that remote, unless he had seen her card on the warden's desk, and was lying, or teasing. Sometimes on rush evenings a pile was left to be seen to later. She remembered the warden's sharp and weatherworn face, neither young nor old, and she couldn't imagine him in any other job, evil demon on the one hand, wonderful wizard on the far side of the face, she would never know which.

Stanley's dark hair was combed straight back, so could she trust him? She had been blonde. His sly smile suggested that she might fancy him. 'It's a lot of nonsense,' he said, not entirely motiveless.

She had been reckless on the trek at times, going over the rocks and scree like a goat, so thought she must be careful in this. 'What time of the day?'

'A quarter to four. My mother swore she heard the tea bell as I popped out.'

Other hostellers listened as if to a tale of suspense, and she knew she turned pale, hands clasped, hoping she was too young for a heart attack.

'Are you all right? Have I said something I shouldn't?'

'I'm tired,' she said, 'I suppose.'

'Aren't we all? What time were *you* born, then?'

Her father had noted in his diary, which he later showed with inane pride: '1545 hrs. Baby born. Seven and one half pounds. Call her Jane. No, Sally.'

'Oh, I don't really remember.'

From then on she tried to keep out of his way, but they were married in six months, drawn moth-like to the flame of zodiacal coincidence, which ever since had kept them in a firm matrimonial grip, or prevented them ever getting to know each other. Occasional quarrels were not enough, she thought, to justify his glib assertion that 'We disagree so much that we get on like a house on fire.' All the same, their meeting at the hostel seemed as fated as any arranged marriage, and they had either never been unhappy enough to separate, or at times too unhappy to separate, while the casualty rate among their friends had been so appalling that they knew no one who was married for the first time.

A black pantechnicon stalled in a bank of mist beyond some cottages, only one rear light visible and no blinkers going. She was so distracted by a man crossing the road that her car glanced the side of the stationary vehicle. To pull up would have left her half on the road, and being just over the summit of a slight rise there was the likelihood of cars overtaking at suicidal speed and crashing into hers. The only safety was in going on, wanting no argument with men who might be even more unpleasant because she was a woman. The barely audible glancing suggested that any damage was little more than superficial to both parties. She wondered in fact whether any contact had been made at all, and that she hadn't imagined a touch of the car against the stalled and lurking monster.

Nevertheless, she was trembling, no lights anywhere but her own, snowed-up hedges like loaded camels by the roadside ready for the trip to some Samarra of the North Pole. The weather babble had not prepared her for a blizzard. Or maybe it had, for she had kept the radio on most of the day, but hadn't taken in the vital words. The flash of a bare tree frightened her more than the thickening carpet in front, though from confidence that the car would get her anywhere, she was afraid of becoming entombed.

Stuff and nonsense, she laughed, going back to baby language in a crisis. Trundle trundle great big teddy bear car, are you going very far? Far enough, on such a night, the engine sturdy and the dashboard bright. There were no lights in houses passed, dead walls side on to the road, and any that could be seen were as dim as if those inside already sat around a candle.

Snow made the world raw, sent everybody back to the cave age, and though kids might think it fun, all in all she did not like to be out, which was hilarious when you mulled on how the country seized up in six inches of snow. Even Mrs Thatcher's true-blue Britain hadn't solved that one, though you'd think it wouldn't be so difficult, with so many people on the dole.

Islands of snow, in which shores were indistinct and flattening at the glass, were pushed aside by wipers turning more and more sluggard. A corridor of winter trees dropped bomb pies from overweighted branches. Or the wind flicked them, hard to say what the hell in such an ambush, catapults at all angles turning the air to chaos.

Brakes on, the wheels locked, windscreen showing what she hardly dare drive into, feet controlled by the strutwires of instinct. A group of buildings dimly along the road, but could she slide the bumps that far? Lights called her on to keep going, play the feet and hands, piano and violin to win even a metre, a few rolls forward.

How safe the place was, good or bad, she couldn't know. It wouldn't have to matter, she had to weave along the snow, white woolly ruts building around the tyres. The gates came close, she grazed the post and then after more manoeuvring was in, following the PARKING sign and across the courtyard between two other vehicles forming the dead end of a white glove thrown down from she didn't know where.

FIVE

After setting out on the road Daniel never wanted to stop, though he hated driving at night, and therefore would like to do so as soon as practicable. The simplicities of life are all that matter, he mused, if only we can find them and keep them pure. The plan was to deliver the van in Coventry, and hope they would have a car to get him home by midnight. What, he smiled, could be purer than that?

The heater worked. He took off his cap and, bald head perspiring, managed a look at the mirror: pale thin face, bushy greying moustache. White-blue eyes blinked before returning to observe the road. As if there was a slow fire in the clouds, though he couldn't smell the smoke, a flake of grey came down like burnt paper, the remains of God's manifesto floating oddly into ashes. Too cold for snow, he had thought, but it wasn't. A few more became moisture, their weight bursting bounds to make runnels, a system of watery freelanes till he turned on the wipers to a cleanliness that was almost next to a God he couldn't afford to believe existed.

Leafless trees were tinselled with hoar frost. To look backwards and check that the cargo hadn't shifted would be perilous, even more so if a shadowy ice patch caused him to skid and jolt. The prime-timing mechanisms were fail-safe, they had said, but then they would say that, wouldn't they? 'We're professionals,' they smiled, 'none more so, by now.' He knew those icy smiles that meant death if you didn't take them seriously. 'We get what we need and we know what to pay for. The Libyans and the Czechs are the technological tops in the business.'

Danger was one of the simplicities of life right enough, pure and unadulterated on this leg of delivery, fail-safe never sufficiently safe no matter what they said. But the amount of time between him and Coventry was not hard to live with, two hours of over seven thousand seconds, each a possible full stop on the future. Which particular white-scorched second would it be? The purity of that speculation was also hard to beat, good for a sweat and a fairly wry smile on any part of the trip.

He would be back at his teacher's slog in the morning, you had better think so, someone else would drive the van to London or wherever, and he would be waiting to hear the radio squawk on about another pinprick of death and injury for the Cause in terms of *terrorist atrocity*, whereas he and all who so nobly fought knew that if there were enough of such attacks the elephant of oppression would eventually bleed to death and let them go their justified way to freedom and self-government.

Oil and grit coated the screen with a subtle paste, melted flakes not enough to take it off. Pressing the button to ease the squeaking wipers, no liquid shot out, connections to the bottle blocked. He slowed, not wanting to stop and wipe with the rag but, his prayer answered, more snow came, melting till he saw clearly again.

The van ran easily, maintaining the ruts, soothing rhythmical bumps under the treads. He had an easy score to keep, not like those clear-eyed heroes who sniped from blocks of flats or drove a laden car of mercurial juice to outpost or point of ambush. Mayhem was their purpose, and bloodshed their policy. If he looked in the mirror again his eyes might encounter the tactical success of visionary techni-colour.

More than the heater was making him sweat, more than the promise of a terrible explosion. Those who set bombs or fired Arma-lites had neither the imagination nor the intellect to appreciate the picture of reality they created. Reality for them was planning in cold blood and watching television, whereas for him the spectacle on the screen was no reality at all, his TV being reality itself.

He regretted that his courage wasn't tested directly, but even so, the load was itching his feet, and he wanted to speed up time, and be floating homewards with mission accomplished. If the police stopped him he would be locked up for twenty years, an aspect of the struggle he didn't care to think about, though how could anyone imagine that such material was carried in this ordinary van? Elation one minute, deadly fear the next, snow indicated a simplicity of life he felt little connection with, the van an impermeable boat taking him along a powder trail to destroy the villainous enemy. He would read about the attack in the common-room *Guardian*, salt tears

25

smarting his cheeks, and the exciting thumps of a heart that would never kill him.

He enjoyed using his courage and faculties in a lost cause, if so it was, because you could not be a hero if you won. If you strove too keenly for victory, success would elude you. You would become careless, make mistakes that would destroy the precision of action. The only way to erode the enemy and finally defeat him was to live from day to day, as if there could never be an end to the fight.

At school he spoke to the children about patriotism, and the comfortable virtue of loving your country. The English could not conceive of anyone born there wanting to destroy its tolerant sanctity, so it was a perfect arena for the oppressed to do their work in. The children listened quietly to his sermons because it was the only time he went into a rage if they disturbed him.

While he spoke he believed ardently, otherwise how could they? But when he went into action for the Cause he was equally in thrall, and had neither tears nor audience for that. He became part of a plan on receipt of a coded message, kept to it no matter how circumstances might turn against him, decisions from Brigade HQ seeming to have been his own.

Fate got him moving, luck pushed him through. He drifted along so as not to interfere with the issues his subconscious laid out, his subconscious being more familiar with the unadulterated simplicities of life. Trusting his subconscious was a way of testing himself, controlling a mind that might otherwise be careless, the one-time sloppy faculties that had led him in a pub to mouth the sentimental fact that he was proud of having had an Irish grandmother.

His wife joked about it when he told her, but he always took seriously what others laughed at. Two years later she fled for ever from the tight-packed darkness of his aura, a flight he had known to be inevitable because with her, after the first few months of telling their dreams, it had become as if every day they met for the first time, unable to reach that second day of familiar relaxation, though he had never stopped hoping it would become possible.

If they had attained that phase, and then split, he might have been less tormented by her memory. Or maybe not. He knew nothing except that he had never been able to replace anguish by love and peace, survival in such a situation being the hardest of all to achieve.

His senses became vague, he was unable to think clearly, and he only felt alive when motoring to a rendezvous in some lethal vehicle, thankful of his offhand remark in the pub when he wasn't to know that McGuinness stood by his elbow and would later talk to him about it.

Momentous events happen whether you want them to or not, for why else would you get into something so thoughtlessly? You could betray your mother, but not the grandmother whom you had never known, and who propelled you towards your destiny. A wonderful concept — destiny. Who would be born without one? There was no other way to explain such action except to say that you must have been born with one, and given such thoughts by the purity of white fleeing towards his windscreen and obliterating names on the signposts.

Maybe they would give him a few words of thanks, as if to a soldier like the rest of them, after he had struggled through, though there was no danger as long as he followed the map photocopied into his brain. The aptitudes required for the Cause fell into place and never abandoned him, and he was a harder man than to need praise, which was for children, as well he knew, just as hurry was for idiots. Intelligence must keep the passionate conviction under control, and you altered the course of history by combining the patience of the snail with the cunning of the fox.

Two cars had collided, tank traps to his direction, half obscured by steam and smoke from metal entrails. One driver battled with the steering to disentangle. Spinning wheels dug into the ruts, and help was needed to push.

Hearing shouts above the noise of his engine, he eased through the gap. At top speed the wiper blades performed too slowly to beat the blizzard-and-a-half, if ever he saw one, but he spat a curse at the pinkboned menacing fist in his rear mirror, and saw his way onwards. They could not know their luck, because any fool rounding the bend at fifty into the back of his van could send all of them heavenwards.

The engine laboured at thirty miles an hour, lace-curtain flakes descending, the air so fudged he got a window down and a towel of cold air lapped his cheek. A long pull of breath cleaned his lungs, but the damp chill set him shutting it out. To jack up speed would be to show a panic which was not part of him. As long as the tyres bit and the wipers went he would soon make up time.

He remembered childhood pictures, they were printed on the myriad snowflakes before being swept off the windscreen. His father came home from clerk's work at the bank and talked to his mother while six-year-old Daniel played on the floor with a long-armed crane, swinging the hook over redcoated soldiers on the crenellations of a wooden fort. His mother was crying, mutely so that he might not notice, and he didn't see his father again because he was sent to prison for taking other people's money. Then Daniel and his mother lived in rooms where there were no new toys because she worked in a shop and saved all the pennies so that he would stay at school and one day go to training college.

She stopped him playing with scabby street kids, and drummed him through one exam after another, treating him as harshly as if he were his father. Or she coddled him because he was part of herself and she wanted him to work where no temptation could ruin him, a pendulum which robbed him of knowing who he was till after she was dead from cancer at fifty.

Then came his marriage, at the beginning of which his wife told him that if you didn't dream you had no spiritual life, implying that you were an inferior person, and he loved her so much that even though he hardly ever dreamed (except for one terrible recurring nightmare which he would never be able to describe to anyone) he decided to make up dreams rather than have her think so little of him, so that at breakfast he would say: 'I dreamed I was smoking a big Havana cigar all night.' Or: 'I dreamed rain was pouring through the roof and saturating packets of banknotes.' Or: 'I went out to the car because I was being chased, and all the tyres were flat.' Or: 'I was walking through a forest on fire and didn't get hurt.'

'It's good you've started dreaming,' she said. 'I'm getting to know you a bit more.' Her dreams were no more or less vivid than the ones he fabricated, so that he wondered whether she wasn't making them up as well: 'I dreamed I met a tiger in a wheatfield and it chased me across a railway line where a train nearly ran over me.' Or: 'I was at a circus and an ape escaped from its cage and turned into a woman in tights, and then the tent fell in.' Or: 'I was in an aeroplane and the pilot said I am now going to peel off the roof so that you can see the stars.' She had one every morning, and he felt it a matter of honour to match them. When he ran out of dreams and used some of the early ones again, with slight variations, she didn't seem to notice. 'You have a rich dream life,' she said. 'That's nice.'

'It's only since I married you. You've done me a lot of good.' He kept a notebook at school in which to put down any ideas for dreams which came to him, tried to concoct one a day, but on good days made up two or three. The 'Dreambook' stayed in his desk because it would never do for Evelyn to find it, though if she did he would explain that they were notes of dreams he'd already told her, and he had written about them because — 'and forgive my vanity in saying this — I find them very interesting.'

But he still couldn't remember the dreams she really wanted to hear about, because they were the totally uncontrollable sort that controlled him, which vanished back into the swamp of his subconscious on opening his eyes every morning.

After a few months the stream of his imagination ran dry, and Evelyn also lapsed in the telling of her dreams — for reasons unknown to either of them. With little else to talk about, the marriage deteriorated into a contest of mutual insult and spite, and when that phase burned itself out there was nothing to hold them together.

A damburst of light from what seemed like an enormous furniture van flooded his eyes, a burning of pupils and orbs that forced him to drop gear but, as if the juggernaut needed to see from one county to the next, its driver flicked on reinforcements, one high-intensity beam after the other sweeping the way clean.

King of the road, the black pantechnicon trundled on, a bandstand blast of its klaxon responding to the squeak of terror from Daniel's horn as he expected the van to be struck along the edge like a box of matches. He swung clear in time, and the length of a lay-by sent him safe along a band of gravel.

He wanted to chase the vehicle, stop it somehow, and murder the driver. He might even know him: one of the dimwitted pig-ignorant kids now grown up whom he had laboured to educate and civilize. He cursed the driver because on the swerve Daniel had screamed in fear at the explosion he thought was inevitable, and now above the noise of the engines he imagined the driver and his mate or mates laughing at his panic, gleeful at what they had done, nothing in front but heaven's white light, a joke to last the rest of their shabby lives.

He had failed the test, except that he had survived and therefore had not, needed to steady himself with a couple of doubles, but the stench of his breath would tell them, and booze on active service was punishable by injury or worse, the rules stipulating nothing less than the whitest probity.

The engine was throaty, but healthy enough, yet gave a roar on him pressing the clutch, as if the plates needed looking at. He increased speed, hating the pestilence of swarming flakes sent to torment him alone.

Asking where Daddy had gone his mother told him: 'He's dead and buried.' If she had said only: 'He's dead,' he would have understood, but dead and *buried* showed his father in a coffin and never entirely dead, struggling in the dark and unable to breathe.

Ribbed snow lay where no car had made a mark. If they had, it was soon covered. The sides of the road could no longer be seen, though he glimpsed a tree, all but its head buried, cold arms and rags of white scurrying in the wind.

He couldn't tell her of his horror in case she thought him soft like his father. When she questioned him as to how he felt he knew she would like to hear about his terrifying worries, even if only to show that he loved her and was for ever part of her. But he had never talked to her openly, as afraid of her as if his father had been born again in him.

A scuffing along the belly made the van feel like a boat speeding through turbulent water, every mile saturating his underclothes with sweat. He crossed from rut to rut, sculpting new ones, a skidding zigzag yet staying afloat. She died because he had never spoken. Dig your own grave, and others fall in. She had fed him, bought his books and clothes, but she dug the grave, fell in first. She dug her own grave right from the start, ran from her family and was cast off because they were Catholic. After his Protestant father was sent to jail she went back to the Church, though never to her family. You didn't need to dig your own grave. Others would do it for you.

Wheels fought the deeper snow. He hadn't thought so gloomily on other trips, only by himself in his room, but when called to action he regained clear thinking, a purposeful alacrity. Maybe the snow was an intimation that he was going to die. Their intelligence section hadn't accounted for the weather, or the task was so urgent they knew they could rely on him to get the stuff through. But a white-out was different and, after a nervous unforeseen slewing across the road, a snowbank pulled him into a lay-by and wouldn't let go.

He jerked the van back and forth in its soft jaws, raced the engine, swore, banged the dashboard – and maligned God. Attacked by the impossible, he closed all systems, and sat a few minutes through the silence he imagined his father enduring in the coffin. He pulled painfully at his moustache so as to stay in the world and think, while a white veil covered the windscreen.

There was a light in the distance. He couldn't tell how far off, whether house or farm. He would shelter and use the telephone, though it seemed no longer a matter of getting through but of saving his life, so he fought his way along the road like a swimmer, bitter cold pushing wet and then icy against ankles and knees, abandoning an amount of explosive that, if touched off, would at the worst blow the empty road apart.

SIX

Eileen took a Michelin map from the glove box, its colours suffused by the light of his torch. 'I suppose we're heading for Bakewell?'

The car trundled under a railway bridge. 'That's right.'

A winding valley of snow caught in the mainbeam didn't like their attempt at straightening. 'I could buy a tart,' she said.

More traffic, so he dipped the headlights and slowed, put them on again, but again had to dip. He seemed to have been in the car for ever. In the office or at home he could go the regular time between meals, but when motoring he felt sick if he did not eat every hour or so. Every feeling should have been coloured and distorted by the fatal fracas at home, but it wasn't. He could forget for minutes at a time that it had happened, which made him happy and afraid in turn, a rhythm slowly changing him to a state of weary indifference. 'The shops will be closed,' he told her.

She supposed he didn't want to talk, but what the hell? 'When I was at school we put on plays.' He smiled at her embarrassment at having been to such a place. 'I liked acting, though. I got second prize one Christmas because I helped to stitch the clothes as well. My part wasn't big. All I had to do was run onto the stage with my hair flying and arms akimbo – that's what it said: arms akimbo! I thought I was supposed to be Dumbo the Elephant! – and then I had to shout at the top of my voice: "Fire! The place is burning down, and you'll all be killed if you don't leave by the nearest available exit!" That was my part. By the time I'd finished they'd all pushed by me, and I still stood there, as if I was sniffing the smoke. Then I ran off. It was a comedy, and because everybody laughed at me I got second prize.'

Snowflakes drove horizontally, ones and twos burning up into the beams like moths, drops of water on the windscreen tackled by the wipers. He was glad when she became too fascinated by the sight to talk. Then they ran in dozens, like soldiers on patrol searching out weak points along the runway of lights. 'I've always hated the stuff, even when I was a kid. Others loved it and ran out in it to play, shouting and squealing, as if it weren't cold. But I got chilblains, and hated it.'

Legions of flakes pelted in, the space in front shaped like a cone, the steering wheel at the narrow end. He made tracks along the whitened road, hard to see the edges or gauge the true lie of the camber. Caution was coated with anxiety as he slowed and hoped the tyres would grip. 'It's like a canal of milk,' she said. 'We should have brought our skis.'

'It's not thick enough.' Now he was glad of her soothing chat. Gwen would have implied that the weather was his fault, which in a way it would have been, since he had been aware of its advent before turning into the hills. 'But I forgot mine. Why didn't you bring yours?'

'They're at the cobblers,' she said, 'being soled and heeled.' Headlights burned from behind, so he slowed enough to let the car race on into the storm. 'The suicide club. The world's full of 'em, especially up North.' She took off her jacket. 'It's as warm as toast in here. I was going to learn to drive once, but my boy friend had to sell his car because he was on the rock.'

He thought of Gibraltar. 'The what?'

'The rock and roll – the dole. He only got twenty-five quid for it. A real old cronk, all rusty and no MOT. But he wouldn't teach me how to drive. I think he hated me. He didn't even want me to talk. He was bone idle, though. Even when he had a job he took the day off whenever he felt like it. He would sit all the time. When he wasn't sucking fags he was supping ale. And when he wasn't supping ale he was sucking fags. And when he wasn't doing both at the same time he was shouting at me. He was bored, I suppose. He didn't even take much notice of me when we went to bed.'

She wasn't thinking unless she was talking, so it would be unjust to condemn her to silence. As long as you encouraged her to speak you would know what was on her mind, such as it was, and in any case her patter could be quite amusing. The road forked without his noticing, or he went as if in a dream thinking it didn't matter. He could only go on, regardless of which blue-white sock of the land he went into, as long as the car kept its mobility. Navigating unknown country in darkness was like being at sea: the nose of the vehicle had to go with winds and currents, and you hoped it would sooner or later get you somewhere.

At a wide bend and steep hill three cars at different slants had been scattered by a black pantechnicon. Or, with lights on and exhaust steaming, they had failed to get up the skid-patch of the hill. He thought she was asleep, till she said: 'What's happened here, then?'

'You'd better start praying.' The sight of the sombre enormous van chilled him more than the snow, but he grinned it out of his psyche and winkled through a gap to begin a lone cavalry charge up the slope, bottom-gearing as he got higher, anxious to put distance between him and the enormous van, though not knowing particularly why, just a fear still lingering over the heart. There were more twists than had been apparent from below, a straight run to start with, but a sharp turning at the top.

She put her palms together. 'I'm good at praying, but only to myself.'

The car slid off course when he released the accelerator before a bend, a drift building up in the cutting, the top of a hill elusive and ever far away. 'If we get stuck it'll be for a long time.'

She looked at the perilous world unworrying. The car would lie banked up in silence, but they would have shelter from the icy wind, be warm in fact, eat from the yummy stocks somebody like him would have in the car. They would only have to wait until rescue came, sleeping or telling stories about their different lives (maybe he had a few funny jokes she hadn't come across) and hearing the radio now and again. A chap like him might not even bother her with sex. Trevor said that such blokes couldn't get it up, though most of the time Trevor hadn't been able to, and even when he had it was just bang-bang-bang and off to his pubs and car sales in Dreamland. You might as well sleep with the cat for what good it did.

The steering fought back as he played the circumference with his palms, wheels a slow zigzag. 'It's like a ballet,' she cried. 'I hope we don't have to get out and push.'

He pleaded with the car to keep moving, sure they would die if forced to a stop. He wondered what might be wrong with that, but called out: 'Come on, get going!'

She threw her arm forward as if whipping a team of huskies: 'Mush! Mush!'

He pulled out of the swerve, iron-willing each roll of wheels to grip, but nothing would help if the powdery softness robbed them of bite and drifts built over them. The technically perfect car could balk at its chosen moment: brakes fail, power collapse, engine pack in, a tyre burst. Machinery was a god but you could never figure God's mind, only fight off stupid fears and let Him do the thinking, it made no difference anyway.

She locked into his system of alarm, but hope didn't die on seeing another bend in the headlights. To park would be sensible, before he was forced to. He was afraid of skidding back or being whammed by a farmer's Range Rover coming blithely up at top speed. He would take a chance, and not surrender to the snowstorm, maintaining twenty-odd miles an hour, too intent at the wash of snow to register the dashboard.

Going on into the bend he again felt the familiar swing at the back and the slewing in front. A relaxation of feet and hands went with it, treadling at the right points, wipers on fast, all systems in full option, engine sewing a line of calico. He moved out of the swing and around a wider bend, sweat crawling over the backs and knuckles of his hands. The road ran straight, faint tracks not yet filled.

He wanted to stop, make tea on the stove, put biscuits into the munching machine, but he didn't fancy the fight with spade and sacking to dig wheels out of the ruts. Hands shook as he passed the cigarettes. 'Light me one.'

'Can I smoke as well?'

No one else would have asked. He didn't need her any more, but if he stopped, and strangled her, and was then unable to get the car out of the lay-by, what a laugh that would be. He wondered where such notions came from. 'Please do. We've both earned it.'

She laughed like a child. He was thanking her, oh so fucking politely. Oh no, thank *you*. Who did he think he was? 'Lovely fags. Thanks.'

'That was a close call. Let's hope there won't be any more.'

Hot water burned her bladder, cold always making her want to piss pints, but it wasn't the time to speak. With Trevor she wouldn't wait for anything, why should she, though that mean beer-belly would never give way to anything she wanted no matter how next to nothing her request might be. This bloke was sweating blood to keep the car going, so she would cross her legs and keep her trap shut, otherwise he might chuck her out.

The road went fairly level, easy enough to take, but flakes thickened, falling as if someone was gleefully splitting eiderdowns above. How could that be, but it was. Maybe it wasn't his car, belonged to who he worked for, yet it seemed too good for that, though some firms did give such motors to their reps.

Globules on the warm windscreen were swept aside, like people, she thought, asking for money on the streets to buy a cob and a cup of tea. As for him, each turn of the wheels meant more time that would never come back, and he couldn't think that was anything but good.

SEVEN

Bowlegged fire irons supported a basket of logs warming the lounge of The White Cavalier Hotel. A huge copper bucket of wood stood in reserve, while a chimney hood big enough to suck up an ordinary room drew out the smoke. The fireplace was backed by a wall of small bricks that had once been red, Aaron surmised, spreading his large hands towards the heat. Most were now fairly blackened, but the pattern of mortar was plain.

Beryl had given him top marks for common sense when he had telephoned that he was stranded for the night, but the news she had passed on in return was not good, suggesting that his career as a bookdealer and manuscript merchant might be over. He didn't care to think about it, after escaping the peril of being iglooed up for as long as nobody could tell.

A man whom he supposed to be the proprietor came down the stairs. He was short, with a solid girth, the jacket of his pinstriped suit showing a waistcoat half undone. He had a healthy spherical face with narrow eyes, large ears, and a grin that most of the time he didn't know how to turn off, though the expression may have been more from nervousness than humour, showing teeth so even they could hardly have been his own. Thick ginger hair was swept back over a broad head, and after buttoning his waistcoat with deft fingers he picked the cellophane off a small cigar and began to smoke.

Ivy plants and aspidistras grew from plain terracotta pots along the corridor, and Aaron felt like a snowman standing at the reception desk to ask for a room. He knew the place wouldn't be cheap, but on a night like this there was no alternative to the bed-and-breakfast rate of twenty-five pounds, as he signed the ledger, and wrote his address in perfect block capitals, so slow about it that the landlord impatiently shook a small length of ash from his cigar.

'It's a nice old place.' Aaron screwed the top back on his pen. A few inches had matted the road on driving into the courtyard towards the line of garages that had once been stables. So many outbuildings gave it the aspect of a hamlet which, when lit up, would draw benighted travellers from miles around.

'It is,' the landlord answered, 'if you know how to run it. Nineteenth century, it seems. And well preserved as well, much of it.'

On the lounge wall by a window was a peacock, with an enormous green grass brush of a tail speckled with royal-blue medallions on brown almond patches, the extremities of its fronds shivering due to a slight draught through the window fittings. The head was long, and deep blue wings joined the body like strongly hunched shoulders.

Aaron stood before it. 'What a wonderful specimen!'

'You like it?' Fred the landlord's chest expanded. 'So do I. I wouldn't part with it for what tea there's left in China. I don't think I've got anything I like better. Everybody comments on it. I got it years ago from an auction, for next to nothing. I don't suppose anybody knew what to do with such a thing, but I did. I thought of changing the name of the hotel to The Peacock, but it would have meant too much paperwork.'

Aaron looked at the bar through the doorway, with its plain chairs and tables, and the empty dining room opening off from the reception area. 'Are there many people in tonight?'

Fred grimaced, as if not caring to fraternize with a possible tax inspector. 'We do mini-breaks on some weekends. It's busier then, even in winter.'

To one side of the fire a wooden settle with plain arms set against the wall was padded with a fitted bolster of flower and acorn pattern. A bare bulb in the large fireplace lit up hooks and fire irons, a copper fender gleaming in front. By the settle was a small round table, and the armchair in which he sat. A dozen other tables were scattered about on a fitted carpet of deep marine blue peppered with small rosebuds. The walls were white, bordering on cream from generations of clay pipes and large fires.

What luxury to have a pot of coffee promptly served (albeit watery) and a plate of (tasteless) turkey sandwiches. The folded *Sun* and *Guardian* hadn't been opened, so he read both, having forgotten to buy a morning paper. Above the fireplace hung a large framed print of *The Great Western* in full steam and sail on a menacing green sea. Strange to see nautical pictures in an inn as far from the coast as you could get. At a seaside place the subject would probably be green fields and thatched cottages. A square-faced grandfather clock with superb Roman numerals chimed dully as if tuned not to disturb the tranquillity of the guests.

He felt grateful for this unsolicited break from reality, until morning when mechanical shovels would clear the road. Warmth and food powered his sense of wellbeing, life's little (and some not so little) anxieties seeping away.

Two people came into the lounge and he tried not to stare, despite the excuse of being stranded. Her face suggested an oriental mixture from centuries back, but quintessentially English features sometimes did, especially in women. Most evidence was in the eyes and the shape of her pale cheeks, an unusually small mouth and thin lips. Perhaps such faces had come over from Siberia before the island was snapped off from the mainland. She was about thirty, and while the man flopped wet and exhausted to the fire, she sat with a large black mock leather briefcase by her legs as if someone might manifest out of the wall and snatch it.

'Just our rotten luck.' The man's cap thrown violently into the hearth hissed on the hot bricks. He was about fifty, and bald, with a large florid face and downcurving wide lips, dressed in a checked pullover and a sports jacket, and wearing steel-framed spectacles. A row of coloured felt tips decorated the top of his lapel pocket like medal ribbons from some war of long ago.

'At least we didn't freeze to death.' She wore grey trousers and, when bending to take off her laced shoes, nondescript hair straggled over a thick Fair Isle sweater. Wet stockinged feet went towards the blaze. 'Only nearly. Some poor souls must have got stuck. It's like the Antarctic out there. I wouldn't like to be in their shoes.'

The man turned, unwillingly diverted from the fire. 'Why don't you go and rescue them, then? They'd appreciate it, I'm sure.'

Aaron put his newspaper down, to let them know that someone else was in the room. 'We've certainly found a nice little refuge, all the same.'

'Who the hell wants your opinion?' the man said to the flames, his only allies at the moment.

'I don't know, and I don't very much care,' Aaron replied, 'but if you want to know who's giving it, my name's Aaron Jones. Maybe we'll be stuck here for a week, in which case I hope you don't mind if I ask yours.'

He hudged even closer to the fire. 'Ask all you like.'

The woman pulled her woollen gloves off, stage by stage, as if at earlier times she had been used to dealing with far thinner ones. 'Nice to know you. I'm Jenny Groves, and I happen to be his secretary, of a sort, and for the time being anyway.'

'Tom Parsons, that's who *I* am.' He put out a hand, regretting his surliness. 'I thought I'd tell you before she called me Dracula. We've been cat-and-dogging it all the way up from London. Getting stuck and having to plough through half a bloody mile of icing sugar was the limit. I'm sorry if I was a bit sharpish just then, but the trudge wore me out. Even if I just stood in it I'd start to lose weight. I'm not a lad any more.'

True enough, Aaron agreed. 'I can recommend the coffee and sandwiches. The dining room won't be opening for meals, so I was told.'

Tom laughed. 'A pint of Greattorex's Bitter will warm me up more than the coffee and tea piss they serve people in these places.'

Curtains of white still fell beyond the window, a faint moan of wolf weather from the wolds of snow. Aaron thought it strange that a wall and a few squares of glass could protect the cosy parlour so completely from annihilation.

'When I was a nipper I ran around in plimsolls and no topcoat. Not even a bit of jersey on my back. Then I worked twenty years down the pit. Well' – his laugh was grating – 'at least down there I was warm and well enough shod.'

'Stop showing off,' Jenny said. 'You're wearing good shoes now, aren't you?' – which Aaron thought was unfair because it had nothing to do with what he was talking about.

You couldn't trust his humour, though. He was amiable one minute, brittle and offensive the next. 'I've got to be well shod nowadays. The lads wouldn't own a Union official as didn't have good elastic-sided boots on his feet. I'd go down the pit again any day, but they need me more at this job. Order me some sandwiches and a pint of jollop, love. I'm famished after that little struggle outside.'

She put her other foot towards the heat as if not able to bear the sensual comfort of warming two at the same time. 'Why don't you ask for it yourself? All you have to do is move your lips.'

His power lay in moody silence, in gesture, for he turned his bullocked shoulders to the fire, hands outspread, until she gave in, and walked out of the room. 'Get some supper for yourself as well,' he called after her. 'Secretary she's supposed to be! I've shit 'em — before breakfast.'

Aaron looked up from his reading. 'Perhaps she's tired after the trouble of getting here.'

Parsons yawned, worn out by his emotional power skirmish. 'Near half a mile we had to walk, the blizzard coming right at us, but I made her get behind me, and I took every inch of the blast. I'm not a brute. Still, I suppose you're right. But everything I ask her to do she does as if it's a hard grind and she's too good for it. Maybe I don't make allowances. You have to make more allowances than you did in the old days. Not that anybody ever made any for me.' He laughed like a good-tempered overgrown boy, hedgerow eyebrows moving up and down. 'Anyway, men and women's supposed to be equal these days, aren't they? I drove the car up from London, so I don't see why she shouldn't order me a pint and a few sandwiches.'

Jenny came back. 'They'll be here in ten minutes, Mr Parsons.'

He stood, arms extended, like a cat finding the radius of its physical limits. 'In the meantime I'll go to the back, for a you-know-what.'

'You've driven up from London?'

She nodded, a hand still on the briefcase. 'He nearly got us both killed once or twice.'

'It's not exactly motoring weather. I set out from the south coast this morning, and it got worse every mile.'

'It always does, summer or winter.' She gave a bitter smile. 'That's my experience.'

He puffed clouds of wellbeing from his Schimmelpenninck. 'You don't seem to like it. Sorry I can't offer a cigarette.'

'I like the smell of cigars. Do you?'

'I don't mind it,' he said. 'I smoke them.'

'I mean, like it up North?'

He laughed. 'I live there.'

'You weren't born there, though?'

'Well, no.'

'Nor me.' The conversation seemed to refresh her. 'I'm from Guildford, originally.'

'And I was born in Devizes.'

She drew her eyes along the titles in a tall mahogany glass-fronted bookcase containing antiquated volumes of the activities of the county hunt, dusty school classics from before the First World War, and a few battered copies of *Who's Who* and *Burke's Peerage*. 'I thought I caught a bit of the accent.'

He mentioned a couple of bookshops in Guildford which he had rummaged through. 'I can't afford not to, though it's so hard trying to park I'll give them a miss from now on. It took half an hour to get out of the place yesterday. But why do you live in the North if you dislike it so much?'

'Marriage, of course. Bloody marriage. My husband, as was, worked for an estate agent. Imagine trying to sell houses in a mining town! Then he left me. At least he hasn't gone off with another woman, I thought. Then I heard through the usual grapevine that he was living with my best friend. Funny I haven't heard from her for so long, I was beginning to tell myself.'

He noticed that she had jettisoned the wedding ring already. 'Life's like that.'

'How do you know?' she snapped.

Similar experience, he could have answered, cursing himself for making such a flippant remark. 'How do you know I don't?'

'Dunno, really. So then I got a job as a general dogsbody for the local Union branch. Then I sold our biggish house and bought one at the end of a row. Don't know why I'm telling you. You're not saying much about yourself.'

'I haven't had time.' He was annoyed at being attacked in such a way that he was unable to defend himself. She had obviously had much practice and experience, or she had been born that way. Then he was annoyed at being annoyed.

'It's because you're a man, I suppose.'

'If you believe that, you'll believe anything.'

Parsons came back. Knowing himself to be the centre of the world – wherever he was – put a light on his face that Aaron couldn't wish him free of. 'I thought I would never stop peeing. Didn't even know

I wanted to go. It was like the River Nile! It must be the bloody weather.'

A girl came in with a tray, and stood as if not knowing which of them to throw it at. 'Who wanted this, then?'

'Over here,' Jenny called.

Parsons lifted his arm, the immaculate cuff of a white shirt showing a gold link. 'I'm the starvo, my love.'

'I'm not your bleeding love. My name is Enid.' The mouth of her bony face was made smaller by forward-pushing teeth, though Aaron noted signs of a fine figure under her apron. Her puffed-up, copious hair was a glorious russet, as if a light shone from inside, so Parsons hoped she was nice enough to risk a joke. 'I thought you'd gone off to grow the wheat, and kill the turkey.'

Plate and pint mug clattered down. 'If I'd known we was going to be so busy I wouldn't have come in tonight. I could have been chewing pills with my boy friend. It would have been better than rotting in this cemetery.'

'Never mind, love, we can go back into the snow and have a nice time dying, if it'll make you happy. Give the lass fifty pence for her trouble,' he said to Jenny.

She opened her purse, souvenir of a holiday in Morocco with Raymond, and put the coin on the tray. Enid walked out, head tilted as if she had been insulted.

Parsons turned to Aaron. 'If anybody had given me a tanner at her age I would have thought it was my birthday. Not even a thank you. I suppose the little trollop's got so much in the bank she don't know what to do with it.' He rubbed his cheek with the gold ring as if it might bring her back in a better temper. 'Would you like some of this sandwich?' He offered it around, then sank half the pint and eliminated the supper as if it had strayed into his cleverly laid ambush.

EIGHT

It *would*, Alfred said to himself. It would, for all the good that could come of it.

Well, it would snow, wouldn't it? Something like this had to happen, on the journey of a lifetime.

Wouldn't it, then, you silly old so-and-so?

But the silly old – he could think of many things worse – was his eighty-year-old father, Percy Joseph, sitting beside him like a ventriloquist's rag-and-putty doll, as flocks of white came against the windscreen like horses at Aintree ridden by the cleverest jockeys in the world.

His poor old geriatric dad stared as if happiness hemmed him in and there was nothing to worry about. And so here he was, Alfred, taking the useless old bore to where he could die in peace and be no more bother.

A man such as himself, fifty last birthday, should not be beholden to this batty old chap who had gaffered him since birth and only stopped now that he drooled and forgot what he said from one minute to the next, though he sometimes came to and recalled in marvellous detail what *his* old so-and-so of a father had said when he was five years of age.

His eyes might not see much but he had wandering hands. 'I can't put up with it any longer,' Betty from next door said. 'I don't mind tidying the place up after him and giving him his dinner, but he puts his hands all over me when I'm standing at the stove cooking his stew. He touches me – well, you know, in all *them* places.'

Sexual harassment, wasn't that what they called it nowadays? 'I'll have a word with him.' His sigh would have blown down Parliament.

'I wish you would.'

'I'll tell him to put more time in on his garden. That'll give him something to take his mind off it.'

'Yes, do tell him. I try, but he don't do as I say.'

Well, he wouldn't, would he, because you're only the cleaning woman, aren't you? And why he should want to touch a fifty-year-old slag with five grown kids and a figure like a bag of Nutty Ashless God alone knows, though I suppose he thinks you're Joan Bakewell or somebody like that.

'Do you know, Father, I think I'll take you to see our Brian down in Bournemouth for a few days.'

Percy looked up from a topless dolly on Page Three, eyes glinting at the prospect of seeing some real ones on the beaches. 'I should like that. Bournemouth's a nice place, or so I've always heard.'

He leered, fingers already roaming. Alfred slapped them down. You had to be sorry. You might be like that yourself one day — though he hoped he'd be able to blow his brains out first — but at the moment he was a bit of a pest, causing so much bother when he needed every minute to organize the coming and going of his dozen lorries, keep them on the road every day so as to make the firm pay. Finding a woman willing to look after him had meant all sorts of trouble and expense, but now he had to be put away, helped to pack his suitcase for the longest weekend ever known in *his* lifetime.

He hadn't been senile while sorting his kit, because he thought he was going to see Brian. He imagined pivoting a telescope onto the beach — as if women sported nude in midwinter, and him not feeling the difference any more between hot and cold. His wavering hands indicated the snowflakes. 'Are we there already?'

'I think we're going to be stranded.'

'I love snow. We used to play in it when we was kids. We chucked it at each other till we couldn't feel our fingers. Do you know, Alfred, we used to put stones in the snowballs, or bits of coal. Caught each other a treat on the noddles. Gang against gang it was. Ah, you're only young once.'

Tell me another. Alfred glanced at him. He had been a pit engineer, a tall strong man, with five kids who no longer wanted to own him, and a wife who was dead and buried. Alfred recalled him in his domineering glory, a pain in the arse to everyone with his mixture of beer-swilling and womanizing when he had half the chance, and now there was the job of putting him out of the way because he could neither be looked after nor take care of himself. Brian was in Bournemouth, Ted was in Australia, Arthur was dead in a car smash, and Phil in Scotland was like the rest who wanted nothing to do with him. So he had to be boarded out, and wasn't going to Bournemouth at all, but Bognor, though he wouldn't know the difference once he was among the other geriatrics.

It was hard to say when they would get there, with this little lot coming down. He didn't relish getting stuck, because even though the old man might perish as quietly as a lamb, maybe he himself would go under as well, which wasn't on the cards at all if he could help it. They would have to stop at the next civilized outpost, and set off again in the morning. 'Are you cold, Father?' He changed gear, hoping to get up the hill. 'Cold, Dad?' he shouted.

'All right, don't break my ear-drum. I'm as warm as toast in here.'

You would be. No sense, no feeling.

'Are *you* cold, Alfred?'

The old bugger was normal again, which pressed on Alfred's heart and made him fit to weep. 'No, Father. I'm OK.'

'A bit o' weather makes me feel young again. I courted your mother when it was like this. Kisses warmed us both. The smell of her coat with melted snow on the cloth, and flakes of it on her lovely fair hair. You can't forget things such as that, not till the day after you're dead, Alfred. Her lips were cold, but her heart was hot and rosy. She had breath like strawberry leaves.'

'You've had a long life, Father.'

He touched his son's hand on the steering wheel, held on warmly. 'Not long enough, my old son. Anyway, I feel young still, don't you worry.'

He was relieved when the grip relaxed. I suppose everybody does, till they kick the bucket. Percy showed himself awake, to prove he hadn't been asleep, or inattentive, or in any way wandering. 'The cottages we lived in when we was young shared a pump, and I would take a bucket out at five in the morning to dip my head in before walking three miles to work. It livened me up no end.'

Alfred felt close enough to follow his thoughts, knew the great effort made by his father, who in turn sensed that Alfred had understood, so he laid his head back into a rest he reckoned he deserved because of the willpower used. Nobody was going to think him senile if he could help it.

Alfred saw lights, and the hotel sign. It wasn't safe to go any further. He turned into the courtyard of a posh-looking hostelry called The White Cavalier Hotel, making his own tracks and parking between a car and a van. What the hell there was – or had been, or would ever be – to laugh about in this wide world he would never know, but lugging your semi-crackpot of a dad from one end of the country to the other, a man you had loved as much as yourself and even more – and hated even worse, at times – was no joke at all. Tears came while saying: 'Come on, wake up, Father. We're here, for a while, anyway.'

NINE

'Send a St Bernard dog if I fall down and sprain a kneecap.' Eileen pantomimed a sluggish curving track towards the distant glimmer, nothing important in life except wanting to survive, a force buried deep enough to be undisturbed by any levity. 'I would drink its brandy, then send it back for more while I had a little zizz.'

'You'd die,' he shouted, finding her tone more acceptable when she was trying to be funny, 'from hypothermia.'

'Who's he when he's at home? One of them Latin doctors?' She clutched his hand. 'If I died I might wake up and live. I've been waiting all my life for that.'

What else she said the jealous wind took away. The cold went through his boots, a poultice of water against flesh. Her feet must be beyond stone, though at twenty years younger he supposed she felt yet didn't feel.

Steely-tipped dust stung his cheeks. She pulled him because the wind had gone mad. Let her think she was helping, but the foot-deep icy floss clutched her knees as they pushed a way to the door. Under the outside light he watched her bony face, deprived for generations, a phosphorous intensity in her visage that he might only witness again if they passed whatever was left of their lives together – a strange idea. Their faces close, he touched her cold lips with a finger, then she drew closer and they kissed, she holding him tight, both wondering why, even whether they had kissed at all in the bitter flurry of the wind.

Feet on fire and arms aching, she wanted shelter and warmth, drew apart and pulled the dopey sod on so's they wouldn't be all night in the deep freeze. It wasn't so bad for him with a warm coat and solid boots, but for her it was chronic – as she gave her best smile and hoped it would have some effect. Her fingers found the latch, and when she vanished before him he followed inside.

The flagstone corridor was bordered by dark panelling, beams crossing above. They shook off the snow by an umbrella stand and a rack for walking sticks and guns. 'Like two dogs!' She imagined a woolly-bully cuddle with an amiable beast, far from the snarling Rotties that Trevor had hoped to get into his furnished room.

The dyspeptic short-arse of a landlord asked what he could do for him, not looking at her, so that she felt like telling him to crawl up his own hole and die, except that the pong would kill everybody inside ten miles. He could see they were caught in the storm, Keith thought, lighting a cigarette. 'We'd better take a room, I suppose.'

'A double with bath will be forty pounds, sir.'

'Bank card all right?' Mr and Mrs Robinson would do in the book, though he couldn't think why it shot into his mind. Usually it was Smith.

'What about your luggage, sir?'

He put keys on the counter. 'It's outside, in the BMW. Have someone bring it in, and take it to our room.'

'I'm afraid I can't, sir.' Fred smoothed his waistcoat. 'Our chap hasn't come in tonight. Nor has anyone except the girl.' He nodded towards the window. 'You can see why.'

'I'm not blind.' He stilled his rage. 'Why don't *you* do it?'

'There's too much on, I'm afraid.' Fred realized the danger, seeing this face blazing like red mercury going up a thermometer, so he turned away thinking how hard a night it would be if more such types came in.

Eileen gargoyled her features, zipping up her jacket. 'Don't bother. I'll go.'

If she wanted to pay him back for the ride it would be churlish to stop her. 'Are you sure?'

'No sweat.' A score of solid and heavy keys fitted the grapple of her fingers. 'I said so, didn't I?'

'There's a small brown case in the boot. Just get that.'

Their inward track was smoothed into yeti hollows of white between door and car. Head down, she pushed her shoulder against the malign force. Overhead a big door stopped her seeing the stars, someone up there holding it shut, a grizzly-bearded old bastard in his warm cottage whose starving slaves outside worked at wind machines, perishing everyone in the wilds of earth to let them know, as if they didn't already, that life was hard. She hated snow more

49

than anything, but whatever you hated was bound to come more often than anything else.

Clearing the keyhole saturated her fingers to deadness through woollen gloves, dreading to drop the key-bunch and not find it again, at which the grizzly-bearded old bastard up top would laugh his guts out till breakfast, if he ever laughed at anything, and if he ever had breakfast, since somebody like that would be scoffing all the time. Such a pack of keys would sink from their weight and not be found till the thaw, so many keys to unlock cars, houses, suitcases, but she had never opened anything in her life that belonged only to her, wouldn't mind such a key letting into a house all her own, though you had to unlock a dream first, and how much would that key weigh?

Eartips frozen, the boot lid sheltered her till the case was out. Hand dashed to feet and clutched the keys immediately when they dropped, fingers burnt and sticky as they went into her pocket. She pushed the sluggish case like a sledge to cut a channel through, effing and blinding at the sting of air, and her brittle left arm, wondering what he had in luggage that would be heavy even if it was empty. She had seen him sign the hotel book, curious as to what her name was for the night, didn't mind what she might be in for, because though he was a stranger the kiss was still on her lips and he wasn't bad-looking, it seemed she had known him weeks already, and fancied him a bit, licking the sting till it warmed her, blue with hunger, white with cold, black with a zest for adventure if she didn't peg out before getting to the door, which had never seemed as far off as any in her life, saturated as she was to the waist and bleeding to death inside but warmer and warmer in the drift that suddenly seemed taller than herself.

Keith stared into brandy the colour of amber and tasting like the one-star throw-outs of a supermarket decanted into a VSOP bottle, foul to that in his flask, but after fighting the storm it was good to sit down and be served by no less than the landlord himself. Such hostelries, as sham as they came and shamelessly expensive, at least kept the rabble at their Berni houses and in bed-and-breakfast bungalows.

'So *you* got stuck, as well?' An idiotic cheery face poked a finger towards the window. 'It's enough to freeze the balls off a brass monkey.'

Keith had never come across such a primate in his reading of natural history, though why dispute the point with someone who would certainly have lodged at a cheaper place had it not been for the blizzard. As it was, he would be so much out of pocket after being benighted at The White Cavalier that he would drink no lager for a month. 'I suppose it is.'

Tom's smile colonized the rest of his face, at this jumped-up smarm-chops whose nose was at the back of his head, barely deigning to pass a civil word in his direction. 'It would have had mine off, if I'd stayed out a minute longer, and I wouldn't like that to happen, because even at my age they still have their uses. In other words, I would positively miss 'em, though I suppose there's some as wouldn't.'

'I'm sure you would.' It was a feeble riposte, but he wanted to stay undisturbed, ruminating on a life that had led him into the cul-de-sac of an endless swamp. His ambition had been to acquire so much money that he no longer needed to work, no matter how hard he must work to achieve it, and in the last ten years he had put enough by to make it possible. To live, yet not to work, to meet only those people of his choice, and live in a climate where thoughts came out of yourself instead of bouncing from the mediocre minds of others. Ambition had driven, energy was fierce, brain deft, hand and eye in trim for every chance. Ninety thousand pounds a year was his salary, and shares brought in enough from the Cayman Islands to beef up his various accounts. Ingenuity pointed a way out of the tax trap, and using talent to the full generated more energy by the example it set, and the more energy there was in the country the more prosperity for everyone.

The foulest pig-brandy or not, it mellowed the steel in him, because wasn't it a fact that a country was like one big extended family? You had every right to relax, much being permitted within it, and you did not abandon a good country for selfish reasons like avoiding the ubiquitous taxes. Or at least you should not, and no doubt he wouldn't, but he had to get out now because his passion had turned violent and ruined everything. He would go as soon as the snow cleared. Gwen wouldn't be found until the au pair returned from

Germany, so he had time to reach a place where he could not be brought back.

'The roads get blocked every year.' Tom wouldn't take silence for a put-down. 'Farms and villages are cut off, but this time it's a real clinker. You'd think the county council would be a bit more ready, wouldn't you? I sometimes don't know what we pay our rates and taxes for.' He wondered why he let himself complain before a shitbag yuppie-mug like him. The sweat he had doled out in his time on PAYE must have paved a good few roads and cleared the odd drain. Society was run for the common good: good for him, good for them, good for everybody, and you had better think that way, otherwise it was back into the trees, the undergrowth a tangle of Tory aspidistras.

Keith was unable to resist saying, though he smiled: 'I saw on the road that they had declared this area a Nuclear-Free Zone. It's a pity they can't do that with the snow as well.'

Jenny took out a little circular compact and tapped powder onto her face, hoping a heightened colour would improve her aspect on looking into the mirror. The toilets were clean, not like some on the way up from London. She stopped using make-up after Raymond left but, feeling at the bottom of her handbag, as if playing a game of lucky dip, fished some out and used it, didn't know why. Hard to know why she did anything the moment it was done. Her tights had become twisted, so she opened her slacks to adjust them.

The make-up burned, caked her skin so she wanted it off, skin as well for preference, her fingers would touch, find what was underneath and, knowing at last, start to live again. She wondered where he was, what he was doing, not even three years had rubbed out the wound of loss. The more rotten he was the more he was missed, but would he have burned for her if she had gone first?

Returning to the lounge in such a state, Tom would notice, and start in on his baby talk. She stood in the cold-floored corridor, her smile a crack down her cheeks that no make-up would obscure. By the back door she heard a thump on wood, the wind having hands as well as feet. Raymond was trying to get in. The blizzard was eating him alive, as if he were on fire out there. She would let him die – if only it was him. Maybe the snow would freshen her burning face.

The day before leaving he said: 'Whatever I do in my life you know

I shall always love you, Jenny, don't you?' And she had laughed: 'Of course I do, sweetheart,' and thought no more about it, as you often don't with someone you know you can't entirely trust, not even when he had gone, not for a year afterwards, by when she had soaped the ring of fidelity from her finger, not till the shock had become a normal condition, and she trawled through every second of that final day. She never knew why he had said something so unnecessary and cruel, unless it was to imprison her in eternal hatred.

Often in the morning, at the mirror, flesh on her bones turned sulphurous white, agony that her bones were rotting. Two people got married, joined by whatever it was called – so, maybe, love – in an offensive and defensive alliance to make existence in the world less arduous, but his betrayal had robbed her of peace for ever, destroyed all hope. Decisions came not by thought but instinct, turmoil making life unbearable and actions out of control. Perhaps that was real life at last.

Opening the door, a body fell against her legs, pushed by a blast that cleansed her face, cooled fire, caused her to laugh with surprise.

The living person, like a demented cat set free by the wind, reached for a shapelier object behind and kicked its dusty covering off, scattering flaps of dull white over the floor and walls. 'I couldn't undo the bleeding handle.' She swung her arms, red-raw hands out of her gloves and clapping. 'It's all right, I'm not a ghost, though I nearly turned into one. What are you doing here, anyway? I only went outside to fetch his luggage, and I expect he'll say it took me long enough.'

The case held her weight when she sat on it, lips at an angle of such resignation that Jenny was ashamed of her laugh. 'Are you all right?'

The pale but pleasant face emphasized a vein down her cheek. 'I'd better take his stuff in.'

Jenny bolted the door against the weather. 'He should have fetched it himself. Men are so bloody selfish.'

He had rescued her from the moor and brought her to this cosy place till the thaw let them go, so it was only right to fetch his case from the car. 'I'm not frightened at a bit of rough weather.' She rubbed her nose. 'All I need is a cold, though. It'd make my day.'

To take the case in was the least she could do for the poor girl. 'You should get yourself warm. Do you have a room here?'

Eileen pulled it from her. 'I'll give it to him, if you don't mind.'

Who wouldn't want a pat on the back for effort? 'Suit yourself.' It was mean to envy her reward, as to a dog after fetching a newspaper, the dog turning into a doormat at a smile of appreciation for having been allowed to become of no more significance than a rag to wipe some swine's car down. She saw it all, but couldn't think of how best to explain it to the exhausted girl, who walked into the cigar-smelling warmth as if she had brought the case from the South Pole.

The newspaper slipped from Aaron's fingers as he dozed. 'Would you like to see the room?' Keith asked her, the key tied to an oblong piece of bone swinging from his hand.

He sat as if with nowhere to go, though in such clothes he fitted into this sort of place. It was hard to be sure where *she* belonged, clad in her everyday gear, a mixture of Oxfam cast-offs and stuff from home not yet worn out. She nodded, hoping her smile was bright enough since it needed some force to put it there.

'You had better warm yourself before we go up.' He took a hand from the side of his face. 'Have a drink, and something to eat.'

Jenny made space by the fire, but there was plenty of room. Keith knew he ought to get into his car and drive on, but the weather hemmed him and all of them in. On the other hand there was justice in being unable to leave, after what he had done. He had betrayed Gwen many times and had been betrayed by her in turn, but neither of them could survive without loyalty, and had used betrayal as a weapon to destroy the other. What began as love had ended in murder, and he could expect neither pity nor forgiveness. The only fit response was to die, because to live on under such a burden of guilt and failure tortured his pride.

He pulled the heavy leather-backed chair across the floor as if it were cardboard. 'Sit down and dry yourself.' When she took her shoes off, the landlord looked as if she was plummeting the reputation of his hotel, for which shade across his sanctimonious mug she would have told him to drop dead if Keith hadn't been present.

He didn't even turn while asking: 'Bring a double whisky, and a plate of your best sandwiches.'

'Yes, sir.' Though Fred the landlord knew his place he would have liked a please or thank you with his orders. Business might be business but he didn't think much of the crew that had dropped in on him. The only gentleman guest, with the young tart he had obviously picked up off the road, hadn't got a by-your-leave or smile of gratitude in any corner of his vocabulary. Such types hadn't much altered since the old days when, as a lad of fourteen, he had cleaned the boots left outside their doors, and got his rabbit-arse kicked by the gaffer if each one didn't glow like the moon. Nowadays you neither buffed up their footwear nor slopped out their pisspots. You could hardly get a willing wench even to serve drinks, like that stuck-up bitch who sulked behind the bar because she couldn't go off to meet her gormless boy friend. You couldn't chuck them out these days, either, though he supposed he would be seeing the last of her soon, because they never stayed long. She even blamed him for the blizzard, as if he was God Almighty Himself who had whistled snowballs down from the sky.

TEN

Sally didn't know, nor would she ever, how the car got within range of the hotel. Her consciousness went into abeyance while fighting a way to the door, worrying more about the car being lost in a drift than Stanley feeling abandoned on not seeing her unreal smile at the airport. Values had swivelled false side up; he had become renewable while the metal of his favourite vehicle turned precious beyond all imagining, which was not the strangest notion that had lately got into her head.

She glanced into the lounge, glad not to be the only woman staying. Aaron smiled, and a young girl near the fire held the hand of a man who might have been her father, while another with a red face tilted his head in ecstasy (unless he was going into a fit), the liquid of a pint descending into the desert sands blocking his throat. The landlord, or maybe head waiter (if there was such a person in this place), who looked as if he also had downed more than one or two, gave her a key and pointed the way upstairs.

The carpets had been scuffed by myriad shoes, runners loose in places, and the only modern aspect about the corridor was a white light in a green frame saying FIRE EXIT above a door which probably landed you in a snowdrift twenty feet below if you were foolish enough to go through it. Fire would certainly be a glorious way for the fine old place to end its days, though not – she put the key in the door – while I'm in it.

Heat in the pipes was feeble, and thin curtains barely met, so anything like a bath could wait. A cold splash from the tap would clear her face of exhaustion, after which there was nothing to do but sleep, or read the Bible found in the drawer of the commode.

The bed sagged like a hammock, but how could she complain on such a night? Not knowing what to do – nor wanting to settle down, since it was only nine o'clock – she decided to take advantage of company in the lounge before the power cracked up and left them in squalid darkness. She could also phone a message to the airport telling Stanley where she was stranded, otherwise he would worry. Funny she hadn't thought of it before coming to her room, and even less funny to feel guilty, as if the blizzard was her fault, not knowing that the more money you paid the better forecast you got, as he had once joked.

A man in the hall needed the payphone more than she did, anxiety crushing his thin face. He leaned against the wall as if about to ask for mercy before letting the tears rush out.

Clutching the phone between cheek and shoulder, Daniel lit a cigarette, dropped the still-flaming match from shaking fingers and put his well-polished shoe on it. 'It's safe.' He was trying to talk so that no one else might hear. 'I left it about half a mile away.' He listened a few moments. 'What do you mean? Timed for what? I can't hear you. Timed for when? And primed for what, for Jesus Christ's sake? Eight o'clock, did you say?'

She speculated that he was an entertainer overdue for his performance, or the props he carried would be late for the opening scene, and he was getting it hot from someone in a warm house, generous with blame for a victim of the weather.

The voice rasped, the rhythm lifting in its bleak insistence that if the van did not get to its destination in a couple of hours an avalanche would bring darkness everlasting on him and anybody else who happened to be within a few hundred yards. 'So get back, and drive it out. Get on the road. Is that understood?' They wanted it by midnight, so that someone else could take the cargo to its place of devastation.

Operation Stromboli they called it, and strings on maps from point to point allowed for no hitch in the weather. Blood sweated down the inner linings of his stomach. 'I left it safe, and it's covered in snow. There's nothing I can do. It's an Act of God.'

'You're bigger than God,' he heard, 'or you had better be. So dig it out from under the white stuff, push it free, drive on, we're waiting. Get to work.'

Work is noble, his father had said, who had never worked, or so Daniel imagined he had heard in those days of no date.

'I'll do my utmost.'

'You'd better mean it.'

The receiver burned his dampened hand, and he put it down. Fight the blizzard, and you would disappear for ever. Forgive them, Lord, they knew not what they said. But they did, and if he didn't try they would kill him, so as a fillip to his morale he meditated on the joyful scene of destruction as the van went up, felt that lilt of the heart when, should the excitement be increased one more ratchet, the heart would cease to exist, as would the body which relied on it.

The back window showed him curtains of snow shaking into banks against the walls, oblong tombs where cars had been. In the lay-by his van would be indistinguishable from landscape, and a thermal suit would be necessary to walk on the moon of snow and search for it.

A car appeared, as if to deny notions of anyone venturing out, sepulchral engine sounding through the gale, slid towards the hotel door, stopped a few inches before the treat of metal-crunch against the wall. An overcoated wendego drudged across the headlights, regardless of the battery running down, and opened the other door, mouth calling yet silent in cross-hatching flakes.

Daniel looked on as at a theatre, at the big man cajoling, in the middle of an argument, or impatient because of the snow. He ran back to turn off the lights, a muffled door-slam, then he was pulling another person out, protecting him as if he were wounded, and planting him one foot before the other towards the inn door.

Daniel helped to get them in.

'Thank God,' Alfred said. 'I couldn't see a thing. That was a kindly action on your part. Thank you.'

He stood aside, hating the thank you while knowing he could never be thanked enough. 'What's wrong?'

'He's a bit frozen, that's all.' Nothing the sight of two shapely tits wouldn't cure. 'And he's tired. He's an old man.'

'You were lucky to get here.' Daniel felt light in the brain: Jamaica Inn, full of wreckers. Or is it The Laughing Cavalier? He spoke like the quiet schoolmaster again. 'I only just made it myself. I had to leave my van down the road.'

In the corridor Percy pushed them aside and walked on his own. 'I'm not so doddery, you cheeky pair of devils. Still on my pins, any road up. In the old days rough weather like this was ten times worse.' Emerging from the straitjacket of his overcoat he was tall enough to stare Daniel into evasion, steel blue to cold blue, knife to knife. 'Who's this damned lunatic? I wouldn't trust him an inch.'

The daft old card would insult anybody, after being fairly quiet all day. 'He's only a kind man trying to help us, Father.'

A framed hunting scene showed a Derbyshire pack taking the stone wall, close in up the emerald hillside, a man leaning on a gate to watch it out of sight. 'Steer clear of him, that's all I say.'

Alfred nudged, hard. 'Why don't you keep your stupid trap shut?'

Back in the world of the humanly vivified, touch cloth, press flesh, feeling nothing but worry and exhaustion, Daniel forgot the lethal package of his van. 'We could do with a glass of something hot, I think.'

Percy leaned against the wall. 'Are we there, Alfred?'

'Halfway house, Father, providing they've got a room for both of us.'

'I'll get some help,' Daniel said.

'No, don't bother.'

'It's no bother at all' – thinking how lucky a man he was to have his father with him in middle age.

'We'll manage.' The less people saw what a shameless old load he was carting around the better. Daniel offered his cigarettes, and Percy's hand reached out, the three of them lighting up like mates after a long journey back from the away-game. 'You're stranded as well, then?' Alfred said.

'Who isn't, in a place like this?' Two big soft boxing gloves held it fast. 'My green Commer got stuck in a drift.'

Percy's drooping fag straightened as his teeth took hold, an alert countenance shining back into the land of the living. 'We passed it, didn't we? Three bikers in their leathers doing a fandango. I rode a motorbike thirty years ago. I used to take you pillion, didn't I, Alfred? We often went to Mablethorpe. Even Llandudno once. Bloody good times, weren't they?'

Daniel, in his sweat of terror, could only think the stupid old grandad truly gaga, surreal images from his deliquescence floating in the icy fagsmoke. He joined in the son's dislike when the old man went on: 'Young 'uns have got the energy for doing a knees-up outside a Commer van in the snow. It's nowt to young lads. It looked a treat, though. I just caught a flash of them as we went by. Alfred didn't see. Well, he wouldn't, would he? All eyes on the road. He didn't want to prang with his dad in the car, did he?'

A loving reach for his son's cheek was driven away. 'Come on, let's get you inside.'

Pain in the brain, Daniel thought, as Percy's face bunched into a cry. Even I would treat him better – still longing for his own generous long-dead disgraced father dying by inches in his bury-box, the father his mother had robbed him of, having brought him up according to the rules of emotional predators.

Alfred's bullying of his father was humanly acted, out of a normal up and down life that time had warped. He clutched him, a fist in his armpit, which might have been painful, but it set him moving towards the reception counter. Waiting for the manager, he put an arm around him, then turned him roughly across the way and flopped him into a chair as if he were a ventriloquist's doll after an unsatisfactory performance.

'I want no drunks in here.' Fred's arm went out like a signpost. 'Blizzard or no damned blizzard.' His pink-dotted bow tie was a compass needle stuck at east-north-east, eyes shot with blood at rage unexplainable, jacket stained from a spilled drink.

'He's not drunk, you bloody toffee-nosed fool. He's all-in, can't you see? We want a room for the night.' The threatening arm drew back. 'Two beds in it. We'll be on our way first thing in the morning. And get us a couple of whiskies while you're about it. We're frozen stiff.'

Fred saw his mistake, too late to right it, but told himself: never apologize. The more battered his dignity the straighter his back became, though it was hidden somewhere in his short and corpulent body. And one for myself, he decided, on such a night, and with this bloody mob around my neck. 'Just sit in the lounge while I sort things out. How was I to know? You'd be surprised at the sorts we get in here.'

Nothing had ever been enough for Alfred, and such driving had unthreaded his self-control. 'He's my father, and he hasn't been drunk in his life. So get that into your aspirin brain.' His height and weight were something to thank his father for at least. If he didn't hit out he would lose all self-respect. A man works his guts to pieces running a transport business, and this whisky-nosed pugdog takes his father for a drunkard. The stance was of a panther ready for the leap: 'I'll rip you to pieces if you don't show him some respect. I'll break your china-pot head.'

Aaron stood up. Everybody existed on such a short fuse these days, ever ready to curse or lash out with boot and fist. In Bexhill, on opening his door in the parking place, he had accidentally touched the next car, and the sort of woman who in olden times might have welcomed the troops back from Dunkirk with cups of tea and a cream cracker, harangued him for not having respect for other people's property, so bloated with rage – and still ranting as he walked away – that if she'd had a gun he felt sure she would have killed him. 'That wouldn't be wise, because who would look after us if you did?'

The low tone, not unpleasant, dispelled Alfred's fit of wrath, though Aaron added: 'I'll give you a hand with him, if you like.'

Percy stood as straight as a soldier. 'I don't want any help, thank you very much. It's a shame though that a chap can't have forty winks without everybody thinking he's gone senile.'

'They said you was drunk, Dad.'

'I wish to God I was.' At the counter he took a Biro from his inside pocket, head hovering over the book as he asked: 'Where do I sign?'

'You don't need to,' Fred said nervously, sensing he wasn't yet free of peril. 'It'll be all right.'

He'll pocket the takings, Aaron thought, or it's a tax dodge. Everybody's on the fiddle in Mrs Thatcher's Britain. But then, they always were. It probably started when they fleeced the Normans. Or the Danes. Or even the Romans. They'd practised on each other since the Flood. He felt it in himself.

Percy's hand slewed over the counter. As he was coaxed into the lounge by his son, Aaron caught them up and put the pen in the old man's lapel pocket.

ELEVEN

A bleak sea going through the motions of stormforce, then the underwater cables broke, lines down in the wilderness. The thin-faced, rather fanatic-looking man had had the final word with the world beyond the snow. She might try later, in case a miracle-working company of weatherproof mechanics with fine hands and unassailable expertise had righted the poles and scuffed icy fluff off the wires to make them sing again.

Stanley, in the meantime, would stay bereft, the little-boy vacancy willed all too easily into his eyes. It was hard not to laugh at the distinctly faxed picture, yet she was undeniably grateful for this heaven-sent separation. He would park himself, providing the aircraft had been able to get down, and had not been rearranged to Paris or Frankfurt (and then what would he be doing?) in some neon-lit airport, putting away wash after wash of dismal coffee, gloomily mulling on the postponement of her sexy reception when, after bolting all doors, they hurried to the bedroom for that quick, yet usually satisfying, wrestle of reunion.

In her dreams she had always wanted to find, behind the false door of a bookcase as in old movies, a hall of people dancing under the glare of white lights, inebriated by delicious wine as they circled through the smell of their own warm sweat, half-naked men and women carried beyond fine talk into manic licentiousness, as unreachable by everyday domestic worries as they in this ghastly gimcrack hotel were from their destinies beyond surrounding snow.

Strange hands stroked her adequate breasts, subtle fingers finding every orifice, till her voice joined others in orgasmic chorus, an orgy she had never partaken of but would have run into had such heady music sounded from the neighbouring room. She would disgrace herself, alone in the corridor by the dead telephone, but didn't want to release the too vivid scene, unearthed from parts of her that must always have existed, their whereabouts unknown to her and certainly to Stanley, though perhaps he had sensed it and was unwilling to touch it off, to let her go body and soul on her own into that very special country, which struggle accounted for his little-boy look of all-round defence.

Shrugging – the thrilling vision sucked away, as all such visions must be – she went into the lounge, to see who might be interesting to know. A girl preceding her with a tray of drinks set a pint by that same middle-aged, middle-sized befuddled man staring at the flames as if he had lost something. The man who had been talking on the telephone took his whisky and went to gaze through the window with an expression that might have been on Sally's face if she had looked out, focusing on the monkey-puzzle of Fate. She found him interesting, though knew as she sat down that she must not look too obviously, since he seemed the type who might be easily offended.

A tall man with large features and longish greying hair was reading a book like the Bible, a bottle of wine on his table, calm face suggesting he would sit out the isolation no matter how long it went on. The serving girl put a pot of water and two large whiskies between an old and impeccably attired gent in a suit and tie, while the younger man who was obviously his keeper poured so much water into his glass as to lose the alcohol entirely.

A woman of about thirty, short mousy hair, wearing baggy trousers and sensible-type shoes, slept in an armchair, more wantonly displayed than she could be aware of, feet out and an arm above the back of her head, a breast lifting into an attractive curve in spite of the thickness of her sweater.

A raddled fortyish man was talking to a girl whose look turned close to adoration after she stopped laughing, and Keith lifted his drink to say: 'Here's to you, then.'

'You're trying to get me sozzled,' Eileen said. 'But I don't care. I like to get a bit tiddly now and again.'

'You've certainly earned a drink.' Glasses touched, and were drained. 'Let's go and see our room. You can tell me whether you like it or not.'

The true exit was the window not the door, Daniel decided, to watch and see yet not to go, a picture of the outside which would torment but not elucidate, rather than a door which, inviting him to action, would surely kill. His courage was exposed, determination found lacking, sight battened on snow flocking down, nothing to do except wait and hope. To open a door and run into the elemental trap would release him from civilized anxiety. He liked the window because he could see and not act, and his attachment to duty gave way to an acceptance of the unusual peace, nothing to be done but enjoy comfort and be calmed by the falling curtain of snow, like the weeks prior to a marriage that promised everlasting protection and ease, before the wagons of doom as in grand opera rumbled over the cobbles.

He would be killed for failure, but deserved to be whitened as utterly as the window for the butcheries he had helped to bring about – not much to take credit for, if credit he wanted, knowing well enough what he had done. You couldn't pay for the sins of your father, though his mother had set him on a course of thinking he ought to, so that he had committed sufficient to bleach his father's crime sheet white.

The snow had saved his soul in burying the van with its radar time-locks, directionally-set detonators, the quarter-ton imperial weight, rendered the box of technology so harmless that a muffled volcano would lift only ice and darkness. His eyes widened, as if the white-out shielded more mysteries than he could conceive of at the moment.

'Is it still snowing?' Percy called.

Daniel came from the window. 'Less than it was, whatever that means.'

'None of us will get away tonight,' he cackled. 'We'll be here till Doomsday.'

Alfred opened all the buttons of his dark cashmere overcoat. 'Finish your drink, Father.'

'I'm right, though. You'll see.' The swallow went skewwhiff, splashing his collar. Wiping himself, he took the watch from his waistcoat. 'We've been here an hour already, but we'll need a calendar by the time we've done.'

Standing in the garden outside the kitchen window Alfred had heard his father talking to himself, which he supposed was understandable if no one else was living in the house. But nowadays he was beginning to talk to himself even when other people were close, and that couldn't be good.

Sally asked the serving girl what wine they had in the cellar.

64

'What sort do you want?' She spoke angrily, tongue going over her uneven teeth.

'What do you have?'

'How do I know? We've got all sorts.'

'See if you can find me a half-bottle of nice Bordeaux.'

Enid put the few coins on the tray into her apron pocket, drying fingers up and down her thigh. 'I expect we've got some somewhere. But he don't like me rummaging through the wine. He thinks I might knock a bottle off. As if I would!' She laughed. 'The best vinegar in England! A chap once sent some back, and Fred nearly went bonkers because nobody had done that before. But it tasted like rotten plonk, as well, when I finished off a glass somebody left on their table.'

She smoothed a pale cheek, which turned momentarily rose, and when she walked out with swaying hips Tom Parsons said: 'She wants her arse smacking, that one does.'

Sally doubted it, but not the sincerity of his desire, supposing the world to be full of perverted men, though the dancing people of her dreams might not laugh at such notions, at Death in his cap and bells, at her in his wake, but always their love and lust combining, turning as swiftly in their priapic gyrations as space in the great hall would allow, under the light of candelabras, fuelled by the fumes of wine and the subtle odours of sweat, she not knowing where the vision came from, but half her body was in it, heart and left breast and leg caught in the swirl, the other half about to be dragged helplessly after, as she in her deepest being wished to be.

Her husband or mother might say she was going mad, but the stunted man's words somehow connected to her peculiar spectacle of obscene revelry.

'Revolting,' she said, shaking the picture from her mind.

Daniel, surprised at such a fervent reaction to Parsons' jocular remark, looked at her with interest.

TWELVE

The lee side of the van was better for comfort, but not much. Fore-heads to the tin, they pissed yellow holes in the snow deep enough for any midget to crawl into and survive the winter.

Garry passed the bottle. Life was only worth living if you were half cut and riding the bike, though being in the blizzard on his vibrant seven-fifty wasn't the best way to be either. 'Windy tonight.'

Wayne pulled his growth of beard out of the slipstream and wiped his lips. 'Where's it coming from?'

'Heaven, you cunt.'

'Hell, I reckon.'

'It'd melt then, wouldn't it?' Lance argued. 'It would be rain. Or steam.'

Wayne flicked a drop of whisky onto his cock. 'Don't say I never give you owt.'

'Shall I tell you summat?' Garry said.

He zipped up. 'As long as it's dirty.'

The Commer van bumped against them. 'Well,' Garry said, 'we're stuck. The bikes'll never get us out of this fucking lay-by.'

Wayne moaned. 'You mean we're going to die?'

'Too fucking right.' Lance plucked a duet with the wind on an imaginary guitar:

> 'If you sleep in the snow
> You won't hear yourself go:
> Or so I have heard.
> You get warmer and warmer
> Like a humming-bird.'

Wayne bumped his head in despair. 'It's all right for you: you scribble songs and want to go to Music City. You hope you'll be famous one day, not like us hopeless gets.'

'I ain't had a fuck for three days,' Garry said. 'I don't want to die

66

a virgin.' He belched. 'Them fucking chips is repeating on me again. Proper bloody Winchesters. I suppose the fat was off.'

'It's the beer, not the chips.' Wayne drew a rag from his jacket and wiped the headlamp. 'There, I won't let you die, Black Bess.' He kissed it. 'You've served me well. You waited eighteen months while I was inside and didn't go whoring off with a Harley Davidson. I'll stand by you.'

'Silly-born bastard,' Lance said. 'You only nicked it last night. Some pimply-faced kid broke his heart when he woke up this morning, till his old lady promised him another for Christmas. He don't know Santa Claus can't get down a chimney with a BMW sticking out of his bag.'

Garry passed around more booze. 'You're pissed out of your flowerpot.'

'We're all pissed.' Wayne kicked snow from the van wheel. 'Three piss-ants, and no fucking work in the morning.'

'Yeh, let others work,' Lance said. 'I'm generous like that. I only want to glide around on my BMW.'

'BM-fucking-Ws,' Garry said. 'I've shit 'em. Only posh fuckpigs arse around on BMWs – Bleeding Middle-class Wankers.'

'It's better than Jap crap,' Lance said. 'They break down all the time.'

'That's why we love 'em.' Wayne's empty bottle fell silently into the snow. 'If they didn't break down now and again we'd never learn owt. Still, are we going to die or not? When the boss wonders where I am in the morning he'll have to shift his own castings onto the lorry. I hope he breaks his fingernails.' He tried a handstand at the side of the van, sank in the snow and came up licking his lips. 'Lovely! It tastes a treat.'

Garry wiped a snow flurry from the side of his face. 'Do you want some sugar in it?'

'We'll fucking freeze to death,' Wayne said. 'I don't like the cold. Me mam got me some thermal long-combs, but I'm still freezing.'

Garry lifted three bottles of Pils from his pannier and handed them out. 'Sorry I forgot the Ogri mugs, lads.'

'Best cartoon character in the world, old Ogri.' Lance took a magazine from his topbox. 'I always laugh when I read that stuff.

You never see him in the posh papers like the *Mirror*, though. I don't know why.'

'I love him as well.' Garry tapped his bottle on the Commer mudguard. 'But seeing as we ain't got no Ogri mugs you'll have to suck on glass. We'll live five extra minutes. Not that we want to live for ever, do we? We wouldn't know what to do with ourselves. Fucking awful prospect.'

'It's all right for you,' Wayne said. 'You're thirty next birthday. You'll be too old then to do wheelies up Mount Everest.'

'It looks like we'll have to walk out of this ice cream,' Lance said.

The wailing of the others sounded above the wind, broken by Garry. 'Did you say *walk*? He *did*. He said *walk*. Did you hear that? *Walk!* Fucking walk, he said. Walk! Us! Bikers! Whoever heard of real live bikers walking? My heart wouldn't stand it. And if it did I'd never live it down. Walk! I'd get cramp. People would laugh. You must be out of your one-stroke mind. I'd never walk. I haven't walked since I was a baby. What *is* walking, anyway? Isn't it that funny little waddle people do when they want to get from A to B? And then they're only on their way to catch a bus.'

'Bus!' They latched arms so close that heads touched, laughing till the tears froze.

'We've got to move,' Lance said, 'and the bikes won't do it. They've hudged closer since we stopped. They know it's all up with them, poor things.' He cried bitter tears. 'We'll have to go from one to another with a gun to blow their brains out, so they won't suffer too much.' He sniffed, back into manhood. 'My old man'll have to open the stall in Uttoxeter market on his own tomorrow.'

'What we need,' Wayne said, 'is a nice big van to get us out of this freezing shit.'

They thought on the matter.

'You might as well wish for the moon,' Garry said. 'We can't even see the road. In the meantime, though, is there any more gut rot? No? We'll have to start on the petrol, then. A cup o' four-star, anybody?' He unscrewed the cap, dipped a finger, held it to the wind, and licked. 'The bastards would water tit milk if it came out of a can.'

'A bad year,' Lance said. 'Our Ken works down the pit, and when he got his NUM diary not long ago it told you the best years for wine. But after that Scargill strike it didn't tell you any more. Nobody could afford even vinegar. A real fucking killpig of a strike that was. He had to sell his car. But everybody was getting rid of theirs as well, so he only got fifty quid for it.'

'He shouldn't have come out,' Wayne said.

'He had to, didn't he, bighead?'

'Well, you don't have to do everything people tell you to, do you?'

'Yeh, but we shouldn't have come out tonight, should we? But we did, and in this bleeding weather as well. Who would believe it?'

'I wonder what the forecast is?' Wayne said. 'My leg's like a bit of old pitprop. Fancy coming for a spin on a rotten night like this.'

'No time's perfect.' Lance looked around the back of the van, barely able to stand against the peltering snow. 'If we push out into it we won't last five minutes. Maybe we can get this thing going.'

Garry considered it for the extended time of one second. 'It's been dumped. Somebody nicked it and flogged it along the road till the petrol ran out.'

'Got any tools?'

'Tools? You're off your fucking cowpat. I wouldn't know what to do with 'em.'

Lance cleared the snow from the handle, wrenched the door open, and clambered in. 'At least we'll get our arses out of the snow.'

'Eh,' Garry exclaimed, 'lad's clever. He'll get his fucking O Levels next.'

'He might even learn to walk,' Wayne said. 'I hear they teach you at night school. You only have to totter twenty-five yards in the test.'

'Then he'll meet another little walker,' Garry went on, 'one with tits, and happen after a while they'll get wed, and have a gaggle of little snotty-nosed walkers. They'll go by us long-haired greasy biking bastards with their little piggy noses stuck in the air. Walkers! I hate 'em, nearly as much as buses and taxis and cars.'

Lance pulled wires from behind the dashboard. A smoky roar blurted from the engine, lights dimly yellow on the snow. 'Get in, for fuck's sake, but kick a bit of that white stuff from around the wheels first.'

Tyres scuffed and spun. 'Push, you idle bastards.'

'Ah,' said Garry, 'push! That's different. Bikers might not be able to walk, but they can push all right. Come on, let's get this wagon moving.'

While Lance coughed himself breathless, Garry took a turn in the cabin and kept the engine lively, got them a few feet forward. 'One more heave-ho, and we're in the clear.' He roared the power to encourage, till hot gas from the exhaust set the pushers screaming that they would kill him if he didn't stop choking them alive. 'It's warming you up. Make you drunk quicker than booze.' He put on all systems in well-timed operation, the van swaying onto the road.

Garry stayed at the controls. 'Come on, my beauty, don't let us down.' He slid the doors back. 'Shake the snow off your boots before you get into my nice van, you flea-bitten deadbeats.' He weaved, threading the drifts at a crawl.

Lance noticed a decrease in the snow, a slight drop in the wind. 'We're on the move. Maybe God won't let us snuff it, after all.'

Wayne laughed. 'God? Did you hear that, lads? God! God's dead, you daft get. I knocked him flying at a Belisha beacon last week. His fucking pension book went all over the shop. You should have seen the look on his face. A wonderful sight. Eh, we're going quicker, do you notice?'

'Eight miles an hour,' Garry said. 'It'll take us all week to find a phone box.'

'We'll get the Chief Constable to send us a chopper,' Lance said. 'Ask him to take us back to Chesterfield.'

'I want a nice cosy boozer.' Garry kicked the clutch, and rattled the gears from slot to slot. 'We can play darts on the landlord's poxy face. It'll warm us up a bit.' Smoke and rubber reeked as the wheels spun. He pulled a spade from the space behind. 'Get digging for victory. That'll warm you up.'

They scooped snow aside with a stiffbacked motoring atlas, kicked and breasted it till the shovel hit tarmac. 'Push again,' Lance shouted, red-raw hands taking the wheel.

'I feel knackered,' Wayne said. 'I won't be able to kick a pub to pieces, even if we find one.'

'It's nearly stopped snowing,' Garry told him. 'And then it'll fucking well freeze.'

'We're getting there. If anybody spots a light,' Wayne said, 'let me know through the intercom.'

'You won't see any lights around these parts,' Lance told him.

'They shut 'em off in case anybody knocks at the door to ask for a cup of water.'

Garry laughed, head back. 'Do you remember when we ripped a door off that hotel in Paxton and chucked it over the bar? And that old bastard saying we ought to be called up into the army? I sent my pint o' slurry over him. He said we ought to be flogged!'

Lance banged his fist against the windscreen. 'But nobody would buy us, I told him. You wouldn't even get ten pence for us.'

'Then we slung a few chairs into the saloon, just to show willing. Posh punters didn't know what was happening. They thought the fucking revolution had started.' Wayne passed his fag packet. 'At least we can have our last puff before we die.'

'We had to run, though,' Lance said.

'Of course we had to run. Twenty to one, wasn't it? You don't fight twenty to fucking one.'

'I wonder what's in the back of this van?' Lance said. 'Why don't somebody take a look?'

'Boxes,' Garry shouted. 'They're full of fifty-pound notes with the ink still wet. No, it looks like hi-fi stuff.'

'We'll have a shufti when we're in the clear. Then we can set it going and have a dance, a bit of old ragtime.' Songs went through Lance's mind ten a minute, but they hardly ever finished. 'Dance with the snowflakes, more like.'

'The battery wouldn't last. Still, we're moving, aren't we? What's that light over there?'

'You need glasses.' Lance waved cigarette smoke away. 'It's a farm, and they've already got their shotguns trained on us, you can bet.'

'It must have been the glow of our fags in the windscreen.' Covered tracks were harder in the frost, and the van crawled healthily. 'Where did you learn to handle this sort o' thing, Lance?'

'My old man's a lazy bastard. He makes me drive his wagon all over the shop, up hill and down dale, taking stuff to farms. I get stuck in the mud sometimes, so it's good practice for snow.'

'I hope we don't find our bikes have been nicked in the morning,' Wayne said. 'Whoever took 'em, I'd chase 'em to the ends of the earth. Anyway, I'd know its cough anywhere.'

'My little beauty is even taxed,' Lance said. 'And insured. My old man made me see to it. If I break the law he goes white and starts to shake all over. He was in the last war, so he can't stand me getting into trouble with Old Bill.'

'Road tax – I stick a Guinness label on mine,' Garry said, 'and even that's out of date.' He leaned forward. 'Ah, that *is* a light. And it's getting bigger.'

'He's right,' Lance said. 'There ain't been any power cuts yet.' Snow melted patchily off the bonnet, warmed by the engine, and water from the roof waved down over the wipers, bringing the van back to shape and colour. 'Oh, lads, it's a pub. Or maybe a hotel. Aren't we in for the treat of our lives?'

THIRTEEN

He had been in such rooms often, wondered whether Eileen had, couldn't imagine where she had in fact been, what furnishings she'd live among. Terylene curtains wouldn't keep out light, cold or noise. There was a small writing table, built-in cupboard and drawers: chintzy bedlamps, an open plastic coffin in the bathroom. He felt a wildness in him to break the place apart, as if he wanted to rearrange the clutter of his mind into some sort of prelapsarian order. He wouldn't know how to begin, the seismic change had been so complete, and in any case he had left his ice axe in the car and didn't fancy sending Eileen out again. Maybe she didn't care for his company, beyond the benefit of the lift off the moors and a bed for the night. He hardly knew whether he wanted to be with her, but there were two beds, which gave them a choice. 'Close the door.'

She sat in the armchair. 'I thought we would get a four-poster in this highwayman's hotel.'

'I'll arrange it next time.' Water from the tap was rusty and chill, but he washed his hands as if he had last done so ten years ago. 'Your face is dirty, by the way.'

She pouted. 'You're a sarky old sod, aren't you?'

'Well, it is — a bit streaky from your travels. You should be happy I told you about it. Anyway, you don't need to be afraid of me.'

She knew that already, otherwise she wouldn't be here, would she? She looked at him, his teeth uneven, hair tousled, rolling the towel round and round. He wasn't much of a picture, either. 'The room smells musty, as if a squirrel died in it, but I like it. I've only ever been in a bed-and-breakfast before, not a proper hotel like this.'

'I didn't realize I was being sarcastic.' He unbuttoned his waistcoat, more to be at ease than with any notion of undressing. He wanted to sit at the table and write a letter, but Gwen wouldn't be able to receive it. Every time he went away he hoped she would go off with another man, their relationship painlessly settled by the time he got back. And she, he knew, had never wanted him to return.

Eileen took off her shirt, showing a larger bust than he had supposed, but an off-white brassiere. Well, you couldn't get into bed with your clothes on, could you? 'I hate it when you laugh at me like that. You're always doing it.'

'Am I?' She was beginning to sound like his wife, surprising how little time was needed. Maybe it was his fault, after all, though he didn't want to think so. 'I was amused at my own thoughts. Not at you, believe me.'

She unhooked her brassiere and let it slip forward, caught the straps and threw it onto the bed. 'How do I know, then, if you don't tell me?'

'Now I have.'

'Not much.'

Turning off the main light left a basic glow between the beds. 'It's a start. You can't deny that.' He felt he could tell her anything, but was it because she was nothing, or because he was?

She let the tap run till the water was as warm as it would get, washed her hands and face, glad to have heard more talk from him in one evening than had been squeezed out of her boy friend in days – and that had cost her a black eye and a twisted arm. She hated the term 'boy friend' because there had never seemed a time when one had been friendly in the way people ought to be. 'You can tell me, then, if you like. You might not have me for long.'

He took off his shirt and vest, disappointing her when he opened his case, as if only to change. 'What exactly do you mean?'

'I'm here just for the night, aren't I?'

'I hadn't thought about it, to be honest.' Tomorrow wouldn't exist from now on for such as him. 'But do we have to make an issue of it?'

A shadowy triangle of hair showed through her pink pants. 'I don't know about you, but I do.'

He put clean clothes back in the case and closed it, as if pondering every action beforehand. 'Perhaps I do, as well. When something good happens to me I like to imagine it's going to last for ever. And why not, even now? So I will, if you don't mind, and if the idea doesn't offend you.'

She smiled. 'I like you more and more. How funny, though, I

thought you'd have lots of hair on your chest, and you have. It tickles!'

His arms were around her, the wonderful feel of her flesh and the cool young breasts. She had been thinking about him to that extent. 'When did it first cross your mind?'

She drew away. 'I suppose you think I'm nothing but a dirty slut?'

He grimaced: not another neurotic woman. Surely she's too young to be in that trap already. He plugged into some corny television play to remark: 'And I suppose you think I'm just a dirty old man out for a good time?'

She was smooth and pale, with the loveliest young woman's figure, neither wrinkles nor stretchmarks, as he stood back to look at her, though her teeth wanted seeing to, and a little civilized polish would do her no harm. Nor would a feeling of security for her battered soul. Such tinkering would make a different person, and would he like her more or less? It was too late to find out, so he wouldn't be the man to know. If he made her pregnant would something interesting come out of it, or a recidivist monster?

'What I would like to know,' she said, 'is why you've got that long knife in your case?' She picked up his packet of cigarettes. 'Can I have one?'

'Please do. I thought I'd left it in the car. It's a survival knife. Very useful for all sorts of things.'

'As long as you aren't going to cut me up with it.'

He laughed. 'Whatever could give you that idea?'

But she was more interested in the lighter. 'It's nice' – flat, gold and effective.

He ought to tell her: it's a present from Gwen. Have it, he should say but – Where's that cigarette lighter I gave you for your birthday? Gwen would surely have asked. I lost it, he'd tell her. I left the car door open and somebody took it out of the glove box. Tell me another, she'd say, if she could say anything any more. 'I'd give it to you, but it's a present from my father. He would be sure to notice it had gone.'

'You mean your wife gave it to you.' She didn't want his lighter, nice as it was. She could always buy a box of matches and read the joke on the back. 'I don't care. All nice men are married.'

'Are they?' He sounded so angry that she wondered what his wife was like, and how his wife's face would change to wild and fierce if she suddenly opened the door and saw what they were about to do. And then she thought maybe we shouldn't do it, it's wrong, but nothing can stop us, she told herself, whatever we think, because I love him and he loves me, and it's all right for his wife to turn funny about it, but she's got all the nice things of the world and I've got nothing but this and me and where I am, though whether I really love him I can't yet tell. 'Married men know how to look after women, don't they?'

'I'm not so sure about that.'

'Well, they've had practice.'

He hoped her assumption would turn out to be right.

'You *are* married, aren't you? That's why I said it. I don't know any other married men. I never have. I just supposed.' She seemed upset, a blush showing the promise of some sensibility.

'I feel as if I've known you a long time,' he said.

'Why don't you take the rest of your kit off, then?'

With women more or less of his own sort he would have had them off in an instant, but because he had never known anyone like her he needed to take more care, to seem polished and reasonable in his behaviour. He couldn't decide why. It would be easy to flash-fuck her, and leave it at that. 'You're the most beautiful girl I've ever seen. I mean it.'

'Hold me, then. Nobody's said that to me before. I thought you thought I was awful. I thought you thought I was a bucket of Aids or something. Anyway, I'm not, I'm clean. I've never been with anybody like that.'

He kissed her lips, not caring to be a lousy bastard who gave such an impression, and she gripped him as if never to let go, teeth pressing against his lips.

'Your cigarette's burning the table.' He eased her away. 'Put it in the ashtray, or' – he conjured up something she would understand – 'it'll be another fifty pounds on my bill.'

'I'm sorry.'

'Not that it would faze me.' He wanted to make amends. 'But it's a pity to ruin the table.' He was going to add: as gimcrack as it is, but he didn't because to her it might seem the best of furniture. While she carefully pressed out her cigarette he took off his trousers and pants, drew the curtains. 'To stop the snowmen peering in.'

'You look good with no clothes on.' She eyed him from across the room as if he were a specimen she hadn't seen before either. 'You aren't fat, are you?'

'I try not to be.'

'I mean, at the belly.'

'I take exercise.'

She smiled. 'With dumb-bells?'

'I jump up and down. I go swimming. I play squash.'

'Whereabouts?'

'At my club.'

'Just so's you won't get fat?'

'I do it to keep healthy.'

She was staring again. 'Your nose — it's got a bend in the middle.'

He laughed. 'So it has. I got it broken a few times at boxing.'

'In the ring?'

'No, at school. And in the army. I broke a few, as well.'

'I'm sure you did.' She drew him onto the bed. 'It makes you more good-looking!'

FOURTEEN

Daniel's mother had said that a watched pot never boiled. He had proved her wrong. The saucepan spilled over and the stew was ruined. When she said a clock hand didn't move if you looked at it he spent the hour of her absence making sure that it did. Recalling such wayward experiments of childhood, the sustaining fire at his back and the soothing timemark of the grandfather clock demanded that he act instead of mindlessly waiting.

A glance through the window showed the snowstorm in a state of St Vitus's dance, a growth in the all-enclosing drifts. His resolution was broken by knowing that to go into it meant death. Though patience beat the stew to the boil, and forced the minute-hand of the clock to move, living at such a slow rate if you wanted something to happen was tantamount to sloth.

His patience was born out of a rock, solidified early on after fire had come into collision with ice, indicating that he was in no way the same as other people. Anything which set him apart helped to make the disguise, to consolidate the split which enabled him to live as a schoolteacher while devoting his other half to the Cause. He distrusted anyone who assumed they had something in common with him, lest they divine his infinite capacity for patience and probe into what he was trying to conceal. Being two people allowed him to peer out through a facade that others assumed to be all of him. He spoke, but his real voice stayed silent, the voice he used being a cover to keep the other quiet. Such mechanism made plain hinted that his ability to dissimulate might be about to desert him.

'The only thing to do on such a night,' Parsons said, 'is to get a few drinks inside you.'

The third whisky which had encouraged Daniel towards speculation also told him that *they* must know by now that he would not be delivering the van. He was lost, and they had no way of getting at him. 'You're probably right.'

'Probably!' Parsons said scornfully. 'There's not much else you can do. I wouldn't mind a party, though. A real slap-up raving mad-night to shiver the floorboards and flip the roof off – no holds barred. What do you say, Jenny?'

'Make your own party. I'm tired.'

'Why don't you go upstairs for a kip, then?'

'I'll go when I'm ready. I'm not your wife, poor thing.'

'I ought to nobble you for that uncalled-for remark. I love my wife, and she loves me.' He drained the rest of his jar and, when Fred showed at the door, asked for another. Fred came with alacrity, deciding that the best he could do was let them drink themselves sleepy (it was also good for business) and then go off to bed, so that he could put all lights off and turn in himself.

'I'm a full-time trade union official,' Parsons called to Aaron, 'and she's driving me back to nappies. She thinks I'm after her.' A hiccup jerked his whole head, hand to his mouth while pulling the chair closer to Aaron. 'Well, who wouldn't be? I ask you. I'm only flesh and blood. Or I was last time I looked.' A whisper, but clear enough for her, as he tapped his breast pocket. 'I've still got near two thousand quid in union money, and I would give every last penny for ten minutes with her. But ten real minutes, you know. A handful of lovely fifty-pound notes with our dear Queen's head printed on them – all ready for disbursement! Come on, my duck, lift your pretty finger and say yes.'

He had disturbed her desert heart, as most men did when they spoke to her. 'Leave me alone.'

Percy appeared at the door, white hair wispy as if his head boiled and steam came out. His blank eyes took on a sudden glitter, cheeks putty-like, a scrap of pink paper resting on a small circle of blood from a shaving wound below the left ear. Lips pursed, as if about to whistle a tune out of bygone years that no one in the room could know, he walked erect and steady to the nearest chair, and held onto the back.

'You should be in bed, Dad.' Fred just avoided a wave of his arm, wondering whether the old codger wasn't either drunk or mad.

'I want a double whisky and a black-and-tan,' Percy said. 'And don't call me Dad. I'm Mr Stone to you, and never forget it.'

'At least somebody knows how to knock back the booze,' Parsons said, as if any recruit would be valid for his wild shindig.

Daniel also called for another whisky. 'It's rare to find someone who knows what he wants.' And lets nothing block his way till he gets it.

'I've always known what I want,' Parsons said with drunken pride.

'How about you?' Aaron asked Jenny.

'I'll have some coffee, then.'

'Coffee!' Parsons screamed. 'Well, I never! Why don't you thaw yourself out with a brandy at least? Or a nice tot of rum?'

'Because I don't want to.' I love my desert heart, she told herself. It keeps me safe.

'Ladies should only drink champagne,' Percy said.

'By God, you're right. Why didn't I think of that?' Parsons said. 'Champagne! I'm too bloody slow, that's my trouble. A sheltered life I've had, well, except when me and the lads went on delegations to Communist countries, then we had some fine old times, I can tell you.' He let his head roll, and looked at the ceiling as if a map of his travels might be printed there. Then his eyes came back to the horizontal: 'What good times they was! But they don't do it any more, I'm sorry to say. I've been smashed in Moscow, sloshed in Sofia, kay-lied in Leningrad, paralytic in Prague, blindo in East Berlin, and blotto in Bucharest. A group from our area went to Lake Baikal once. They took us on a bus from Irkutsk. We was already drunk, and still had two bottles of duty-free. When me and a bloke from Barnsley fell through the ice we was still singing "The Internationale" when the Russians fished us out! The sturgeon and the caviar we scoffed, and the vodka we put back! It don't bear thinking about, except that it does on a lousy night like this. The comrades used to try and drink us under the table for the sake of international peace and friendship. Drink to this, and drink to that. Toast after toast. Working-class solidarity was all the rage, and we meant it, though it's all over now. But we could hold our own with the booze, I can tell you. We used to drink champagne as well. Yes, my love, I'll get you a bottle of bubbly, but real French, none of that Russian stuff. There's nowt like it to cheer you up.'

'Don't bother.'

'"Don't bother" she says. It ain't no bother.' He set a fifty-pound note on the beer mat. 'That's for us. And don't say I never look after you.' He wagged a finger, which she found common and hateful.

80

'I'll try not to,' she said wearily.

'Because I do. You're never out of my mind. I always think of others. That's the way I was brought up. My mother, God bless her, she used to din it into me as a lad. "Always think of others," she would say, "then somebody will be there to think of you when you're in trouble." She was lovely, my mam was. "You only get out of life what you put into it," she told me, and she was right. She worked her fingers to the bone, she did, but a lot the old man cared.' His voice broke, as if a cinder burned in his throat which needed the liquid of a sob to put it out. '*He* only wanted his pint, or a quart if he could get it. He treated my mother like dirt — till I grew up and put him in his place.'

'You're maudlin.' Percy was loud and clear. 'Drunk and sentimental. The worst thing a man can be. A person's only as good as what a person gets, that's all I know.'

Enid came in with a tray of sandwiches, and the old man put his arm out like a train signal, a brush at her skirt happily unnoticed except by Aaron, who dwelt on the fracas between age and beauty if by any chance the hand had touched her legs.

FIFTEEN

A hum came from a refrigerator, lulling yet melancholy, otherwise silence. At half-past nine no one was willing to go to bed, as if all that could happen hadn't yet done so: reading, dozing, staring into space or up at the ceiling to create their own versions of past and present. During his marriage Aaron had worried about his sister Beryl, which may have been why he did not stay married long. And yet, forcibly kept from her by the gale, instead of thinking about his uncertain future, he felt wonderfully calm. The whisky had subdued his toothache, and he knew that he should observe whatever went on so that he would have something to tell her beyond another dull garnering of books along the staid south coast.

What he was waiting for he did not know. To have neither plans nor hope was a living death in this uncanny tomb of snow, but because he was a forger of signatures and a falsifier of manuscripts the police would be waiting when he got home. Even so, for the moment anyway, he was unable to care that the future was murky and uncertain.

Fred drew the flimsy curtains, as if to protect them from prowling nightmares beyond the glass. Outside the range of the fire the air was bleak, unless you had a few tots glowing inside you. Aaron's feet were so cold he got up to pace, but it was like walking in buckets of ice.

No windows fastened flush. Cracks brought singsong windtone, a cat's moan for kittens doomed. He went up the creaking stairs and into his room for a packet of cigars, then out again, a drone of talk and a girl's laughter from behind a door. His weight did not let him tread lightly. Back from a dead end along another corridor he heard a prolonged high cry as if out of a bad dream, though he couldn't be sure it wasn't a trick of the wind in this old Aeolian harp of a place.

A small window looked out of the back, and his nose almost touching drew a snow smell through the glass. The frosted oblong bulb above the shed door cast a glow around the nearest drifts, cars only recognizable as vehicles on the lee side. Snowbits diagonally floated then turned up as if seeing no purpose in completing their journey, an advance guard of spies with enough to report.

A light shone, and he heard the grind of an engine, and a van pulled slowly into the yard, stopped side-on against the wall, and three men in helmets and black jackets jumped into the snow like a local police team wanting to see that all was well at the hotel. Or they had come for him, to get him even here, except that there was no blue light, and the men were scooping snow to throw at each other, stick people supernaturally animated, he couldn't think from where.

One filled his helmet and tried putting it on the head of another, who avoided it by leaping away. They were like soldiers who, having subdued a strongpoint, were celebrating that they were still alive. He marvelled at the resilience of the young, let the curtain go, and went back to the lounge, where two flattish glasses on slim stems waited, one on either side, as Parsons turned the bottle slowly clockwise, pressing the ball of his thumb forcefully against the steel-capped dome of the cork, easing it so subtly out of the neck, Aaron and Jenny assuming that at the precise second he would remove the cork then calmly decant the amber liquid.

Fred recognized his nihilistic glint. 'If you damage my ceiling, you'll pay for it.' Enid ran for the door as if it wasn't the first time she had been close to such an experiment.

Tom could let the cork out silently, with a skill he had often seen in others, when the opening smoke preceded the tamed liquid into a glass, or let the cork fly along any spectacular trajectory of his choice.

Aaron considered the uncertainty to be half the fun, and when Tom tilted the bottle as if it were a gun the cork hit the fireplace like a shell exploding in the desert, sending up a cloud of ash. Then by a twist of the hand he put the spout over a glass and didn't lose a drop.

Percy looked up from his whisky and water. 'Nowt but a show-off, if you ask me.'

'Here's to you!' Parsons beamed good luck on them all. 'There's no better drink this time of the year. A tot of the old bubbly, and then to bed. When we wake it might be summer.'

She clinked his glass, a bare touch but he was more than happy.

With her you had to measure progress in millimetres, which was something good to be said for metric.

'I expect it'll make me sleep,' she said, but immediately recalled something close to a giggle as she heard her voice say it.

Aaron stood at the bar. 'It's amazing that people are still turning up. I can't imagine how they get here.'

A splash of whisky onto wood, and Daniel couldn't speak for a moment, gripping one hand with the other to stop the shakes. 'People? What people?'

'Oh, three lads. Would you believe it? They're throwing snowballs at each other. It must be marvellous to be young.'

'You're never anything else,' Tom Parsons shouted, 'if you're worth half your salt, eh, Mr Stone?'

But Percy was in the desert of the wandering, head back and mouth open, mind gone to where no one could guess. 'Just leave him,' Alfred said. 'He's never much trouble.'

Daniel looked out of a front window, drifts building across the road. A single snowflake had lost its way, so went back up as if to join the Gadarene rush elsewhere. Such a winter seemed new to him, though he took it as a sign of getting old when you thought the weather patterns were changing. From feeling free of trouble he was overwhelmed by anxiety, and went back to the tables. 'How did they get here?'

'They looked like bikers,' Aaron said, 'but I think they came in a van.'

'We passed 'em a few hours ago,' Percy called. 'I told you already. A Commer van in a lay-by. They were having the time of their lives, but who wouldn't? I got up to some right tricks at their age. I never told you, did I, Alfred?'

Parsons poured Jenny a second glass. 'It's the one drink that makes me want to live for ever, and I hope it does the same to you.'

'I only want it to put me to sleep.'

'Sleep! She wants to sleep! You'll get all the sleep you need after you're dead. Life's for wearing yourself out, for the big cosy bed in Heaven!'

'I wish you'd all go to sleep.' Fred had heard on the radio that there were twelve-foot drifts in the county. If he jumped into one from the roof he would be lost to the world, as if he had never existed, because there would still be seven feet under him. Yet he didn't want to sleep, either, as if psychic emanations from the vast padding of snow were keeping the eyes open, the senses expectant. In the last big snowstop of a few years ago, all those stranded had gone upstairs like zombies by nine o'clock, unable to stay awake. It was hard to say what made this fall so different.

Daniel peered out of the back window into the beautiful pure world, thinking of the dismal black slush when the thaw came. Where had the bikers gone? Maybe people were imagining weirdos and jack-o'-lanterns shaped out of the snow, clothed and given life by some malignant god to torment him alone.

He turned his head, and the van was there. He hoped it was fantasy, or there were so many of that type it could be anybody's, except that the last three ciphers of the numberplate marked it as the one he had driven. Snow was building up against the wheels, and the door beckoned him to go down and sit inside, turn on the engine and say goodbye to the world. Or stay with it till the cargo exploded.

The world outside was dangerous. Thin glass, painted over by his breath, kept him from it. Hard to think he would ever lift that latch and get back to the zany territory of the Cause. Before collecting the van he had gone into the upstairs room of a terraced house (at Warrington. Of all towns it had to be Warrington), not even staying in the parlour whose door opened onto the pavement. The room had a disassembled bed pushed against the wall to the right of the window as he went in, an electric heater instead of a fire in the grate, a table under the window, and a couple of chairs and a stool. Their looks were distrustful because he wouldn't sit on their grubby chairs.

Maybe they had sent him off with a load either to get caught or be killed. He picked the van up at specified traffic lights, while on red changing with the driver, no one the wiser. 'Whatever you do, don't be in this van at eight o'clock,' was all the other said, the laugh something Daniel could have done without. Just one of their jokes. They think I've betrayed them sometime in the past, so they've set me up. There was no reason for them to think any such thing, but no reason could blossom into every reason, like when they had got Smith who was never proved guilty.

The bikers must have gone, so what was the sense of that? Perhaps there had been two vans and they departed in the other, but how, in such a blizzard? The van was so close to the wall that when the stuff went off the hotel would become a crater in the landscape. It was the end of the line. If he told them, they would stay and be blown to pieces. Heads they lose and tails they lose. There was no saying which was worse, since he would lose as well. His father might have been able to give him an answer, but he was long dead and couldn't have known the difference between right and wrong even when he was alive.

SIXTEEN

Fred locked up and bolted because nobody else could be expected, unless a phantom of the Labrador snows blundered in, but who could believe in a thing like that, though he almost did when the thump of a battering ram made the building shudder, followed by a series of cannonball blows, a rhythm of impending doom swaying the lights. Parsons uptilted the last of his champagne. 'It sounds like the rent man.'

The veins of Fred's temples stood out like leeches about to burst, cheeks reddening as if fed by them. In the silence he had no voice, and they were startled by a tall, broad (and balding, as would be any long-time biker) man of about thirty, with his Belstaff black wax cotton jacket open to show an American-style backwoods shirt. He wore cowboy boots and gauntlets, and a black noddy bucket shone in his left hand. 'Aren't you going to let my mates in? They'll be dead in the snow if you don't, and if that happens you'll be lying on the deck bleeding all over it – for a start.'

To Aaron he had the kind of face you couldn't tell much about until he did something to make people realize what he was like, and then he would know a little of what he was like himself, and be satisfied with the recognition. His deprived yet intelligent features would not become refined or even more harmonious for centuries – if then – something he wasn't to know, while everyone else did, though he was as happy with himself as he could ever hope to be.

'My name's Garry, and you spell it with two Rs. I never got the third, so don't try and tell me which one's missing. Now then, who's the landlord of this poxed-up pub?'

Fred fastened the last button of his waistcoat, and switched from amiable penguin to fighting cock. 'This isn't a pub. And if it was it wouldn't be poxed-up, not if I was running it, which I am. For your information it's The White Cavalier Hotel, and it also happens to be closed for the night.'

'How can it be?' Percy added to the seed of Fred's distress, who at least had supposed the other clients would be on his side. 'He's in, isn't he?'

More blows at the front door rattled every pane, as if they were driving a dumper truck against the wood. Garry set his helmet on a table, and pulled a brass Zippo from his top pocket. He had a trick of throwing a cigarette from waist level and catching it neatly between his lips before lighting up. 'If you don't let my mates in, I'll push a table through a window and they'll come in that way. Then you'll sit in a draught all night, and you wouldn't like that, would you, Frog-chops?'

Fred backed a pace at the difference in their heights. 'I've told you, we're closed.' He wasn't having such riff-raff on his premises. People like that didn't freeze to death anyway: they were unkillable. And if they weren't, then it could only be a matter of good riddance. He hadn't made his way so painfully up in life to tolerate such dregs as that. They would come in only over his dead body. 'You'd better clear off, unless you want me to phone for the police.'

'Let them in,' Parsons called, 'on such a night. If you don't, I'll do it.' He turned to Aaron. 'That short-arsed bugger would have us all up for murder.'

They kicked snow from their boots when Aaron pulled the door open. 'You'd better keep back, Mr Scumbag-Landlord,' Garry warned.

In for a penny, in for a pound. 'Get me another bottle of champagne,' Parsons told Fred, 'if you want something to do.'

The drink had made Jenny drowsy, but her senses sharpened on seeing the three bikers at the bar. Fred, like the sensible man he decided he had better be, asked what they would care to order.

'A foaming pint, for a start.' Lance faced into the room, tapping a rhythm at the wood behind his heel. The thick coat with a full range of shoulder tassels came to his knees, and Jenny didn't feel as wary of him as of the others. His thin face looked more sunken with weariness than she supposed it might normally be. He was sallow skinned, though his full lips seemed about to say something which would justify his presence on earth, making her wonder how he could possibly have teamed up with the others.

'I could eat a hoss between two mattresses,' Wayne said, 'if you've got it, though that lovely bit of stuff will do to be going on with,' he added, when Enid came into the room. He stroked his beard, and smoothed the hair tied back in the shape of a little saveloy. Jenny wouldn't trust him an inch, with his preening and his mean mouth much obscured by hair. Under his biker's gear, well laced with studs, he wore a suede jacket and a white highnecked collarless shirt.

Enid turned a deadly-nightshade glare on Wayne, her mouth shaping into as fine a sneer as Aaron had ever seen. The crisp-coated burial mounds outside made the silence so profound that everyone seemed more individual, a silence ended by Enid's knife-sharp request for him to: 'Fuck off! If my boy friend was here he'd have your bollocks off and roast 'em over a slow fire as soon as look at you!'

Percy gave a weird hyena-ish laugh. 'That's right, my old duck, you tell him. Anybody would say the same. Come to that, who the hell *are* you lot?'

Lance's pint had gone down, and the tattoo heeltap changed to a banging on the bar with his glass as he smiled at Jenny, who looked away on being caught in her scrutiny. 'I'll tell you who we are. We're our own special club of bikers, Knights of the Arterial Road – the KAR Club. We used to be The Magnificent Seven, but now we're The Three Musketeers. I expect we'll be The Lone Ranger soon. And then I'll slop tears!'

Darkness came down like a curtain on their laughter, as if he had been godsent to entertain them in their isolation. 'It looks like the blackout's come back,' Percy said. 'Or maybe the dam's burst. Too much sand in the cement.'

'Shut up, Father.' Yet Alfred was happy at the old man's return to more ordinary consciousness since nature had put them up against it. Maybe he hadn't gone senile after all, either that or there was a case for geriatrics being sent to areas of high disaster incidence to keep them a few more years in the land of clarity.

'You'd better search out for some lamps and candles,' Aaron advised when the lights came on again. Fred felt as if it would be safer to remain a statue for the rest of the night. But that won't do, he told himself. A statue is something that dogs piss against, and you should never let that happen, though you're half-pissed already, more, even, if they knew the truth. But who wants the truth in this imperfect world? 'I'll see what I can do.'

'And you,' Wayne told Enid, 'bring us three turkey sandwiches –

and I don't mean tomcat – with plenty of meat spilling from between thick slices of granary bread!'

She dipped, and folded, and nodded, then uglied her face to an extreme, as if to liquefy the features and pour them in a poisonous acidic stream in his direction. 'Yes sir, no sir, three bags full of shit, sir, you . . .' The word-bin was empty, but the bin itself was made of words, a chipboard container of words which, though brittle, would not be snapped off.

'Little moxy's cross,' Garry said. 'Is this a public house, or in't it?'

Daniel spoke for them all. 'Why don't you ask her properly?'

'They want sandwiches,' Enid's voice stayed envenomed, 'and booze, but who's going to pay for it? That's what I'd like to know. I know your sort. I'm surprised you got the beer. I suppose Fred only did it to stop you cutting his throat, but I'm not frightened of a pack of ratty highwaymen like you.'

Garry held up a plastic bank card. 'What's this, then? I've got a wallet full, and they weren't nicked, either. Maybe they'll be useful to buy a car with one day, but I won't get one of them tin boxes for a cripple till I'm over the hill at forty. Meanwhile I'm an emergency plumber who goes everywhere on his ton-upper and panniers stuffed with tools. That's my job. I answer phone calls so quick my customers love me, though they pay double time because I'm on twenty-four-hour standby. I've got plenty of money in the bank, and I'll have even more when this lot's over, fixing all the burst pipes and blocked faucets. I'll be a millionaire for a few days, anyway.'

'I suppose you'll each be wanting a room?' Fred, mollified by the sight of credit cards, set a camping lamp on the bar, and waited for an answer. Not knowing who had money and who was a tramp didn't make his job easy these days.

'We might.' Garry lit a cigarette that hadn't been machine made. 'Then again, we might not.'

'Herbal fags.' Percy sniffed. 'They smell nice.'

'Have one, Dad.' He lifted another from his tin and took it across. The air was filled with a bucolic aroma.

'Perhaps it'll thaw in an hour,' Lance said, 'and then we can float away under the stars. We'll turn the van upside down and paddle it down the road.'

'That van is mine,' Daniel said. 'I left it in a lay-by where I thought it would be safe. You seem to have got it going and driven it here. For which I suppose I ought to thank you, though it's hard to think how you did it.'

'We thought it belonged to a mob of spivs up from the Smoke. The back's packed with hi-fi stuff.'

Daniel congratulated himself on feeling so calm at a time of danger. These types were fresh from Eden compared to those he usually dealt with. They still had pips on their lips.

'Which fell off the back of a lorry,' Lance said.

'A bloody juggernaut, I expect.' Wayne looked closely at Daniel. 'I've seen you somewhere before.'

'In borstal,' Garry said.

'No, but at some bloody school near enough to borstal. You was a teacher at Matchwood Comprehensive. I hate faces, so I never forget 'em!'

Many potential yobbos had sat before him, faces dead and smirky in turn, vicious or asleep, passive or threatening, but always a few who could spell before they left, which was much to be said for them, though not so much for the system. He had never agreed with those bearded beer-drinking so-called benign instructors who moulded their accents to put the kids at their ease, then lulled them into believing that it didn't matter how you spelt as long as the words could be understood, and that arithmetic was all right provided the answers came out close enough. Try telling that to a shopkeeper you went to for a job! It had changed for the better now, though the one called Garry might have been a victim of such beliefs.

'You're right,' Lance said. 'Would you believe it? How are you, Mr Butler, sir?'

The stench of cannabis was as if they were caught among burning stubble after the harvest. He had once taken some from boys in the playground and flushed it down the toilet. 'Didn't I teach you about rhyming?' He shook the cold strong hand. 'You were interested in writing pop songs, if I remember.'

'That's right,' Lance said.

He had tried to guide him towards poetry, suggesting Yeats and Tennyson, but that was a stage Lance had not aspired to, fearing the scorn of his mates, which told Daniel he would never do any-thing worthwhile. Even so, without preamble, he had one day read

'Byzantium' to the class and, a few lines in, no face moved, frozen images as never to be forgotten as the verse itself.

'Can I buy you a drink, sir?'

'All teachers should be shot,' Garry said, 'though maybe not when it's snowing and we're up shit's creek together.'

'Not Old Ferret,' Wayne said. 'That's what we used to call him. We liked him, though, didn't we – sir? We'll drive your van anywhere you want it to go, being as we're the only ones who can. Anything to do you a favour, after all them years you tried to drum knowledge into our big soft heads.'

They were amiable at the moment, boasting, stoned perhaps and soon to be drunk as well, the best the world had to offer, except that they were on the wrong side, as far as he was concerned, the worse side because it was no side at all.

'It depends what's in the van, don't it?' Garry said. 'We wouldn't want to flog our goolies off if it wasn't important, would we?'

'Forget about it, for the moment,' Daniel said quickly. Perhaps they did have the grit to get it to Coventry. He could telephone and say it was on its way, and if they argued for not having got it there himself, that would be their problem, though it would be his as well when they caught him. Then he recalled that the telephone lines were dead.

'We can have a rave-up,' Lance said. 'To think we met our old teacher when we got stuck in a blizzard.'

'I always wondered what became of you,' Daniel said. 'You were different to the others.' He couldn't stop his tongue from being the schoolmaster, Mr Chips of the slums, the man his mother had decided he would be, and what the greater part of him in those days had wanted to be. Looking at him from Heaven, the only place for her, if she was anywhere, she would be happy in that shark-like possessive way which had ruined his life by forcing him to be something which was not part of his nature. But he became even more of what she had in mind, a caricature in fact, to prove to himself that he at least had some independence. Therefore he could allow himself to enjoy being the schoolmaster, idolized by two old boys, rough and common as they were, who recalled what he had tried to do for them.

They stood as if expecting wisdom that only he as an old teacher could provide. He was sorry to disappoint them, yet they took the blow calmly, he thought, tamed at the moment by his presence. What he wanted – and craved for them to desire, though it was an accolade he knew he could never have, and therefore a blessed state that they could never have though he hoped for it against all odds nevertheless – was to be a god and run their lives from birth to death on the principles of love and justice and the mellow rules of sweet reason, till the world became perfect for teachers and taught alike, the harmony of the just and the elect to prevail over all rough beasts, pain and bloodshed banished for ever.

SEVENTEEN

Sally felt culled by the hair, out of a doze between icy terylene sheets, as if barbaric assailants were at the castle drawbridge of her dreams, vandals spilling in for rapine and plunder. Eyes pinned open, and sleep impossible, she would go down and find out what mayhem had broken loose.

It was a poor show, she thought, not having the wherewithal in her luggage to change from skirt and blouse into a frock: stockings and knickers instead of tights: her favourite amber beads and a Liberty's silk scarf. With a state of mind so altered such formality would have kept her within range of who she was, and stopped that happening which she might not like to remember. No, that wasn't how she felt at all. What she really wanted to be clad in was her leopardskin trousers, highnecked white shirt (opened a button or two) and black high heels. Stanley hated a rig that was outlandish enough to get everyone looking her way.

Standing in the doorway, she observed Daniel's ruminations, his eyes beamed downwards, deepening as if some recollection was coming full thunder on him, a pushing out and drawing back of the lower lip, and a more subtle alteration of his visible cheek. He was at the point of speaking to himself, or action of some sort, or even – a notion that caused her to hold back a laugh – a mild kind of fit.

She supposed the state of people's souls was marked on their faces, especially when they didn't suspect scrutiny, though Stanley's smooth visage showed so little he had to talk for her to know what was on his mind, and whatever was revealed proved that he didn't exist at the intensity she sensed in Daniel, whose differing layers of expression only increased her curiosity.

He looked up at this rangy blonde holding the bannister just outside the door. He had never known whether he was quick to show the red face on being surprised out of his reflections; or whether he was generally calm at any disturbance, always unable to decide which personality to use. With the short-fuse version he sometimes felt close

94

to madness, and for that reason rarely employed it, knowing it was his responsibility when he did, and having no sympathy for people who couldn't control it (like some who also worked for the Cause) and might therefore be considered mad. To be mad was a matter of choice, it seemed to him, because on losing his temper he could watch himself doing so, and revert to a calm state easily enough.

He thought she was the sort who might laugh long and loud if he showed irritation at her gaze meant only for him. 'You seem to be curious about me.'

'I'm sorry if it annoys you.'

'I'm flattered. Let me get you a drink.' It was always hard to bring the fascinating conversations in his own mind into the open. Women suspected such concentrated silence while he wondered whether he should and how he could do it. Or they were bored, or took his inability as indicating that they themselves were at fault. They might question what the man was trying to hide, though you weren't expected to talk nonstop either, because that would be worse than silence. But, above all, and this he felt from the most bitter experience, he must never mention even the mildest of his dreams.

'I'd love a sherry. Dry.' She sat at the nearest table, much better than staying in that draughty bedroom. The storm was so dreadful that no one could complain about their accommodation, however. Poor Stanley would wish he hadn't left Singapore, though she shouldn't keep thinking of him if she wanted to get the best out of being marooned. 'Cheers! Here's to getting out – sometime.'

'You seem uncertain about it.' The English loved a crisis. Even the bikers were quiet, sitting before their drinks and heaps of sandwiches. 'I expect we'll be on our way by tomorrow.'

Percy, jived by some chemical engine, swayed away from his table. 'We're on the way to Heaven. That's our destination.' He smacked the middle of his forehead. 'I can feel it here. It's a wide road into the blue beyonder. A lot of light up there. You'll enjoy it. I can't wait, talking for myself, though I don't know if any of us deserve it.' He lurched towards the bikers, caught a chairback to right himself. 'We'll all go together when we don't, won't we, lads? No matter how old you are you always look young in the mirror.'

Garry reached for another sandwich. 'I reckon you're a teeny-weeny bit stoned, Dad.'

'Never felt better.' Percy flailed away. 'You won't stone me, young 'un. That's what them Arabs do when you're caught having a bit on the side.'

'I have this awful feeling' – Sally knew she could say it, since his behaviour at the telephone had indicated that his life seemed to depend on getting out as soon as possible – 'that we'll be cooped up for days.'

There was nothing to do but smile, except that he couldn't. 'Since I can't get out in the next couple of hours it won't much matter if I'm here for weeks.'

She gulped the sherry. 'Crikey, it's like that, is it?'

He had already had several whiskies and a few more would make him drunk, yet he was disappointed not to feel any clouding of the faculties, since that would be some relief from the horror which seemed to fill his stomach with cold water. 'Would you like another?'

At least he was losing his look of frantic worry. 'Please, but I ought to pay.'

Fred came in with another load of wood, the cane of the basket scratching his jacket as he set it by the fire. If he didn't do it no one would, and he wondered how much fuel he would use before they took themselves off upstairs. Still, it was his job, what he was here for, though if this went on for several days he might yet show them who was the gaffer.

On the second load his arms straightened as he went forward. After the butt at his ankles he let the woodbasket shoot ahead to the floor. He swayed sideways and, with a few workings of the legs, grabbed a table and righted himself. 'You bloody fool!' he screamed.

Wayne straightened himself at the bar. 'I hope you don't mean me, because if you do we'll use your swede-head for a game of soccer. Won't we, lads?'

'You bloody tripped me up.' Fred gathered the logs. 'And you know it.'

'Did I?' Wayne smoothed his beard. 'You're making a mistake. If I had, you'd still be on the floor.'

Aaron had seen only enough to make a definite accusation difficult. It could have been the sheet of coconut matting which had one of its corners turned up.

'I'm not daft. I felt your toecap.'

'Did you? I didn't. My toe wanders off on its own, though, and gets me into all sorts of trouble. I give it a good talking to now and again, but it don't make a blind bit of difference. Shall I get my left foot to apologize? It makes people feel better, after it's been naughty.'

Fred stood at the fire, with his back to them. 'Forget it. But I bloody well know what happened.'

'Does he know he's talking to the Wheelie Champion of the World?' Garry said. 'Somebody ought to tell him, in no uncertain terms.'

'Not yet.' Wayne gave a sinister, self-confident grin. 'We've got all night to think about it.'

Nor did Sally like his smile, and wouldn't trust him an inch. She turned to Daniel, thinking that the truly liberated woman (whatever that might be, because if ever it came about, she told herself, we would have the truly liberated man) would go straight for the man and get his trousers off, letting the devil take the hindmost. I suppose you would frighten most men, though not a real one – whatever that might mean as well.

Daniel saw laughter in her eyes, but they also had that slightly troubled look of the woman who is worried about her husband. He had learned a lot in his short but turbulent marriage. Strange how much part of the world he felt, but he was calm, almost grateful to her. Threatened by the biking hooligans, he had become more like his old self before enlisting for the Cause, no longer involved in damaging other people's bodies from a distance with Semtex. The blue cold glow of snow outside, and talk with an attractive woman who so obviously saw things about him that she liked, took him from thoughts of the cataclysm nobody knew was on its way.

'I think we're both ready to burst out laughing,' she said, 'and I'll bet neither of us can think why. Or if we are, we aren't saying.'

He liked her, because she knew his thoughts, and didn't unreasonably demand that he know hers, which promised a viable relationship, though one that had come too late.

Percy reamed out his pipe, black dust chuting into the ashtray. Better than nodding off, he thought. Well, I've got a right to nod, haven't I? Prodding and scraping with a little silver penknife made for the job, he fought the oppressive snow by lingering on memories of summer weather, rich black elderberries over a glassy pond not far from the colliery, the sun so warm and mellow through the trees that he only wanted to lie down and sleep on the bank. Birds with their hot little hearts whistled among the leaves, and there was a smell of wood ash from a fire where kids had been playing. You couldn't call them happy days. Happy wasn't a good enough word. But God had been on your side a few moments now and again in your life, whatever other troubles you had. And then as an engineer he had overseen the drainage of that pond on Coal Board land, trees uprooted, declivity filled, and buildings put where none should be. He had taken many a sweetheart there as a youth, remembered it as vividly as in reality, and so it was, memory being everything, to judge by the smile on his face which he felt duly grateful for.

'Why don't you have another fag, Dad?' Garry called. 'That old pipe'll choke you.'

He paused, smiling widely. 'I'm up to your kids' tricks. You're trying to get me even more stoned than you are.'

Alfred had been glad to have his father off his hands for a while. 'Don't press him. He's never been used to that drug sort of thing.' We don't want to turn him into a hophead at his age, though it might not be a hard way to go, which idea made his reprimand a mild one.

She put a hand on Daniel's sleeve. 'Have you ever indulged in hash?'

'I have more respect for my consciousness' (or my immortal soul, he was too shy to say) 'though I can't be that much of a prig, can I, if I drink and smoke?'

'I'm wondering how much it would relax me if I took some.'

Garry wiped crumbs and turkey fat from his lips, flashed his Zippo, and passed her one. 'The opium of the masses. Well, we've got to have something, haven't we? What's good enough for the middle classes is good enough for us.'

She coughed as the fibres lit. 'It's my first time.'

'Let's hope it isn't the last.' Wayne looked closer into her face than Daniel liked. 'How did you manage then, up to now?'

She pushed him away, and took Daniel's hand, his fingers warm and slender, acting so forwardly because she didn't want him to imagine later – when she had gone further, which she fully intended to do – that smoking a bit of pot had been the cause. 'Do you mind if I kiss you?'

He would like it more than anything. The back of his neck tingled, and his face went close enough to meet her lips halfway, the delightful pleasure of flesh on flesh causing him to smile.

His lips had been cold, but she would soon warm them. *Warm hands – cold lips* must mean something. 'I never know how to act when I fancy someone. I rarely do, of course. I see very few men I could fall for. I mean, it's not a normal thing with me.'

'You have a lovely voice.' It was the sort of upper-register English trill he had always loathed and distrusted, but he didn't mind it now because he couldn't care less what she said – he told himself. Just to hear her talk was enough, being already in love with her even if only because she had made the first move. Otherwise, how had it happened?

'When I first saw you by the telephone I was attracted by your face.' Such a wonderful face, she wanted to say. 'The expression was so interesting.' That didn't seem right, either.

He winced, no longer in control of the situation, couldn't stop the flicker in his cheek, swore to himself. She put down the half-smoked cigarette, which he thought was sensible, considering that she wasn't used to it, and was probably talking in an uncharacteristic way. But she only relinquished it to free both hands for his shoulders, and drew him into a longer kiss.

Aaron turned away, as at a bride and bridegroom on their own after a wedding feast. 'I wish I'd got my guitar,' Lance said. 'I'd play 'em a nice tune.'

Wayne looked peevish and unsettled. 'I wonder where that lovely little waitress got to? I wouldn't mind settling her bit of hash. We might be dead tomorrow, and then where will we be?'

Not much of a philosophy, Aaron thought, though it's the needle tip of all the philosophies ever created by indolence out of chaos, which people like him inherited in his blood, and so doesn't need to write a book about.

'Come on, duck, let's get to the end of this bubbly.' Parsons pulled Jenny by the arm. 'It won't keep till breakfast.'

'I don't want any more.'

'Oh, it's like that, is it?' – seeing her gaze at Lance. 'Go over to him, then, if you want him. If you've made up your mind, there's nowt I can do about it. I'm just another fifty quid down the drain.'

That's the end of me when the lads at the Union get to know. In which case I suppose I can buy another couple of bottles. We'll have a proper party, and them as can't get laid can get pissed.'

Sally was relieved at having gone too far to pull back. 'If I go up to my room will you follow in five minutes?' Even without the sherry, or the few intakes of bindweed from the cigarette, she would have asked, not knowing how it had begun, though she trembled that it had, hoping he would sense it yet not be deterred. 'My room's number five, halfway down the corridor, on the left.'

Jenny felt helpless from lack of sleep yet couldn't sleep, kept even more awake by willing the biker they called Lance to come to her table. She liked him. She wanted to talk to him. He stood, nonchalantly observing, and she loved it when he looked quickly by on his sweep of the company – with his regular, almost Latin features. Why were the men she could like so foolishly shy, at least the best of them, and often with a self-deprecation that made them revel in loutishness – or make friends with louts?

'We all look a bit dressed up with nowhere to go, don't we?' Lance sat at her table, so that getting what she wanted came as a pleasant surprise. 'Is he your husband?'

Parsons' head jerked, every word a superfine Gillette. 'No, he's bloody well not.' He turned to Aaron. 'Can I borrow the newspaper?'

'Take it. I've just about wrung it out.'

Parsons smiled, then put a hand over his mouth because he knew his breath was foul. 'Even the crossword. You must be brainy to do this one.'

'I've been struggling with them for thirty years.'

He was rueful, envious. 'There's something to be said for a regular life.'

Aaron felt a twinge of sorrow for him. 'I suppose it can be less painful, but it also makes time go too quickly.'

'Ar, there is that. You can't have everything, can you? But if it's painless, and gets life over quickly, well, I suppose that's best.'

Enid came in, stood with hands on hips, eyeing them in turn. 'What a deadbeat lot!'

'I swear her skirt gets shorter by the hour,' Parsons said in a low voice, aware of her wrathful nature. 'It'll be up to her armpits before midnight. It might be worth staying up for.'

'Anybody want owt?' she said. 'Don't think I get commission, though, because I don't.'

'Get me a pint o' Greattorex's, duck.' He unthreaded his black and purple tie, folded it neatly around his broad palm, and put it in his pocket. 'I need summat to chase that champers away.'

'The same for me,' Aaron said.

'Christ, I'm run off my feet.'

Garry pulled her to him. 'I'll have a bit of *you*, duck. Bring yourself in on a tray, all trussed up in pink ribbon with a vibrator in your mouth and a garnish of furlined zip-fastening French letters near your toes.'

The five minutes Daniel was expected to wait were the longest of his life. He had looked twice at his watch, a bare minute in between, every second precious and never to come again. Who but the lowliest sort could regret the passing of time? The distance between one second and another was filled by a smack of bone on flesh so decisive that everyone looked to see where it came from.

Garry stepped twice back along the bar, a hand to his face. 'You rotten little cowbag. I'll break your neck for that.'

Enid's fist stayed high. 'Just because I'm a woman the leery fuck-faced ponce thinks he can do as he likes. If you come near me again you'll get some more, in your scabby bollocks next time. A fuckpig like you ain't going to shit on me.'

'Her vocabulary,' Parsons smiled, 'ought to be the envy of the uncivilized world.'

Wayne applauded, but Garry went towards her with a flat hand uplifted.

'Leave her alone.'

The tone stopped him, but for how long, Aaron wondered, noting the parallel bars of his brow, the wicked glint, the alarming swivel of the left eye. Enid hurried to get the drinks, imagining she would see Aaron looking a different person when she came back.

'What did you say?'

'It was a fair fight.' Aaron was not going to be taken at the disadvantage of sitting down, and to make his stature more apparent, lifted a log in one large hand and held it firm. 'Well, wasn't it?'

'We'll see about that. No fucking trollop's going to do that to me.'

'If that's all you ever get,' Percy said in his high, hectoring tone, 'you'll have life easy.'

'All's fair in love and war,' Parsons said. 'Eh, Jenny?'

Garry looked around, as if for allies, but too many of his own sort seemed poised against him, so he would wait.

Five minutes had gone by. Daniel walked to the stairs. In the dim room, with only one bed light on, Sally looked at him from under the blankets and sheet. 'Get undressed, my love. It's freezing in here, and I want some warmth.'

EIGHTEEN

Enid set down his pint. 'I like old men.'

Aaron thanked her for the compliment, though not aware that he was so far gone in years.

'You stood up for me against that bully, and I'll never forget it. Don't pay for the beer. I'll make it right. There's nothing else for me to do at the moment, so can I sit down?'

He pulled out a chair. 'You really swore at him. I've never heard anything like it.'

'He tried to feel me up, and I can't stand that. You might not think it, but I'm twenty-six, and I've just about had my lot, what with one thing and another.'

Garry lay in an armchair, legs spread and head back, mouth open at the ceiling. 'He's clapped out,' Lance said. 'But no wonder. He works all the hours God sends.'

Jenny turned from the sight. 'He doesn't seem your sort.'

'Maybe not, but he's one of the best, when you get to know him.'

'Have you been friends long?'

'Long enough. I remember how we met, on a sliproad on the M1. I'd just clogged it back from London, and my bike had broken down. It was a boiling July day, and I hadn't got no AA or RAC insurance. I was out of cash, though there was enough juice in the tank to get me home. But the engine had blown its top, or near enough. I just lay on the gravel, black and grimy in the sun, thinking that when it got cooler I'd hump the bike to the nearest garage and phone the old man. Either that, or I'd flog it for a tenner and hop on a bus. The next thing I know, somebody's pulling at me, asking what's up. I tell him, and notice his all-black roadster purring a few feet away. "Can you wait an hour?" he said. "Then I'll be back. Rely on me. International Rescue. Bikers' Law." He took a flask and some sandwiches from his topbox, and let me have 'em for company. Then he rode away. I thought that might be the last I'd see of him, but the tea was the best drink I'd ever had. An hour later this big van drives up, and there's Garry, opening the back. He pulls out a plank and in no time we've got the bike inside and we're driving to my home. I was a stranger, but he did that for me, no strings, not even knowing we lived in the same town. He would have done it for any stranded biker. He said if I wanted to pay him back I had to do the same for somebody else.'

'He must have been lonely,' Jenny said.

'We all are, when we're on our own.'

'What makes him so rough?'

'Who knows? I'm rough, as well. I suppose it's because we're bikers. Everybody's against us. We're young, we're free, and we're mobile. People hate us for that.'

It all sounded so romantic, though everybody's romantic life wounded somebody. But she tried to sound positive: 'I suppose it is a good time for you.'

'When we're all out together, riding over the dales, nobody can touch us.' He reached for her hand. 'Are you married?'

'I was.'

'How did you kill him? Poison, a knife, or a gun? I wrote a song like that once.'

'That's what I like to hear.' Percy woke up. 'Lovely no-holds-barred peals of feminine laughter!'

'Perhaps I'd better take you up to bed, Father. We've had a long day, and tomorrow might be even longer. You must be all in.'

'I like it down here.' His eyes glinted. 'I might miss summat if I'm asleep. There'll be plenty of time for sleep when I've popped my clogs.'

'He left me,' she said.

'A nice person like you? He must have been insane. You didn't lose much, if he was that stupid.'

'That's one way of looking at it.' She felt as exhilarated by such talk as he must feel when flying across the landscape. 'I got pregnant, and wanted to have the baby, but he didn't. He said we couldn't afford it, and that he wasn't ready for such a responsibility, whatever that meant. I couldn't figure him out. So I thought: if he isn't ready, neither am I. It would be a disaster to have a child under those conditions. I got rid of it, and now I see how wrong I was. He'd still have left me, but I'd have managed. Women do. And then he went off with one of my best friends.' She wanted to be free with him, yet saying such things might put him off. 'It's because I like you' – which was as far as she could go.

He had had plenty of girls, but not a woman like her. 'I love you, as well. It's good to trade stories.'

'Have you written a song about it?' She laughed, touching his face, laid her palm there, winning the dare with herself to do it.

He kissed her. 'I would have looked after that baby. I know I would. I hope the snow keeps us here for ever.'

Kiss my tears and taste the salt. And I'm not even drunk. But she felt sick from the champagne, a vacuum forming in her stomach. 'It doesn't matter.'

'It does, but you might as well forget it. Worry is no good for anybody.'

'What made you so wise?'

'You should ask my old man that. He'd laugh till he died. So maybe you should. It could be the snow.'

'I've been looking at you all evening,' Enid said, 'whenever I came in and out. You didn't see me, though. I like you. You're more interesting than anybody else here.'

Aaron wondered how she had come to such an amazing conclusion.

'I like older men.' She wanted to make good her previous mistake. Her grey-green eyes shone. 'Older men have been through a lot more. Young 'uns make me sick. Older men have learned how to treat you better.'

'How do you know?'

'Well, I don't, do I? But I'm sure it's true.' She looked at his hands. 'Your nails are clean.'

'Why shouldn't they be?' He was never allowed to come to the table unless they were, and such early inculcations didn't die.

'I hate dirty nails. That's the first thing I look at in a man. That pig's nails was black, every one of 'em. Didn't you notice?'

Thank God he was asleep. He wanted to keep trouble away as long as possible, dreading that they would wake up and fight among themselves. 'He's probably been working on his motorbike. Everyone's nails are black at some time.' Her nails were clean, but eaten to the quick. 'I always look to see if a person *bites* their nails.'

She drew them back, reddening in a way he found charming. 'I know,' she said. 'I can't stop. I try, though, honest I do.'

He wondered why she was working in a place like this. 'How long have you been here?'

'About three months.'

'Do you like it?'

'I live in the next village. I don't want to milk cows or chase sheep all my life. It pays my way here, but it's not a career, and that's a fact. I've been to secretarial college, and I can work computers. I've applied for fifty jobs in the last few months, in Sheffield, Nottingham and Derby – all over the place. Sometimes I get as far as the interview, but then I don't hear from them again, I don't know why.'

Nor did he. When not battling to preserve her self-esteem she looked sad and serious, her faraway expression of not entirely belonging to this or any other world making him feel sorry for all young people who had to get used to the brickbats of life. 'I run a second-hand book business with my sister. It's the usual thing of buying cheap and selling as dear as I think we can get away with. We put catalogues out a few times a year, and by the end we've made enough to justify our efforts.'

'It sounds nice work. Especially if you like it.'

He held her hand, his heart at a faster rate when she looked at him as if not wanting him ever to let go. 'It's hectic, sometimes. We get a lot of orders in and they all have to be packed and posted. In fact we've often thought of getting somebody to give us a hand.'

'Come on, Father, it's time,' Alfred said, 'the sort that waits for no man. If we don't get into our beds soon they'll run away and leave us for them as needs 'em.'

Percy stood up, and took his son's arm. 'Aye, we don't want that to happen. I must get my beauty sleep for when we get to Bournemouth. There'll be a lot to see, won't there?'

The older he got, the more pity he felt for his father. 'There'll be all sorts of nice things, I promise you.' Alfred waved good night, but Percy wouldn't leave till he had shaken a few hands.

'Have you got a room here?' Lance asked.

'Of course she has.' Sweat fell from Parsons' nose as if he had just run ten miles. 'Nothing but the best for such as her – the best that my money can buy.'

'Let's go, then,' Lance said. 'I love you, you can tell that, can't you? You're nicer than anybody else here, because I don't know anything about you.'

She laughed at his ambiguous compliments. 'I'm ready when you are.'

'She's nothing but a bloody tart,' Parsons called tearfully.

Unsteady on his feet, he sprawled backwards at the first blow.

'Oh good,' Wayne yawned, 'the fighting's started.'

Jenny was sodden with pity and regret at Parsons having helped himself to the Union money, not at all encouraged by her. He had been in a funny mood the whole trip, unlike his usual self (whatever that was, she now thought), as if he had made up his mind to spend the money beforehand but hoped she would save him from it, and show that she cared. She hadn't guessed his weakness till too late, and if she had it would have been impossible to stop him. She pulled at Lance's arm: 'Please, leave him alone.'

'He'd better keep his trap shut, then,' Lance said, 'or my boot'll fill it.'

'Pack it in.' Aaron lifted Parsons, though without much sympathy, into a chair, blood falling onto his sleeve.

'Nobody can take a joke,' Parsons muttered. 'The young 'uns always win. That was bloody well uncalled for.'

Lance hooked into her arm as they walked away.

'You could take a job with us,' Aaron said to Enid. 'We certainly need someone.' Living a quiet life produced unseemly fantasies that might one day turn magically real. He imagined she looked at him with love, while knowing himself to be older than her father. He would take her home after the thaw like the top prize gained in a raffle, and Beryl would give her the spare room, and slowly they would train her to the business, and he would marry her. He had never had children, and would be an old father, the world not short of such cases.

'I like you,' she said, 'but you don't have to fix me up with work.'

'We need someone, and you would learn.' What was power if you couldn't use it for good? But when Beryl said that the police had called, it could only be for one thing. She would look after Beryl while he was in prison.

'I want to go to bed with you,' she said.

'The snow seems to be taking everybody the same way.' Parsons, unabashed, swabbed the cut lip with his handkerchief. 'You'd think the booze had been laced with Spanish fly. Or maybe it's the snow itself. Though I suppose it's the booze: you never know what the landlord gets up to.'

'Dirty old sod,' Enid said. 'They're all the same.'

Fred came back from his own quarters, happy at seeing half the guests gone to bed. 'What are you sitting down here for? You should be behind the bar, serving the clientele. This isn't the Barbary Coast. What the hell do you think I'm paying you for?'

'I suppose you mean me?' Enid sneered, stood, and marched close. 'Well, do you know something, Mr Fucking Frog Belly? I don't work for you any more.'

'I'd want a month's notice, if you didn't. So do as I say, and none of your lip.'

Aaron thought he was about to slap her, though the twitch of his hand might have been the onset of DTs. He took her by the elbow. 'Sit down, Enid.'

'You'll get no notice out of me. I'll be off first thing in the morning.'

She wouldn't be easy to replace, bad as she was at her work. Most girls in the area were barely out of the Stone Age. 'You can't leave me in the lurch like this. You wouldn't get a reference, anyway.'

'You can stuff your reference. I've already got a job.'

'You won't have when I tell 'em how you left me.'

'He won't mind. He's sitting here.'

Fred took it in. 'Well, that's the bloody limit, when the guests come and take my labour away.'

Aaron saw that he was right, but it was done, and he would stand by his offer, though he was sorry she hadn't let Fred know more gently.

'I'd like a drink.' She sat down. 'Tell him to get me a drink, Aaron. I feel like celebrating. We can drink to my new job.'

He wasn't sure it would be tactful. 'I'd like two whiskies.'

'Not for her,' Fred said. 'Anyway, the bar's closed. The towels are on. I'm not having any more of this. You can get out into the snow and die of the cold. This isn't a pothouse – nor a knocking-shop, come to that.'

'Oh, stuff it, then.' Enid pulled Aaron by the hand. 'Come on, let's get up to bed. I'm dying for a bit of sex, after all this excitement.'

'Can I come as well, duck?' Wayne called when they reached the stairs. 'I'll be ever so quiet!' He felt lively after the sleep, no longer hungry, and certainly thirsty due to the state of his pigsty mouth. 'Get me a pint, mate. I want to console myself.'

'One for me, as well.' Garry stretched, and belched. 'I ain't had a drink for an hour.'

'The towels are on,' Fred told them. 'You're welcome to sit here until morning, but there's no more to drink.'

'It's only ten o'clock,' Wayne said.

'My watch says ten minutes past. Everything's closed up.'

'How much more of his fucking lip are we going to have to take?'

'I might as well clear off to bed myself.' Parsons' face still ached. 'I've just come to the end of the longest day of my life. Good night, everybody.'

Fred wished some guests had stayed down, as witnesses or assistants should it come to violence. 'I run a respectable house, and when I say time's up, it's up. I mean it.'

'The best thing you can do' – Garry took him by the lapel in such a way that if he struggled he would choke – 'is sell us a bottle of whisky, and then get to bed yourself, where you'll be safe. I can't say fairer than that.'

'You can't frighten me.' Fred pulled free. 'I'm going to phone for the police.'

Garry sat in an armchair. 'Do you have a secret CB radio in your room? Because that's the only way you'd get through tonight. Me and Lance yanked the wires out before we came in. We're dab hands at that, though I expect the line was down already. In any case, don't you know that our lovely lads in blue are at this moment in time supping tea with their toes up against a stove? And who can blame them? Be sensible, and rustle us up a few drinks.'

'I've told you. My mind's decided, and when it is, it stays that way.'

Garry turned. 'Where's Lance?'

'He's up in a bedroom, having it off with that woman.'

'Pity. He's going to miss this.'

NINETEEN

He had said nothing, a muteness she deserved perhaps, and didn't mind because he had moved in such a way during their lovemaking that she'd had her pleasure each time. She lay on her back, eyes opened in the dim light, clothes to her chin. Curled by her side, he seemed asleep, in the shape of a shorthand symbol studied in her teens.

But he wasn't asleep, his voice startling, as if it were a facility which he'd never had before. 'We're all going to be dead by the morning.'

'After that' – even her laugh was dry – 'I don't think I'm going to feel alive ever again.'

'You don't know what I mean.' Half out of bed, he reached for cigarettes in his jacket. 'The joy of it is, nothing can alter the fact.'

'Are you telling me we won't see each other again?' She hardly expected it, though to continue the adventure might be interesting, and certainly pleasant, albeit dangerous, unless she confined her activity to while Stanley was away.

He turned to her, leaning on an elbow. 'I mean exactly what I say.'

'But why say it so soon after such a good time? Wasn't it marvellous for you as well? It seemed so to me.'

He held his cigarette away while kissing her. 'It was the best thing that's ever happened. I don't mind dying.'

She supposed it was the old bite of sadness after sex – weren't men said to feel it more intensely than women? – though he was putting it a bit strongly.

'It won't make any difference,' he continued in the same weird tone, that she hadn't picked up in him before coming to bed. 'I wish it would, but it won't. We might just as well lie here and let it happen. There's no better way.'

She stroked his hard flesh. 'Darling, tell me, what is it? Talk to me. I love you, don't you know?' And who wouldn't, caught tightly in this blue world of snow? It must be snowing again, since even I sound different to myself.

He felt an unfamiliar contentment, dwelt alone on a confined levitated plane, which state he didn't want to spoil by too much talk. 'I'm happy, that's all.'

'So am I. It would be strange not to be.' But she wasn't, not entirely, recalling his anguished face when he had been on the telephone, the expression of a person in such trouble that he was afraid for his life.

His disembodied voice came again. 'I never imagined my existence would end in happiness. I have to thank you for that. You're the glorious person who will make it possible for me to die happy.'

'I'm glad for you, if this is the effect I've had.' He was being more poetic, even profound, about the experience than Stanley could ever have been. 'I feel wonderfully satisfied as well, but it seems to have been more interesting for you. Tell me more about it. I love to hear you talk.'

'You could hardly be expected to understand.' His protective mood of detachment had been broken into, violated, though he wasn't able to care. 'It would make no sense.'

She borrowed his cigarette, as she had seen lovers do in films. Stanley had been irritated when she once tried. 'Maybe you're right. Why spoil our lovely time?' Ease came back. No reason to feel guilty of a little affair in the night. What the eye didn't see the heart didn't grieve, as her mother used to say, but about things far less important.

His voice again sounded as if from a little box in the stratosphere, out of timbre with reality, and she didn't want to lose him. 'I don't know,' he said. 'I never did know. I suppose it's the human condition that we can never know till we die what it's essential to know, and by then it's far too late. My mother was convinced she would go to heaven, but for me it will be hell, like my father.'

Oh, that stale Catholic stuff. As far as she was concerned she wouldn't go anywhere. But let him talk, it must be good for him, almost as good as it was fascinating for her to listen. Perhaps he had to make up for his unnatural silence during their exquisite session of love, though what he was saying was hardly flattering.

'I don't know whether I should tell you,' he said.

'All right then, don't. I'm happy just lying here' – floating listlessly between utter wellbeing and a concupiscent desire to make love again, touching him, smoothing his flank, but softly so as not to disturb his obviously fragile spirit while he struggled to get rid of some burden clearly impossible for her to comprehend.

'I don't know whether or not I can trust you, you see.'

He was so serious that she knew she had better listen, a faint alarm that she hadn't known him long enough to rely on his sense of humour. 'That's for you to decide.'

'I want to trust you,' he said. 'I need to. I suppose I'll be compelled to, anyway.'

'How do you mean?' Talk, muffled or garbled according to distance, came from other parts of the hotel like waves of far-off traffic, as if the snow had now gone and the roads were dry and open, motors speeding in all directions. Then silence again, except for a sudden jolt of the ancient plumbing system. They were in a structure of enormous weight that would be part of the world till the world itself came to an end.

He sighed, as if about to put on the little boy act. He wasn't that sort, plainly. His face showed no illusions, though there was more than a hint of them having worked their way out. 'I was brought up to walk in the path of the righteous, to know the truth and to speak the truth. But given the way I must have been before I was born, it was a fatal course. I was bound to be the opposite when I grew up and got to know myself.'

'What caused it?'

'Let's say that it was politics.'

She wondered what he saw in her features, though guessed it wasn't half as much as what she was beginning to see in his. 'We all have to mature in that way.'

He paused awhile, then: 'But not the way I did.'

The closer he came to words of importance the more relaxed was his voice, but his body was as tense as a loaded crossbow. She had never imagined such talk after making love, but she hadn't foreseen being stranded, either. In her fantasies she would have been in a sunfilled bedroom, or strolling through beautifully dappled bluebell woods for more dalliance with her ardent lover. 'It strikes all of us differently.' She wanted him to continue talking, so as to have as much as possible to remember him by, fighting the faint echo of desolation which told her she might not see him after tonight.

'I swear you to secrecy, though it won't be for long.'

Her surmise was right, yet his words sounded like some kind of boyish ceremony. 'That goes without saying,' she said.

'Nothing ever goes without saying. At least it never did in my life.'

'All right, then, I promise.' She tried to sound nonchalant, so as to encourage him to talk. He frowned neat furrows along his brow, and she knew she must look serious, and even feel so, however difficult at such a careless time, since he was in a state to detect it if she didn't.

'When I woke up this morning I wasn't to know that in twenty-four hours I would cease to exist. On the other hand, I have the consolation of knowing that the same applies to quite a few other people.'

'You can go out of your own house and be mown down by a juggernaut ten minutes later, but it doesn't do to worry too much about it.' She had never got anywhere near such a conversation with Stanley, which fact made her curious as to who Stanley did have his heart to hearts with.

'That,' he responded, 'is pure petty chance.'

'So is the blizzard.'

He seemed to think about that, and then said, disappointingly forlorn: 'Is that all there is?'

Didn't you know? she wanted to ask, which would be flippant, something Stanley often accused her of being, whereas she had thought it a virtue to make fun of the futility of life. With Daniel she decided to be more guarded: 'Well, it could be.'

'There's always a moment when the bomb begins to tick.' He saw, in her lovely rawboned English face, that she didn't understand. He wanted to tell her everything, unable to stop even if only because he was unwilling to do so. 'It began when those damned bikers turned up.'

He didn't seem so timid as to be afraid of them. 'They're stranded like us, that's all. I expect they're harmless enough.' Her arms were stiffening, she wanted to get dressed and go downstairs for a drink, see what was happening. Someone passed the door on their way to bed, as if the party might be over already.

'Oh, you're right there. I taught them at school. They're the usual louts, but nice enough when tamed. The fact is, though, they found my van in the lay-by and brought it here. That's the crux of the matter. God knows what evil intentions allowed them to get it through the snow. Perhaps they saw it as just a lark, and didn't know that they were God's chosen in what they were doing. If they hadn't got it here everything might have been all right.'

To find out what was in the van she would have to be quiet. Her skin had cooled even more, and she pulled him closer so as to stop shivering, and as if to recall their passion. He hadn't made love for months, he had said, and fucked her till she was limp and empty. How lucky to find someone who had been so taken with other matters that he had forgotten the divine urge!

His tone was so faded she could hardly catch the words, breath warming her ear when she put it close. 'The van is loaded with high explosives, timed to go off at eight o'clock tomorrow morning. It was meant for some street or other in London. Or maybe Birmingham. I don't know their plans exactly.' He felt the vacuity which was nearer still to happiness, his only wish now to disembarrass himself of treacherous words and stop talking. 'It began a long time ago.'

In silence she might have been distraught, and let him sense her terror, but he was talking still, so she encouraged him to talk more, as if only that would help, since he was a madman wielding his power and trying to destroy her as well. But he had the wrong person, which she hoped was true, dried up inside as she now was, the medieval ballroom of spectacular dimensions and lubricious debauchery a long time faded. Married to someone eminently sane would help her to deal with this situation. Even to be herself was enough.

She listened to him telling her why he worked for terrorists. She said yes and no, feared to nod her head but stroked the warm hard limbs as she rehearsed the story to Stanley, about how she had coped oh so wonderfully with this lunatic trying to scare her by saying his van of explosives would blow them and the hotel to kingdom come and halfway back again, a dreadful tale with not a grain of truth in it, but so convincing in his mad, intimidating way that she had been half frightened out of her life, it being his kooky idea that she should be, of course.

She would not be able to tell Stanley, and her eyes welled as if tears would fall. Stanley was her husband, and he wouldn't stay much of a friend either if she told him how she had got into such a fix. For all she knew he would call her a slut for the rest of her life or divorce her on the spot, and that would be that, an outlook worse than hell itself, though if what Daniel was saying was true she wouldn't be able to tell her adventure even to herself because she and the rest of them would be dead. Stanley had always made a great thing of loyalty, which was why she had never quite trusted him, so it would be better not to confide in him at all.

TWENTY

Eileen lay with legs apart, and he stared at the dark patch and lips. 'Aren't you cold?'

'Is that all you can say? I love you looking at my cunt.'

He passed a cigarette. 'As long as you're warm enough.'

'You won't have any left soon.' She blew smoke, which he boxed away.

'I expect there are plenty more downstairs. Do you think I'm mesmerized by your charms?' he smiled.

'I might be if I was where you are, only I couldn't be, could I, because I'm a woman. Trevor would never look at me when I was starkers like this. It frightened him, unless he was drunk.'

He frowned. 'I don't want to hear about him. Ever again. Do you understand?'

'All right. You're my boy friend now.'

'Aren't I too old?'

'How old *are* you?'

He told her.

'Well, it was lovely being in bed with you. You made me come.'

'I couldn't stop you. It's good when it happens. It means a woman's in love – though it might not last more than the time it takes. But it's good, all the same.'

'I don't come with a man. Only when I do it myself. I must have been wanting it. And I love you.'

'No, you don't.'

'You said that's why it happens.'

He lay by her side, not wanting to smash the place to pieces any more, getting more kisses from her than ever in the same space of time, which left him feeling he also might be in love.

'It sounds as if they're having a barney downstairs.'

'Shall we go and take a look?'

She came to him. 'Not yet. Let's be together again. I don't want the night to stop. I never knew a day to start so rotten and finish up so good.'

'Nor me.' He was truthful for once, needing her smile. After Gwen's body was found he would have no life for twenty years. Hanging was too good for murderers, he had always said, which was why Gwen had supposed he would never do it. Her intuition ought to have told her that only a man like him would.

'You know I love you,' she said, 'don't you? I love you very much, in fact, and when I say it, I mean it. I don't care whether you love me or not. But I think you do a bit, don't you?'

It didn't hurt him to say yes, especially since it seemed more than likely to be true, certainly as much as he had ever loved anyone. 'Of course I love you.'

'No, you don't.'

'How can I convince you?'

'I don't know. I believe you when you laugh like that, though. What a terrible rumpus is going on down there. It sounds as if they're breaking up the happy home.'

She had a way with phrases, the 'happy home' always to be smashed by those who had moulded one out of impossible circumstances. To build and break was the armature of ambition, to find love and, while you had it, look for another love to avoid the heartbreak of when the present one went rotten in the sun, the worm at the heart of the fruit. Such thinking had led him into a cul-de-sac from which there was no turning back, so all he wanted to do was enjoy the time left. 'There must be some new arrivals.'

'A pop group called The Abominable Snowmen,' she said. 'Who else could it be in weather like this? Or the police have arrived in a chopper and they're clearing the bar. Your laugh turns strange, sometimes.'

'How do you mean?'

'As if you're frightened. You don't look like somebody who could be frightened, though.'

Silence was golden, and if that phrase hadn't been in use for thousands of years he would surely have invented it in this situation. 'No, I'm not. I only know that it's a miracle being here with you. Life's very simple: you find whatever you need when you won't be able to enjoy it for long.'

'We enjoyed it *then*, didn't we?'

A straight yes was easy because his body had plainly said so, and she accepted it as spoken without thinking that the lack of a word might be insulting. Nuance and telepathy had over the years been replaced by the venom of belligerence, when his determination to say nothing invariably ended in a spiritual bloodbath. Such anguished battles were not part of his temperament but had become so, whereas Gwen had thrived on the bold stance, the lit eyes, the triumphant mouth at having harried him to become someone he was not, imagining she could always drive him to the brink of violence and then induce him to pull back.

'Didn't we?'

He felt benign, in his own world again – for however long it would last. 'I'd get you some flowers if I could pull them out of the snow. You've made me happy.'

'Talking will do. I love talk. At home they used to tell me to shut up, I talked so much. But it wasn't all that much. Only *they* thought so. It wasn't that they didn't talk, though they didn't talk all that much, either. It was just that I wasn't supposed to.'

He laughed as she stroked him between his shoulders.

'You can monkey-jabber as long as you care to with me.' It was more than comforting to have someone you were half in love with talk and yet say little. Only in saying something – the telling, the asking for explanations, the no uncertain demands for an answer – did affection fade. 'I can't hear your voice enough.'

'You'd better be careful, or I'll never leave you.'

'You might have to. Things happen.'

'Well, you lousy sod, if I have to I'll have to. But not until.'

He kissed her lovely pliant lips. 'That's what I hoped you would say.'

'Every time you open your mouth you make my day. I've lived a year with you already.'

He stroked her nipples with his lips. 'This is how I like to open my mouth.'

She shivered against him. 'I'm not cold. That's all I want you to do. That's right. Just there. You know how to do it. It won't take long.'

He was roused enough to go into her when she had finished, but work as he might he couldn't ejaculate, and at last flopped out. 'We need distraction.'

'Well, we can't go to a dance. Buses aren't running.' She wiped between her legs on a corner of the sheet. 'We'll be in this room for ever.'

'I wish that were true.' The walls shuddered, telegraphic thuds resounding, followed by a scream and the breaking of glass. He jackknifed off the bed to reach for pants and trousers. 'Mayhem's got loose. Wait while I see what's happening.'

'Not likely.' She pulled her knickers on, was dressed before he had buttoned himself up. 'Where you go, I go. I'm not going to be left on my own.'

Oh, but you are, he thought, you are. 'On your own head be it. Come on, then.'

Fred's squinting eyes led people to assume he was sharp enough to miss nothing of what was going on around him. His solid girth and spherical face gave the impression of a sergeant-major who knew how to take firm control of that part of the world in which he worked.

Though Fred did see what went on, as far as his all-embracing pigeon vision would allow, he never imagined what might be around the corner, or try to guess in unusual circumstances what the next five minutes would bring. He had always assumed that the host of an inn had the authority of a ship's captain. Backed by the law, *his* word was law. He couldn't put anybody in chains, or hang them from the yardarm, or maroon them on an island of clinker and ash, but he could certainly refuse to serve anybody who, he had reason to believe, was drunk, lousy, delinquent, or not the right kind of person to inflict on the other guests.

The English ship and the English inn were unique and special, and a hotel- or innkeeper was responsible for the wellbeing of everyone within its walls. Any violence, either threatened against him or others in his own house, was rank mutiny, an end to ordered life if not of civilization itself.

When Garry and Wayne, one at either end, lifted the wooden settle bodily above their heads, he was unable to speak. As they swung to face him, part of it smashed into the print of *The Great Western* on its turbulent sea, glass and frame crunching under Wayne's boots. 'Where shall we hurl it?'

'Over the fucking bar, if he won't serve us a drink.'

'I can't hold on much longer.'

Fred gave a strangulated cry, a hand raised. 'Don't! It's an antique. It's real. I'll get you whatever you want.'

'Lad's being sensible,' Garry said, 'so we'll put it down. Over to the left — right?'

Two tables and a chair were flattened, a crash that shook the rest of the furniture, and rattled bottles behind the bar so that two fell forward and smashed. Logs displaced in the fire sent sparks up the chimney, rushing as if they would rather join the snow outside than stay in this madhouse.

'You vandals!' Fred saw a brace of gibbets, two swaying dead men surrounded by an approving crowd and overlooked by the wrathful features of God. 'I'll get you twenty years for this,' he screamed. 'Your feet won't touch the ground between here and Strangeways. I'll show you. You won't get a drop now, unless I can find a bottle of three-star poison.'

'He's hysterical,' Garry said. 'What shall we do with him?'

'Chop him up for firewood, except we've got plenty.' Wayne took a bottle of whisky from the bar and poured three glasses. 'You only won the hotel playing at Monopoly. Here, drink this, and calm down.'

Fred knocked the glass away, and went after it at a swing from Garry's fist. 'Waste not, want not, you daft prick. What a way to behave.' He turned to Wayne. 'Cheers, then, mate. Now we can get stuck in.'

'I even put a tenner in the till,' Wayne said, 'so he needn't have refused to drink with us. We was only being polite, but he must have been dragged up. Do you think he's hurt?'

'He deserves to be,' Garry said, 'the unsociable bastard.'

Fred rubbed his pained elbow, and would say no more. He dragged a chair to the bar and sat down, nothing to be done at the threat of such force from the scum of the planetary system, who must in any case know that justice was always done. Or was it? But he would get every brass farthing back, and maybe even a bit to spare.

Four years ago, after Doris had come into a legacy from an aunt, he decided not to manage a pub any more, nor she to be the drudge of a publican's wife. His life savings nearly equalled her windfall, and the rest of the money for The White Cavalier was raised by a bank loan. But last year Doris had had enough of the even worse toil of keeping a hotel, and departed with the cook to run a fish and chip bar in Brighton. She wrote now and again, to make sure of getting her share of the money, because Fred had talked of finding another place.

Since taking The White Cavalier (which Doris in her more bitter moments had referred to as The White Elephant) they had been hoping to get the establishment into *Michelin* or *The Good Hotel Guide*, but some detail was always not quite right when the inspector called, or maybe they had just been unlucky. To be favoured by one or two such prestigious lists would put Fred's asking price up no end, though now he wondered how long it would take to fix the damage these savages had wrought.

'Look at the miserable sod.' Garry poured half a tumbler. 'Dead from the neck up. Deader than that stuffed bloody peacock on the wall. Just because somebody wants a good time. He can't stand that.'

'Lance's still having it away upstairs,' Wayne said. 'She took a shine to him because he writes them leery pop songs. He's letting the side down, the bloody traitor.'

'Good luck to him,' Garry said. 'We'd do the same.'

Wayne aimed a splash of whisky at the peacock. 'You have a drink as well, my old bird. Imagine walking into a disco with that on your arm.'

Garry kicked a beer tin across the lounge. 'We ought to slip it in his bed. It'd frighten the life out of him, all them feathers. Her, as well. She'd think it was her husband back from the hat shop. We'll pull the sheets off and throw it in. Come on, let's get it down.'

Fred walked towards them, fingers twiddling at his waistcoat. 'Don't touch that. I draw the line there. It's part of the hotel.' He didn't want the ship to go down without a fight: the deck raked with grapeshot, all rigging splintered, a glowing cannonball sizzling into the magazine, and when Garry reached for the peacock's tail he broke an empty whisky bottle against his skull, blood trickling through sparse hair.

Garry, not realizing how wounded he was, or that he was wounded at all, turned from the resplendent bird and went with murderous hands towards Fred who, gasping at what he had set going, stepped back in the direction of the fireplace. He had only imagined the action, but now that it was done, and in so little time, he changed tack and skittered between tables to the door that was blocked by Wayne as if keeping goal.

'Let's kill the bastard,' Garry said.

She put off the light and packed the bedclothes gently around him, lulling his body in an Aga patch of heat, taking no chances on letting the cold alert him. He would sleep while she found someone to tell.

She slipped her pants on, tights wrinkled but they would have to stay, one nipple caught but the bra soon adjusted, everything in silence, hardly moving, then the shirt and skirt put on while he slept. She had to stop her teeth clicking from fear or cold, going with shoes in hand towards the door. Thumps and screams from below might not disturb him but a mouse-creak out of the worm-eaten boards would bring him in a mad leap across her path. 'I can't sleep, I'm going for a walk,' she would say, if hands gripped her wrists, or fingers pressed at her throat.

He sat up, stark and clear in the darkness, as if filings of phosphorus glistened around him. Perhaps he saw her only in his crazy mind, imagined her still providing the heat, for he lay on his side as if to face her for more of the comfort she had given – and began to snore.

The latch took time to lift, no one to hear as she drew the door slowly towards her, sufficiently to slide her body out and be gone. Who would believe her? Would *she* give credit to someone who with manic eye buttonholed her in a hotel lounge and said that a huge amount of terrorist's explosives parked in the yard was due to go off in ten hours' time? She would think them a fugitive from the local funny farm and run a mile.

While standing outside to mull on it, and rooted by another cacophony of animal rage from downstairs, the door snapped open, and Daniel caught her by the arm.

'Where are you going, without me?'

TWENTY-ONE

Enid took her hands from his wet and languid penis. Strange how it was such a bulltup one minute, and small like a cat's the next. 'It sounds like those bikers are killing poor old Fred. I hope so. He asks for it sometimes.'

He thought it nothing less than miraculous that she had given her pale and exquisite body over to his adoration. 'We can't let them, then. You stay here, while I go down.' From thinking he would be able to pass the night in unaccustomed bliss, the noise from below would not let even the most dedicated morphetic sleep.

'Not likely,' she said. 'I want to see.'

A screech could have been man or gale, the pitch-note ending in a thump at the gables, suggesting a body landing after being hurled. 'Get dressed quickly, then. The central heating system seems to have packed in.'

He kissed her when she pressed against him to ask: 'Do I still have that job?'

And more, whatever Beryl might say, and she would surely have plenty. Every time he went away she teased him how he would one day come back with a wife. Some hope of that, he had to reassure her pleading grey-green eyes, so deep the attachment between them that she would turn murderous if it happened. Well, the worst always did occur, after you stopped thinking about it, the time never of your own choosing. 'Yes, you still have the job.'

When they walked hand-in-hand along the corridor, Keith and his girl friend came level. 'I suppose you're on the same expedition?' Aaron said. 'We have to do something.'

Sally, never so glad in her life to hear voices halfway sane, broke Daniel's grip: he slid back into his lair – or that was how she would tell it a few weeks later, which was impossible, since the women she knew were friendly with Stanley, as indeed were their male acquaintances, not the sort to condone her minor though disastrous affair.

She followed them downstairs, as another jack-in-the-box scream came up to meet them.

Keith launched himself on a two at a time descent, a flight through the bar which caught his hip on the hard wood, turning him from the joy of action to rage as, after righting himself, he felt the pain and, in order to diminish it, was in the space of a few seconds manifested before Garry whose neck he held in a grip no one could break. 'You'll be dead if you don't drop that poker.'

'Don't move' – Aaron placed himself between them and Wayne – 'or you'll have me to reckon with' – fists raised and pushing him further and further away from the action with blows of his stomach. The threatening but disembodied voice got through, Wayne forced so far back he fell momentarily into an armchair.

Only one button was left to Fred's waistcoat, but strongly enough sewn by Doris's loving hand to prevent his shirted belly coming through. A sleeve of his jacket had been scorched by the poker, and hair lay over his forehead like weeds unwatered. He got up from hands and knees, eyes bloodshot with outrage and mortal fear. 'The lot of you must have been dead from the toe-nails up not to hear what was going on.'

Keith was just audible to Garry. The cold exuberance, after a time which had spent him to the marrow, so cleared his mind that he would indeed have murdered if the weapon hadn't fallen. He looked around, till it was plain that the horrible smell of burning flesh had been no more than the stink of peacock feathers. When the neck was near to breaking, he let go. 'Make trouble from now on, and you'll be the loser.'

Wayne stood up, fists moving apart as if to bracket into oblivion any foolish head that got between. 'I'll have him.'

With a madman's breath at his ear, Garry knew they had met someone who was dangerous, a man serious about killing and not out for fun alone: the instinct to get into a senseless fight had to be crushed. He took Wayne by the elbow, tapped the end of the settle with his boot. 'We'll get this back to where it belongs' – telling himself to keep his dignity, never let anyone think you were hurt, either in mind or body. They should only have dropped into a place like this on a summer's evening, the bikes primed outside for a quick getaway.

Aaron put chairs and tables upright – those which would stand – Fred gazing moodily at his lounge coming back into some way ship-shape. 'Bring us plenty of coffee,' Keith said to him. 'We'll all need it. Make it double strength. I'll pay.'

'Leave it to me,' Enid said. 'I'll brew it as black as the ace of spades. Another day's wages won't do me any harm.' The wrecked room, the approving noise of the blizzard, and the phenomenon of men clumsily putting the place in order, made her employment seem more interesting.

'Do it, then, while I clean myself up.' Fred was glad she had altered her notion of leaving. 'Then I can make an inventory of the damage.'

'It'll give him something to do,' Wayne jeered. 'I'd like a fag, though. Mine have all gone.'

Keith threw his packet.

'Still got my Zippo at least.' He ignited it, and smiled. 'Thanks, mate.'

Eileen walked across and retrieved the cigarettes so that Keith could offer her one. What a terrible thing they had done, to make such a mess of the place. They probably came from nice homes. Bikers often did, though you could tell from the faces of these, and the way they were dressed, how much they loved causing trouble.

'How did you manage to get here?' Keith wanted to know.

'We had to leave our bikes in a lay-by, about half a mile away,' Garry said. 'But we found this van, and set it going. I'll never know how we got it here.'

'It belongs to an old schoolteacher of mine,' Wayne said. 'He must have made his way on foot. He's sleeping it off upstairs. Funny van, though. It's full of weird stuff. None of us could figure it out.'

'Explosives,' Sally spoke up. 'I'll have a cigarette too, if I may.'

Keith gave her one. 'What do you mean?'

'He told me, upstairs, after I – slept with him. All fused-up and primed to go off at eight in the morning. It's supposed to be in London by then.' She felt a pinch of guilt at betraying his secret, but it would mean little if they assumed her to be mad or a liar.

'You deserve top marks for trying to entertain us through the long evening,' Aaron said.

'I'm only telling you what he told me.' She was arguing with a face that belonged to someone else, rubbing hard across her mouth as if to bring back her own features. 'And I was convinced.'

'Were you?' Keith smiled.

'I wasn't for a while. Then he gave the details in such a way that I couldn't not be. He tried to stop me coming down to tell you. Luckily, you showed up in the corridor, and he had to let me go. He said there was enough explosives in the van to demolish a block of flats, maybe enough material for a whole campaign.'

Aaron, by the tail of the peacock, looked through the window. The wind's subtle knife found cracks and, rubbing mist from the glass, he cupped hands around his eyes to see heavy flakes of falling snow.

'It's in the back courtyard,' Garry said. 'I wouldn't be surprised if it wasn't buried by now.'

'You mean' – Keith walked to her table as if in a dream and someone was handing him a prize he had always hoped for, yet which would turn to dust before he could use it – 'we either sit here waiting to be blasted, or we go out into the blizzard and freeze to death?'

She smiled at his speed of thought, but had told them, so would say no more. They could take it or leave it.

'I hope she's having us on.' Enid stubbed out her cigarette, as if that would be to blame for whatever might in any case happen. 'We get that sort now and again, real fucking jokers. A man came in once saying he was Jesus Christ. The world was going to end in half an hour, he said, a big smile right across his clock. It didn't, though, but we had a good laugh over it. He paid his bill next morning, and even left Fred a big tip. Old Fred didn't know whether to throw it back in his face or run away wagging his tail.'

'I've never been blown up before,' Eileen said. 'I wonder what it will be like? As long as I come back together again, I don't suppose I'll mind.'

'My bits wouldn't know how to find each other,' Wayne said with a smile.

'So what do we do?' Garry said to Keith.

'We'd better see if there's anything in it. Would you and your mate like to do a little job? It shouldn't take long.' He turned to Sally. 'What's the room number?'

They seemed to believe her, so she agreed to talk again.

'Do it with as little rough stuff as possible,' Keith told them. 'And that's an order.'

'You can trust us,' Garry said. 'As long as he's a good lad. If he ain't, we'll pull him down in his birthday suit.'

He had to fasten the knot of his tie three times before the two ends were of equal length. In the old days he wore a brass tie-pin, but such things weren't used any more. He only knew that the Cause was lost, or his part in it, if ever it had been found. The light before the mirror wasn't good, and trembling hands didn't help. She had gone down and told them everything, and now he must flee into the snow, curl up in a hollow and never see morning. The experience was so real he seemed to have done it already and come back to life, so now he needn't do it, but he must still save himself, because if they believed what she told them they would kill him, and they would certainly believe such a 'right sort' of good-looking Englishwoman like her, accept it from her honest and open face as readily as he had been deceived by it. She deserved to be killed, but everyone would die anyway, therefore it didn't matter. He should have begged with all his soul for her to stay the whole night, a decision to be regretted for ever because there was no explanation for it, the sort with which his life had been only too full.

He found himself at the top of another descending staircase in the large and complicated house. Where it led he didn't know, but it must be a safer place than the one he stood in. They were surely out to find him. He hadn't lived a double life not to know when the air was throbbing with danger for him and him alone, so he would get to some place of concealment, and rest until the whole establishment disintegrated, a blinding wave of flame and smoke.

When he was eight and a gang of rough boys from school cried out that they were going to get Daniel and have some fun, he ran into a wood of which he had always been afraid because some said it was haunted and others that it was full of snakes, but the bushes parted for his frantic passage, streams narrowing for the leap, giant elms smoothing their boles to draw him deeper into shadowy gloom till the boys were so far behind he could choose his hiding place. They soon tired of looking, but one boy, stout and cunning, the school bully, was more diligent than the rest. Daniel in his hideaway sharpened a stick to needlepoint with the penknife his mother had given him so that he could cut his daily apple at school, and pushed it with all his scared force into the boy's leg after he had stood for some minutes wondering what direction to go in. Daniel jabbed again and again, like St George's lance at the dragon, then dropped the crimson stick and ran from his howling victim. Before reaching the edge of the wood he was fearful that the boy would bleed to death or get gangrene so that his leg would have to be amputated. Daniel learned that the cunning have their pride and the vicious have their freedom, not knowing which word fitted him, but hoping now that he was both, and able to deal with anyone who was rash enough to get in his way.

'I'd like to sleep with you for ever,' Lance said. 'You're all the songs I've ever known rolled into one.'

'You're lovely as well. But we must get up and see what that racket was all about downstairs.'

He laughed. 'You mean I'll never see your lovely body again? I love your marvellous tits when you bend over me.'

'Thank you very much. I'm sure you'll see them whenever you like. And I'll see you as often as I can.' She couldn't be sure of anything, but it was a delight to have someone as young as this, biker or not. She didn't think he'd had many women before, but it was good all the same, making the past with Raymond seem less important which, she thought, was nothing short of brilliant.

'It sounds like somebody's at the door,' he said. 'Or is it a dentist's drill for a pterodactyl's toothache?'

She got into slacks and jersey, but Lance had nothing on when he let them in. 'Oh, it's you two. What's up, then?'

'It stinks like a Texas whorehouse in here,' Garry said. 'Have you seen that shitbag of a schoolteacher?'

'He was downstairs, wasn't he? What are you looking under the bed for?'

Wayne opened the wardrobe. 'He ain't in here.'

'We want him,' Garry said, 'dead or alive.'

'You've got to be joking.'

'No fucking way. Did you know that that clapped-out van of his is full of explosives and Christ knows what else? About five thousand tons of it, and if it goes off we'll give the world a bigger fucking show than the Dam Busters, except that we'll be the ones to get busted.'

'Half of Derbyshire, which includes this hotel, will go to the moon and back,' Wayne said.

'Old Ferret a terrorist?' Lance stood on the bed to get his underpants on. 'I can't believe it.'

'You'd better. He told it to that tart he slept with.'

'You mean *woman*,' Jenny said.

'Yes, I suppose I do. We're on the lookout for him. He ain't in the room we were told he was.' He threw Lance's trousers and they snaked around his face. 'You come with us as well. And you'd better go downstairs, miss. Maybe they'll save you some coffee.'

'Somebody's having you on. Explosives in that van! We drove it here, didn't we?'

Garry laughed. 'Yes, and don't expect anybody to thank us for it. Weren't we the world's biggest twits? When we get hold of that schoolteacher we might be able to find out what's what. He's bound to be in the hotel somewhere, and whoever finds him had better sit on him hard till the others get there. You can blind him, if you like, but don't make him dumb. He's got to talk.'

TWENTY-TWO

Parsons' head was a globe of the world, four-fifths water and five continents clonking around — or was it six? Boiling lava was in the middle of it all, and he couldn't lift it from the pillow, try as he might. Beer and champagne never mixed, as he ought to have known, and in spite of having lost count of the buckets he had put into himself his only need was for water to slake those fires in the middle of his globe.

He couldn't even blame Jenny — the baggage. He had loved her since she started working for the office, but naturally she wouldn't have anything to do with an old fartbag like him, though one or two young girls had before her. As for Kitty, his wife — well, she's fifty-five, and acts like an old woman already, saying that the carpet they've just had laid (the best bloody Co-op Axminster) or the new coat he had got her from Griffin and Spalding's in Nottingham, would see her out. I ask you! *See her out!* Who could live with that and not go after a bit of crumpet on the side now and again? At least if he packed her in and took up with a young woman he wouldn't hear things like that. In any case, even if you were young you could be dead in half an hour, but at fifty-odd you don't want to be reminded that a new chair or carpet will *see you out*. At fifty-odd you want to think you're going to live for ever. Nevertheless, he loved his wife and kids, and you couldn't live with a woman all that long and not think the world of her, no matter how mad she drove you now and again.

Enjoying his little think, he cursed himself for forgetting to flip the catch on the door before climbing into bed. 'What the bloody hell do you want?'

Daniel looked into his eyes. 'I'm sorry. It's the wrong room.'

'You'd better go out and find the right one, then.'

'I will.'

Strange chap to be on the loose, but the hotel seems full of 'em. He cooled his face at the sink, but it made no difference to the lava within. He didn't suppose anything would, not this side of forty-eight hours. He had got pig-drunk, and ruined his life, and didn't have enough money in his bank to make up for the spending he shouldn't have done. At least there wouldn't be new things going into the house which would *see them out* – and that couldn't be anything but good.

'Have you seen that schoolteacher called Daniel?'

'Don't anybody ever think to knock around here?' It was beginning to seem like Billy Ball's Taproom. 'He was in a minute ago, but he went along the corridor.'

'Left or right?'

'How should I bloody well know?' he cried, putting a jacket on to go downstairs.

Snow gusted over when he looked out, nothing to see but blue-black haze, Keith forcing the door shut on the steely cut of the cold, unwilling to be refreshed at the cost of frost-bite. Freeing the van and moving it might be more than anyone could do, though he would try because he had the least reason for wanting to live. On the other hand, heroes being old-fashioned, it would be wise and natural to sit in an armchair with a bottle of whisky and wait for the end. But he wasn't born for such a course, and helping to save the others would give him the pleasure of being as near to himself as he could get before the iron gates closed for what he might just as well look on as for ever.

The large square room was cluttered with tools and benches, a maze of tables, a jumble of barrels, an interlocking of broken chairs, and buckets in which paint had set brick-hard with age. An old motorbike with flat tyres leaned against a wall, and a bicycle minus its saddle lay on a pile of folded sacks. Stacked boxes of lemonade and beer bottles took up a corner near the door he had come in by.

The overall stink of icy damp was reminiscent of the rooms his mother had sometimes rented. But for him the hunt was on, because hadn't he heard that ageing yuppie lout say what he would do when they caught him? During times of not being pursued or threatened he hadn't cared about dying, but now that the danger was real he would fight his persecutors to the end.

The room was too perfect to hide in. If they came at both doors they would sense he was there, and close in. There was no benign forest at his back in which he could hide from the world.

From the long ladder by the wall he looked at the ceiling, where a narrow trap door indicated a way into the roof. Noting its position, he took out the light bulb, and climbed the aluminium steps in darkness. Opening the trap, sawdust and grit sprayed down. Only a thinnish person could get through, and to avoid breaking the lath and plaster he had to find two beams inside and pull himself up by his arms. Exercise every morning had prepared him, and the manoeuvre was easily done.

Flat on his stomach, clinging to the beam with one arm, he reached down and drew the ladder through, laying it silently to one side. From bits of broken lath he chose a slender enough piece to wedge into the crack between the trap and the rest of the ceiling, so that no one from below would see that it had been opened. The only clue would be the missing ladder, but it was too late to worry about that.

His Ronson and a few matches would provide light when necessary. Making a way between struts and beams, black cobwebs brushed his face. He trod so that the weight of his feet would not go through the ceiling or be heard from below, measuring the extent of his kingdom which went over the bedrooms. At one corner, if he pressed his ear to the floor, he could make out what was being said in the lounge, because like all frightened people they spoke loudly.

In his dark attic he felt even more to be one of the elect, and if those who did not share his ideals had to suffer the catastrophic fusion of beauty and violence, then so be it. The elect suffered to keep those ideals sacred for the future, so why shouldn't the mob unknowingly contribute to this stored energy for the good of mankind? God worked in many ways His wonders to perform.

'You mean' – Fred put it to him straight – 'that the whole damned lot is going to go up?'

Keith had looked into the van, and known the contents for what they were. 'Us as well, unless we can think of some way out.'

Fred regretted that he would not be alive to collect the insurance. 'We'd better get our thinking caps on, then.'

'And lateral thinking it may have to be, to be effective.' Aaron didn't altogether believe in their predicament. 'A bit of pro *de Bono publico*, I should say.'

Sally laughed at his punning. No one was going to die. It was inconceivable, impossible, a piece of instant theatre they had cooked up, sheer genius on somebody's part, maybe even Daniel's, after all, who might really be the actor she had thought on first seeing him at the telephone.

'Are there any cellars here?' Eileen sipped her coffee as if it might be the last hot drink on earth. 'We can make an air-raid shelter, stuff it with tinned grub and candles, like in the Blitz. I saw a film about it once. Me and Enid can brew tea and sing "The White Cliffs of Dover".'

Percy, frail and bewildered at being dragged out of sleep, sat in an armchair with a blanket packed around him. 'I've lived too long to be blown to smithereens. I'll go and cut myself a hole in the snow, like we did when we was kids. We'll be as right as rain in the morning if we all do that.' Maybe he *was* going crazy at last, Alfred thought, who had never supposed, from the way he often felt himself, that you were ever too old to go off your rocker.

'Why don't we set fire to the place?' Wayne suggested. 'This dirty old drum would burn a treat. It'd melt the snow for miles around.'

'Shut your face,' Fred said bravely, while he longed for the morning. The snow plough couldn't come soon enough. 'If we could catch that bugger whose van it is, maybe he could tell us something. He might let us know how to defuse the stuff.'

'We've looked everywhere,' Garry said.

Lance reached for Jenny's hand. 'Maybe he went out in the snow to die from gangrene. I read about somebody called Captain Oates once, at the South Pole.' His face at times reminded her of Raymond's when she first met him, though Lance's didn't have the same restless untrustworthy intelligence, and there was nothing lacking in his feelings.

'That'd be the best thing he could do,' Garry said, smacking one fist into the other.

If he suddenly came among us they would turn into killers. It doesn't take much, and who would blame them? 'He's in the hotel somewhere,' Keith said, 'that's all we know.'

Fred stood. 'I'll look. Nobody knows the place better than me.

You three lads come as well, though. We'll start from the top and work down bit by bit.'

'We'd better take our helmets,' Lance said, 'in case somebody drops on us.'

'And gloves,' Wayne thought.

'All I need is my fists,' Garry said, amused as they went out that they were now protecting Fred as if he was their new-found mascot. 'I'll knock the snot back up his nose. A fucking schoolteacher pulling a stunt like this. It don't bear thinking about. We'll be dead silent, though, until we spot him. And then it'll be tally-ho!'

Fred brooded as they went up the stairs that he might lose everything: my whole life – all the work me and Doris put into it. Maybe I won't even get any insurance, if they don't pay out for acts of terrorism. I must look at the policy, and if it's so I'll be on the dole, not to mention having the rest of the mortgage over my head. I'd have to go back to sea, that's what, but where would I get a ship, at my age?

After looking everywhere else they went up another staircase and came to a door without a number. 'This is the junk room, and if he's not here, he must be out in the snow – which would be good riddance as far as I'm concerned.'

He flicked his torch, and saw that the bulb was missing. He had always been careful about lighting, keeping every socket active to illuminate all corners. If the Duke of Edinburgh came to inspect the hotel (for the winner of The Hostelry of the Year Award) Fred would want the lights shining to good effect on his creditable handiwork. His passion for white-lighting began after staying with his Aunt Liza who lived at the seaside. Farmed out as a child to her guesthouse he had wet his bed, and been locked for two hours in a dark cupboard to remind him that he had better not do it again, a punishment he could never forget. 'He must have taken the bulb out, the bloody villain. But why would he want to do a thing like that?'

'We'll stay by each door till you get another.'

Fred shone the light again, a black spot in the middle surrounded by a ring of illumination. His immaculate brain was an inventory of what he owned to the last splinter or shave of metal. 'The ladder's gone, as well. That's the bloody limit.' It was only by such limits that he knew himself. They were dear to him, and he was proud of them, because being unique to him they set him apart from everybody else.

'He just came in here,' Garry said, 'and vanished up his own arse. But where did he go after that?' Fred went to his store for a new bulb and a ladder, while Wayne and Lance set out for one more nip around. In the silence Garry heard a creak in the ceiling, a vagary of the wind perhaps, then something like a knock in the plumbing except that there were no pipes up there.

Fred returned. 'I'll need help to lift the ladder, then I can get the bulb in.'

'What's in the attic?'

'Nothing. I couldn't get planning permission, otherwise I'd have had half a dozen rooms up there. Birds get in now and again.'

'With shoes on? And what bird weighs ten stone around these parts?' Fred turned pale in the dim light. 'Don't worry, though,' Garry said, 'me and the lads will have him down. Is that the only way up?'

Fred beamed the light. 'It's the builders' fault. I told them to make it three feet square, but they left it oblong. I haven't paid them yet, and I won't until they come back and make it a lot bigger. It's too narrow for anyone to get through.'

'He got up. Then he pulled the lid after him. Not very clever, to box yourself up in a blind alley. Lance can get through. Or we'll get a sledge-hammer and rip out a decent hole. The three of us could shoot up then.'

Fred wagged his head. 'I can't allow that.'

'The whole fucking hotel's going to be blown to bits,' said Garry, exasperated, 'so what's the odds? That bloke up there is off his trolley, so it won't be right to send Lance up alone, will it? And then it'll be hard enough to batten the looney bleeder down, even with three of us. And when we do, how are we to get him through that little hole if he's unconscious? Turn him into fucking toothpaste?'

Fred saw some reason in this. He offered his cigarette case, and Garry took one. 'Even so, it would be a shame to rip the ceiling out unnecessarily.'

'I don't like unnecessary work,' Garry told him. 'I never did, because generally you don't get paid for it, and even if you do you don't get a very good rate. I can spot unnecessary work a mile off, but necessary work I can see coming for a hundred miles, and it strikes me that to enlarge that hole so that the three of us can get up there and storm that madman is like the SAS doing the Iranian Embassy: one isn't enough, because you need one from the back, one from the front, and another down his neck. So it's very necessary to enlarge that hole. I've been in some tight corners as a plumber, but you wouldn't see me trying to get my beer-gut through that letter box. I would just end up getting stuck so that the bastard could kick my bonce in.'

'Maybe he isn't up there,' Fred suggested. 'You hear all sorts of noises in a building like this. Doris, my wife, thought she heard a baby crying once, but I told her it was a ghost, and after a day it stopped. If there is a ghost, though, maybe that'll get him. It'd save us a bit of trouble. Still, it might only be a squirrel looking for its nuts!'

'He's up there,' Garry told the others when they came back, 'so watch that trap door while me and old Fred get a ladder. It's going to be D-Day all over again.'

'Why don't we smoke him out?' Wayne said. 'Nobody can stand smoke. He won't know whether it's poison gas or if the place is on fire. He'd soon come down coughing with his hands on his head.'

Fred knew that Doris had taken to the cook because she had found out about his passion for Nellie, the waitress who had come to work for them from Nottingham. That one thing always led to the next was the simple mechanics of human nature. You sowed what you reaped, and no mistake. When you stood a set of dominoes on edge and in line, and pushed the first one, even if only lightly with your little finger, all the rest in turn fell down.

Likewise, as a result of the blizzard, a group of people had centred on the hotel, one of them a terrorist whose van of explosives was primed to go off and blow the hotel and all who lodged in her to pieces as small as the snowflakes, except that they would be red and wouldn't melt. That meant him, as well. Was he the last in the line of dominoes whose face would fall flat on the earth and in more than one million pieces? He would give a lot to know whose finger it was that pushed the first domino in this cock-up and got the whole line going of which he was such an insignificant part. But unless someone came up with a very good story there would be nothing he could satisfactorily believe in. The only way to go on was to forget that rippling line of dominoes and decide if anything could be done about it. Everything was certain, but nothing was sure, and in the end you did what you could, no matter how cocksure the grin on God's face.

Of all the people in the hotel he thought Keith was the one most likely to get them out of trouble. Keith was the right kind of guest, a person who was sure of himself, no doubt well educated, well connected, wealthy, hardworking at the same time: a family man and a man of good family. He looked all of these things, and Fred would trust a man of probity and position who had obviously at some time been a soldier, and had never been in prison or in trouble of any kind with the Law. He might even go to church once or twice a year. The only flaw was that he had picked up this young tart on the road and taken her to bed, but if you thought about it that's just the sort of thing somebody like him would do, and it only reinforced your views about him rather than otherwise. He would have a good time with her one day – and who wouldn't want to? She was a lively bit of stuff – and chuck her out of his car on a windy moor the next. The hardness of his features indicated that he was well capable of pulling them through this situation unscathed.

'Well,' Keith said, as if Fred was a little dog that had walked in wagging its tail, 'have you rounded him up yet?'

'Not exactly, sir. But he's in the attic, and can't get down. He pulled the ladder through the trap door after him, and we're getting another in position. The biking lads will be ready to go up any minute.'

'So there's a desperate man – for all we know – waiting for the first person to show himself? If he doesn't have a knife he'll take a running kick at the head. Call them off, except one to keep watch. We'll go up in our time, not his. It's only midnight.'

'Yes, sir. I'll tell them.'

He threw a credit card on the table. 'Then you can go on supplying us with coffee and food. Or drinks, if anybody wants them.'

'He'll charge you double,' Eileen said when he had gone.

'No, he won't. If I paid in cash he might short-change me, but not this way.'

'I don't much like him,' she said.

'You don't have to. All he has to do is do as he's told.' Any man who couldn't do that wasn't worth his salt, because everyone had to do as they were told at some time or other in their lives, and the present situation demanded it. All the same, he didn't want her to think he was too harsh. 'I'm not sure whether I like him either, but there's only one way to get things done.'

If he hadn't been so good as to give her a lift in his nice car she wouldn't have landed in this hotel with some madman who didn't know Guy Fawkes Night had already gone. Even if what the man in the attic had said was true, and even if what the woman said he had said to her was true, it either didn't bear thinking about, or it was going to be the funniest thing that had ever happened to any of them. If Keith hadn't given her a lift when she was walking across the moor she might have been dead in a drift already, so she still had a lot to thank him for and would only have a bone to pick with him if she got blown to pieces, which would be too late anyway. 'What would you do if there was no Fred or Enid to make your coffee?'

He looked surprised. 'I'd have to make it myself, then, wouldn't I?'

'And burn your hand like you did on the moor? My dad never made his tea. Other men I've known didn't, either, not if a woman was within a mile. All the men I've known were bone idle.'

He wondered what other men someone like her could have known, but didn't say it, because she was so young, and could only have been familiar with her own sort. Men are idle when they have no interest in their work, though when they do have they usually get on and out. 'Your father couldn't have been idle if he brought up a family.'

'He did as little as he could, and grumbled every time he lifted a finger.'

'I'll bet he worked hard, all the same,' Parsons said. 'Only you didn't know it. Kids never do. What work have you done, anyway?'

'I worked nearly two months in a knitwear factory. Then I got laid off. There ain't much work to go round any more. What world are you living in?'

'Everyone lives in their own.' Keith put a hand on her arm. 'There isn't much to be done about that.'

'I'm over the rainbow,' Percy cried, 'because I'm on my way to

Bognor. Who wouldn't be? In fact I must be a few miles beyond, because it's snowing!'

He's going again. Alfred's face reddened when Enid – the little bag – laughed. I shan't be able to relax till I get him there, if ever I do. If I could get my hands on that bloody maniac in the loft I'd gladly squeeze the life out of him.

'I've been happy all my life,' Percy said, 'even when I was unhappy! I've had work I was interested in, a good and loyal wife, fine kids, and a roof over my head. So why shouldn't I be over the rainbow, eh?' he asked Garry, who came in and stood by the fire to light a cigarette.

'I'll only be over the rainbow when we've got that prick-squeak down from upstairs. It's marvellous what can happen when you come out for a spin. One minute you're free, and the next you're stuck in a place like this and might be blown to bits. When I was twenty everything I did was because I wanted to live, and now that I'm thirty I do it because I don't want to die.'

Keith felt as near happiness as he had any right to be. Various solutions drifted in and out of his mind, but it was hard to avoid the notion that, whatever happened, he couldn't allow himself the luxury of thought.

TWENTY-THREE

Daniel, squatting simian-like between two beams and not caring that his persecutors registered every move on the radar screen of their feeble minds, told himself that he nevertheless had them at his mercy. All my life I've wanted to have a say as to whether people should live or die, but only in order to do them good because that would allow me to call it a victory. Now I have achieved it, but at the sacrifice of my own life, so what kind of a victory is that?

One had to make a choice between good and evil, whatever power you had, any middle way a paralysis of the moral sense. If your opponents considered you evil you could deceive them by simulating good, then engulf them in an evil demise when they weren't expecting it. You opened yourself to certain defeat when you allowed people to pride themselves on being good by assuming you to be evil.

Sun Tzu said it was a mistake to attack at the strongest point, that the weaker party should create uproar in the east so as to strike unexpectedly from the west. Such homespun maxims of senseless violence were only relevant when you believed that your cause was just, but if evil was with the weak (as it was now with him) then the ploy was false, and you became paralysed. Revolutionary cracker mottoes were coined for those without the intelligence and moral subtlety to ponder on the finer strands of good and evil, and needed their convictions reinforcing by slogans fit only for simple minds.

He had set out on his journey to take a load of high explosives from one point to another, an automaton who nevertheless felt the joy of being evil, which he could not give up because to do so would empty him of any reason for having been born.

Cold tears fell on his wrist, and he fastened the buttons of his jacket. Stop thinking, wait for the fearful bang and split-second flash of oblivion. Would it be evil, to let it happen to them all? Some could live another fifty years, but what was that compared to eternity? There might be so much suffering in those fifty years that a painless death now would be a blessing. Blind chance had brought them together, but 'blind chance' was only another name for God who was testing his servant Daniel with one last problem.

Knives of cold came against him from the shrieking blizzard. The vast attic was his inheritance. Life was good because God said so, and so had his mother. She had given him his name because there were three men in the Bible who had found favour in God's eyes: Noah, Job and Daniel, and she had made him promise that he would try all his life to be like one of them. During his nightly prayers, impossible not to say yes to his mother, an obstinate inner voice out of his childish self said: 'I won't do as she says. I won't' – words spoken without gladness but enabling him to hold on to the unique spirit he had inherited. Having been born, he could have given no other response, and the memory distressed him more than the freezing isolation of his attic.

To be physically destroyed would deliver him from turmoil, but to die before solving his dilemma would damn him for ever. Even if there was no place beyond life, those who were left behind would judge him. You did evil because the world would not extend its love to you, but that was because you had no love in you for the world, and so could only go through life consumed and consoled by evil.

Knowing yourself rarely brought the good that was supposed to inspire a change for the better. He lit a cigarette and, letting the match drop, watched its flame shrink, as Lucifer's mark abandoned him. The pain of displaying his iniquity lessened the terror of waiting.

She felt angry at the sudden recall of Stanley's disapproving expression. He would hardly credit her with the power of bringing the blizzard on herself, but his features might imply that with a little attention to the met. office and a scrutiny of the AA Route Atlas she could have diverted to east or west of hilly features and cut in towards the airport.

He didn't belong in a place like this, and she objected to thinking about him. Why must he follow her everywhere? She certainly hoped she wasn't wherever *he* was at this moment, but not being interested in where he was by no means meant that he wasn't interested in where she was.

She contrasted the breast-like mounds of bluish snow beyond the window to the scene of springtime at their place in France. Buying the house had been her idea, because Stanley would have liked a chalet on the English coast. He had never said so strongly enough to stop her getting one in France, but did nothing ever after except try to disillusion her about all things French, not knowing that since she had never allowed herself to become sufficiently disillusioned by him to do anything about it, he hadn't a hope of disillusioning her about the house in France. We aren't as happy together as out of stupid pride we lead family and friends to believe.

'Your paradise' as he scathingly called it, was some way from a village, but he always complained about what to her were acceptable everyday sounds, even when they were sitting at the garden table with a bottle of wine and a dish of olives in the evening. If it wasn't traffic it was an occasional aeroplane, or the faint clash of knives and forks from the villa down the road, or the harmless tinkle of their radio. And then some brainless dog that couldn't tolerate the silence would begin to howl.

'Oh, for God's sake stop whinging all the time,' she said on a superb day last year, putting him in a foul mood for a week, though he did stop complaining, which she was glad of, because out of all his faults (though she had hers, too) that was the one she could sooner or later divorce him for.

She had been brought up not to fuss, as no doubt had her parents. Whoever had reared Daniel must have instilled the same virtue into him, for she could not imagine him complaining either. If they were free of the blizzard and this ghastly hotel she would take him clandestinely to France, so that after a few days in the house and under her tender care he would become (as would they both) amiable and easy-going, different people to what they were now.

She had got to know Daniel more in a few hours than she had Stanley in twenty years, and ought to tell him that no man had to turn himself into a self-aggrandizing liar to prove that he loved her. She needn't have succumbed into believing that what he had said was true, and certainly should not have blabbed to the others in a ridiculous fit of weakness. A terrorist with a van of high explosives! She wondered how she could undo the damage, while he (she was sure) sat in the attic laughing so much at her gullibility that he was getting stomach cramps, which pain could nevertheless be seen as an accolade for his gift of storytelling, a wonderful parlour-game kind of yarn made up solely for her who like a fool had retailed it to everyone else.

And look at them, in earnest conference as to what they should do, either frightened out of their paltry little lives or enjoying the situation in such a way that they would hardly notice the rest of the night go by. No longer bored, their existence has a purpose as they go for lights and ladders, saying what they will do to Daniel when they get hold of him. The men treat it like a war film, the only lack being a few extras coming and going in German helmets. She could see the plot turning into something very nasty indeed, so it seemed only right to try and make up for her gaffe, and save Daniel from their wrath.

'You're so full of shit,' Garry said, 'it even comes out of your mouth.'

'Well,' Parsons laughed, 'shit fertilizes, don't it? And it brings forth plants. I expect it says that in the Bible somewhere. I've always believed everybody's got a right to work, and I'll always say so.'

Garry spread his legs, and made another neat roll-up. Keith liked their chaffing, otherwise how could you know what people thought? You couldn't get such raw material from television, though maybe those who wrote for it went out to pubs and sat over their pints of lager with a tape recorder strapped to their legs. Or maybe the Japanese had invented one that fitted into an earring.

'When I wanted work,' Garry said, 'I found it.'

In spite of Garry's foul language and adolescent passion for motorbikes, Parsons suspected him to be halfway intelligent. 'There are only so many jobs to go round, though.'

'I don't know about that. I've done everything. I delivered papers when I was a kid. Then I tried snow shifting, and tidying people's gardens. Anything to get money in my pocket. When I left school I worked in a radio shop for a year, so I even mend the odd wireless now and again. Then I went down the pit to get more money, but I packed it in after six months because I didn't like being a cave dweller. I did lorry driver's mate, pirate taxi driver, brickie's labourer – everything I could. Then I cottoned on to the plumbing racket, a real cowboy till I got to know how to do it well. Now I'm good, and everybody knows me. I found it didn't need much more time to do a good job than a bad 'un, so I undercut the cowboys on the make.

But I've never been on the dole, and hope I never will. My brother was on it for a month, no fault of his. He said that whenever he went to collect his money he couldn't find anywhere to park. When he got talking in the queue he found they sat watching the bloody telly all week.'

'Are you saying those poor buggers out of work shouldn't have a car to get around in,' Parsons said, 'or a TV to watch? People have got higher expectations these days. Blokes like you think everybody ought to live by the law of the jungle.'

'It's the only law that gets things done, as far as I can see. If thousands of unemployed were out shifting snow for their dole money we wouldn't be holed up in The Cheapjack Hotel, with some bloody looney who's gone and parked his bombed-up van outside.'

Fred set a tray of coffee and sandwiches between him and Parsons. 'It's not as cheap as you might find, if you took a room like any other guest.'

'I like value for money, monkey-brain, and hotel rooms don't come under that category. We take tents, and camp in a field. We pay the farmer a couple of quid, except when he lets us off for nothing, then we trade with him for eggs and fruit.'

Keith listened to the storm between their words, heard it whether he would or not, talk mixing with the blatant howl from outside. He thought of Daniel not yet found, the terrorists' delivery boy who didn't know how much of their prisoner he was.

'Last year,' Garry said, 'we went to Spain, and stopped in a little inn. They're cheaper over there. Well, the plumbing in the toilets was all shot, and we couldn't stand the stink, so I fixed it. The man wouldn't let us pay the bill. When we arrived, though, with GB plates back and front, he didn't want to have us. Next year we might go to Yugoslavia. There's nowt like a bit of travelling, though we behave ourselves overseas because we can't speak the lingo, and don't want to get good old England a bad name. Anyway' – he drained off his pint, and turned back to Fred, who no longer saw anything unusual in sitting among the guests to drink his own coffee – 'when are you going to ask everybody to settle their bills? The balloon might go up any minute, and even a half-p piece will be in twenty bits.'

That's one way out, because how can I face the lads when they ask me where the money's gone? 'Touch a penny of that dough, for liquorice allsorts or fizzy lemonade – or even cream buns – and don't come back here again.' Jack Montgomery's joke was laughed at by everybody in the meeting, Parsons included, who liked a hee-haw as much as the next man, though there would be no such jollity when he got back, so he might just as well make the best of his time in Fullstop Alley and get senseless. 'Another bottle of champagne, Fred.'

'He thinks God takes care of sots and kids,' Percy said, 'but I wouldn't bank on it. God only looks after those who think summat of themselves. You can get blindo in your own house, but to booze yourself into a wet cabbage when we're all in such dire peril, well, I reckon the Almighty wouldn't countenance a worm like you. If He did He'd be no God.' His fist waved, and Parsons' head subsided under the onslaught. 'Look at him. He knows who I mean. Only the lowest of the low don't care whether he lives or dies.'

'Everybody's entitled to do what they like with their lives,' Jenny said, thinking what an awful old bore he was.

Her remark stirred up more of Percy's venom. 'Nobody can back-slide into not wanting to keep on keeping on, not even me, and I'm the eldest here by a long shot.'

'Now stop it, Father. Don't overexcite yourself.'

'Overexcite myself be damned.' He was off again. They looked on, wanting to stop him but unable to do anything about it short of, Keith thought, killing him, though if he went on much longer that was precisely what he would get up and do. 'I'm just showing a bit of responsibility, which seems to be seriously lacking in this snow-bound den. I'll bet he's got a wife and children, though I expect they hate his guts, and think him the biggest ninny in the world, and wish he wouldn't come back whenever he goes out of the house. Still, he ought to stay sober and help the rest of us.'

The old man's breath was grinding for renewal, and Sally thought his problem might be over sooner than most, though it was a pity he was using Parsons to commit suicide. The total attention he demanded made it difficult to get the conversation back to Daniel who, she knew, was thinking of her in his cold attic, and wanting to be comforted in his loneliness.

Percy lay back, head sculptured against the armchair, face drained of life, a noise out of his mouth like fingernails scraping along zinc. Keith thought he was becoming a nuisance, because you couldn't tell who he would begin to demoralize next, and his death wouldn't be much loss. In any case, if they had to run into the snow he wouldn't live, so he might do well to snuff it in relative comfort.

Parsons found no joy in drinking the champagne. The first wash into his mouth could have been Dandelion and Burdock for all he knew, though Sally said it tasted fine when he pushed a glass disconsolately across. Alfred unlooped his father's tie and pulled the collar apart, the old man's eyes blue like the flame out of an acetylene welding torch, which he flashed again on Parsons. 'God gave you life, and only God can take it away, and you're seeking refuge in the product of the heathen Bacchus. He won't help you, no matter how much you might think so.'

Parsons became more himself as the champagne took effect. 'Mind your own business. It's got bugger-all to do with you. Nor with God, either, as far as I'm concerned.'

A touch of pride had coloured Alfred's overweight face at his father's renewed tirade, and he placed a hand on his shoulder to stop him getting up. 'He used to do a bit of preaching at the chapel, but the young 'uns didn't take to him, when there was anybody there at all. He was a bit too straight for them.'

Parsons should have known he'd been a bloody old Bible thumper. Nevertheless, he had betrayed a sacred trust of the union, which was the nearest to God he himself would ever get, and spent a few hundred quid of the money which a benefactor had insisted should be collected in cash. Now that he had done it he could only tell them he was sorry, though *mea* bloody *culpa* would cut little ice.

Wayne came in from sentry duty looking petulant after his inactivity in the half dark, furthest away as if, Sally thought, to have a good view and decide who he should be unpleasant to next.

Parsons' bottle had been more than half emptied by Jenny and her biker pal pledging their love, so he asked for another, thinking he might as well be hung for a sheep as for a lamb. If he had to sell up his furniture to pay the Union back, what was another chair more or less? At least it wasn't something that would see the wife out.

'He's even brazen enough to laugh at what he's doing.'

'Have a drink yourself,' Lance called. 'You've had some pot already, Dad. Chase it down with a tot of bubbly.'

'Don't encourage him,' Alfred said. 'It's not right.'

'He's over twenty-one, ain't he?'

Wayne was bored, as well as tired and cold. 'A hundred and twenty-one, if you ask me.'

Halfway out of his chair, Percy smiled at the joke. 'I can still give you young 'uns a run for your money.'

'Let's have a trot round the room, then,' Lance said. 'It might warm all of us up.'

'Leave him alone,' Alfred said.

Percy reached for the glass which Lance pushed across. 'I can take care of myself.'

'Like a cat in a sack in a river,' Wayne laughed.

'He's a good old sport,' Lance said. 'He should have two pension books at his age. I'd vote for it.'

Before Alfred got to him, Wayne leapt over a chair and knocked him back along the floor. 'You were going to hit my mate, weren't you? That's naughty. It's not on.'

'Sit down,' Jenny said to Lance.

'You young bastards!' Alfred called. 'I'll have you for that.'

Keith prevented a second hit as Wayne went forward again. 'Leave him alone. Save it till we're out of here. If you feel like it then, it's up to you.'

Wayne hadn't done halfway towards enough. If you thought something was enough you were weakening, and you did yourself no good at all. Alfred was used to bossing people around, but if he couldn't take a friendly bit of chaff about his own father he should stay in his bungalow with his dogs, and make sure the fire extinguishers worked, in case there was a nasty accident one dark night.

'Don't think I won't settle the score,' Alfred said. 'This isn't the end of the world.'

'It'll be the end of you if you don't stop threatening me. We were having a joke. We weren't hurting anybody.'

'I think you should be quiet,' Keith told Alfred, which set a momentary silence over all of them. Percy's face, in sleep, lost twenty years of his age, and he wasn't awake to comment when the lights went out, and stayed that way.

TWENTY-FOUR

At the sound of fighting, Daniel spoke to the palpable ghosts he imagined were crowding him in: Let them kill each other, and when they're dead I can go down and make my way into the countryside, where it will be better to die than stay here in the dark, though a dozen fleecy sheep in the lee of a Derbyshire wall might still save my shepherd's life.

The chimney structure was warm from the fire downstairs, though his feet were cold. Time had no value. The air was bleak in the space he could sense but not see, more space than he had ever possessed, his body slowly expanding to fill it. He would be here for sufficient time to reach the bounds and burst through. Only then would he know why he was on earth, a boon never to be conferred on those who quarrelled while deciding how to dispose of him.

Unfamiliar with the discipline of faith, they did not know what they wanted to do. Only faith could guide them into defeating him, but since they did not have it (and he did, both in himself and in his Cause) he would stay safe long enough to become the vanquisher.

He had already been through many lives in his refuge, saturated himself in the past so as to be reinforced for what future he could make. Out of the past all answers come. Only the past tells you what you are, and how to act in a crisis. Pure faith and hardness of purpose make it unnecessary to distinguish between good and evil.

It was dark except for the inner light such thoughts provided. To escape and survive he had to deal with brutal people, the squalor of conflict which no one consumed by pure ideals could avoid. So far he had only contributed by driving a van of explosives, but now he was trapped, and to escape would mean contact with the lowest form of an impossible-to-enlighten enemy, who killed the believer only for what he believed and not out of what they believed. They were as unthinking as the blizzard which had them all trapped.

Sooner or later they would come to get him, but they could only squeeze through the trap door one at a time. Strait is the gate which

148

would save him, because when hand or head appeared he would smash them with a post of wood which the attic had providentially provided. Strong enough to cause confusion among his assailants, the first to try his redoubt would never forget how foolish they had been. The brutalism of the idealist would defeat the savagery of the unbeliever.

His mother had also said: 'As long as you believe, you are safe.' Fighting for survival might muddy the distilled water of your ideals, but belief survives and the water will become clear again. She may have meant her words to be taken in a different spirit, but whenever did those who spoke the Word have any control over how others interpreted what they said?

'First you tell us,' Keith said, 'then you say you think you made a mistake.'

'Yes, I was convinced. But now I'm not so sure.'

'Nor was I, till he locked himself in the attic. Then I went to look in the van, so I know that what you said in the first place was right.'

Fred turned the gas lamp to a white glow on the bar. 'I heard him going walkabout just now, so why don't we get him down?'

'Not through one little trap door,' Keith said. 'It's too dangerous to go up one at a time.'

'We've got helmets,' Garry said, 'and thick gloves. It's no problem for The Queen's Own Biking Hussars.'

'You never attack head-on.' Keith wished he had taken such advice for himself in the past. 'You create a diversion. Since there's only one trap door, we'll make another, break a hole in the plaster. One man goes up sharpish through the one our terrorist can't defend, and we've got him.'

'Let me be the spearhead,' Garry said. 'Lance can go through the other, because he's got thin raps. And Wayne can catch him when we drop him down like a sack of spuds.'

'I'd like to go up and talk to him,' Sally said.

Fred was uneasy about the structure of his hotel. 'I don't want you breaking up my ceiling. There's been enough damage done already.'

'If the police did the job,' Keith said, as if to reassure him, 'they'd have the whole roof off. At least we'll try to do it neatly.'

Wayne extinguished the nearest candleflame with his thumb. 'Tear gas would be best, if we had any. A smoke canister lobbed in. Then we would shut the lid and wait. It'd be better if we chucked in a couple of thunderflashes first. We could go in like the Israelis. The bastard would really get the chop.'

Sally became more and more scared of their talk. 'I could bring him down peacefully. You wouldn't have to make the other hole in the ceiling then. I'm just thin enough to get through. That would save him or anybody being injured. It's got to be tried.'

'Common sense at last.' Fred stood by a candle to light his cigar, favouring a solution to stop further vandalization. Gas lamps and a scattering of candles didn't sufficiently illuminate the room, and gave a sinister urgency to their talk.

Garry turned to Keith with a grin. 'I apologize in advance for swearing, but if you ask me,' he said to Sally, 'you're fucking barmy. You're totally unrealistic. If you got up there and tried to talk to that looney he would either butcher you, or take you for a hostage. Then we would really be in the shit.'

The virtue of keeping quiet and letting others state your opinion was not new to Keith, and he was gratified at hearing his own views so tersely put, needing only to add: 'If he took you or anyone else hostage we would have to tear the ceiling apart and really go in and get him. Nor would anyone worry overmuch if the hostage was killed in the process.'

He spoke so quietly that Sally hardly heard. She did not know what other way there was but couldn't believe theirs was the only solution, though she recalled the half-whispered implications of Daniel's fervent monologue and again began to believe that what he had said may well have been the truth. Yet to get him down with the enjoyable and ebullient violence which had taken hold of the others didn't seem the proper course.

Keith held Fred's arm, and drew him to his feet. 'Bring that ladder from Trap Door Number One, and provide us with any saws, hammers, crowbars and axes you can find.' He felt luxuriously in harmony with the crisis, but in the hallway at the bottom of the stairs at home he had done something which had put a stop to his existence, and made all that he was doing now seem like the action after death of an animal still making sound and movement until the millrace of the blood finally abandoned the heart. Her head crashed against the bannister again and again into a mass of blood and hair and brain, her astonished then horrified face fading into death.

He held his hands together, as if to stop them vibrating uncontrollably, but they were still. 'And you,' he said to Alfred, but indicating Aaron and Parsons as well, 'can stay one at each door down here to look after the women and the old man, in case he tries to make a run for it. Sit on him if he does. We'll hear the racket, and come right away.'

Aaron, at his ease, thought that if Daniel tried for a getaway the kindest action would be not to hinder him. When he had phoned Beryl to say he was stranded she told him that the police had called that afternoon, wanting to interview him. They had asked where he was, so the only thing for him to do, she went on, was get back home as soon as possible.

The charge would mean ruination whether or not they made it stick. It wouldn't be difficult. The buyers and experts were understandably enraged, and chemistry would do the rest. He would be lucky not to get jailed, but felt defeated more than guilty because knowledge and skill, rather than his conscience, had been called into dispute.

He had worked patiently night after night and, if one reckoned up the hours of labour spent on his various forgeries, he had netted no more than a few pathetic thousands. It began when he went to inspect a cache of books for sale in a local vicarage. Let into the attic to root among shelves and in trunks, he came across several quires of paper a century old when, for example, Conrad was getting into his prime. The manufacturer's date was still on the packets, the watermark plain. The vendor willingly put them in with the books he bought.

His steady hand had gone scores of times over a signature until no one, or so he would have thought, could have said it wasn't written by the celebrated writer. The edition of the book, the paper and ink had to match (no problem for a man of his old trade), as had the date, the place, and the inscription of friendship. Then came the letters . . .

The challenge of the game had been more tempting than the profit, his only incentive to return being that in court the evidence of the prosecution would show how he had been found out, as if the explanation of his failure must be so interesting that it would make up for his chagrin at being a felon in the dock.

Beryl had suggested the forgeries as an amusing pastime on winter nights after the catalogues were finished and the last orders hauled in canvas bags to the post office, but he would not hint that she had been involved. Nor would she expect him to, therefore he must return before she implicated herself. She now knew the name of the hotel, and when the police came again she would tell them, though he doubted they would send a helicopter to pluck him out of the blizzard.

He didn't want to go back. Enid was sleeping nearby, and if it hadn't been for the snow he would have driven south with her and had a good time in the days that were left. Paradise would never come again, so it would be going against life not to take advantage of it now.

If Daniel broke free it would be merciful to let him escape into the snow, and also sensible to do the same himself. He felt comforted to know that there was more than one option open.

TWENTY-FIVE

The box room cum linen cupboard at the end of the corridor on the second floor was the best place from which to excavate another entrance into the attic. Keith set a Calor lamp on a chair to light up the exact position. They were, he told himself, laying siege in medieval fashion, by opening a way into the fortress from below, before mounting their final attack.

Fred took out sheets and blankets, sidling in spite of his girth around the angled ladder to reach the shelves, yanking down loads as big as could be carried and leaving them in haphazard positions along the corridor where they would be safe from plaster.

His activity amused them, but Keith made way for him when he could, however inconvenient (and his rescue of the precious linen said much in his favour), because he liked his populist and splenetic spirit that would never countenance the likes of the man upstairs. All terrorists and their helpers should be put to death, Fred had signified, preferably at the point of capture so as to save hearing the garbage of their crackpot slogans from the dock.

A mighty blow from the top of the ladder sent Garry's crowbar through the plaster, Fred wincing as if the cold steel had entered his own flesh. The odour of un-aired long-stored linen, pressed against his nose as he took it out, brought poignantly back how he and Doris had worked night after night in their own small sitting room when the guests had gone to bed, hemming and repairing, folding and smoothing with almost obsessional neatness, writing letters or totting up the accounts between them, while the wireless played mindlessly on low. Hard days with never a moment to spare, and not much time for sleep either, were recalled as months of happiness because there had been no slot of idleness in which to quarrel.

Fred looked through the doorway, the air so full of flying powder he saw only the outline of a muscled arm drawing back for another exultant smash. Keith brushed bits of wood and dust from his clothes, and when there was a hole big enough for a head to go through Garry lifted the visor of his knightly helmet and called down: 'We'll be there in a bit.' He paused to sneeze. 'I'll need the axe, though, to snap these bits of lath off.'

Lance in the lumber room slotted a carpenter's saw between the edge of the trap door and the ceiling, and cut through the wedge holding it in place. When it fell open towards him he immediately thrust his saw into the space like a weapon should anyone jab down. 'He won't surrender, I know Old Ferret. He was a strict bastard at school, the only teacher who wouldn't let us arse around.'

Wayne at the foot of the ladder spat, and dodged the ricochet. 'And now we know why. A killer, that's why. Here's the hammer. Knock it around, to make him think we're about to have his guts for garters.'

'It's a claw hammer.' Lance tossed it from haft to head as if it were an ivory-handled gun in the Wild West, then banged a jungle rhythm around the gap. 'A real murder weapon. He was all right, as well, though. He tried to teach us summat.'

'Yeh, about how great England was,' Wayne said. 'He used to cry a bit when he said it, just so's we'd believe him. As if we needed that wet prick to tell us what we already knew. Here, let me have a go. I'll make his fucking tripes jump.'

At a signal, Lance came down. 'They've smashed a hole in the other place,' Fred whispered, 'and everything's ready. But the Captain says you've got to be dead quiet.'

Wayne pressed against the ladder to keep it firm. The only sound was an uneven moaning of the wind from beyond slates and walls. Lance went through the trap door slowly so that his leather jacket pressing at the edges wouldn't give warning by its squeak.

Reaching for the cosmos, you had to shift slates from between the rafters, and pull them out as do prisoners in hencoop Victorian jails. He would root a way through, roll in a blanket of snow, and go down the sloping roof, no stars in the blizzard to light his escape, moiling clouds holding them off. He would fall through space into the yard, break from his shell and fight each hypothermic step till a safe haven was gained.

While the vivid scene comforted, he restrained his stave from smashing the first slate, knowing that whatever he did could only bring the end closer. The fearful banging began, and because it wasn't feasible to defend two places at once, he would gladly descend peacefully if they would let him, knowing that his ex-pupils turned yobbos could be dealt with – though not the man Keith, who had them under his barbaric control. If the bikers had not succumbed to such a person they might have merited redemption at some future hour, but they had found their natural ally and master, and been set on hounding someone whose mission had crosswired into a dead end because his mother foretold it.

Hearing her mini-mouth saying that God had turned his back on him, he recollected with loathing her theological platitudes. Regardless of cuts at his numbed fingers, he pulled shards and shavings clear so that he could unhook more slates. A flat undersurface of packed snow broke into crystals and fell against eyes and hair.

Light from far off picked out the beams, as he frantically pulled at the covering roof, showing himself to heaven before the pack closed in. There was no time to climb through and escape, but he would wreck as much of their refuge as he could. He stabbed into the snow, lunging as if to draw blood from the Almighty God who would not use His power to save him. Heavy and sharp, the slates became easier to rip away, till water ran down the warmth of the chimney, larger pieces of snow slopping around him. He sent a slate spinning, which broke to pieces on hitting a strut, the noise making him smile and forget his peril.

A wet sleeve turned his arm heavy and cold, the second slate falling uselessly between the beams. 'When you are sent on a mission you're on your own, but we assume you will get there. We're mature people at the game, and nothing is expected to go wrong through human error.' They had come up through the ranks, so who could deny them their purblind assumptions, their power? They weren't an army fair and square for all to see. They were an underground gang or gangs, as much on the hooks of fate as he was. Things went wrong, by chance, or betrayal, sudden inexplicable despair, or excess of confidence, or because of the weather. In the beginning was the word, and the word was luck. In his memory of arguing with them he always spoke with an Irish accent – ever perfecting his shibbolethic passwords – but he hadn't, not at all, not in actuality, because some-how he had neither the mouth nor throat for it.

He laughed, as if testing his humour as a weapon against them. They wouldn't find him, in spite of their torches. He launched slates lethally one way and then the other at advancing light. The beam struck when he altered stance. Slates in reserve were as sharp as razors and as weighty as claymores, chilblains plaguing his fingers, however, when he touched them, ready for the well-fed confident hunters.

They had warm clothing. Their voices threatened: find him, get him, kill him: curses and futile exhortations. He flung with all his strength, a scream of rage as a slate struck, one of them out of the game. A boot went through lath and plaster. Someone laughed. 'Come on, Ferret, it's no good. We've got you cornered. You can't get away. Be a good lad, Ferret, and stop chucking slates about. You've hurt my mate, so isn't that enough? Come down with us and get warm. We won't hurt you if you do.'

He knew how to care for himself in his own kingdom, had been here since before he was born. Let them gain it by inch and foot. He forced himself not to answer, or explain, or plead that they leave him alone, change sides, help him. They had retreated, turned lights off and vanished, silence but for the ever-wailing blizzard.

Unbelieving, he skimmed more slates as a test. They were cunning, well trained, patient under fire, wouldn't let him know if they were anywhere at all. They would hear him breathing, so he breathed as if he were dead, too rarefied and superior to need air in his lungs.

From the wet chimney wall he heard the far-off belly-scraping of a large rat dragging towards him. Sleep was what he needed, and dreams. He breathed again, to stop his lungs bursting, because what was the use? Dreams had been his only freedom, exquisite or horrible didn't matter. You could always wake up from dreams. The worst dream, which he'd had more than once, was when he was going to be hanged. Why or what for he didn't know, but he felt dread in every bone, the horrible fear of the end about to be inflicted on him. Had an ancestor suffered this, in a fight against the dastardly English? Then, still in the dream, he was able to tell himself it was a dream, only a dream, even as the hard rope was put around his neck. In dreams you were free because nothing was final. You always woke into a world where no situation could be as awful as the one in the dream.

He was wrong. This wasn't a dream. It was events in life that you had to be afraid of, because they happened inexorably, and you didn't have the freedom to wake up from them. Murderers should be hanged, his mother had always said. He screamed at her phosphorescent face filling the whole attic and advancing slowly towards him. Two black helmeted figures leapt up from before his feet.

Part 2

TWENTY-SIX

'Old Ferret, all present and correct, sir!'

They bundled him into an armchair and gave imitation salutes. Twice lucky seven were back in the same room. Huge logs burned so that it was impossible to get close. Nobody spoke, as if they were one family after the enormous dinner of a Yulish reunion, in that lull between the pious intake of calories and the explosion of distilled venom from grudges ancestral.

Fred turned out two of the lamps, and Aaron thought how much more interesting faces asleep or in repose were under candlelight. 'We might be here for days, and that means nights as well,' Fred told them. Keith nodded, glad to have such details taken into account. No one seemed to worry about the van outside, or they didn't believe what it meant, or they were so disorientated that reality couldn't get through. If no one did anything they were within hours of death. Gwen's lifeless face stared at him in triumph, an image he prayed for his will to push aside. It would never depart, and being with her again in a few hours, even if in oblivion, did not seem strange, only horrible, and so he would do all to avoid it. He didn't want to be whatever she was, nor where she was, because who could guarantee that she might not be waiting somewhere? He was ready to act, but the others wouldn't help until they were as terrified and determined to stay alive as he was.

Daniel felt as if the limits of his face were several miles out. He had never been in this country before, where the flesh ached dully from collision with boot and fist, and the body no longer belonged to him. Trying to touch, he couldn't reach, one eye covered by the blue mountain of its swelling, his right knee a nodule as if the bone had been taken away. It was all too distant, only the blur of pain transmitted from the centre of his damaged fortress, the crenellations a wavy line, the moat a rubbish ditch, portcullis crumbled. He found a patch of stiff and bloody hair from a crack in the skull, but the

161

twinge was momentary. He told his hands not to move. His audience might see, and not like it.

He had escaped being kicked to death because the dogs' keeper had ordered them from their fun. Another minute and they would have been impossible to hold, savages only sated when they had drunk his blood.

Old age, Percy knew, was never as old as it was supposed to be. Full of purpose because he was among people he could feel safe with, he walked in the direction of the fire, a criss-cross of heavy timbers in a white blaze hotter than Hell itself the closer he got, so, being forced back by a pain at his eyes, he swerved towards Daniel and stood over him with a hand on his chin as if wondering what he should do now. They soon knew.

After the second vicious smack Wayne leapt up and pulled him away. 'Keep off, Dad, he's our meat.'

'No,' Percy shrieked, 'he's not meat any more,' and turned back to his chair, where he dozed with the assurance that when the time came his instincts would serve him as well as anybody else's. He cat-slept, in and out of comfort, coming into noise, going back into silence or dreams. The spit of burning logs, or the anguished baby moan of the wind, brought him sometimes into the room.

Alfred's eyes stayed as open as oysters under a rain of lemon juice. He could run into the snow as well as the next man, get as far from the van as would save his life, but the question was: how far would far be if he had to carry his father? No-bloody-where at all, should he collapse from a heart attack under the weight. Half the roof and three quarters of the main wall might crash onto his napper before he reached the gate, the sort of joke he wouldn't be able to enjoy. The kindest thing would be to leave the old so-and-so to the explosion, and hope he would go suddenly and without pain, better than living months or years as a cabbage-brain, bossed and tormented by a pack of sadistic old bags in a cheap south-coast nursing home.

If he got clear and his father didn't, the blessing would be on both sides. What a way to think about your own flesh and blood – but when he put a hand to his cheeks to see if there were any tears the dry flesh made him smile. Tired of jumbling the same ideas, he imagined talking the issue over with his brothers, his wife, his children, even his neighbours and friends, and knowing that everyone would call him a merciless villain.

He had read the word for it somewhere a long time ago, in a history book most likely. *Parricide*. Well, there would be a word for it, wouldn't there? The fact that you couldn't get away with anything convinced him he would never have the guts to do it, though having considered the matter at least deserved a dummy run for when the time came.

She feared to touch the red and purple bruises, but held his hands, fingers folded into the palms, and kissed his lips, which seemed the least damaged part of him. He was some person found on a raft after twenty days adrift, one man left from the many who had perished. He made a smile, but she saw pain. Only pain would come if he tried to speak and say how wrong she had been for causing his distress. Her screams from the room below had buried his own cries at the fear of death, as well as the dreadful blows drummed onto his poor body, forcing Keith up the ladder to pull them away.

She had done with shouting, hoped her insults would echo in Keith's mind till the day he died. As for those biking goon-bullies, nothing could move them to feel regret, though if it was true that 'vengeance was the Lord's alone' she hoped He would take care of it sooner rather than later, that they would find their Nemesis under the wheels of a hundred-ton juggernaut, and live only long enough to realize why it was that the Lord had done His work. As for that vile Jenny who had been to bed with one of them, and was stroking his greasy hair, and no doubt whispering praises for his part in the disgraceful riot, she would like to kill her and not let the Lord have the pleasure.

'Everything's going to be all right.' She pressed his hands gently, seeking a response in his eyes, and speaking so close that no one would hear. 'Whatever happens, I won't leave you. I love you. We'll always be together.' Yet the statement was hard to believe, only her way to try and help him bear his suffering.

The room was filled with lovers, Garry saw, everyone paired off except him and his mate Wayne. There weren't enough to go round, that's why. His fists were his lovers, and they'd had a sufficient piece of action to last a few nights at least. He couldn't remember yesterday, nor care less whether tomorrow came. If what that bag Sally screamed about him had been true he ought to wish it never would, but she hadn't had a slate go into her thigh like a sabre. Without his leather trousers the leg would have been sliced off, and even then the gash was too deep to bear thinking about, though he didn't want to bother anybody now that the job was over.

Fred wound an old sheet around him soaked in a bottle of iodine, and the bleeding seemed to have stopped, so he lay in his underpants like a wounded swaddie in the Falklands, bare legs thrust in front. Though the flesh was chilly there was the danger of getting a hard-on, and then where would he be, with everyone to see it?

He reached for his jacket, covering himself in case it happened. The fight had been more equal than Sally could have known. Lance would have been left headless if he hadn't worn a helmet, and Wayne had a bruise as big as a headlamp from his forehead hitting a beam. They had taken enough damage between them to add up to as much if not more than Daniel had got, so he couldn't feel bad about having put the boot in.

He had only intended getting him down after a couple of thumps to calm him, but the shock from the slate sent him a bit loco, the same with Lance and Wayne when they saw what happened. His laugh brought a glare of rank detestation from Sally, which made him laugh again. If Daniel had been killed he would have asked her to marry him, or take up with him. It must be wonderful, wedded to a woman who not only cursed like a navvy but mixed her spiel with words you hardly knew the meaning of. It would be an education listening to her, and the thought of such a future stopped pain drumming at his leg for a few minutes. Daniel, warped from birth, had still been lucky enough to shaft a nice big lovely woman with a vocabulary like a dictionary, which dirty video he'd better stop running through his brainbox or there would be more than a hard-on under his jacket.

Pity she won't look at me, though not many of her sort would unless I chatted them up all evening and got them more than half seas over with a conveyor belt of short drinks. And where would I meet them, in the first place? The only way Fred the Landlord knew how to dress was to put on a white shirt and navy-blue suit, but even a happy walker like that must have better chances with women.

She had fallen for that schoolteacher all right, though when it started I don't suppose she knew what she was getting into, no more than I did when I gave the lads a bell and asked them out for a spin. On a night like this! Well, I'd been sweating my bollocks off all day, and didn't even have the tranny on to tell me the weather because the woman at the house said it interfered with her work at the word processor. You can't win 'em all, but it would be nice now and again to win one.

Keith told himself he must look sharp, pull his finger out, do something for others' sake as much as for his own, though it was hard to rouse his faculties or the energy. Inert in the brain, he knew he need only stand up for full power to flow back, to scratch his head and look as if in thought, able to settle every problem, for those around him to assume he was their man.

You felt more powerful after killing someone. He hated himself for it, yet could act and be strong, as long as he didn't question. He went between sickness and wanting to live. His mother had died when he was seven, and everyone said that his father had killed her. Disease did not run in the family, but tragedy did. Every fatal illness began with someone thinking they had caught a cold. Maybe it still does. She was dead before anybody could do anything. His father had gone away with a woman, his Aunt Virginia said. His father later married the woman, who brought Keith up. 'Your mother died from broken love,' his aunt told him. Broken love? Did that mean suicide? He still half wondered what it meant though yes, he certainly knew. 'She wouldn't have done it but for your father betraying her. He was an absolute rotter. If he had only pretended to love her she might not have died.'

Keith was the age his father was when he'd had that devastating affair, killing his mother as surely as he had battered the life out of Gwen. His father still lived with the woman, because nothing can break a love affair started in such a way. At sixty-five, the old man was retired, and healthy, went to church every Sunday with his upright wife, the eternal lovers of a storybook Hertfordshire village.

His mother receded into dreams, and then was forgotten because he had grown to adore his father, the bitter injustice not striking till much later. He hadn't even disliked Helen, who had looked after him like her own child because she couldn't have any. Maybe that was why his father fell in love with her, never easy in body or mind with children, though when Keith was older he taught him to shoot at his rifle club, took him walking, boating and cycling, horse riding and skiing, visited the zoo and all the museums with him, and when Keith at fourteen wanted to be with his friends, his father left him to himself without the slightest fuss.

He would no doubt convince me with tears in his eyes that what happened thirty years ago hadn't been his fault at all, Keith thought, and wondered how much his father's life would be smashed when his only son was arrested for murder, which alone would be worth surviving any explosion for.

The click of Garry's Zippo interrupted his speculations. 'We've got to do something with that murderer. We didn't get him down here for nothing.'

Wayne leaned across to share the flame. 'That's what I keep telling myself. If we're going to be blown up in a few hours he ought to be made to pay for it.'

'We'll put him on trial.' Garry was glad to turn his mind from the picture of Sally's naked and active body, but he also wanted to torment her, as if she was responsible for the grinding pain in his thigh. 'We'll find him guilty, and then put him to death. Our helmets are black, so one of 'em will do for the cap. A bit of good old English justice, an eye for an eye and a tooth for a tooth. I don't want to die without somebody paying for it.'

'How do we know we're going to die, though, till we're dead?' Lance who had been listening opened his eyes to talk. 'We might execute him, and then be alive tomorrow to tell the tale. That would put us in a fix. Not that I'm against killing him, mind you, even though he was my teacher.'

'It's a problem,' Garry said, 'and I don't like problems. We should kill him for that alone.'

'It's even worse,' Lance said. 'It's a *moral* problem. If we put him on trial, and then execute him for being a terrorist and killing us, or killing any of us, we'll be guilty if we're alive tomorrow. But if we don't do him in for killing us, and we get blown to smithereens, and he doesn't, he'll only get twenty years in clink. He'll be free and on the streets again in fifteen, back at school teaching kids.'

'But what if *he* gets blown up as well as us?' Wayne said.

'Dead men tell no fucking tales,' Garry said, 'so we might as well top him. There's some lovely beams in the attic, and I saw a coil of rope in that spare room.'

'It's still a moral problem,' Lance said. 'You can't get away from it. That's what moral problems are like. He used to talk to us at school about moral problems. Just think of it! He was shunting fucking guncotton all over the shop, and he talked about moral problems. Not that I understood a word of what he chuntered on about, so we can't try him on that count as well.'

'It'll only be moral if we hang him.' Garry made another roll-up. 'Even if none of us die we can make him swing, just for having a load of bombs that he knew would blow people up. He might only get six months in a court of law, not twenty years, but to me it's a hanging matter. I mean to say, I don't have fuck-all to do with his politics. Nobody does here. We're just innocent bystanders, aren't we?'

'Too fucking true,' Wayne said solemnly.

'We top him, then,' Garry said. 'Right?'

'You can for me. He'll swing a treat.'

'I expect he ought to be tried first,' Lance said.

'Oh, we'll try him all right,' Garry said. 'We aren't fucking heathens. All square and above board. Then we'll hang him. After all, his bomb load's outside, ain't it? We should know. We drove it here.'

'That means you're the guilty ones.' Sally's words were loud enough to suggest they were indisputable. Daniel shook from the icy cold that was his alone. 'At least he left it in a place where it wouldn't harm anyone.'

'Except a few passing motorists,' Garry said.

'Or bikers,' Wayne jeered.

'*You* deserve to die, as well.' Garry altered position to ease his leg. Ferocious ants were gnawing at it. 'You took his part, so how do we know you aren't one of them? You was in it from the beginning, and followed him in your car to make sure he got to where he was going.'

'I arrived before him,' she said coolly.

'What difference does that make? You only went ahead to make sure the coast was clear. Terrorists use people like you because nobody would dream of suspecting you. You can't fool me. It's only shits like you who help terrorists to blow ordinary people like us to bits.'

'I don't suppose they even get paid for it,' Wayne said, 'apart from expenses. They do it for kicks. I dream all the time of making a fucking great blaze in the middle of Chesterfield, but I'd never do it. I might hurt somebody, or get put inside if I was caught.'

She couldn't plead for Keith to hold them back, though he would be happy to hear her do so, for he was her sort after all, and would stop them sooner or later. One minute she loved Daniel, to a pitch never felt before, a melting together of temperaments that pushed tears to her eyes. She fought them, also, then became still, with a desperate uncertainty as to where such weakness would take her. A few hours ago she was driving to the airport, no one closer than dull and familiar Stanley.

Wayne pushed her aside to reach Daniel. 'Your van's full of explosives, eh?'

Words came thick and distorted out of his battered features. 'It is. I wish it wasn't, but it is.'

'When is it due to explode?' Keith, needing them to hear it from the Devil's own lips, pulled him by the arm to make him sit up.

The world and everyone connected to it was meaningless, too far away from Daniel, except for Sally's warm hand, and even that was taken from him. Sharp aches ran through his legs and head, and he smiled because his limbs were becoming real again. 'Eight o'clock is what I heard. I'm not supposed to know.'

'Stand up,' Keith said.

Daniel knew an order when he heard one, helped up through the climbing frame of pain which would prevent him falling once he was at the top. He feared the three savages who had pulled him from the attic, but Keith was more dangerous, merciless grey eyes close to his face: 'Where were you supposed to take it?'

'Coventry.'

The fist showed a large ring with an aquamarine stone, dull in the candlelight. 'I want an address.'

He had photocopied the town plan in his mind. 'Fourteen Dants Street.' Even in the dark he would have found it.

'Then where would it go?'

'I don't know. Probably London.'

Keith believed him. Whoever it was meant for were safe, but they in the hotel were not. Fourteen dead would surely satisfy them for a while. Hearing the news on the radio the terrorists would be laughing and hitting each other on the back at their bloody brew-up, then arguing for the privilege of the phone call to tell the world who had done it.

'So when do we put the rope around his neck?' Garry scooted his cigarette stub towards the fire. Fred picked it up from the mat and put it in an ashtray. 'You must admit he deserves it.'

'It's half-past one,' Keith said, 'which gives us a few hours to decide how to get away, but no time to think about killing anybody. He'll be dealt with when we're safe.'

'We'll get into our kit and leave at five to eight,' Wayne said, 'just far enough to watch the explosion. Then we can come back and sit in the ruins to keep warm.'

'I won't make it with this gammy leg,' Garry said. 'Look how it's swollen up. I'd like to kill him just for skimming that slate. I expect he smeared poisoned pigeon shit along the edge. He would have danced a reel and two jigs if he'd killed me.'

'We'll rip a door off and carry you on it,' Lance said.

'Not my weight you won't. I've put back too much ale in my life. But I'll be all right. Nobody gets the better of me, not even a fucking snowstorm.' Nor will they, whatever O Levels he hadn't got. He didn't remember his father because he was knocked arse over backwards by a concrete mixer on the motorway and killed while doing his stuff as a chainman for the surveyors. The emptiness of infancy was normal, but when he was two his mother married again, and he knew the man couldn't be his father because Garry got a kick every time he went close. Henry was his name, and in the beginning he waited till Garry's mother was out of the house, but later he didn't care, and when his mother told him to stop kicking Garry he kicked her as well. In three years the man spent what was left of his father's insurance, and then lit off, leaving his mother with two more kids.

She lived on National Assistance, and slutted after what men she could get while the kids ran around wild and half starved. Some nights they waited on the steps of pub or bingo hall hoping she would come out with lollipops or a bar of chocolate. A fancy man might chuck fifty p to get them out of the way. All men were bastards, so it paid to grow into a bastard yourself and keep them in their place. And all women were bitches who had anything to do with men like that. Only you yourself were left, and all you could do was find a couple of mates you could trust and have as good a time as you could. The rest was bullshit.

He never forgot insult or injury, and twenty years after the toe-capping Henry came to see his mother but she threw him out. A few weeks later Garry saw him in a pub on Saturday night, standing at the bar over a meagre half-pint. Garry clapped him on the back in friendly fashion and talked of the good old times when Henry had been kind to him as a three-year-old, and Henry had the gall to say: 'I'm glad you remember. I was good to you, wasn't I? But that's how I am. I allus was good to little kiddies.' The man's face was ageing and spiteful, but a few pints even got him talking again about his mother.

Garry said goodbye but went across the road to wait, and when Henry came out swaying and swearing to himself, he followed. At the end of a dark street he pulled him from behind, and while Henry lay half stunned in the gutter Garry told him how his infancy had really been. Then he gave every kick back that he had ever got.

And now the king-sized bastard of them all had come with his clapped-out van of explosives to do you and your mates an injury, even to kill you. If there was no justice in the world you had to make it, that's all Garry knew.

TWENTY-SEVEN

'I'm stiff all over.' Eileen woke from her dreams so troubled she thought they were real. 'I suppose I should go upstairs to bed. What are we doing down here, anyway?'

'We've just got to sit,' Parsons said, 'until the crack of doom.'

She yawned. 'Believe that, and you'll believe anything. He's only saying the van's full of bang-bangs to frighten us. He's like one of them poxy hoaxers who phones an airport and says there's a bomb on a plane. It makes him feel good. Then he puts the phone down and has a good wank. The dirty bastard's the same as a flasher. There's plenty of them around, as well. You see 'em all over the place.'

She stood, and bowed to their laughter, as if she was acting in that play again at school, only this time it looked like being real, because if that beaten-up old flasher was to be believed, the whole lovely hotel would soon be on fire, which was a shame because it was one of the nicest places she'd been in. Maybe they should have kicked him in a bit more up in the attic, though they hadn't done a bad job, to look at him wincing and twitching. No wonder Trevor had been such a numbskull, with teachers like him knocking around. Keith must have had better schooling, not to mention the mam and dad who brought him up. He knows how to talk, and I'll bet he's got a good job that pays lots of money – as well as being tall and strong, and standing no fucking nonsense from anybody.

But there was a sense of violence about him that made her afraid. When he was angry, from habit it seemed more than reason, his eyes were sunken and closer together, nose almost hooked, a bit like an eagle, as if violence was mustard to his meat. Even when there was no reason for violence you could tell he was hoping for it. He had done something, or something had been done to him, or he had done something *because* something had been done to him, and he couldn't get it out of his mind. He was tense in look and limbs, always ready to spring – as he had up the ladder to pull those bikers off Daniel, when, if he hadn't got his own way, he would have killed the lot and enjoyed it.

She felt love for him but did not know whether she ought to like him, though she did because she wanted to. She wondered who his wife was and how they managed together, hard to imagine him easily in love with anybody, but she could understand women being in love with him. He was the sort who kept too much of himself secret, a man women love till they know better or get fed up with him. On the other hand he couldn't be so rotten, because he had brought her to this hotel, so that instead of twenty-five pounds single it had cost him forty quid double. Maybe he might think it worthwhile because she had been to bed with him, but she had enjoyed it as well, so he'd still been generous.

He hadn't done her such a favour if staying any longer meant getting blown to bits, but he wasn't to know, because he had got himself into the trap as well, which didn't seem to worry him all that much, and that was strange, as if something funny nagged at his mind, unless that was his way, and he was too proud to show he was upset like mad at what he had driven into. Not everybody screamed and swore if things went wrong, like her father and some of the men she had known, lashing out left, right and centre when they couldn't think what to do, and only making things worse.

Keith seemed like a clock that could take care of anything to do with time, though sooner or later the springs would break and the whole thing split apart. There were moments when she wondered who he was, and she didn't get very far but at least it was easier than trying to find out who she herself might be, which became impossible whenever she tried to try, though maybe that was the same for everybody, and it was easier to see other people, if that was easier at all. She thought she ought to stop thinking, because if you got ravelled up you would have a hard job starting again, which must be worse than not having started at all.

Keith liked her affectionate smile, the perfect girl friend who would never question him, because in her apparent mindlessness she thought it would be no use. And he wouldn't ask anything of her, even though he might want to. In any case they were far from being empty-minded, but out of love and good will towards each other (that rarest of attitudes between men and women) they could become devoted because it was no effort to be so.

Such dreams were of little use, dangerous to you and others if you strove to make them real. Daniel had tried, and turned into one of those who blew limbs off people but had never cut their own finger. Without experience or imagination his ideals had been easy to maintain, though you had to curb your contempt for such types if you believed it was right or useful to understand them.

He knew he must get on his feet for what he had to say. 'I assume you can all hear? We have to think about getting out of this place, beyond range of that van, because there's enough stuff inside to demolish the hotel. I take it that none of us wants to die?'

Wayne pulled Daniel's hand vertically like a railway signal. 'Here's one who does.' He let it fall, which pained Daniel more than the lifting and made him cry out. 'He ought to, anyway.'

Sally's flat hand swung so quickly he wasn't able to dodge, two fierce slaps chasing each other, though he hit back with equal force before she could run from what she had done. 'No bloody woman, or anybody else, hits me and gets away with it.' He was breathless with surprise, and holding her wrist that was hinging out for another blow.

'He's helpless,' she cried. 'Haven't you done enough?'

'We thought we had.' Garry's leg throbbed, and he wondered if he would be able to ride his bike again, saw himself sitting when the others had gone, sucking on his last fag and waiting for a flash whiter than any snow. 'We haven't started yet, if you don't behave yourself.'

Her breasts were rising and falling, breath grinding in her throat with passionate loathing. The bones of her skull were ringing with pain, but she took both hands away, sat by Daniel and stroked his arm. 'Don't worry, everything will be all right.'

She wasn't sure about that, in her misery, heart keening at such injustice, and at the stupidity of Daniel for involving himself in a cruel and useless cause. He was a child who had been led astray by the balloon man, with no matter what justification, dazzled by the hot air filling their plastic gewgaws.

Enid's face was pinched with the anxiety they all felt. 'My boy friend's supposed to pick me up in the morning. He said so when he dropped me off in his car this afternoon, so I didn't bring a proper coat, only this cardy and what I stand up in. I'll freeze if I have to go outside.'

Aaron put an arm around her. 'You can use my coat.'

Keith smiled. 'We all want to live. That's understandable. There are a few options, which I've been thinking over, so I suppose it's time I shared them. The first is that we stay in here and don't do anything. After all, the van might not explode.'

'I'm not going to be a sitting duck, or play snowman's roulette,' Alfred said.

Nor was anyone. Daniel's state of half-sleep dimmed his pain. He heard, but didn't want to show that anything concerned him in case they baited him for being the cause of their peril. Tied to a chair, he wouldn't be able to move, the only person in the hotel. The pale and leaded sky of dawn was showing. They had abandoned him, and fled to save themselves. His evil latched on to a greater evil in them, so who would be the first to suggest the fate which he pictured? What they didn't realize was that fuses, being what they were – if there had been clumsiness, or carelessness, or any subtle fault whatever in the connections, or the timing, or the wiring – could send the van sky-high any minute. To assume all would be well until eight o'clock was optimistic.

'So we put the kaibosh on that one,' Keith said. 'Still, it might have worked, to get together in a room furthest from the van, and hope for the best. The trouble is that the van's parked halfway along the hotel wall, which would reduce our chances somewhat. So that option, such as it is, would be too much of a gamble, every life being precious, mine included. Even his, who got us into it. Though he never knew a moral twinge in his life, he's as valuable as the rest of us, and we can't abandon him. When we're safe he'll have a long enough time to think about how brave and clever he's been.'

'You should have been a bloody parson,' Garry said, 'with all this jabber.'

'You wouldn't know what to do with a bagful of words if they was put around your neck in a stable,' Eileen shouted.

They were like brother and sister, Keith thought, when she laughed and sat down. Cousins, perhaps. He was amazed at how well people of that sort got on. Quarrelling was a way of them getting to know each other. They would have a set-to and then start laughing and talking about the good old times. He felt more connected to their verbal liveliness than to the glum mood of the others.

Alfred liked the way Garry wasn't afraid to throw in remarks against big-headed Keith. He would have said the same himself, but Garry had got there first, so why waste your breath? 'You're a plumber by trade, then?'

'What's it to you?'

He glanced towards the fire to be sure his father slept, then knelt, not wanting anybody to know his business. 'I bought a nice plot of land near Matlock, and I'm going to have a bungalow built for Janice my daughter. She's the eldest. You understand?'

'I'm not deaf, am I?'

'I didn't think so.' Alfred smiled. 'I'm sure there's nobody less deaf. Nor less sharp, either. Are you all right, though? You look pale.'

'I've got a bit of gyp in my leg, that's all. Just get on with it.'

'This bungalow's going to have a lovely view over the Derwent. I want it to be a little gem.' When the old man kicked off there'd be more than enough to pay for it. He would be in clover, though the death duties would drop it by plenty. 'I've got to have a man of your trade to plumb the place up. A nice kitchen and bathroom. I know a plumber, but I don't trust him, neither his prices nor his work. Could you give it a try? Make a good job, I mean?'

A house was a lot to take on, even if only a bungalow, but you have to start somewhere. 'You mean you want an estimate?'

'That's right. Can you do it?'

'Don't keep asking me if I can do it. Do you want bloody references or something?'

'Oh no, just an estimate. I've had one already, and if yours is anywhere near, you've got the job. You don't get into a situation like this and not make friends you can trust. Anyway, I like to give a hand to somebody who's up-and-coming. I was very happy at the way you sorted that bastard out upstairs. If I had been thirty years younger I would have been with the rest of you, believe me.'

Garry was laughing inside. A whole house to play with! 'I'd have to take on extra help, but I'll do it.' He would go to the library and get an instruction manual, swot up a bit, take it little by little. He had already fathomed the basics, and you didn't need A Levels to be a plumber, not a good one anyway. Apart from anything else, once he had made a start Alfred wouldn't be able to get rid of him, though he'd be sure to do as good a job as he could because if it was known that he had fixed up one house it wouldn't be hard to get a contract for another, and soon he would have his own firm. When things got hectic and he had more work than he could handle he would take on people to help him, and become one of the youngest big employers in the Midlands. He would do it all on the quiet, a deal with each chap so that they would pay no tax and he would buy no stamps, everyone in it for love and money. After a year or two he wouldn't even need to get his hands dirty but would send his men out in little rainbow-coloured vans while he sat in a centrally heated office during the winter with his feet on a desk, winking at a gorgeous secretary in charge of the paperwork. The house he lived in would have the plumbing done by one of the best firms in London. There would be a Harley in one garage and a BMW state-of-the-art bike in the other. The picture built up in a few seconds, all pell-mell but vivid and desirable as a future, even to the extent of getting his old mother out of that damp rat trap in the valley and buying her a proper set of teeth.

'Shake on it, then.'

Alfred was glad to, because though Garry was only a jobbing plumber, he had a notion that he would see better work from him than anybody else.

'Another option' – Keith had been some time thinking about the matter – 'could be to wait till half-past seven in the morning, then make a run for it. The blizzard might have lessened, but at least it'll be light enough to see where we're going. Five hours will give us plenty of time to kit ourselves out for the elements.'

'That might be cutting it a bit fine, because what if they put the clocks on during the night?' Eileen joked. 'I mean to say, it would just be our luck, wouldn't it, not to have heard the news? All of us arsing around at half-past seven when – bang, we're dead.'

'They don't alter the clocks in the middle of winter,' Lance said. Whether they were dazzled by his expertise or stunned by his imbecility, Keith found the simple badinage hopeful in facing whatever peril came with the blast. But the more optimistic he was, the most despondent also. He would have as much talking to do to the police as Daniel when they came. I had no intention of killing her, I just wanted to give her a good shaking because her words filled me with an agony impossible to bear. Accident it was, manslaughter if you like, but not murder.

She obsessed him more now than when she had been alive, unless he was talking. 'To run for it would be the worst possible thing. Perhaps I do sound like a parson, but I don't want to get you either to Heaven or Hell one minute earlier than necessary. Nor do I want to go, before my time. Even a blizzard has its charms.'

She loved him. He was a card, a comedian no less, no tension in him while addressing them. He didn't altogether believe in his talk, you could tell (or she could), but he was thinking and at the same time trying to entertain them so that they wouldn't be frightened.

'If we went out now, in which direction would we go? The nearest farm, according to Fred, is half a mile or more. To struggle through twelve-foot drifts, which was what the newsflash said they were, before the batteries of the radio ran out, would mean death from exposure. And those who wouldn't be able to keep up, what would we do with them? Leave them behind?'

'I could climb on the roof and send an SOS with a flashlight,' Lance said. 'Somebody might see it, and pass it on.'

'Yes, God,' Garry said. 'He knows Morse code. The only thing is, I thought He'd snuffed it.'

Daniel's words were wrenched out because it was more than any bodily pain to keep them in. 'He can't be dead, otherwise I wouldn't be here. Neither would you. It could only be God who brought us to this.' Who else had held the friable arms of the timing mechanism apart for so long? If he didn't think that God alone was responsible he would run for the wall and bang out his brains in despair, though he felt something near terror at having broken his silence when all rights to do so had been taken away. 'God decided, and drew us together for His higher purpose, just as He made me do what I did. Everything that happens is part of His scheme.'

His words were English, but the outlandish language grated so painfully on Aaron he wanted to get up and strangle him. Perhaps the hatred was from a *déjà vu* dose of his own slipshod way of expression when he was young and writing poems, something he had ceased to do when the future closed its doors. The flash of similarity blinded him to pity unless, he thought, it was pain from the rotting tooth once more on the attack, but if so what had made it reassert itself? Calm so far, enjoying the rarity of being marooned (in any case, he had problems to solve), his sudden craving for violence against Daniel was only stoppable with the greatest effort.

Not everyone bothered to hold it back. A heavy ashtray spun by Daniel's head and hit the lintel of the fireplace. 'You shitbag!' Garry's effort made him gasp at the pain in his leg, and he was even more enraged because he had missed. 'You'll be in jail soon, not fucking church. Or you'll be dead, if I have owt to do with it.'

'No, I won't.' When Sally tried to stop him talking he pushed her away so forcefully that her back struck the chair. 'If anyone should try to get us out of this, it ought to be me.'

Parsons peered at the maelstrom of snow. After twenty years down the pit his ears could pick out any sound that was different, and he swore he heard the churning blades of a helicopter. Yet it couldn't be, came from his fantasy of hope perhaps. Pressing an ear to cold glass, the uproar of the blizzard heightened the ante of cyclonic wildness.

Daniel fell from Keith's push at his chest. 'There's nothing you can do to help. If you want to be safe, stay quiet.'

Sally was not part of such people, never had been. She belonged with Daniel, sat by him to be loathed as part of him, marked off from those who thought themselves much in the right but were as culpable as anyone because all they had in mind was to kill. Daniel had done what he had done out of an idealism he had never clearly understood. 'It's your responsibility that nothing happens to him, and I'll hold you to it, believe me.'

'Not a duty I take too heavily, I might tell you.' Keith turned from her. 'The next question is whether there are any bomb-disposal experts among us, who can fight their way across the yard and tackle that tangle of wires and fuses? Well, I knew it wasn't on, but I had to ask. It's the only thing that would save us, though even a bomb-disposal expert can make the wrong move.'

Parsons wished somebody would, in his lower moments, because what could he say when he got back to Ashfield? His life was finished, so he didn't much care whether he did or not. There would be nothing but scorn from the lads, even if they didn't have him prosecuted, and there were more than a few who would want to. I'm over the hill, rotting from the inside out, and I can feel it speeding up, doing its stuff with every minute that passes. If I had to run a hundred yards for a bus I would drop dead before grabbing the rail. Twenty years ago, when I was ripping out coal underground, and was a dedicated servant of the Union, I made up my mind I would get to the top in that set-up at least, but somewhere on the mountainside of endeavour I began donkeying around in circles. I'm bloody sure that was a helicopter, unless it was a chimney falling down in the wind, or drainpipes cracking under the weight of snow. And then what did I do? Spent the Union's money in a Soho club, fifty quid for a bottle of stuff they called wine but tasted like the worst vinegar in England, and then off to bed with a woman who wanted to whip me because I couldn't get it up. 'It's nourishment I want,' I said, 'not punishment.' On my way to meet Jenny at the station I found she'd robbed me blind. Christ, I'll tell 'em it fell out of my back pocket. 'I was mugged,' I'll say. 'Don't kill me just for that.'

TWENTY-EIGHT

Keith stood by the fire, a hand in his pocket as if it were full of ideas and he couldn't decide which to bring out next. 'The question is,' he said, 'whether one of us can't get to the nearest house or phone box to explain matters, and call a bomb-disposal specialist in by helicopter.'

Fred's map, fished from what he called The Information Drawer, was an old one-inch clothbacked provisional edition hurried out for use by the Home Guard during the Second World War, a relic picked off a junk barrow in the market for ten pence. All but falling to pieces, its only use was in showing that if you went left from the hotel the road undulated for miles until it reached a valley and the nearest village. If you turned right it did the same for an equal number of miles and led right into the fangs of the gale.

'We're up the creek,' Eileen said, 'without even a soup spoon.'

Joking in face of peril, feeling no responsibility for getting out of it but waiting for someone to tell you what to do, must be paradise to them, but for Keith such a state would be torment. To them it was normal, but he had been born to show people and think for people and, when necessary, to lead people. At such times he was most alive: people trusted him, and wallowing in their dependence was like a tonic – though finally he must justify their faith.

Your secrets were your own, until you let them out. Look into people's eyes and, however frank you appeared, they could know nothing unless you told them. In a crisis, when it mattered to conceal what you were thinking (so as to mull more effectively over your choice of what to say), you were one person hidden and for yourself alone, then another for those with whom you had to deal. So he could hope to be their saviour, while guilty of murder. Such thoughts were necessary for his strength of purpose – pausing only to seem more caring to his audience, as if to imply that a half-concealed scholarliness mixed with the man of action.

His tone was one of impatience at Eileen's remark. 'Not too far up it. I saw a pair of skis in the junk room. They weren't exactly new, but the rats hadn't eaten the straps as they did the leather of the Assyrians' shields. The runners look straight, so the only question is who, apart from myself, is able to ski?'

The bikers couldn't, he was sure, and Aaron would be too old to plunge through such conditions. As for Parsons and Alfred, the same for them with knobs on, even if they could ski, which he doubted.

'I can,' Sally said. 'Ever since I was old enough to stand on my feet. My parents insisted I do everything: type, swim, drive, ride — and also ski. I can do it as well as anyone here, if not better. The snow must be above the hedges by now. It should be plain sailing.'

Keith remembered a white-out near Bluedale Tarn, when with all his weight and strength (and experience) he could hardly stand against the wind which was blowing from the direction he needed to go. The only way was to have the wind with him, though it pushed and buffeted, and more than doubled the distance to safety, with moments when he thought he would never reach his hotel. A local farmer lost in the same storm was found dead a month later, in spite of building himself a shelter in the lee of a wall.

The expression was eager in her offer of help, but he considered it useless to sacrifice her. 'It's nothing for me,' she went on. 'I can do it easily. It's a brilliant idea.'

He sought a way to refuse that would not drive her to try more persuasion, which he might not be able to resist. He understood why she pleaded, and even felt envious at such a gallant way of cancelling her mistake with Daniel, but he couldn't let her absolve herself at the cost of her life. He told them about Bluedale Tarn. 'If the wind drops, I'll think about it. Nobody can live in this weather, skis or not.'

'You don't trust me.' She struggled not to cry or swear, or do both. Her face was dirty and bruised where Wayne had hit her. He mustn't let that happen again. All of them looked like street cleaners in for their tea break, except for Percy and Fred. 'You think I'll get to safety, then leave you in the lurch,' she said. 'What a mind you have. As if I could leave *him* to your rotten schemes. You don't know anything, however clued-up you might be in other ways.'

Gwen had come back to life in her, so to kill again would be easy. Let her have the skis, and go. Her death wouldn't be on his conscience. But the matter was finished, and he felt better at disposing of it. Experience had scored into him that in the face of irrelevant accusations you either stayed quiet or set further talk off at a tangent. 'The map was printed in 1942, so I wonder if any new buildings have been put up since? There could be a place closer than we think.'

'Not that I've noticed,' Fred told him, 'and I know the area well.'

'You can't put me off,' she said. 'I still want to go.'

'Have a dekko through the window,' Parsons told her. The blizzard mocked their isolation, bumping around salients and inlets with the noise of despairing travellers trying to reach safety. 'Or the back door. It's an inferno.'

'She wants to run the whole show,' Garry said. 'Keith's the only one as could make it, but he can't go because the gaffer's got to stay at the controls.'

They were silent and waiting, but he hardly knew how to proceed, lit a cigarette and looked at their faces, features shifty and uncertain where they had once been clear. He assumed his to show the same puzzling blend of uncertainty.

'It sounds like the wolves are after us,' Lance said. 'Eh, Ferret, what rhymes with wolf? I'm in the mood to write a song.'

'There are no rhymes any more.' Daniel took the cigarette that Sally had lit. 'Neither rhyme nor reason. We're beyond all that. Whatever he says, nothing will succeed.'

Daniel's unwillingness to hide his glee enraged Wayne, who opened the short blade out of a Leatherman pouch and jabbed it towards him. 'If we try, and whatever it is doesn't work, you'll die. I'll make sure of that. I'll slit your fucking throat.'

Keith, not as successful at keeping anxiety from his face as he thought, wondered how long he would be able to hold them in check and, if the final panic took the form of a blood bath, whose side he would be on. 'Tell your boy friend to keep quiet,' he said to her.

She smoothed her cheek over Daniel's lips, held his hand and whispered that she loved him. His tormented features filled her with a longing to be with him where they could renew the delight of when she had known him yet not known him. He wanted to die and didn't care, lived in a void and loved no one, which was why she would protect him even at the cost of her life, would die with him because there could be no life after him, no going back into the appalling emptiness of the past.

Percy startled them with his razor-honed pronouncement. 'Them as can, do. Them as can't, teach.'

'I thought you were asleep, Father?'

'I never sleep, you know that. A pit engineer catnaps. He can be called out any minute. When you turn the gas on, water pours out.'

He hated those who laughed. 'Your mind's wandering again,' Alfred said.

'And your brain's zigzagging around the maypole if you think that plumber's any good. You'd be better off getting a monkey from the zoo. He might be all right on a motorbike, but he couldn't plumb a Wendy house.'

Keith wondered who would want to go on living with a father like that, with the chance that you would end up like him. Maybe others among them were also thinking that the effort wouldn't be worth it. He had to persuade them otherwise by unrolling the last possible option.

Alfred seemed about to put his father into a sleep he wouldn't wake up from. The old man's only safe, Aaron thought, because we're here, otherwise Alfred would have smothered him by now, though if we weren't here he wouldn't be so embarrassed and want to kill him. 'I don't need your opinion about my business,' Alfred said, exasperated. 'So go back to sleep.'

Garry had known it was a dream, to fix up a whole house and get himself into business. Even so, if anybody died in the snow, should they ever get that far, he hoped it would be the old man. The idea of the house had been good in hiding the pain in his thigh, which now came back as if hooked hands were inside and trying to rip a way out.

'If you had taken my advice from the beginning you'd have been a lot richer than you are today,' Percy went on. 'And who was it got you started, anyway? Me. Who told you what to do and how to do it? Me. And who lent you five thousand quid to get your first lorries? Me. Without interest, as well, because I never expected to see it back.'

'You did get it back, though, didn't you?' Alfred said mildly.

'After twelve bloody years I did. You held off as long as you could.

You had it in the bank making interest, because you hoped I would die, and you needn't bother then. But I didn't die, did I? And I won't, either. I'll see you out, you see if I don't.'

Aaron stood. 'Lay a few more bottles out, Fred. A double whisky for me.' Not so much for conviviality as for his tooth. Tormented by draughts and chill, Hell was where you had toothache, and Paradise where you didn't.

Fred was pleased to take orders, middle of the night or not. That was what he was here for, such action a sign of normal life, placing glasses on a tray and balancing their weights to keep it even, a tuneless whistle at the thought of the till ringing. Hidden from them at the other end of the bar, he told himself that if Doris was here to share the work, life would be fine. But she wasn't and, considering the mess, it was just as well. If she were here she would never stop nagging – and I would never stop swearing. If only I hadn't learned to swear! But then, I shouldn't have been six years a sailor, because sailors swear, though when you think about it, who doesn't? The only reason women don't swear as much as men is that they nag and men don't.

He flung the white towel over his arm, scrawled fingernails through his hair, took a sip of Aaron's whisky as if to be sure it was a good brand, and strode into the lounge like one of the best waiters in the business.

TWENTY-NINE

How does a common fly get to where it is? Why does it land on any particular spot? A big black confident muff-footed specimen rested on the back of Keith's hand, hairs for a jungle and between the veins for valleys, a summer fly that had survived the autumn in some warm cupboard and now came out sensing that there was no safe place even for a scavenging fly.

He couldn't understand why everyone looked so cold: caps on, woolly hats donned, coats pulled together, overcoats buttoned and belted. He felt neither one nor the other, more proof (should he need it, though he forced himself not to) that he was different.

'Our only hope is to start the van,' he said, after they had settled with their drinks, 'and get it as far from the hotel as possible. Fred tells me there are spades and tools in one of the stables. Two or three hundred yards should be enough. Then we shelter in the strongest room to escape the worst of the blast. I'll drive the van myself, but I'll need volunteers with spades and mattocks to clear the way.'

He had come to the point aimed for from the beginning, the cul-de-sac of action in which he hoped to find the dream of youth which youth had waited to spring on him like a giant well-poisoned cobra in middle age, something about to happen which would erase the significance of all that had gone before. He had wanted such an event for a long time, had sensed it was inevitable and never been unduly worried whether he won through or not, since it was hard to imagine life after the snow. A dream beyond the dream could not exist when the present was so important. He wondered if the others felt anything similar, or would object to him drawing them into his adventure of redemption. They were talking all at once, and he let them go on, because that also was part of working towards the final plan at his own circumlocutory rate.

'I'll drive the van,' Aaron said.

'Another fucker wants the George Cross.' Wayne spat. 'I'm willing to dig, though. I'll dig from here to Australia to spite that bomb-carrying fuckpig. I once dug my old man's garden over in one day. He swore I couldn't, so I bet him five quid I could. He thought I was as soft as shit because I was a biker. I knew the cunning old bastard only wanted to get the garden dug over for a fiver, but I proved I could do it, all the same.'

'I don't care what I do,' Lance said. 'Dig, drive, dance a jig. I'm willing to get at the wheel, though, because I'm a biker. When you're doing a ton on the motorway, every second can be your last, and who wants to live for ever?'

'Everything in the van must be melting into a jelly,' Daniel said. Never getting to the drop-off point was the peril of the trade, a flash, and only a few bits in a bucket were left, after a couple of days finding them. He considered himself back in the comity of cave-land society now that the last hope had been proposed. 'You would be wiser not to listen to your guru, and try getting through the blizzard to safety. It would be better to die in the cold and be in one piece when they found you, than have your bits scattered so that they'll never know who was who if they do.'

'We'll need as many spare lights as we can get for those who go in front to clear the snow,' Keith said. 'Also, wear every scrap of clothing you can wrap around your bodies. Are there any chains we can put on the wheels?'

Fred sat writing a list of the wanted items. 'Not for a van. The wheels are too big. We can try them, though.'

Daniel pushed Sally's hand from his mouth. 'You won't even get to the gate.'

Fingers moved among bottles in the half-dark – wine, beer and whisky – chose the solid neck of a champagne bottle and grasped it as firmly as to uproot a tree. Keith at the window tried to assess their prospects, but behind the wind there was discordant singing, like a woman wailing her heart out, calling him. At the back of the wind, a multitude of people on the moors and hillsides howled as if a terrible disaster were about to overtake them. He was hypnotized by the noise that went on and on intolerably, but he stood it out, couldn't turn from the cold glass, forced himself to listen, moments like days, to the endless wailing of cosmic despair breaking the heart of that part of the world which thought itself safe, as if all beyond the hotel was a vast Pompeii being earthquaked out of existence. A real and immediate scream filled the room, a heavy object smashing dully against flesh.

Daniel's blood raced him to the floor.

'He opened his trap once too often.' The jagged glass went again at the injured head. 'I told you to belt up.'

Parsons and Aaron pulled him away, and Wayne sat down but kept the bottle in reach as if for another bout at the time of his choosing. Keith stood over him, staring the crazed face out, the mind behind peeled of all sense.

'He asked for it.' Wayne burned bright with indignation at Daniel's gloating pessimism. 'If he opens his mouth again, he's had it. We don't need him any more. I feel like a massacre. Fuck the van. Let's have fun. We'll fuck the place up before the van does. Let's take a few happy walkers with us.'

'We've got to stick together.' Garry spoke softly, and Keith was appalled at his pallor when he held a light close, glad the candles had been so low on the illumination of his suffering. 'We'll shift that snow,' Garry said. 'We didn't have so many tools when we moved the van before, did we? If we wreck the place we're on that Daniel's side. We got the van here, didn't we? Well then, we'll get it away again.'

Hands over her head, sinking to the floor, Sally knew there was nothing to be done, either for Daniel or for herself, only to go down at his scream of pain and despair. They would murder him, and then kill her, both lost if they didn't run away, no one willing to help. The hideaway under her arms and inside her closed eyes was dark and warm, a last protectorate formed by cutting out sound and light, as the howl from someone she hoped was not herself went on and on.

Fred came in with a bowl of warm water and a pile of hand towels, busy as on a summer's day when a kid had gone uncontrollably headfirst from one of the swings in his garden. He had been meaning to cull stones out of the playground, but then gravel was just as bad to the palms and knees of a falling child. 'In my business you have to be a jack of all trades: plumber, carpenter, electrician, even a doctor, like now. Come on, Mr Daniel, let's see the damage. We'll soon have the bleeding stopped. But that screaming's a bit of a nuisance, isn't it? What's got into her?'

'Kill the bitch,' Garry said faintly. 'She's getting on my wick with her racket.'

Fred pulled Sally's arm out of her lock, the flat of his hand ringing against her face. She stared, then discovered where she was. 'You ought to be all right now, miss. I'm sorry I had to do that, but I'm sure you'll understand now you're back to normal.'

Lance stretched himself and reached for his leathers. The jacket was heavy with studs and belt but Jenny held it high enough for his arms to go in, getting her amiable strong guy ready for his labours. Enid and Eileen fitted up Wayne with trousers little slimmer than his legs, boots well zipped and buckled to the knees, jacket fastened with press studs and thick belt, helmet with visor set on his head. 'Look at that fussy old bastard dabbing at that little cut I gave Old Ferret with the bottle. He'll still be at it when the balloon goes up.'

Fred scissored another strip off to tie the bandage, then stood back to view his work. 'You'll be all right now.'

'I wish you'd stop my leg bleeding,' Garry said, 'instead of wasting your time on that pair, though if he's as all right as you said I was he'll be dead in a couple of hours. His troubles are over, if he did but know it.'

'He's right,' Enid said. 'Look at that blood on the floor.'

A pool had spread in the shadow, and when Fred took off the swabbings blood pulsed bright red from the wound. 'We'll do a tourniquet. I've seen worse at sea.'

'I suppose you dragged the poor fuckers behind the ship in salt water,' Garry said.

'Only for a week.'

Keith lifted the telephone on the bar, in case it had mended itself, but there was no sound. He hammered it against the desk.

'That's always the first to go,' Fred told him. 'That, and the power. I meant to get a generator in last year.'

'Then you would have had enough light to operate on my leg,' Garry said. 'No thanks.'

Fred tied the ligature, and the bleeding stopped.

Which was good, Keith thought, unless gangrene's the result. 'We'll look at you when we get back.'

Percy stood up, staring ahead, clean and spruce as if he had just finished a long dolling-up for a Saturday night at the pub with his wife. 'Aren't you going to take me? I fancy a walk on Bournemouth's lovely sands. The sun's coming through the window, which is funny, with the blizzard going on. Still, I'll bet some lovely nurses are sunbathing out there in their birthday suits.'

In one swift walk, before Alfred could get to him, he was stroking Sally's hair, a grin on his ancient maniacal face, large immaculate teeth fixed in her sight for ever. His hand roamed her shoulders and went down to a breast, gripped so hard she cried out and pushed him away, the fall-out of his body shaking the floor.

Eileen looked at Keith, and he felt that to kiss her would be too much like saying goodbye, an impression he didn't care to give. He smiled and touched her hand. 'We won't do it all at one go. We'll have to come back for more help.'

'I love you,' she whispered. 'I've never loved anybody so much in my life, honest. I know that now.'

'I feel the same. Don't worry.' And that would have to do, as he turned from a sweeter farewell than he had ever received from Gwen, or given her. But then, I never loved her — though in the beginning he had been infatuated, and eventually obsessed by her as she wove and stitched and knitted him into her possessive web, and he had gone along with it, not knowing that one day he would kill her. Or maybe I always knew, he told himself, as they went into the blizzard.

Part 3

THIRTY

The back door was as much in the lee of the tempest as any part of the hotel could be, Keith nevertheless leading Wayne and Lance into a meteorological topsy-turvyness similar to when he had yachted with boat-loving colleagues in gales around the Orkneys. The spirit was with them and the flesh was also willing, but icy snowbits drove against their cheeks, and Keith wished he too had a helmet instead of a balaclava around his head. Wayne and Lance wielded their spades and chopped a footpath through waist-high snow till a blade clanged against the back door of the van.

Lance mouthed a joke no one heard, the flashlight brushing his visor, sound stopping all but their own Royal Banshee shouts of glee. Keith did not know who was who: one at the side door hammering with the spade handle to break the ice that crusted it shut, while whoever other it was slid between the van and the wall and after a few uppercuts with the handle opened a door.

He got in and lay flat across the seat, pulling himself up like a spayed animal. One out and one in, between them they forced the other door to slide back, a thud that sounded out the wind. They sat in a row, damp upholstery and mock leather smelling above the cold, snow padding the windscreen. 'Now what?'

Lance turned the key in the ignition, and the dull red spot came on and then went out, a lifeless click on trying a few more times. 'Just what I thought. The fucking battery's as flat as a pancake. Now we're fucked, and no mistake.'

Keith cleared water from his watchface – at four o'clock. There were two possibilities, he told himself. Only two, but listen, he said to them: 'Either we find a car ready primed with a full battery and a set of jump leads in the boot so that we can start the motor from a boost out of the good one, or we unload the explosives and fuses into another car in which the engine will start, and drive that one away.' But there were two disadvantages to consider. The first was that while manhandling the lethal cargo they might disturb it and – goodbye all.

'Not yet,' Wayne said. 'I love the world still.'

The second snag was that a car would be less able to negotiate the snowdrifts than the robust van. So they must get back in the hotel and find out whose car had a full battery, or who thought their car had, and whether or not it was equipped with a set of jump leads to make the transfer of power. The prospect of finding that other car, supposing it existed, and assuming it could be found, and uncovering it from the snow, and manoeuvring it into position to get the two engines close, then opening both bonnets and attaching the jump leads with freezing clumsy fingers was, to put it mildly, awesome.

'Let's get moving, then,' Lance said. 'My nuts are knocking from the cold, even though they're twenty-two-carat gold.'

They tumbled into the snow like black polar bears – if there were such things in the Far North – and went back to the porch, while Keith stayed to make certain that the van doors weren't entirely closed so that they wouldn't lose the same sweat getting in again.

Wayne kicked and Lance thumped, but the door to the hotel held, their efforts silent in the high pitch of the wind. Keith pushed at solid wood. If every little operation took so long they would still be arsing about by the deadline of eight o'clock. The Yale latch had been on when they came out, and had clicked behind. What they needed was luck, and you put yourself in the way of that only when you worked your hardest. They were willing and capable, so could afford to be hopeful, though all the force they could muster wouldn't move the door.

Aaron sheltered the last inch of his drink, as if a man out of the desert would come in and slurp it up. He wanted to make it last. The day was dire, he had known from the start that it would be, because every time he saw a word on a signpost or shop door he had tried to say it backwards. He often did this for amusement and to cultivate his dexterity with anagrams, but when the habit persisted, and he was unable to stop, it meant that something irritating or just plain unlucky would occur before the day was out.

Duffle coat, scarves and gloves were heaped on the carpet while he waited for Keith and his myrmidons to come in cursing and exhausted, and tell him to have a go. He did not want to, saw no reason to, they were trapped and there was nothing to be done. The besetting sin of the English was idleness. At least Robert Burton had said so, and Burton should have known, writing but one book in his life. Maybe that makes me more English than most, he thought, because the others are labouring hard enough.

Beryl worked harder, never still, even now she would be sitting at home in the room with the old-fashioned miner's grate which shone because she black-leaded it every day to make it look *traditional*. At the table she would check the titles and prices for the next catalogue, or make sure the house accounts were in order. She took note of every penny spent, and of every pound that came in, a rigid framework he liked. Into such a dream world of work, love and lodging he would introduce Enid.

He drank the last of his whisky. He thought it might come back up, but his stomach, like an old friend, let it rest. It was all lies, a pitiable deception of a lost and honest girl, because the offered job did not exist. The police were onto him for forgery. Even without that upheaval Beryl would have said we can't afford her, the spare room is full of books, she will be more trouble than she's worth. And he would have to tell her she was right, for to lose Beryl (and she was always threatening to go) would make life untenable. Any rift between them, and she would die, she said at the same time. So might he, the dread of the hostile world on him, because she had become his and his alone.

Every month she stood for hours at the parlour window looking at the moon, weeping at the emptiness of her life, always after days of sullen complaint against everyone she had known: their parents, friends, him — most, he thought, not justified. Or she would rave about slights that had happened so long ago they did not deserve to be remembered, brewing herself into a pitiable crisis of nerves, raving as if a wolf were loose in her, possessed by a longing for the side of the moon she would never see. No inducement, persuasion, or show of affection could break that barrier, every fit as painful to him as if he were witnessing it for the first time.

The end was always the same. Exhausted by unexplainable suffering, she allowed him to lead her to his bed, which he did with intense feelings of shame and joy. In the morning her eyes were clear, brow smooth, heart calm, levity for herself and subtle commiseration for him, and a wistful kind of gratitude that he had helped the storm go by. For him one evil cancelled out another, but what would happen if he took Enid home?

The fire glowed between two half-burnt logs that would never sufficiently meet to give a warming flame, kept that way by Fred's attack of manic parsimony. Alfred put his father close, laid his cashmere coat across to keep the blood from coagulating unto death. The old man's teeth clattered like Ezekiel's bones, stopped and then began again, eyes intently shut as if to let him listen more appreciatively to the rhythm. Alfred eased up his trousers, and the flesh above the socks was of a cold that would keep rising, an ice age in reverse going towards the warmer Pole.

Jenny knew there wasn't, but had to ask. 'Is there anything I can do?'

'He needs a warm hospital,' and the sight of a lovely-looking nurse or two.

She wondered at the smile when his cheeks were wet with tears. 'So might the rest of us, before the night's over.'

Percy's eyes took time to settle and focus. 'I should be out there, giving the lads a hand.'

He'll get at me with his last breath, Alfred thought. He means why aren't I with them. They don't need me yet, he could say, but it wouldn't make a blind bit of difference.

Percy called out in self-reproach: 'But I'm not up to it. I've got these awful aches in my shoulders.'

'Try to rest,' Alfred said. 'You'll be fit to travel in the morning then.'

Aaron thought they should get him upstairs to bed, but Alfred waved him away: 'I want to keep an eye on him down here.'

Enid was putting the various drinks together, like to like – beer, whisky, wine, gin and sherry. 'We always do this when we clear up. Fred tips the spirits back in the bottles, but he lets me have the other dregs before I go home. The beer and wine makes me sleep better. Only I'm not going home tonight.'

'I'll never get to the palm trees,' Percy sighed. 'I know it's a geriatrics' home you're taking me to, and who wants to go to one of them? I twigged we wasn't going to our Brian's. I'm not so bloody daft.'

A ship had come, to pull Alfred away from the island where he had been marooned with his father since birth. Or that's what it seemed. The old man was dying, and he wanted him to, but at the same time he hoped he would go on living. 'I was only trying to do what was best.'

The rattle in the throat declined to a cynical laugh. 'Oh, I know you was. I was a pest at times, wasn't I? Everybody is, though. You'll be a pest one day. Maybe even a bigger one than I've ever been. If you aren't a pest to somebody you aren't alive. And everybody's alive, so everybody's a pest, aren't they?'

His hands seemed to be searching around the inside of a refrigerator for his favourite leftovers. 'Sing "Greensleeves" to me, Alfred.'

'I can't sing, you know that.'

'I allus loved it. It brings everything back. Your mother loved it, as well. There's a lot to say goodbye to. Life's a bit of a pushbike at times, ain't it?'

Why don't you die, you old bastard? — which Alfred didn't entirely mean, Percy's words (and his) a row of taps releasing more tears. 'Don't leave me, Dad.'

'I'm not going, you silly sod. What makes you think so? It's just that I don't know where I'm coming to.'

No one was going anywhere on a night like this, Eileen thought, the gale thumping and bumping at every brick. She should have stayed in Buxton. Even a doss in a shop doorway would have been cushier, though the police might have prodded her on a few times.

Fred came in with a heap of blankets, the captain of the ship once more, or The Flying Bloody Dutchman, though even that was something to smile about. 'It's too late,' Aaron said, 'though you might as well cover him. But it was more than blankets he needed, so don't feel bad about it.'

'Oh, I don't. We expect casualties on a trip like this. Even though I run a tight ship you can't stop the odd accident. We crossed the North Atlantic in such weather once, and lost three chaps. One died of an ulcer, one had a brain haemorrhage, and the third disappeared over the side from no apparent cause. It was the worst crossing I'd ever been on. I left the ship as soon as I could. I trod on a bloody great rat as I went down the gangplank.'

'Did you?' Eileen said.

'You should have heard it squeal. I had a heavy kitbag on my shoulder, and I weighed more than I do now.'

Eileen sniffed. 'Poor bloody rat.'

'I didn't think so. I hated 'em.'

Alfred took the other end of the blanket, to spread it over the body. Talking right to the end: I might have known. If he could talk, and get on at you at the same time, he was alive, nobody more so. I thought he would never let go of the rail, but he's gone now, back to his tadpoles in jamjars as a kid, and the way sense was knocked into him at school, then to working and college at the same time on the engineering side, living for next to nothing a week and being happy on it because fags were a shilling for twenty and beer a tanner a pint, when courting was courting because you had to be careful of VD and putting a girl in the club – back to hiking and the bike, hard work and cold water, football on the wasteground, the pictures once a week if you were lucky and the music hall when you were flush – back to the happy days you couldn't get back to till you died, and then you were lucky to find anything at all, though he was sure his domineering old bugger of a father would get all he wanted, even on the other side.

Daniel looked around the room as if he hadn't seen it before – limitless in the gloom, people slumped in their chairs as if in the waiting room to Hell and hoping for the doors to open soon. He could do as he liked now that he was doomed with the rest of them, wouldn't bother to tell that the van battery was all but flat, only good if you kept the wheels turning, having barely got it going again when it stalled at traffic lights outside Warrington. He stood, a demented-looking figure with a bloodsoaked towel around his head. 'They won't come back.'

'You look like a real fucking terrorist now,' Eileen said. 'One of them Arabs. But if you don't stop saying things like that, I'll go in the kitchen for a carving knife and finish you off. I won't fuck around with a bit of old bottle.'

Garry raised a fist, as if to indicate that no one would deserve it more. His tongue wouldn't do as it was told. He slept and woke. Words spoken in the room came through to his dreams, and when no one took his advice on what they should do with Daniel he assumed they couldn't hear, being too much in the shadow. In more light they might have heard him better, done something. When Jenny came to hold his hand, a fragment of warmth went momentarily back into his body.

Fred bent from the waist to look. 'This young rating could do with a few blankets' – spreading over him what remained. 'You'll sleep like a top under these.'

Aaron took the flashlight. 'Let's fetch more. They're going to be needed.'

'What for?' Enid wanted to be left alone. Heat was supposed to rise, when there was any, but upstairs it was like entering headfirst into a layer of ice. 'I'm perishing,' she said at the landing.

He kissed her lips, hoping to warm her. 'Go back, then. I'll do it on my own.'

'No, I want to help you. It's like a morgue down there. I'll only go back if you come with me.'

'We'll find some blankets first.' His light picked out the exit sign, which he read as TIXE, then focused on wetness spreading from the corner of the ceiling, the wind sounding as if packs of dogs were assembling to go on a journey.

She gripped his hand, as if the building had been abandoned years ago. 'The place ain't the same any more.'

'It will be, when the lights come on again, and the heat gets going.' He led her into the spare room where the ladder rested against the open trap door. Air streamed from the attic as cold and strong as a river in the tundra. He put a foot on the ladder. 'I'm going up to have a look.'

'Don't leave me in the dark.'

He held her in his arms till she stopped shivering. 'Only for a moment. I promise.'

Sally followed him to the window. The same dull whiteness bulged at the panes. 'What are you thinking about?'

He saw only her eyes, nothing of the rest of her face, so turned to the snow, fatally drawn. 'We must get out.'

She wanted to unravel the towel that made him look as unreasonable as his words. A pocket had been torn from his jacket, his trousers were ripped at the knee. His power, such as remained, was in thinking they had a future. She touched his arm. 'Where?'

'Away,' he said, 'anywhere,' as casually as if suggesting a walk through summer glades, with no more danger than a cooling shower of rain. 'We'll be all right, the two of us. One alone might not be, but two can find a wall, and build a shelter. We'll make a palace in the snow.'

She was cold against him, even inside, ice coming through and freezing the sentiment. The sound of a grown man sobbing by the fire told her there was no more hope. She wanted to shout for him to be his age, pull himself together, it wasn't natural for a man in his fifties to cry because his father had died. No man should cry. Her father never had, and she wouldn't when *he* died. Nor when her mother passed away, come to that. 'We have to stay here. They'll get rid of the van, and then everyone will be all right.'

A palace of snow would make them impermeable to cold, halls of ice for eternal lovers to shelter in. They belonged together. 'I believed you when you said you loved me.'

She stood with folded arms, warmed by her coat. Yes, it had been love, nothing more so, but it would be suicide to go into the blizzard, though whether she would or not if the time came, and she had no way of stopping him, she couldn't say.

No guidance expected, she looked around. Jenny knelt, head on the blankets covering the injured leg of that horrid biker. Parsons' whining snore dominated, until Eileen poked him, at which he stared as if she were mad, then turned into another position and slept more quietly. The old man was dead, his son mourning him like a child who had lost his mother. Enid and Aaron were prowling around upstairs, though God knows what they expected to discover. Keith and his pair of yobbos were in the snow at the back trying to move the van, and Fred was in the kitchen assembling food for their comfort. He would only think there would be less to feed if she ran away with Daniel.

Aaron's light at the beams showed a tile ripped free by the wind, others following like bats in a mass panic, spinning into the turmoil of snow. Much of the roof was uncovered, half-frozen grit on the attic floor. Fred's hotel would no longer be viable after the thaw. Making sure the trap was closed, he was careful to put one foot after the other on the ladder.

'I thought you was never going to come back,' she said. 'That's snow on your coat.'

'If we're here much longer it'll be in the lounge as well. It won't be any use telling anyone.' They went into the rooms to gather as many blankets as could be found.

Spades were weapons of war. Sweat saves blood, as Keith had heard said, such fervour from one old soldier he would believe it for life. Work the body and you saved the spirit, which in turn looked after the body, and so you guarded both. In other words, treat every problem with care. Lavish it with time as well as mental labour, then *sweat* over it by digging into all the possible whys and wherefores. Such meticulous care for detail helped to win people to his way of thinking. You pondered on what intelligence was collected, while they drifted happy-go-lucky along, and when the problem fell into its many parts you fitted them together like the components of a machine gun, till you saw a way through and, with the illumination thus gained, took everyone with you.

The spades Fred had found were barely fit for peace, never mind war, especially against elemental malice in the heart of the blizzard, and when they were cutting at the solid door he was so afraid the handles would snap that he dragged them towards a window because glass was easier, leaded or not, enough particles soon freed from the frame to let them help each other over the sill and into the kitchen, stamping on putty and glass to get warm again.

The lounge was rank with woodsmoke after the outside air, Fred economizing his supply by pulling green logs from the top of the pile. 'He's trying to gas us or freeze us, just in case we get the van safe away.' No blaze, the fire also gave less light, like one you'd made in a wood, Wayne thought, that a keeper or a farmer kicked to bits and chased you away from.

Keith found the place as squalid as a camp in the Arctic after nine months of winter. Where were the brushes and cleaning rags to fight off signs of the crack-up? People in the rear echelons should set to, and present an ordered place for destruction – if the hotel had to go. And if it didn't, what then? Nothing was wasted. A clean front to life or death was all that mattered.

A circle of snow flopped around Wayne when he jumped: 'My

hot-aches are killing me. I'll have frostbite soon, if I haven't got it already. And look at the sweat running down my wrists. It's like being in a sauna inside all this clobber.' He smiled at the shadows, happy with his purpose in life. 'I'd better not undo it, though, or I'll croak from pneumonia.'

Lance crashed his helmet against the table. Jenny kissed him, and leaned across to light his cigarette. 'It's lovely weather for an Eskimo.' He wiped the visor with a beer-soaked serviette. 'I used to want to emigrate to Canada, but I think it'll be Australia, if ever I do, unless I get a call from the Grand Old Opry to go to Nashville!'

Keith felt inexpressibly tired, wrung out, ready to sleep or die: but he knew he must rouse himself, fight free from a sudden onset of total ineptitude. 'We want the keys to the Volvo, because it's the nearest car to the van. I'm sure the battery's good on that, as well.' From shadows by the fireplace came a sound halfway between that of a kid robbed of his toffees and someone who thought he had cut his finger but then sees his hand's dropped off. 'Who's making that noise?'

'The old man died,' Aaron told him.

'Is that all?' Wayne said. 'I wish my old man would. I've asked him to, many a time. He'd never do it for me, though.' He reached a ham sandwich from the tray, then swung his rawboned hand, missing Fred by a millimetre, Fred wishing at the rush of air that they were still on inches and the gap bigger. 'You've been at that titty-bottle again. I can tell. You stink rotten.'

'Leave him alone,' Keith said.

Wayne smiled. 'I was only trying to get my blood going. It's like mud, and it hurts. He's more than half-pissed, though.'

Life and limb wasn't worth tuppence to these types. The only respect you got, Fred knew, for what it was worth, came from people who looked on you as lower than a dog. He levelled his bow tie. 'We've had two away, Mr Blackwell. Three, if you count old Mr Percy, though he's still here, in body at least.'

Food gave energy, beat the tiredness. Keith paused in his eating. 'Who are they?'

'The woman Sally, and her boy friend.'

Murderous fingers gripped his knife, though he couldn't have said whether to slice that incompetent fool or himself. You curbed the impulses of the rabble at your peril. He should have allowed Wayne to kill them both. 'Why did you let them go?'

'I wonder how Garry is, with his bad leg?'

'He's asleep,' Jenny said. 'I'm keeping an eye on him.'

'I hope he's all right.' Lance saw him lying back in the half-dark. 'If he isn't, I'll smash that Daniel to bits.'

'I couldn't stop them.' Fred stood back a few paces, as if to show he knew his place, and also because his place seemed a safer spot at the moment to stand in. Any trouble, and he would be more limber than anyone could know in those electrified seconds before they decided to take a witless poke at him. 'I was in the kitchen doing the sandwiches. The others were asleep.'

'She had the Volvo, didn't she?'

'Yes, sir.' He sensed the rebuke that he should have kept everyone awake with words or threats, but he knew he hadn't the backbone to make a captain, something he had always felt. He wasn't discouraged to be reminded of it, as long as he could act the part now and again. He had often been the life and spirit of the ship with his impersonations of those who were more successful in achieving rank. Funny, how a situation such as this took you back to a time when your next minute also did not bear thinking about. But bosun at least he could call himself. 'I've got the number in the book.'

'And her handbag's gone, with the keys?' His own car would be far more trouble to get into position, though at least he carried jump leads.

'Something smells good,' Wayne said.

Jack of all trades was also a cook, and glad to sidestep the foetid air of recrimination. 'I've got the biggest pot I could find on the stove: the soup of soups. I chucked in vegetables, tinned and raw, a bottle of olive oil, lard, onions, rice and a few spuds, as well as a chopped-up chicken and a pound of bacon. Anybody who goes out into the snow is going to have their bellies full. I wouldn't be me if they didn't. And those who don't have to shake hands with the blizzard will have a breakfast they'll never forget.'

'I hate fucking soup.' Wayne liked fun. Fun stopped him knowing a self he might not like and therefore turn dangerous. He winked at all but Fred. 'I broke my mother's heart over soup, so she had to make stews. I love stew. I love her cakes, as well. She's the best cakemaker in all Derbyshire. She made a big sponge cake for my twenty-first birthday. It was shaped like a motorbike, icing and all, twenty-one candles on the topbox. Dad said she'd never be able to do it, but she did.'

Fred stepped over broken glass to flick a crumb off the table. 'I'd give her a job here.'

'She wouldn't work for a cunt like you. Twenty-one candles on the topbox, and every one of them was lit!'

'You must have been spoiled all your life,' Eileen said, enviously.

'I was, duck. That's why I'm so rotten!'

'Another thing' – Keith turned to Alfred, scornful at such open manifestation of his misery – 'get rid of that corpse. Parsons, Aaron, help him to push it into the snow. I don't want to see it there when we get back.'

Fish slid around the pool, and vanished. But they didn't vanish. They turned a corner and were no more seen. So, little Alfred fixed his eyes on them to see where they went, while his father on the bank took out cakes and lemonade, tea and cheese sandwiches for himself. The sun made them warm and lazy, though not the fish coming out from the muddy bank and sliving towards the middle. This time he followed it, but the cake stuck in his mouth, and when he choked his tall and frightened dad gently banged his back so he would spit it out and breathe again. He had read a book once which called them 'halcyon days'. 'Put him outside? Do you know what you're saying?'

'The body will be better preserved. Open a window and drop him out. You'll find him again when it thaws.'

'We could cremate him,' Wayne said. 'That old furniture in the spare room would burn a treat. Then there's the tables in here. A funeral pile, like in India. I suppose it would stink, though, inside here. And we're not fucking savages, are we?'

Eyes convexed under Alfred's lids, then bulged dangerously. 'He's staying with me. You're not the gaffer here.'

'I am, for the time being anyway,' Keith said. 'Somebody has to be, and I can't see anyone else willing to take over the job. I expect to find that body gone when we come back. And if you don't do as I say you'll be dead as well.' He pushed by and drew the blanket back. They hadn't closed those staring pot-white orbs that had widened at the shock of death: the eyes of the head being smashed again and

204

again at the wooden bannister made him throw the cloth over. There were no rules any more, no laws, only the ones he made. He didn't say that, though they had to know he would slaughter anyone who stood in his way. There could only be one voice in the Republic of Possible Catastrophe, though the illusion of reason and consensus must be fostered. 'It's unhygienic to have a body in the room. We have to live here for the next few hours, maybe for days.'

'He's my father,' Alfred wept.

'He's dead. Throw him outside. Come on, lads, time's running out, and there's a lot of work to do.'

Lance and Wayne donned gloves and helmets, ready for the wind and snow. Watching them go, Alfred knew he had to defend his rights. His father would have laughed: 'You're still a little lad, and don't know what it's all about. Either shut up and let them get on with it, or get the biggest carving knife you can find and take one with you. Two would be even better, but oh, for God's sake, don't whine or waffle.'

Nor did Parsons like a corpse in the room. 'It's bad for morale, and it'll smell soon. If we plonk him out of the back door he'll keep as fresh as a daisy. We'll ask Fred to get a Bible from upstairs and say a prayer over him.'

THIRTY-ONE

Powdery snow thrashed up by the wind made his cock so small it must have gone into the furthest fold of his pants, but his fingers had to find it, since the only way to unfreeze the lock of the BMW was to send out a jet of hot piss. No need to explain, he thumbed around, found the end and worked the rest through: work, you idle bastard, earn your keep for once in your life. Iced tips rattled at his back while the amber stream went like a spinning garden hose, Wayne's torch spot on target.

The door opened as if the car had been six months in the dry, but that was the easiest part. Keith's smile was returned by a thumbs up in their gloves, which he knew was a gesture embedded in himself as well, the old sign of success and complicity crossing all boundaries.

They crammed in for shelter and he turned the engine on, the soft purr a tuning fork to the wind, then a roar as Keith stamped the accelerator. All systems go, the magic wands of the wipers grated over particles of frozen snow and picked up speed.

A gully was created the size of the car, sides of snow mounting as they dug. He hadn't believed work could be done so quickly, but they laboured without discussion, Lance near the boot and Wayne lost in the snow behind, and soon the sunken tracks became apparent and their trenches joined, wider than the car and down to the level of the wheels till a spade struck tarmac.

More space than Keith needed, but more was always better. The heaters cleared all Perspex, and he backed into the space till the rear window showed only snow. Like born surveyors they had set the angle at which the car would come side on to the van, digging as if any minute the shelling would begin, their previous excavation joining the one they worked on now.

Like a heavily-encased astronaut stepping on a Siberian-scaped moon, gravity pushing him around the storm and, hardly able to see, Lance wished for windscreen wipers on his visor, a minuscule motor to turn them, as well as heated clothing like an aviator's as he worked at cold dust and pale blue by the spadeful coming up in woolly slabs and going high to left or right, the snow light compared to soaking worm-laden soil. An intense ache along both arms slowed him, though there would be no honour in resting until they got the van clear and made everybody safe. Cold sweat under his leathers weighed, which was why he thought he might be on the moon, his blood running and his stomach warm, though the body turned so sluggish he wanted to lie in the snow and sleep.

Wayne navvied the spade, gripping the handle, pushing well under, drawing each swaying load towards him and upping it clear. Snow is my worst enemy. Everybody loves me except the snow. They think I'm handsome but the snow shouts that I'm ugly. Snow doesn't love me because I hate it. The only thing to do with snow is make a fire and chuck it on till it melts away, then it wouldn't matter if it didn't love me.

Because I'll never get to the end I've got to go on, but you can't tell in the dark how much is left. If I make a neat roadway at the same time I might push through to sunshine and green pastures. Sweat saves blood, but what I've leaked already matches the blood in my body three times over, enough to sink the bloody *Bismarck*, though I've got to go on till I drop, which I will in not too soon if I don't have a break, I'm even ready for a basin of Fred's stew, except he's put that old man's corpse in, thinking waste not want not, looking at it with that glassy left eye as he stirs it up: as long as I don't break my filling on a button.

They leaned on their spades – cripples and suppliants, wounded soldiers, phantom gravediggers – Keith fixing them in the headlights. Close to dead beat, the last of their stamina was called for. Snow swirled a film over the macadam so far uncovered and, both standing to guide him in, he drove forward, and as he slowly passed they presented arms with their spades like two busby-headed swaddies on guard in Whitehall. In their exhausted state they were laughing, and so was he, out of gratitude at them making fun of the common plight for his and their enjoyment, in defiance of the blizzard, and mocking whatever the explosives in the van could do.

Such an assessment might be sentimental, a summary of his liking for traditional values and the comfort they gave, the refuge they provided whether real or not, yet he didn't care, because in the charade their innermost spirits were sending a signal they knew was acceptable. Nobody could see, the noise overshouted it, and when he laughed again so did they, as if to say: What are we doing here, and what the hell's going on?

They were digging again, if more slowly, knowing that before they could draw the van back till it was head to head with his car they must clear a track behind. He prayed no spade would make a spark, strike the van, metal against metal. Perhaps in their weariness they would curb their new enthusiasm, but he tapped Lance for the spade, who refused and cut another slab from the bank.

Neither would Wayne allow him to take a turn, not caring to have his motions broken. This was his job, not some posh shagbag's up from London who had never held a spade in his lily-white hands, tough nut or not. Wayne hated work, but wouldn't give up a job once begun till it was finished. If somebody else did a bit in between he wouldn't be able to say that he himself had done it, and if he couldn't say that, what would have been the use in starting?

Miniature clouds of snow drove at their coverings, no defence but to shake the head and stumble like the moving semi-frozen stones they were turning into, doing what had to be done before sinking under the weight growing heavier and heavier from the inside. They excavated, shifted, stacked, and stamped down with their boots. Steel claws gripped Keith's feet as if he wasn't wearing socks, let alone boots and two thick pairs inside. When there seemed nowhere else to put the snow he moved the van so that they could shove it from front to back in the space they had made.

He unclipped both bonnets and slotted them safely open, his own battery neat at the terminals but the torch showing the van's corroded to a sickly, almost glowing green. He scraped them free with his penknife, hoping for enough live acid and distilled water within to conduct the jolt to its destination. Positive to negative to make a circuit, he unravelled the jump leads, sorted the black and red ends, and fastened the croc-grips with freezing fingers.

The dashboard glistened red in the wilderness. Jump the red light and you might be dead, but this was friendly and comforting, a means to an end, a red eye you drove through the spot-middle of to get into action. The engine gagged with life after a few spasmodic jumps, power unhealthy and threatening self-extinction any second.

He told himself the odds were too great, but he must keep such ruminations to himself and go on working, mentally thanking them for every effort, as if they were doing it for him alone. Tackling one problem at a time, you didn't think much about those still strung in line ahead like differently shaped and coloured beads waiting to be sorted. You took the setbacks and, prime mover, kept the end in sight, so he put his head down and went on to consider the next hurdle.

A stench of smoke and petrol filled the van. Spades clanked across the windscreen, erasing harder nuts of snow, till the wipers – reluctantly – took the rest. Changing into reverse, the engine slugged dead, but it was easy for Lance to bypass the ignition because, at fourteen, up to no good one day, Albert Green explained the mechanics of hot-wiring, doing it like the best teacher: by example. They were topped and tailed by the flashing blue lights and screaming horn of a Jam Sandwich. His father was an old Desert Rat, no less, who with the rest of his tank crew had shaved and trimmed up to look dead smart for the drive into Tripoli. He had grovelled before the local powers, wearing his suit with the permanent medal ribbons, a believer in war and justice, to prove that he loved Lance his son, a man who always had a good morning smile to any passing copper, and if he hadn't then Lance would surely have landed something more than two years on probation.

He kept a blank slate ever since, and if once or twice he had been close to another scratch of red chalk due to his biking forays, he wondered nevertheless what the old man's face would look like when he learned that his son had been blown to bits, as he himself nearly was a few times in the war.

Keith eased the engine, coaxed it to a roar whether or not vibrations jostled the van's frail insides. If they deserved a medal, and they surely did, what bit of flesh would the Queen pin it on? The laugh got him into reverse and several yards towards the clear, turning sufficient progress of degrees to aim for the gate. Headlamps picked up needles of wandering snow, their way blocked by a bank that even a plough would find hard to shift.

Snow was semi-solid water, an ever-present enemy you had to vanquish. Man would always vanquish, a fight without quarter and even to the death against the earth which had never been anything but his enemy, otherwise how could you believe in God?

Daniel fought his way, made a track for Sally to follow. It was no use turning to see if she did. The demon's howl blocked his ears, so maybe she wasn't there any longer, had gone back to betray him a second time, or had given in by accepting the warmth of endless sleep.

Like thin wet carpets, his clothes drew in the cold and stored it to send to the soft marrow at the middle of his bones. Drifts were crust-hard in places, and sometimes sinking as if he were unable to stop until engulfed, he would flounder in panic, but quickly right himself, as if even in such visibility he was being observed by everyone in the world.

The fire in him could not be put out by snow, though the vicious wind might extinguish it before shelter was reached. He knew he would not die, the blaze giving no say in the matter, a question of live now and perish later if you must, because if the police didn't kick him into a catatonic state or put him in a place for so long that he would wish he *had* died, then the people waiting in Coventry would track him down and, as the awesome phrase had it in order to terrify, 'blow him away'.

So up and over the powdery snow, into a stinging veil of wind that whoever was caught in it felt it was out to get them and nobody else. Followed by a woman so close he sometimes fancied he could hear her breathing even above the tigerish rage of the gale, he couldn't see her when he turned, the sound being his own. As he scrambled hands and knees to the summit of the wave, no energy to spare for looking back, she was the last person in his life, and he must go on loving her for that.

He was the only person in her life, and she had nowhere else to go because her own sort had cast her out, and there was no turning back except that she didn't know how the move had been made, always the blinding light of non-comprehension, snaring her in like a moth trap, the process then carrying her along. She had followed mutely after a kiss, overcoats and galoshes quickly sought in case someone should try to hold them back, then the door closing fatally behind.

Floundering with frozen hands he used an interior compass to try for the lay-by where he had left his van which the unthinking bikers had brought to the hotel, didn't know why he wanted to get to that blemished spot, but followed the markings of the road between wall tops visible now that his eyes were accustomed to the darkness through swirling snow.

Map and compass would be useless in this continent of wild attacks from every direction. He had done orienteering on Dartmoor in winter for the school. A boy in a stream netting specimens had lost a shoe, sucked off by the current. Daniel splashed in bare feet to rescue it, and gave the boy his own dry socks and shoes after yanking him clear. The boy never realized his peril, and Daniel hoped he would not lose his own feet from frost-bite before reaching safety.

He saw flashes as of light bulbs breaking because of too much light, eyes as exhausted as his limbs, eyes unmercifully bombarded that could take no more, pain so great he kept them closed as on and up and through, he had to get there, though no longer knew where *there* was, nor what he would find.

Sally had to draw back so as not to collide with his hunched form, wondered whether he wouldn't collapse before reaching a farm. She was freezing alive, starting to burn in a fire, wasn't tired yet dreaded ice and fire in collision forcing her to stop. Reality had come back after leaving the hotel and its awful people, life had meaning again, the urge to win through. Never had she thought to meet such types (didn't they call them 'punters'?) who wouldn't show the vaguest comprehension of a man like Daniel, no sympathy with ideals which, though leading to unjustified violence, needed to be forgiven. Faced with the unfamiliar, they turned into killers set on murdering him and her as well, so better go into the snow, Daniel had said, as they stood by the window.

She followed him towards the door, the storm drawing her fatally because she wanted to find out whether she could defeat what the elements were able to throw against her. And as for whether she had done right, now that she had done it she must believe that she had.

Absence of landmarks sapped his power, and he didn't know if he would recognize the lay-by when he reached it. He prayed to the moon, a different man to the one who had been in charge of explosives for the Cause: rational, courageous, certain of himself, *unthinking* you might say. Wherever the moon was, knowledge of its existence permitted him to go on, praying to it because it was the last ally he could have.

Hope pulled him as if with a rope attached, told him that in a few days he would be back at school, no one living to connect him to the explosion. Those in the hotel couldn't possibly get the van out of the courtyard, and would be obliterated. Even the men in Coventry would hardly blame him for his failure. Life must go on, but what about the woman behind, who was the only witness?

THIRTY-TWO

If allowed to go on working they would use that reserve of strength which should only be kept for the final effort, so Keith signalled a way back to shelter. 'The snow'll need clearing again in half an hour,' Lance said as they went in. 'Look how it's coming down.'

'It's only dusting,' Wayne told him. 'We'll scuff it away with our toecaps. It won't stop the tyres.'

Arms of light went up the walls and across the ceiling like rapid columns on an army map, flames arrowing almost to the mantel shelf. Lance unzipped. 'Where did all that wood come from?'

Alfred, a hump of grief near the fire, reached for another broken chair and threw it on as if it were the imp from hell that had caused all his troubles. Fred had given up on spinning out his supply of fuel: the wood pile had melted down, and he was rummaging for half planks and bits of old beam, the remnants of builders' rammel coated with dust and congealed whitewash which gave off spectacular tongues of green flame.

'He's already cleared the spare room.' Parsons was encouraged and made cheerful by this systematic gutting of the hotel, and nodded towards Alfred. 'I expect he'll start on the stuff in here next.'

'Not if I know it.' Fred laid soup plates and spoons on three tables put together, which Enid had spread with the whitest cloth from one of his personal cupboards in a box room off the kitchen. Where the devil did she find the key? he wondered but, saying nothing to her about it, turned on Alfred and Parsons. 'You two are like a pack of barmy schoolkids. You should have a bit more respect for other people's property. Not that I expect you to understand a thing like that, though.'

'At least Alfred's making the place a bit more cheerful.' Parsons spoke to Keith so that none of the others could hear. 'We took a kitchen knife off him half an hour ago. He would have done a tidy bit of damage with a weapon like that. Aaron jumped him from behind. It was quite a scuffle.'

With such people the administration of the crisis took on its own momentum, Keith smiled. The bomb maniac and his woman would die in the snow, and good riddance. And that lunatic who'd had his father die on him had given himself the duty of keeping them halfway warm, lips jabbering out the list of his misfortunes.

I must be a fool, Alfred said to his own picture not far in front of his staring eyes, and feeling an intense conviction he hadn't noticed in himself for a long time, to get so upset at seeing my father's worn-out carcass tipped unceremoniously into the snow, when I was wanting him dead during the drive here. That's the proof you love somebody, when you wish every day they would kick the bucket. His, after all, sudden departure for the happy hunting grounds had put the kaibosh on Bognor, and no mistake. I won't break my heart twice a day from now on wondering if they're doing the right thing by him, or forget to post off the monthly cheque. When this bit of bother's over I'll give him a decent burial, and then get back to happy working days.

He took the leg from a chair and hit the frame of one already on the fire. Sparks singed his face but he let them fade out rather than take any trouble in brushing them off, then threw the rest of the chair on, telling the sparks to be more careful with his skin next time round. The fire was a wolf trying to come for them out of the snow, flames its arms, sparks its claws, a raving animal which would stay in its place only for as long as plentiful wood was slung into its jaws, and he thought about the even more than halcyon days now that his father had departed. Funny how you didn't imagine dying yourself till your father had copped it, God in Heaven's way of letting you know for sure that one day the same would happen to you.

Fred, in his cook's white hat, scooped the ladle round and round the large tureen to let the smell of soup fill the room, looking at everyone and waiting for their words of appreciation.

'Oh, wonderful,' it would have been easy to hear them braying, 'wonderful, it'll save my life!'

'Serve it quick. I can't wait!'

'Good old Fred!'

'You can always rely on him!'

'For he's a jolly good fellow!'

Keith ended the silence. 'Wayne and Lance first at the food.'

'Yes, sir. That's understood,' Fred said.

Every part was stone, Jenny couldn't warm him, his ice-cold body at rest, impossible to know where the spirit had gone. Fear ached her, she had sat too long in one position, only half alive herself, panic making her want to run outside, to wait no longer. She had champagned her faculties into and out of sleep, but was awake now and so cold she had to sit at the table.

Wayne placed his elbows to either side of the plate, his stare fighting with blue and white mixing into droplets of snow, still seeing drifts surrounding the cars, squalls continually buffeting. 'I'm not hungry.'

'Nor me.' Lance picked up a spoon, hunger changing his mind. 'A piece of chocolate might do.'

'That'll be for dessert.' Fred was eating: he'd always enjoyed his own cooking. 'I found a few slabs in the stores.'

Keith thought the best way to live might be to regard every minute as your last. Look forward to nothing, and whatever came that was more than nothing would be an unexpected bounty, and perhaps beneficial enough to deserve consideration. If he had realized this from the beginning then that other existence with Gwen might not have seared his spirit.

'It's a lovely stew.' Eileen imagined that if she got blown to bits her father would say in twenty years' time: 'I ain't seen our Eileen lately. Where do you suppose she went?' And her mother would no doubt reply: 'How the hell should I know? She'll come back when she's ready.' No, she was being unjust: they would wait no more than two years before asking the Salvation Army to get on her trail.

'It's a stew to put lead in your pencil,' Parsons laughed.

'If you'd been out there,' Lance said, 'you wouldn't have enough lead left in your pencil to scribble a betting slip.'

Keith tried to eat, but the food died in his mouth. It was impossible to search back far enough in his life and find the turning point which had set him on a course ending in murder, no more than you could wind back the reel of history and sidetrack the wars of the century. He had been driven to where the crime was waiting for him, and he had lost control, the mind becoming a vacuum in which he had for a fatal moment ceased to think, an unforgivable surrender never to be made good. He felt her hair in his hands (that crown of all her

215

glory!) and the merciless mindless banging till the weight of her unconscious body meant that strength had jettisoned reason and she was dead.

Alfred finished his bowl, Fred noting how often he had seen the grieving eat more than most, after they had made the first food in their mouths go down.

'Aren't you hungry, sir?' Wayne said. 'I'm not, but I'm on my second helping, so I suppose I must be. We need a bit of packing inside us for going out again.'

Keith, finding it good counsel, finished eating, and guided Fred into the corridor between lounge and kitchen. Now what? Fred was irritated at not getting a word as to why. These high-handed types got on his bloody wick, but he wasn't able to say them nay, or not listen. To make a fuss would damage his pride more than giving in to their whims. Even so, he would like to tell them where to get off, but knew he never could.

Keith gave him a slip of paper with the make and licence number of the van. 'If we don't come back, give this to the police. Is that clear?'

'Yes, sir. I'll do that. I've thought about it already. We can't let that bugger go scot-free. Not that I wouldn't be surprised if somebody like that didn't manage it, but we'll do all we can to have him pulled in.'

'I also want you to witness this sheet of paper. It's a Will. Sign underneath my signature, and put the date.'

Another trade! Would they never stop coming? Commissioner for Oaths now. They'd heckled him as a mess-deck lawyer a time or two on the ship. 'Is this it, sir? To her a third?'

His tone hardened. 'Will you do it, or won't you?'

'If you say so.'

'I do. Now get me an envelope.'

'Yes, sir.'

You could not live imagining that each second might be your last. Such innocence, the anarchism of the naive, would end civilization. Even to think one hour ahead was a step forward. When men began to wonder where the next meal was coming from, and who might attack them for the food they hunted, the ability to live in the present had gone for ever, though in truth it could never have existed, the state of Eden only tolerable to the mad, who can't or won't see any future. Crimes committed were a price that had to be paid. 'Wait here, till I've been to the toilet.'

'Yes, sir.'

The door wouldn't close. Had one of the bikers kicked it off its hinges, or was the building already subsiding under the weight of snow? He folded the four crisp fifty-pound notes in with his Will, and sealed the envelope.

'Take good care of this,' he told Fred. 'I want your solemn promise.'

'On the Holy Scriptures, sir. If we get through this mess all right, then good luck to her.'

A star was sharp and bright beyond the hole of cloud, but having no others to fasten it to he did not know what name to give. Two made a connection, three a pattern, four a picture, but a single one was an astronomical trickster and to be ignored.

The engine was healthy, chains fitted, and they were already digging a way for him to back into. He preferred them some yards ahead so that if the van exploded they might have a chance. Not much of one, true, but it was the best he could do – every second the final call for me as well, whether I like it or not, and I surely don't. There was only the snow, and the job to be done, glad when the deceptive star was covered, nothing to think about except work.

At the wheel, a cigarette burning, he watched them clearing and flattening so that the chains would grip. Uneven drifts further from the buildings were not more than a foot above the macadam, and when they were close to the gate he went anxiously forward, praying for luck, for the others, and also, he was half-ashamed to note, quite fervently for himself, thinking that if he came through all right he would stay with Eileen for as long as she could tolerate him.

Daniel could no longer feel his feet and hands, but burning faith divided the freezing snow, a forlorn imprint of his passing. The inner glow was brighter now that he was alone. He should have realized from the beginning that only then did you come to full power. Even so, the purest of the pure can be diverted from the clear beam of their inspired way, though not for long. The debilitations of his enormous wound were annulled by him being able to go on, power provided by not knowing where that inner fire came from. Nor did he want to think, eschewing curiosity so that even if he had wanted to succumb to the storm like any ordinary person, he could not.

His inexplicable spirit took him through the blizzard. When the border between his transcendental state, and the reality of wet clothes clinging around even colder flesh became indistinct, he rekindled the light by an act of will, pure will, the victory of the will. He kept the road's edges at an equal distance, fighting for the economy of a straight line along which to measure progress by unfolding a finger for every hundred yards.

Already the others were dying. He would outlive them, being one of the elect. The old man had died, the woman who had so stupidly followed him was dead. So would everyone be, none to unravel the mystery.

Such reflections made the body immediate, reduced him to a moving corpse encased in icy clothes, matted within a miserable cocoon, each foot an anchor to drag now that he had lost count of the paces, which caused him to panic for a moment, because no will could alter the fact that he was a fragile mortal caught in the storm and lost for ever. Tears of chagrin froze onto his flesh, but he went on, veered to one side then back to the other, increasing the distance from the hotel, wanting only to sleep, sensing he was no more at last than a failed and miserable hibernologist staggering to perdition.

Head and body were covered with ice, boots frozen into a stone and feet giving out the purest pain. He leaned against a window half hidden by snow, a window into what was impossible to say and, moaning *hic jacet*, he fell into the drift, a scream when he bruised himself on some metal object which he then tried to grasp. The outlines seemed those of a long hut, and he was wondering how he could get inside when a door was pushed against him and he fell.

I haven't handled one of these for thirty years, Alfred would have said if the gale hadn't assailed his ear-drums to extinction, except to play around now and again in my little bungalow garden, and I didn't have much truck with it then, hard labour being something I decided not to make a career out of. He was doing his level best with the shovel because the flood of the headlights would show him up as a shirker if he didn't. An old football scarf around head and ears held a cap underneath, but his gloves and cashmere overcoat were the sort it behoved the boss of a haulage firm to wear. He worked as well as, if not better than, Aaron on one side and clapped-out Parsons on the other. The bikers were placed up front to draw the oldies on, unless Keith had decided they would be less in danger if the blast came. Thank you very much. What did he have to live for now that his father had gone? He laughed with the joy of freedom, though couldn't help shovelling as if the old bugger still needled him with his gimlet eyes.

Aaron had lifted boxes of books up and down stairs, bending at the knees to avoid back pain or a hernia, carrying heavy volumes into or from the car, and he was satisfied to find enough wind in his pipes for shifting snow. If he had done it straight from the laboratory job ten years ago he would have been on his knees and gasping his lungs out. He liked the cold blaze of gusting snow, the bite against ears and nose. If he went to prison for not having been clever enough with his false signatures he would look on this shovelling as the best of times. And if the flash of obliteration caught him unawares he would not have to decide any more what was and what was not worth recalling.

The door clunked open, and Eileen wriggled across the seat. Before Keith could throw her out or say anything she fastened her lips on his. 'I was fed up in there.'

Stuck-up Jenny sat by that half-dead biker not saying a word but crying now and again, Enid was flopped in an armchair with what blankets were left, and barmy Fred whistled to himself while making little brew-ups and concoctions in the kitchen, telling her to piss off whenever she went in and tried to talk.

'You can't stay here,' Keith said. He didn't want her to go, though the longer he didn't tell her the more certainly she would have to.

'I love you,' she said. 'I want to be with you. My place is here, darling, darling, darling.' She felt herself burning into a blush: such a word would have made any other man laugh: posh, false, not for them, but with him there was no other to fit. 'I want to stay. I don't care what happens.'

The only way was to get her by the throat and bundle her into the snow. Haul her to the hotel and lock the door. He couldn't, and for once felt the same passion. 'I love you, but I have work to do. I can do it better on my own.'

'No,' she said, 'you don't love me. Not like I love you. You don't know what love is. I'm beginning to think no man does. If you did you wouldn't want to get rid of me. You can drive this rotten old van just as well if I'm sitting here, can't you?'

Chains clanked and bit around the wheels as he reversed several yards and then went forward, more precious distance gained. 'You don't know me. You know nothing about me. If you did you wouldn't want to know me.'

'I don't care about knowing you. What does that matter? I love you, don't I? Anyway, what do you know about me? But you said you loved me. I don't know whether to believe you, if you keep on telling me to go. I just love you, and that's that.'

He felt warmer at hearing words of such simple and unsolicited devotion – at this time of his life. 'You have to believe I love you.' Wondering whether she would when he knocked her senseless, he was afraid to hit her, even out of love and protection, because would he be able to stop?

'I want to be with you. After, I want to live with you. I know you're married, so I don't mind if you can't see me often. I love you, but you don't know what that means.' She began to cry, her body moving up and down in its covering of clothes. She seemed to have taken every coat in the hotel, as if really meaning to stay with him in the snow for ever. 'I want you, so let me stay. I want everything. I want to have a baby with you.'

They were level with the stone pillars of the gate, a lion surmounting each. A ditch by the roadside full of snow must be avoided, Lance signalling him clear with a flashlight.

'Do you know what you're saying?'

'Oh yes. I don't always, but I do now.'

'If you love me it would be better for you to remember me than get killed with me.'

'No, it wouldn't. I don't want to live if you get killed. I'll go mad. I'll be out of my brain as long as I live. I won't be able to work, or talk to anybody for the rest of my life. I'll go around not wanting to live. I'll drift from squat to squat with all I own in two plastic bags. I'll be the youngest bag-lady in Manchester.' She was laughing. 'Look at that snow! Life's marvellous, isn't it? Well, I think so. So just let me stay, and don't think about what might not happen.'

Not to think, to accept, to let everything go. She promised paradise, but how stupid if they both died. 'I want you to live, because I love you, and if you live, then I live. Whatever happens, you won't be poor. Fred will tell you why.'

'Oh, fuck off,' she cried, the heart wrenched out of her. 'I don't know what you're on about. I said I loved you, didn't I?'

No one could hear it better expressed — at any other time. He felt eighteen again, unable to trust himself, so said: 'A few days ago I left my wife. I killed her, then I left her.'

'It won't work. Tell me another.'

'No, listen. She taunted me. She said our daughter wasn't mine. She said she'd had an affair at the time she was conceived. We've hated each other for years, and more or less gone our own ways, as far as we were able to. Why she told me what she did I don't know, though it was at the end of a long argument, and I'd said things which must have hurt her as well. So she came back with something to finish all our arguments. I'd thought all my life that no matter how much we loathed each other there was one mark of the love we must have felt at first. But she'd never felt it. She'd gone out and got pregnant by a boy friend, then told me the child was mine. I knew she was right, but in any case she assured me of it, swore it was true, and gave details which I'd suspected all along. I killed her. Then I loaded the car with enough things to live rough, and drove up to the Lakes. I was going back to give myself up, when I met you. I don't know where I was going. Maybe the police are looking for me already, though she might not have been found yet. I didn't mean to kill her, but that won't help me in court. Nor do I deserve it to. I could live with you happily, because I love you, but please go into the hotel, and I'll come later. Then we'll decide what to do. You can bet I'll be all right. I'm in no danger. But give me another kiss first.'

THIRTY-THREE

The high platform was covered with sacks, and when Daniel moved across he saw three men playing cards below, a white pint mug of steaming tea by each. Cigarette smoke mixed with the whiff of fuel from a primus, and he picked out a blackened kettle, teapot, an opened packet of sugar, a carton of milk, a frying pan and plates, an inventory helping him not to scream from pain in every fibre of his body.

'It seems he's awake,' someone said, as if he had no right to be. 'Hey, mate, you up there, welcome to the best little removal van in Christendom, or anywhere else, come to that. Let's get him down, and see what we can find out.'

The inside of the black pantechnicon was lined with plywood tea chests, and a pair of stepladders rested near a porter's barrow by locked doors at the far end. The plates of a split-up Pirelli calendar pasted along the sides had been jabbed by stoves and bedsteads brought in and carried out. 'We pulled you in, when we heard you go bump in the night.'

'Where am I?'

He came up the ladder to Daniel's level, a man in a khaki button-front overall smock. 'Somewhere in bloody Derbyshire, I suppose. We only cut through this way to save petrol, which the gaffer always likes to hear about, though he's not going to be happy at us getting stuck. Do you think you can manage down this ladder? My name's Charlie. That's Bill. Paul, the one who's sneaking a look at my hand of cards, will get knifed when I get back, if he don't put 'em down.'

'It ain't worth it.' Paul was a cadaverous man in a grey three-piece suit, such apparel possibly lifted from some trunk or other during a move. 'I dealt you such a piss-poor hand.'

'I'll be all right,' Daniel said, 'with a little assistance.' Bill came to help, more solid in body than the others, wearing dark-blue dungarees – all three men unified by their Day-Glo scarves and woolly hats against the cold. The van swayed from a heavy fist of wind, and Daniel screamed on slipping down the bottom few rungs.

Bill grasped, to break his fall. 'You seem in a bit of a mess, mate.'

'I'll do another brew.' Paul threw the cards into a common heap, and began cranking the primus. 'We all need it, and he looks as if he'll die if he don't get summat into him. It's bloody perishing, even in here.'

They laid Daniel on the floor. 'He needs a doctor.' Charlie unknotted his tie, then covered him with a dust sheet and several large sacks till only the head showed.

'My car broke down.' The weight of coverings made him feel worse, so he pushed them aside. 'I got stopped. Must have hit a post. Couldn't tell. I was knocked out. I don't know how long for. But then I woke, and thought I'd get some help.'

'Don't worry,' Bill said. 'You're in good hands. I reckon you should have stayed with your car, though. That's what they tell you to do.'

'He probably didn't know what he was doing,' Paul said, 'after the knock on his napper. He just thought he'd get out and walk, poor sod. Look at him. Frost-bite all over. He looks as if he's crawled out of a fire, and fell on a broken bottle. His face's all cut up, where it ain't turning black. There ain't much we can do for him. He's shaking like a leaf.'

'Some tea might help. And what about a couple of aspirins, Charlie? There must be some in that chemist's shop you carry about everywhere.'

Daniel contained his agony, trying to smile. 'I've fallen among Good Samaritans.'

'That you have,' Bill said, 'that you have, mate. We might be common-or-garden removal men, but we're also gentlemen of the road, out to help distressed travellers.'

'Unless he's a social worker,' Charlie snarled. 'We'd draw the line at social workers. They tried to take my kid away once.'

Daniel wanted to tell them he was a teacher, but maybe they didn't like teachers, either. There seemed no hard surface under him, he was floating in distilled pain, his instinct telling him to reach for a tree branch or door handle and stop falling. He tried to compute how far he was from the hotel, and crawled through more and more snow into the nightmare of a sudden thaw, his refuge visible from an upper window, and people coming to get him, each with a coil of stiff hard rope, led by a woman with skeletal head and demented eyes, limbs bare and hands sprouting claws, on an unstoppable route towards him as if all the rage of the world was pouring from her hurt lips at his cruelty.

'His bloody screams are getting on my wick,' Bill said. 'Let's either chuck him outside, or give him his tea. 'Appen he'll choke on it and give us some peace.'

'Wake up,' Charlie said sharply at Daniel's ear.

He looked, eyes swelling with terror. 'Where am I?'

'If you'll stop screaming a minute I'll tell you,' Paul said. 'You're in The Blue Herald, one of Ramble's furniture vans, so you're safe and sound. Lift yourself up a bit and drink this. It's strong tea, with plenty of sugar and milk. Here's three aspirins as well.' He showed them in the palm of his hand. 'They'll do you the world of good.'

He sweated and shivered, but the nightmare had gone, and the lukewarm tea tasting of paraffin nectarized his veins nevertheless, easing him into a sleep in which he only dreamed of being in agony.

'Thank God,' Bill said, 'now we can have another game. I only hope we don't get any more refugees parking themselves on us.'

'Maybe we'll be here for weeks,' Paul said. 'They'll eat all our supplies and take our jobs, though if we do run out of something to eat we can have a game and serve the loser up for dinner. Or we could carve a slice off you know who.'

'He'll be rotten before he dies,' Bill said. 'You can smell him already, even in this cold den. I don't mind starving to death, if it comes to it, but I'm buggered if I'm going to die in agony eating tainted food.'

'We've got to be prepared for all eventualities,' Paul said. 'Don't you recollect what happened to old Jack Bailey and his crew on the way back from Brindisi after doing that Greek run? They took a short cut through Switzerland, and got stuck in the snow for three weeks. Luckily, they'd picked up a hitchhiker near Milan. Jack told me he'd bought a bottle of olive oil and a bag of dried mushrooms in Italy, so that helped as well. When it thawed they sank what was left of him chained to an old tyre in one of them Swiss lakes. Jack'd stop at nowt to get his teeth into a good dinner.'

Bill reached for the primus. 'I don't think I would be reduced to that, though, as long as I had plenty of tea and sugar, and a few cartons of fags.'

'Mind you,' Paul went on, 'if it came to that sort of crisis there'd be no option, would there? Not that I do think we're going to be here anything like three weeks. The cold's not as sharp as it was. Yes, I will have another mug of tea. It's no use offering that poor bugger any. It'll be wasted on him. He fetched half the last lot up.'

The house was bigger than he had imagined, not a bungalow at all, but floor after floor and bits going off in all directions. Somebody had got there before him, because it was already fully plumbed up, unless he had done it in another life and forgotten. Maybe his estimate had been too high, or Alfred had spotted some fault in the details, though you couldn't think so to see how no expense had been spared. The baths were porcelain and the taps were gold, and in every room there was one of them funny little bidets which he had seen in even some of the cheaper places in France where he had stayed with Wayne and Lance. Every bathroom was tarted up like a picture from a catalogue so that you would think the Queen was going to live there.

The trouble was, they had fucked up the central heating, and *he* would never have done that. He couldn't see a radiator anywhere, and as for a fireplace, forget it. It was the coldest house he had ever been in, though there was bright blue sky at every window, and lights on in every room. He climbed a spiral staircase to see what was on the next floor but funnily enough couldn't go any further because some steps were missing. There was no carpet and they were so filthy with broken glass and wet dead leaves he nearly went arse over bollocks. Then his breath was torn out like a flame, and when he tried to jump to where the steps began, instead of backing down like a sensible lad, he fell, and kept on falling.

Clouds were dividing, such gaps showing the Big Dipper. Aaron's pleasing fantasy was to have it turn into an actual scoop, and clear a ten-mile lane through the snow, along which they could walk to freedom. Beyond the gate, Lance and Wayne leaned against the side of the van as if asleep. His watch showed six o'clock, eyes closing, and the ache in his arms total. He went a few paces back towards the hotel and, no coordination in any limb, fell sideways.

The wind beat as if to power the massive sails of a ship, at war with stillness, not the random drumming of the blizzard, but gusting with some new purpose not yet apparent. Alfred and Parsons had given up half an hour ago. The clean and welcome smell momentarily revived him. Drawing his spade out of the snow, like Excalibur from the Stone, he cradled it for fear he would lose such a prime tool of their endeavours.

The even piping of jet engines came from thousands of metres up in blue sky and sun, telling those living near an airport that another ordinary day was soon to start, a sound reminding him that the trap they were locked in could not stay closed for ever.

The van stood out, stark and dark green, coils of pale smoke from its exhaust, almost alive in relishing its power to destroy them all. Keith looked dispiritedly at the ramp of snow, and at the Trojan Horse it seemed impossible to budge more.

Wayne took off his helmet, a smile followed by the gesture of a hand across his throat signifying that he'd had enough. Lance turned his visor towards Keith as if to say that whoever owned the head inside would do no more. But Keith knew there was always more energy where that came from, an untapped abundance in everyone still, that last black rock of reserve waiting to move the van another hundred yards.

They followed him like a patrol of yetis, Lance in the lead, Aaron and Wayne together. The glow of false dawn about the yard faded as clouds closed. Snow flurries irritated his face, a hand sliding over the greased features, stung his eyes that were barely able to see.

He stood alone in the dark between the cars, did not know why. An animal sound mimicked the wind, a note of despair turning to a tone of wonder at surface snow flying into clouds of mist to find a better position and becoming more and more irritable at knowing they never would. The issue of life and death had lost its bite. Utter exhaustion stopped him knowing where he was. Belonging nowhere softened the spirit, till he remembered that the job was not yet done, and forced himself to go in after the others.

Fred needed no help, but Eileen followed him from lounge to kitchen, and from bar to store room – like a little dog, the lucky bitch, because she surely knows about the bit of paper that rustles in my pocket where'er I walk.

He was jealous of his work, work being precious, work being like gold to him. He made each task last, spun it out because while there was something to do he wasn't worrying about past or future, nor the present which could end more abruptly than he wanted and which therefore didn't bear thinking about.

He had never known what happiness was, only that if he worked he was not unhappy. Work was a luxury – especially in this situation – as long as enough money came with it to keep him in food and shelter, and the little packets of those cigars that he puffed with such relish. He had faith that Keith would bring them sound in wind and limb through the night, and keep the bikers working so hard that they wouldn't have the energy to torment him any more.

By dawn, if you looked at the way things were going, the hotel would no longer be habitable. The attics were full of snow and debris, the ceilings of the bedrooms were patched with damp, icy wind was coming down the stairs. In other words, it would be a write-off. He would claim full insurance, and begin the great work all over again – like that bloke who kept pushing a boulder up a hill because God or whoever at the top always rolled it back to the bottom. This time though he would buy a place on the coast in a more benign climate. Maybe he would even start up somewhere in Spain, because Doris would be sure to come back to him then.

'I love the smell,' Eileen said, as he laid strips of streaky bacon from a five-pound pack on a hotplate over the fire. 'It's the best meal in the world.'

'I prefer the smell of roast turkey,' he said, 'when it comes out of the oven at Christmas.' She was complimenting him on his work, so he could almost take to her. 'Turkey and stuffing: it's the best smell in the world.'

She moved from the warm rail to let him throw more logs into the stove, his best dried logs held back from the fire in the lounge. 'Did you have a party, then?'

'At this hotel we did. I set up a Christmas Special, at twelve quid a head. All anybody could eat. And did they eat! It did me good to see 'em, except that they were robbing me blind. They said I made the best garlic bread they'd ever tasted. I came out on top, though, financial-wise. And I didn't mind, anyway, because it was good for trade at other times, except that it's been falling off a bit lately.'

She leaned forward to light some paper for her cigarette: 'I wish I'd been there.'

He struck a large kitchen match for her. 'You should have been.'

'Well, I was elsewhere, wasn't I?'

'Where was that?'

'At my boy friend's. We had a can of beer and a pizza between us.'

'That's not much to celebrate on.'

'We enjoyed it, though.'

'If I've got a place by next Christmas,' he said, 'you can come and eat all the stuff you like. I shan't charge you anything.'

'I don't want charity. If I've got no money I'll do some work for you to earn it.'

'No, you won't. I'll treat you. For old times' sake.'

If what Keith had said was true, she thought, he would either be dead or in prison. She still didn't know. But she had to believe what he had said about his wife, because nobody would tell a whopping lie like that.

'Now what are you crying for? He's alive, isn't he? Listen, I can hear them coming in. It's a good job we've got these bacon sarnies on the go. Everybody loves a bacon sandwich.' It might be better if he *was* dead, though, he told himself, and then she would have his money. The daft young thing don't know how lucky she is. No, she would only lose it in six months, so he'd better stay alive.

The first run they had done was to the West Country, and Lance remembered them belting down the M5 like skirmishers trying to get in front of an army, Garry in front, followed by Wayne, and then him, weaving between the cars of happy holidaymakers with noddy toys hanging in the back and kids either puking up or howling out for water. All three heading next summer for Devon they would gun along in the sun, stopping for a cream tea at a place Garry had known from his earliest roadworthy days. But even with such a picture he felt so dead tired it was a struggle to keep both hands at the bacon sandwich and chew it down.

Fred went with his tray to Aaron and Alfred. 'How is he, then?'

'I wouldn't be surprised if he wasn't dead.'

Parsons lay, mouth fallen open, soundless, eyes upwhite and seeing nothing. Fred used the force of both hands to close the mouth, then pressed on the eyelids to conceal the ghastly stare, and arrange arms across the chest. He was dead all right, but what could you do? We all had to die sometime. 'I can put undertaker down on my list of trades now, and that's for sure.' He spread a blanket: 'A man in his condition shouldn't have been sent out. Anybody might have known he'd have had a heart attack.'

He didn't care how many went, now that his father had gone. 'Try telling it to that stuck-up swine. All I can say is: God preserve us from bloody heroes.'

'I did. Parsons could have got out of it if he'd wanted, but he insisted on doing his turn. He must have known the score. Everybody I've ever known always knew that kind of score. Have another bacon sarnie?'

'Thanks, I will. I thought I was about to cop it as well, a time or two. You won't get the MBE I laughed to myself, but you might end up with the MCA pinned to your chest. That's what they said my brother-in-law died of – massive cardiac arrest. But I've never worked so hard out there, and I hope I'll never do anything like it again.' He ran a hand over himself, as if hoping to find another coat to button up against the chill. 'I might as well chuck some more wood on the fire.' He reached out for a chair and, gripping top right and bottom left worked the legs loose till all the blood from his body seemed to be in his face. He riffled the ashes with a poker and threw the bits on. 'We may be in out of the snow, but I'm still bloody freezing.'

'Why don't you take a hatchet and start on the beams?' But Alfred didn't hear, and Fred knew that you just couldn't get into the haybox of some people, not even with sarcasm as blunt as a cold chisel.

Giving all her warmth to Garry had done him no good, and Jenny felt that she had no spark remaining, not even for herself. Lance's face was coated with grime and grease, eyes deadened with fatigue, flopped hair adhering from sweat. She didn't care to imagine what her own face looked like, on coming to the table, or think about what she had turned into since entering this house of death. She didn't have a job any more, but what would it matter if none of them lived beyond the night? If they did she would go back south and stay at her parents' till she found a job and a room of her own. They'd always told her that Raymond was no good, that she shouldn't have married him, and as for going off to live in the north . . . she would put up with any taunts to live in a more civilized place. No, it wasn't that, because wherever you were you couldn't escape from yourself, always a real Piranesi prison if ever there was one.

Lance thought this is how a soldier feels, not knowing you're going to be alive the next second, though not caring too much either because to do so would break you into a thousand bits even before a bomb or shell could do it. Still, it isn't in the Falklands, and I've got this lovely woman holding my hands, though hell, I don't know what to say to her except: 'Love you, Jenny.'

Jenny was surprised by a smile that she felt improved her features. 'I hope you'll be all right out there.'

'I don't think about it,' he said. 'It's in the bag, though the Chief'll never say so. All the time I was digging I was thinking about us in bed together.'

His inexperience had been made up for by guidance and abandon, and his energy. 'I'm glad. I was thinking of you.'

'Even when you was holding Garry's hand?'

'It was a way of holding yours.'

'He's still asleep,' Wayne said. 'Fancy sleeping all through this. He don't know how lucky he is. It's not like him, though. That terrorist caught him a real packet. I hope he's burning in hell.'

'He's dead,' Lance said. 'You can bet on it.'

She drank her tea, not wanting anybody dead, yet not able to care if they were. It was cold. So was Garry, dead and cold, but they would discover it when their work was done, or nobody would find anybody if they were unlucky.

Keith sat with Eileen, and she held his hand, nothing to say, she just didn't want him to eat alone. Not even a dog should. Though he was in charge, and had done so much, he looked beaten, finish written on his face in streaks and wrinkles, lips more down than when they had been fighting their way through the snow to get here. His eyes were dark and fallen-in, his skin cracked and in places peeling into the grease. Maybe pain made him look at the end of his strength. Everybody else's face was in a rotten state, masks breaking up, except when they smiled or said something. He squeezed her hand, but she held from telling that it hurt, and pressed back gently when his fit of whatever it was had passed.

After one of the last quarrels with Gwen, when everything had been said on both sides to cause the maximum hurt, he went out of their Chelsea bijou gem – as she scathingly called it: she had never stopped telling him how much she disliked it, in spite of the half-million it would fetch on the market, and not being by any means so *bijou* – and drove over the bridge along the Inner Ring Road, comforted by traffic lights opening onto green-go when a hundred yards away.

Lulled by the light traffic he lost himself somewhere in Lewisham, circling but glad to note that for a while Gwen hadn't dominated his mind. Even realizing her absence only brought her back for a moment. He stopped by a pub to orientate himself with his atlas, to find a route out of town for the Kent coast, where he would go to a hotel and sleep the night in peace.

He wound the window down to let out cigar smoke, and heard singing from the pub. All windows were squares of light, and though the singing was hardly the King's College choir, he stood on the pavement to listen. The music rose and fell in waves of boisterous noise, till after a few choruses he made out the words, and began to laugh. *Ain't it grand, to be bloody well dead!* They struck him as well off-centre, for of course it could never be grand to be bloody well dead, though going by the sound of their happiness it might be exhilarating to say so.

Expecting to see harridans with false teeth and candyfloss hair he went inside to find a dozen girls, with punk or otherwise elegant hairdos, sitting at a long table with linked arms, swaying from left to right and singing at the height of their voices, all healthy, confident, with good teeth, nice individual clothes to each.

Men along the bar and a few older women looked as if such merriment wasn't taking place and there was nothing between them and the wall but silence and empty tables. Keith mimed a clap of applause, and one of the girls waved, her smile a flower thrown for him alone, to wear till it faded from his lapel. Sipping brandy and smoking a cigar, he enjoyed the crude yet funnily inspiring songs, as if the girls had inexplicably taken to such old-time melodies for the verve and gusto of their music.

They cared for no one, young women who worked hard and had money to spend, not the sort who would tolerate the marital anguish he was locked into, though maybe they would have to later. When he got home he could answer Gwen's taunts with such equanimity that they went to bed without further quarrelling.

Sixty yards out on the road, the blast would sweep through the hotel like a thousand knives and kill everyone inside, so one more attempt was needed to get the van clear, and at half-past six there was no more time to play with.

'Another stint.' He touched Lance on the shoulder. 'Just one more,' he said to Wayne. 'I want you as well, for as long as you can do anything to help,' he told Alfred and Aaron.

They followed without complaint.

Every trade had a different apron, the escutcheon of skill and industry, but Fred of many trades had only one. He had bought a dozen of the strongest cloth, and picked them out himself. Doris chose everything else, which was right, but the aprons were his. Never let anyone choose your aprons, not even your employers, the butler at his first job had said. If the slave bought his own chains they wouldn't feel as strong.

Funny things you thought of when you could be blown up at any time. He wore an apron so as not to sully his suit, narrow grey and white stripes that made him look a little longer in the body. He listed the trades he had been forced into on this long night which was not yet over. Barman and waiter at the beginning, then cook and bottlewasher, doctor for the wounded and priest for the dying, and undertaker if you thought about it, which he did as he whistled with apparent cheerfulness between the tables, collecting pots and cutlery, hearing the baleful groans of the gale and half expecting the floor to heave under him as it had in the old days at sea. In a great gale he had been aware that the waves were big enough to tip the whole caboodle into oblivion. Any second could come and without anybody's by-your-leave decide to be their last.

So he had been in that state before this awful night, had learned that you couldn't be frightened out of your life for more than a few minutes. And anyway, he had told the young lad with him in the galley, the system could only take so much uncertainty, so you might just as well settle down and forget it, which he had known how to do ever since. All you needed was something to occupy yourself, and you could cock a snook at God Almighty Himself, if you cared to. And then you could rely on the God of Israel to look on you grimly (but with a hidden smile somewhere) and say: 'Carry on, then, lad.' You could always find a place in God's favour if you were working.

THIRTY-FOUR

Eileen felt better if she talked. She had been born knowing that there was no greater way of easing the heart but, if that was the case, why was it that all the people she had known hadn't wanted to hear what she had to say? While Keith was outside doing what he had to do (and she would never be absolutely convinced that he had to do it, no matter what anyone said the danger was), every second that went by was a painful cut somewhere on her skin, so that if she didn't talk there would be so many cuts she would bleed to death.

Maybe she ought to try singing, but she would sound like a wailing cat, and didn't want to frighten anybody more than they were already. Let the wind do that, moaning around like a man who hadn't got any ciggies just before Bank Holiday.

Enid slept on two armchairs pushed together, as far from Parsons' corpse as she could get, a dead body Keith hadn't told anybody to throw out because he seemed too knackered to bother, maybe too disappointed at how things were going. Jenny at the table, hands by the side of her face, looked as if a bit of a natter might not do her any harm. 'I wonder how much longer we'll have to go on waiting?' Eileen asked.

The light from two Calor lamps at different ends of the room barely reached each other. Chairs had gone into the fire, which spat and subsided, as if it had taken umbrage and would warm them no more. The wind through gaps and cracks gave the bit of candle nicked from the kitchen a hard time in staying alight. Jenny looked at this poor young drab in the man's overcoat Fred had found for her. 'Is all this waiting around getting on your nerves?'

'I've been waiting all my life, so it ain't much different now.' She kicked a piece of broken bottle back under the table. 'It's just that I ask myself now and again what I'm waiting for, and how long it's likely to go on.'

Jenny laughed, but it was no laugh. 'I thought you were being serious, for a moment.'

'Well, I was. I always am, though everybody thinks I'm not. The only person I've ever met who took me seriously was Keith. And he's out there with his bikers pushing that van around.'

'They're trying to save our lives. Don't you know?'

'Of course I do. And I'm waiting for it to be finished, and for them to come back, and for all of us to be safe. We ought to be shovelling as well, but they think we can't do it because we're women. I'm as hard as any of 'em. That's what I said to Keith, but he made me get out of the van and come back in here. So I'm waiting, and it's getting on my nerves. But it's like you say, it stands to reason I'll always be waiting.' She was silent for a while, and Jenny missed her prattling, wondering when she would speak again, and thinking Eileen too young to have been knocked about by life, which was why she found it so easy to chatter.

'I don't think that time will come for me.'

Jenny laughed at such gloom from a young girl. 'That's a bit pessimistic. Aren't you in love with him? I'd want to die if Lance was killed, whatever we might mean to each other.'

'I've never been in love before so I don't know. I once told a boy friend I'd never had an orgasm when he was talking about a book he was reading on sex, and then he made me come and said: "That's an orgasm!" Well, I'd had plenty before, but now I knew. So as for being in love, well, with Keith it feels like people say it ought to feel. Only it's no good being in love with him.'

'Why not? Doesn't he love you?'

'He must, after what he said to get me away from that van. I wanted to stay, in case it exploded, because if he got killed I wouldn't want to live. So I suppose that's what being in love is, because I know he wanted me to stay. But he couldn't let me. I thought he was going to thump me and throw me out, like one of my boy friends would have done. But he did it another way because he loved me. At least that's what I like to think. I won't stop waiting till he's safe and we're together again, and then I'll never wait for anything for the rest of my life. Only it's never going to happen. So I'll be waiting all my life, except that I won't. If you wait all your life it's no life, is it?'

'No.' She heard the hard response in her voice, but went on, words coming out that she had often drilled into order: 'You can always make up your mind to stop waiting. It's useless. It's killing. You can just say no to waiting, and start to live.' Then she knew her words were foolish, because she wasn't capable of any such thing.

'I can't.' Eileen wiped her face with a serviette. 'I haven't lived yet, so I won't even try. But if I wait for Keith I'll have to wait a long time, because he's on the run.'

'What, him? He can't be.'

'When the police get him he'll be put away for twenty years. He told me, to get me out of the van. But I know it's true.'

Jenny was convinced that men were worse than born rotten. They had been rotten for generations before they were born, and their descendants – if the world was unlucky enough to have them – will be rotten for generations to come. In fact rotten was mild to what they were really like. Imagine a man like that telling such vile lies to a young girl he had just been to bed with and wanted to get rid of. 'I can't believe it.'

Eileen lowered her voice, though there was no one else to hear. 'He killed his wife.'

'Oh, God, that's too bloody much. I've heard of some tricks, but that's the limit. And you believe him?'

'Yes. And you would have done, as well.'

'I wouldn't.'

'You would if you'd been me.'

'Did he tell you to keep it secret? To tell nobody else?'

'He didn't need to, though I don't suppose he expected me to be such a flapmouth.'

Jenny felt Eileen ought to be protected from such a predatory swine, and though on a night like this he had his uses, she would say when he came in: 'What the hell do you think you're up to, telling a young girl you've just murdered your wife? Is that how you cook up your fun?'

All she had intended was to talk to Jenny, and since Keith couldn't have lied, what would it matter how many people knew? 'He didn't want me to get killed, so he told me the only thing that would frighten me away. It proved he loved me, so how can it be bad? But he still killed his wife.'

'Don't be silly.'

'You're no fucking good to talk to at all.'

Jenny had a sudden dread that the explosion was about to happen. Talk had made her forget, but now she felt tense, almost tearful at what seemed sure to come. She soothed herself with the fact that whenever she had felt a warning premonition in the past nothing had taken place. It was only at those times when no sign was given that the unimaginable happened. 'I'm sorry about that,' she said in response to Eileen's protest. 'It's just that I've learned to believe nothing men say. They're liars, all of them. It's bred in the bone for them to lie. As soon as they meet a woman they start lying, as if to mummy, all over again. Why it is, I don't know. I think every man's afraid of every woman. A person only lies if they're frightened. The only total thing about women is that they have a vagina, but the one factor men have in common is that they all lie.'

Eileen laughed. 'Christ! What a mouthful! I suppose most men *are* liars, but some must be different.' The blizzard changed its tune to a high-pitched continual note, and though the windows stopped clattering the pressure against the frames caused more insidious anxiety. Another fall of debris sounded from upstairs. 'Keith didn't lie, so there's one who's different. My old boy friend Trevor lied all the time, when he condescended to speak. And women lie as well, I know that for a fact. Haven't you ever lied?'

She needed little time to answer, but wondered whether she hadn't missed something in her life. 'No, never.'

'I've had to, sometimes, so that I wouldn't get a black eye, or to calm somebody down.' It would be getting light soon, and she hoped the wind was having its last fling. 'What about Lance, then? Doesn't he lie? I know you went to bed with him.'

She smiled. 'In the time we spent together he didn't need to. Or I didn't give him the opportunity.' She didn't want to think about him or be reminded of anything, good or bad, in her life at the moment. She wanted to sleep, and when she came out of it find that all night-mares had vanished at the onset of daylight.

'I'll bet he fucks like a rabbit in a thunderstorm,' Eileen said.

'Mind your own business.'

'I was once forced by a biker. But I didn't tell the police. Not on your life.'

'You should have.'

'It's none of their business, either. It ended all right. We stayed together three months, and he was very good to me in the end. He looked after me. When I got pregnant he coughed up the money for an abortion.'

Jenny wondered if there weren't more than a few liars among women, the way she told her story. 'And how did you feel afterwards?'

'Lousy. I wanted to do myself in. I felt so rotten he left me. Maybe I got preggers after being in bed with Keith last night. I hope so, because I'd have it. I don't care what he says, if he's here to say it. Anyway, if I do have a kid maybe I'll be able to get a flat out of the social workers. I'll look after it till my dying day.'

She was crying again. Who wouldn't? At least you were living if you could cry. 'Yes, never get rid of it.' It was a hateful phrase, but one that would be readily understood.

'I won't.' She was laughing, sucking in her tears. 'If it's a boy I'll make its middle name Blizzard!'

They were both laughing, arms around each other, cheeks still touching. 'And what if it's a girl?' Jenny said.

'I'll call her Snowdrop!'

With Alfred's spade and then Aaron's to help, Keith made them concentrate on levelling the way ahead so that he would be able to drive a further fifty yards. A range of snowhills from the digging had their own valleys and heights, the escarpment of a cutting mark here and there where human quarrying had been at work. Otherwise white, a blue glow in the dark, a false solidity you couldn't travel over or through without sinking. The stars were paler, and contours of snow beyond their excavations vaguely outlined, undulations more or less flattened. They made their road into unexplored territory, seemingly to no purpose since its colour would never change enough to indicate what they might find.

A short stint, and Keith forced poisonous meditations out of his mind as he motioned them in, arms signalling that for them it was the end with shoulder and shovel, though unexpected energy came from somewhere when they walked quickly through the courtyard.

'After we've had something to eat we'll all move into the spare room, as far away as we can get.' He was amazed at how fresh and neat Fred looked. He had taken off his apron and, cold as it was,

238

wore no more than his smart waistcoated suit. Keith imagined him putting his head under the tap every half hour, spraying his face with a reasonable brand of aftershave, combing his hair, and wiping his shoes with a rag. As the only one able to go on with his normal trade, he was a being apart.

'You ought to sleep,' Fred told him. 'It looks as if *your* battery's drained. It wouldn't do for you to fold up on us, sir.' He turned, and pulled Enid out of her sleep. 'I want some help in the kitchen. And no bloody cheek, or you'll feel the flat of my hand.'

She smiled, no need to give him what-for, though he turned before she could do so. He felt light in the head, at the first pale hint of dawn coming back to the windows. Pulling the curtains open, to be more welcoming to the day, they ran completely off the rails, so with an operatic flourish he scooped them up and threw them on the fire, wondering why the hell he was doing such a thing.

'Now you're trying to choke us to death, you daft old bastard.' Smoke clouding the room, Wayne pulled the drapes clear and ran to the door, black flocks falling as he flung them out.

'What a mess my hotel is.' Fred noted a lilt of hysteria to his laugh, and curbed it. 'You wouldn't think it used to be such a fine old place. All in a few hours.' He walked towards the kitchen, shaking his head and wondering why it was that yesterday seemed weeks away. 'You just never know what Fate is about to bring, do you?'

'It serves him right.' Enid followed at a certain distance, as if he were a wounded animal who, not yet knowing the extent of his disablement, might suddenly realize the pain and turn round to rend her.

'It doesn't serve him right,' Aaron admonished, though gently.

'Not if he hadn't deserved it,' Alfred agreed when she had gone. 'And we've no reason to believe he has.'

'We all deserve our fate, though.'

'Do we? I don't know about that. Anyway, what harm have we done?' He poked Aaron in the chest, which Aaron felt as being too familiar, even vaguely insulting. 'I've got nothing on my conscience.' He had taken Jack Smythe's trade and chased him out of business, but it hadn't done any vital damage to Jack Smythe, who had then obtained a job as a long-distance lorry driver, and had also moved into a smaller house, which surely must be more convenient. There was nothing wrong with that because not being threatened with ulcers, how could he complain?

'I'm in trouble with the police,' Aaron said. 'That's what I mean.'

Alfred opened his coat and stuck a thumb in the armhole of his cardigan, a comforting stance which made him feel more himself, not even the old man's image to chinwag him mercilessly into the slough of indecision whenever he had to do something about the business. After drumming up sufficient respect at the funeral, and arranging a spread of baked meats that the old bugger would be chagrined not to be present at, he would be finally on his own, able to go to the Devil or wherever else the inclination might take him. The mixing of freedom and exhaustion made him feel as if he'd had too many eggnogs at Christmas, and not in any mood to hear another man going on about his troubles. 'Did you knock into another car, and not report it? Ah, here comes Fred with some tea, bless him!'

'Worse than that, I'm sad to say.'

'And he's got beans on toast as well. I can't think how he does it.' He took out his soft leather wallet and put a tenner on the tray: 'That's for my favourite waiter.' Two bob's more than enough, his father would have said.

'I'll see that he gets it.' Fred folded the note in four to fit the bottom right of his waistcoat, then left them talking like childhood pals, himself amazed at how Old Nick's tantrums and the Sword of Damocles could bring such different breeds together. Not that the situation made Enid seem much sweeter when she beamed her needle eyes at him, but she was only a kid so what could you expect? All the same, she was sweet enough on that bookseller who was far enough over the hill to be her father. I don't know how people have either the gall or the luck: but you'd think I was running a knocking-shop the way they screwed each other blind upstairs last night.

'You mean,' Alfred said, 'that you can get more money for a book if you write the author's name in front?'

'That's about it.' Aaron didn't know why he had told him. 'Among other things.'

'And the police can nick you for it?'

'They certainly can.'

Alfred picked up the slice of toast, beans falling as he chewed. 'You're in a bit of a fix, though I've heard of worse pickles.' Having swallowed his food, he laughed wide enough to show a couple of gold fillings. 'You might get off with a caution from the judge if you sign him a copy of the Bible!'

Fred doled out refills from an enamel jug as long as his arm. 'To the top,' Wayne said. 'If we get out of this place in one piece we'll always call here for a drink on our way to somewhere else. We're pals now, aren't we?'

'I reckon so. You'll be very welcome.' Like hell you will, he told himself.

'Fill a mug for our mate Garry,' Lance said. 'It's time we woke him up from his long night's sleep.'

Fred walked away saying he would make a fresh pot. 'He's sure to appreciate it' – wanting to be out of range because too many people in the world were insane, the sort who overtook on the inside lane of the motorway, or walked into plate-glass windows on coming out of a pub at afternoon closing, or hit their wives if the home team lost or only drew – such types as you had to avoid for your own good by staying in the kitchen which in any case was the best place to be alone in.

'I hope he'll bring plenty of sugar,' Wayne shouted to the others. 'If Garry's tea ain't sweet he'll be cross, and I've never seen anybody as happy as Garry when he's cross. Even I get frightened.'

Keith touched Eileen's hand before beginning to eat. An old scar fanning from his left eye had whitened out of the grime. She hadn't noticed it before, normally so blind she needed years to take in what another person looked like, and as for knowing them after forty-eight hours, well, she hoped Keith wouldn't mind if she went on staring, wanting to remember him whether she saw him again or not, because if he got sent down for twenty years that's how it would be, unless he gave her a photo. 'I don't want you to leave me. I couldn't stand it. I never want us to be apart. I love you.'

Words failed at her lips. She hated tears but couldn't stop them.

'I love you.' He did, whether or not she would always remain a mystery. 'Don't worry.'

She was satisfied with that, would have to be, but she would also expect him to let her make up later for her silence, how much later she didn't know, an uncertainty that kept her tongue still. She wouldn't worry either about both of them being blown to bits, or getting carried to the hospital. She couldn't think about it because it was impossible to imagine.

'There's no problem,' he said. 'We'll be together, no matter how long we're apart. Forget the circumstances. They won't kill either of us. Now you're crying again. Please don't do that.'

She was crying for him, in inexplicable rage, about something lacking all significance, crying out of an agony of spirit meant for him alone, and because of what he had told her about Gwen. 'I'm just so fucking happy,' she sobbed.

'So am I. But you'll have to stop swearing if you want to convince me.' He held her warm fingers. 'It's not necessary to swear. I believe you, without you swearing every time.' He thought he would do her a favour, so that she might have some kind of chance in life.

'I'll try never to swear again.' She leaned forward to kiss him, and knocked over an empty glass. 'But it often comes without me knowing.'

'I can't believe it,' Alfred said. 'The signatures are still in the books, whether they're true or false. So what are they complaining about? They aren't going to disappear. They'll give you a slap on the wrist and tell you not to do it again. Nobody gets sent down for a thing like that.' He lit a cigar and passed it across, then ignited his own. 'In two years, maybe less, you'll be back on course, wondering what the fuss was all about. Mind you, a chap like you should never have left that chemistry job. There's too many temptations for people who set up on their own. Don't I just bloody well know it?'

During the snow-shifting his toothache hadn't much bothered Aaron, when it surely ought to have done, but now his whole mouth ached so that he didn't know where the bad tooth was. 'It's my sister I'm most concerned about.'

'Never worry about a woman.' Alfred leaned closer, pale at the idea that Eileen or Jenny might hear and take him up on such views. His married life had been one long time-and-emotion study, which was why he still lived in the usually happy home. 'Women are always all right. Society takes more care of them nowadays than it does a man, which is fine by me, because I'm old-fashioned. Your sister will let it flow over her without too much harm. Anyway, when we get out of here I'll keep an eye open for your case, to see if it gets in the papers. I can follow it up, now that I've met you.'

Parsons was dead, though she wasn't convinced there was any need to feel either guilty or bereft. You can't save anyone from their folly, and to assume any responsibility for it is unjustified pride. She could have helped him more than she had, made it easier for him to cope, but only if she had been another person. If they had put the body out of the room and not left it under blankets she wouldn't expect any moment to see an arm move, a head rise and a mouth call for champagne. The dead weren't dead till they were buried or cremated, and then you couldn't always be sure. She thought of him as he had been when alive, weak and good-natured (unless gerrymandering Union meetings), often kind to her. After Raymond left she had moved into a smaller house, and Tom got a friend's lorry to shift her stuff, all for the price of the petrol and a few drinks. He even made two journeys in his own car to transport the fragile items.

'I suppose my old man's worried to death,' Lance said. 'When I first got a motorbike he never went to bed till I was in. He used to sit all night by the phone in case I'd had a spill, so he told me. He still does, I expect, though I'm not such a madhead any more.'

'Phone him,' Jenny said, 'as soon as you can.'

'You think I won't? I'd send a carrier pigeon if I could. He'd love that. He'd think he was back in Libya.'

'My old man's counting his blessings,' Wayne said. 'He's in bliss when I'm not there. Or he's totting up his matches. He don't trust me, not since he opened my cupboard and saw enough matches to start the Great Fire of London. I was smoking in bed last year and the eiderdown caught fire. It weren't my fault, though. I nearly bloody choked on the smoke.' He stood, on seeing Fred come out of the shadow with Garry's tea. 'I'll take it to him. A cup and saucer, eh? He'll think he's at the Ritz. It's too good for him.'

'I suppose you think we're a rough lot?' Lance moved his chair closer. 'We don't mean anything by it.'

'I know.' Jenny envied him, that they were so easy with each other, and seemed to enjoy their lives. Nobody could fault them for that. The pain of existence would overtake them soon enough.

He kissed her. 'I think you're marvellous. I'd like to live with you. I'll bet you could teach me a lot.'

'I don't know about that.' She would ruin him in no time, as she would any man, though the hope of possible happiness wouldn't leave her alone.

'We've been to bed together, but I don't know you yet.'

What a quaint notion, that you could get to know someone at all by going to bed with them. 'And when you do know me, you won't want to know me.' She regretted what she had said, on seeing his eyes wince.

'How do you know?' he asked. 'How can you be so sure? Even somebody like you. I wish you wouldn't say it.'

Wayne still held the cup and saucer. 'Come over here' – tea splashing over his boots. Then he skimmed the saucer, lethal fragments ricocheting from the back of the fireplace.

'What's going on?' Alfred shouted.

Wayne wanted a suitable target for the cup as well but, seeing nothing worthy of the effort, and no person whose possible injury would lessen the shock, sent it skittling among bottles above the bar. Then he caught hold of a table, and beat the floor with it till all legs were smashed, his bull-like grunts sounding out even the whining bandsaw moaning of the wind. Lance did not know whether to tell him to pack it in, or himself join in a last celebratory bursting to pieces of the hotel. 'Come and see.' Wayne pulled him close. 'I'm sure he's dead.'

Fred pushed broken bottles from the bar with a piece of folded cardboard. 'Even doctors that cost hundreds of pounds a visit have people die on them,' he murmured to Keith, 'and as for me, I did my best.'

'He died some time ago,' Jenny said, 'but what was the point of telling anyone?'

Keith was glad she hadn't, since it would have disturbed their work. But he was responsible, for having encouraged them to attack a madman. He should have let Daniel starve in the cold, put off attacking him for a few hours and left him too weak to throw slates. His instinct had told him to go up himself, but he had played God and unleashed the bikers: 'All right, lads, take him out. One in front, one in support, and one in reserve.' No, that wasn't it. 'You go left, you to the right, and you in the middle.' Not that, either. His heart had never been one for breaking, but you didn't like losses. Call them together. Give them a talk: 'Sorry, lads. The fault is mine.' Another death that can't be made good. Time punishes, because once a crime has been done there's no calling back the good days, the score only wiped out when you die yourself. They wouldn't understand that, either.

'It's not your fault,' Jenny said.

'No, but something else is.' Even one death added up to too much. You lived with whatever you had done, existed with the insupportable. A week ago he was one sort of man, and today he was another. It happened to untold numbers, but they became the kind of people incapable of ever meeting each other. A killer lived with his internal injuries, never able to atone by bringing back the one whose life had been wasted.

'Eileen told me. Is it true?'

One way of getting back to conventional simplicity was to give in to anger, but he curbed the temptation, such a distasteful route leading to mindlessness and defeat. 'I'd give my life for it not to be.'

'What a world.' Nothing more to say, she left him to his breakfast, and looked at Lance moving the blankets one by one, as if not to cause pain to a corpse, until he came to two white legs streaked with blood, all below the waist awash. He had seen no more blood than that of a cut finger. They say you faint at the sight of blood, but I won't. He flopped the blankets aside like enormous floorcloths, knowing it was the stench that put you in danger of throwing up. 'It would have been better to go off the road doing a ton than peg out like this. He was dying while we were outside.'

'We should have let the snow alone, and then we might have gone together.' Wayne groaned. 'His mam will go off her head when she knows.'

'No, she won't. Everybody hated him, except us.' Lance shivered, out of control, legs melting under him, drew a chair close and sat down to cry. 'It's all that teacher's fault. After Garry's death, with my last breath. But it won't work.'

'Ferret's dead,' Wayne said. 'But if he ain't now, he will be. If it thawed we could track him down. I'll get him. Even if he's put inside for life I'll be waiting to top him when he comes out. He deserves to be roasted over a slow fire. But if Keith hadn't got us on snowshifting we could have stayed with Garry, and then maybe he would have been all right.'

'The ifs don't do any good,' Lance said.

'I know, but somebody's done it, and it wasn't us. Keith stopped us killing him when we was up in the attic, didn't he? And then he wouldn't let us hang him, like Garry wanted to.'

'He'd been hit by that slate already,' Lance said. 'He should have gone straight to hospital, and he would have if the snow hadn't blocked everything off. Another if, though.'

'They're right,' Keith said to Eileen. 'Five dead, and I'm still here.'

'Take no notice,' she told him. 'They don't know what they're saying. You can't blame 'em, though.'

One more push, another fifty yards. He would draw the van back, take it at a rush, up the well-prepared slope, then it would be far enough away not to kill anyone, a last effort before coming back to sleep till the storm was over and the police arrived.

Wayne and Lance sat silent, with heads down, settled by misery, flashes of the good times going by. Keith touched Lance's shoulder, and said when he looked up: 'I'm sorry about this.'

'It ain't your fault.'

If there was work to be done it would be easy to get them out, even kindness in it, and they would toil as never before, giving no sign of exhaustion or grief. 'I'd like to thank you for all you did.'

Lance smiled, on hearing his own dead voice: 'Any time.'

'Just let us know,' Wayne said.

He walked to Eileen, wondering what there was to say. Killing puts you beyond redemption, the solution always too late. He kissed her out of sleep. Her hands had gone cold, but she was warm and young. 'I must just go to the toilet.'

'Love you, love you, love you,' she murmured, then smiled and closed her eyes, sure of him at last.

They were frozen and blocked, but he used one. Washing his hands in the kitchen, he turned to Fred. 'Get all of them to safety. I don't care how you do it.'

'I hope you know what you're up to.'

'Another few yards, and then we'll be safe.'

He went with head lowered towards the van, the blizzard come to life again and trying to beat him back.

Eileen waved. 'Love you!' she called, joy in her heart.

THIRTY-FIVE

'We should have landed at Portsmouth,' Charlie said, 'and cut up through Oxford, then we wouldn't have been two hours tangling with the Blackwall Tunnel. And if that CB radio hadn't packed in we wouldn't have copped all this and driven round in circles till we got stuck. So give that wireless a fucking good kick and call international rescue.'

Bill, never lucky at cards, threw his hand in. 'I was trying all the way out. The gremlins must have crawled in it for a rave-up.'

Light came from two windows in the back doors and directly parallel with his sight, the changing badge of a new day that Daniel hadn't expected to see. They had manhandled him up the ladder and onto his mattress above the driver's cabin because of the smell and his disturbing groans, neither of which he was aware of.

The men ceaselessly playing cards and making tea below looked like bandits in a cave whose ceiling he had levitated to, instead of the decent-minded trio who had lifted him out of the claws of the blizzard. He had heard them say they couldn't be bothered with him any more because he was dying, though he felt a long way from it except that the pain made him so tired he wanted to sleep for ever.

'Our job might be easier,' Charlie said, 'when the Channel Tunnel opens.'

Paul stretched out on his mattress. 'There'll be a queue as far back as York to get on in summer.' He nodded upwards. 'If he goes on like this we'll have to tip him outside. It's making my guts heave. No wonder I lose every game.'

'We don't want to dump him while he's alive,' Bill said, 'but we could be here for another week. Some people take a bloody age to snuff it, even if they've got gangrene all over like he has. It might be a kindness to all parties concerned if we chuck him out to die in the snow. In the meantime, let's have some char. I'm as dry as the top end of a bulrush.'

Daniel didn't know whether he was dreaming their talk, or

redreaming their dreams. The drift of their unmusical voices made yesterday seem so long ago he could never have been there.

'I envy that couple near Montpellier,' Paul said. 'They've finished sorting their few sticks out by now, and are on that lovely terrace with a bottle of Martini and a basin of olives.'

'They've worked all their lives for it,' Charlie said.

Bill's laugh was dry. 'Maybe they're train robbers.'

'What? That nice grey-haired woman, and that old gent in his fancy waistcoat? They gave us a hundred francs each to get a meal with.'

'We could sweat two lifetimes and not retire to France.' Charlie handed fags around. 'Who'd want to die among strangers, though?'

'If I could pull off a good job and get hold of half a million quid I wouldn't mind,' said Paul. 'A few palm trees and a rooftop swimming pool would do me. Do you remember that geezer in Morocco, when we was watching them belly dancers?'

Bill choked on half a laugh. 'Them belly dancers was boys, you stupid fucking berk.'

'Well, whatever they was they looked all right in them yeller frocks.'

'Christ, wait till I tell his missis.'

'He wanted to fit the van up with packets of white powder, didn't he?'

'I nearly pushed my fist into his fat chops,' Bill said. 'They throw away the key for things like that.'

'They'd never have found it,' Paul said. 'Not the way I'd have hidden 'em. I've been thinking up a scheme that can't go wrong.' His thin face was raddled by a greed which his ambition had never been able to satisfy, the reason being that bad luck had always made things go wrong, or people he dealt with had a secret grudge against him which he couldn't have known about because he thought he had never done anyone harm. Or it hadn't been people at all, but a timetable he had not read properly, or a list not fully taken in, an inventory not rightly assessed, or a page of instructions his sight slid over, thinking he understood everything when he hadn't by any means, and even half knowing he hadn't because he wasn't that stupid but with more pertinacity and attention to detail he could have been much cleverer — and yet, after all, assuming it would be all right 'on the day' with someone as finally sharp as himself. And neither had he ever called on anyone to be his partner in business, because he hadn't known who could be trusted, not so easy when nobody trusted you. The present scheme, unlike others, would be different, however, would net such a big sum that he wouldn't either have to pit his brains against the world again or work with these two deadbeats any more. 'Thinking about that couple whose furniture we just took to Montpellier . . .'

'Whose mattresses we're lying on,' Bill laughed. 'And I'll be wearing their wellies to dig my garden from now on. So what about 'em?'

'Sometime or other, they're going to die.' Paul's eyes were almost as bright as the gas lamp standing on a box. 'There must be thousands who'll want to get shipped back to dear old Great Britain and have a proper Christian burial.'

'I follow you,' Bill said impatiently, 'but I'm lost. Anyway, they have nice refrigeration trains for that journey.'

'I know,' Paul said impatiently, 'but it would be cheaper for them to use the nice refrigerated van that our set-up would have.'

'If we cut it so cheap, where would the profits be?'

'Now you're talking. Listen, what if the stiffs was filled with them neat little bags of white powder that the bloke in Tangiers talked about? We wouldn't get it there, though, because I know somebody in Marseilles. We'd run the bodies to his warehouse, and a few medical students in need of a bob or two would be standing around trestle tables in white coats, with lots of buckets and hosepipes. They would make enough space in each body to pack a dozen little plastic bags, and when our black van rolled off the ferry and went through the Nothing to Declare slot, HM Customs' boys and girls would stand to attention with hats under their arms and respectfully salute.'

'This pretty scheme merits more thought.' Bill scratched his head, then put his cap back on as if to get started. 'Methinks the corpses would be dancing a fucking jig with all that head-banging stuff inside 'em when we came off the ro-ro at Dover.'

'You're not with me,' Paul complained.

'Too fucking right I'm not. What bad dream did you get that stunt from? I'm glad it's getting light at last, that's all I can say.' He let out a particularly fruity belch. 'We'll have another fry-up soon.'

'It's foolproof,' Paul resumed, though well knowing that if the plan failed they would blame him to the death, and that if it came out right their lips would be too solidly glued to the brandy bottle to spare a common thank you. 'I've worked it all out. We place an advert in the *International Herald Tribune*.' He pulled a stub of pencil and a piece of scruffy paper from the ticket pocket of his suit. '"Does it worry you what will happen when you're dead? We would not be surprised. So why not go back to Blighty by refrigerated lorry? Our competitive rates will be right up your street." Well, something like that. You two see if you can do any better. There'll be so many enquiries we'll need a secretary and an office to deal with 'em. We'll do it for half of what the railways charge, and then . . .'

A light whiter than snow filled both windows, a thunderclap pushing the rictus of agony back into Daniel's head. Pebbled glass swirled like shrapnel, and waves of force travelled along snowdrifts to hit the pantechnicon rear-end on, lifting the wheels so that the heavier front sent vibrations backwards like a dog shaking off water. Daniel, nothing to reach for, fell into the vortex of his screams.

The mattresses were yanked away and, as if with a life of their own, came back and tried to smother them. All three heard shouts of panic and shock, wondering where they came from, and what they had done to deserve whatever was happening, as pots and lamps and the stove flew. They rolled and collided within the doors that had stayed bolted, and Bill found himself clutching the stove, hoping to God it wouldn't ignite as paraffin squirted over his arm.

The receding echo held more terror than the great bang, a malice implying the threat of returning to finish the job. Charlie held the frying pan but was curious as to how it came into his hand, as if he had been placed on guard should anyone try to get in or out. He ran a finger down his cheek and saw blood. 'What the hell was that, then?'

Paul's laugh was as if from a parrot which had just reached out and torn into someone's finger. He took a card from the scattered deck which turned out to be a middle grade nonentity, squinting because the other eye wouldn't open, and trembling that it might stay shut for the rest of his life. 'It sounds like the fucking atom bomb went off.'

They looked at him while the wind, as if awed by the explosion, stayed quiet. Charlie released the frying pan for fear he would hurl it at Paul. 'God took umbrage, and quite rightly so, at your cock-eyed scheme. Corpses! We was nearly able to begin on ourselves.'

'Look at the mess.' Bill smiled at finding he could stand. 'We'd better get some sacks and nail 'em at the windows. If we hadn't been dug into the snow the van would have gone like matchwood. Maybe it was a tanker carrying chemicals.'

A mattress had burst, foam rubber like imitation shards of dark steel scattered among the tea chests. 'I thought it was what's-his-name up there' – Charlie wiped a gritty tear from his cheek – 'but he's down here now, and he's dead.' They looked at the face, and the tortured body. 'I reckon he's better off. Now we can tip him outside.'

'He had a long way to fall, and that's a fact,' Bill said. 'He's broken every bone in his stupid fucking body, by the look of it. Some people just shouldn't come out in the snow.'

Fred whistled, shoes crunching bricks and glass in what was left of the lounge. Another one away, and that was for sure, over the sticks, up the slope, and off to the happy hunting grounds. Them as dies will be the lucky ones, as he'd read somewhere. Maybe more than Keith had caught a packet, because Wayne and Lance hadn't been able to leave their dead mate, due to loyalty and friendship, which wasn't as old-fashioned as he had thought. In their peril they were not provided with the heartless wherewithal to leap for safety, or the sense to drag him after them. God knows, he weighed little enough after losing all his blood. And as for that young tart running out into the blizzard, she must have taken much of the blast when it came. I don't suppose she looks very pretty now, so if I don't see her again I can burn that envelope he left me with.

'That's it, then.' Enid smoothed her headscarf and the borrowed coat. 'That's it at last. Now we can relax again.'

'I'll need a week or two to get used to it.' Alfred, the lower parts of his eyes like saucers filled with blood, needed three matches to light his cigar. 'We're all right, but what about the others?'

The wall was cold at Aaron's back, dust and rubble around his feet. A beam had fallen in the opposite corner, where luckily no one had sheltered. 'I'll take a look.' He stood up to go after Fred.

'At least it's daylight,' Enid said, arms tight across her chest. 'I want to get home and tell everybody I'm all right. They'll be worried to death, I hope.'

'You'd better not leave too soon after the authorities get through,' Alfred said, 'or you won't be on television. You might even get a film contract if you primp your lovely self up a bit.'

'Fuck off, you sarky old bastard.'

'If my daughter Joan had said half as much to me I'd give her a bloody good hiding. But she's well behaved, and I'll have a house built for her as well one day. She went to the High School, she did.'

Fred called from a gap in the wall: 'I can't get through to the bikers. But they're swearing worse than my old parrot, so come and give me a hand.'

'It might be a farm,' said Charlie. 'Somebody else have a look.'

Bill put his spade down, and focused the field glasses. 'The roof's off. It's derelict.'

Paul took them. 'It's a hotel. Or it was. I can see a sign. It must have killed everybody. There's bits of a motor car. Or it might have been a van. We ought to get over there now it's not blowing so much.'

'It's a good half-mile away,' Charlie said, 'though I suppose it might be better than staying in this truck for the next three days. It must have been a hundred tons of gas. I once read about a whole caravan park being wiped out from one bottle.'

'It'd be more sensible,' Bill said, 'to get our engine started, then have another go at the radio. It's got a two-year guarantee, so there can't be all that much wrong with it. If you give me the flashlight I'll try and get a word through to Smokey.'

Charlie put the binoculars back in their case. He loved his binoculars. They made him feel like General Montgomery. 'Let's go inside. We can cook our breakfast and think about it. If we have to trek through the snow we'll need our bellies full.'

'The first thing to do is get that corpse out. I can't stand the smell.' Paul cleared more snow from the top of the van. 'If he stays much longer he might bring us bad luck, and we've had enough of that already.'

'It's changing, though,' Charlie announced. 'I swear blind it's got a bit warmer since we came out. Anyway, let's eat, then Marconi can bodge up that wireless and give the world a bit of Heavy Metal from the tape recorder.'

'Are you hurt?' Jenny said. 'Can you stand up?' Lips at her ears to beat the blizzard's muffle. No blood, and the lion-headed stone pillar by the gate had kept her safe, a lucky chance in her rackety life. She had come out to find her, even before looking for Lance, because she knew he had to be all right. It had to be women and girls together, because no man would make it his first thought to help them. And Fred had gone to look out for the bikers.

The breasts and bellies of snow were pure to one side, but out towards the fields, along where the road was supposed to be, were twisted wheels, black ripped-out pieces of chassis, a door buckled beyond use, a steering wheel like a plastic toy some child had stamped on with disappointment, broken items she could not recognize, pieces of flesh she sought not to, odd bits of tubing like sections of dead snake, a sleeve with an arm still in it, blue striated with red, couldn't not see, scarves of blood, grey guts, a butcher's shambles: bits of cardboard, coils of wire, the half page of a road atlas splashed with red like Chinese writing, spinning over and over in the wind, chasing a scalp, odd crimson rags and half a head.

'Don't go.' Jenny used all her strength to bring her face against her chest. Then she closed her own eyes and said: 'Let's not look,' before being more sick than she could ever remember.

THIRTY-SIX

The place that had seemed so staid a refuge in the blizzard, plugged into the earth and beyond all notions of destruction and, what's more, eternally welcoming with warm punch and womb-like shelter, had in fact been rotten with woodworm, rising damp and deathwatch beetle, as if reinforced only by the faith of those who were stranded under its roof.

Thus Aaron felt as he took off his coat and jacket, determined to pull rubble clear, with Alfred at the other end, and Fred taking position in the middle. The beam was brown below and black on top, a ponderousness pinning laths, plaster, chairs and tables, making a rapidly diminishing prison that Wayne and Lance must be pulled out of before everything slid, because half a bed hung through the ceiling, a counterpane waved to warn or encourage, and foul water descended the wall below a buckled window frame. He would lift the beam or die in trying, though to have survived the explosion and then throw the gift of life back into God's face would be opposing nature.

Fred heaved at the wood. 'The pipes must have split.' Some, against the regulations, had been plastic, and snow melting around them stank like soot.

'Stop fucking nattering,' came Wayne's faint voice, 'or I'll never do a kickstart again. My ribs have gone, and I'm getting snow on my face.'

'Take your sweat. We're getting there.' Fred looked anxious, though not upwards, such a gesture bad for morale. 'The whole lot might tumble.'

The beam was of hernia weight, and Aaron had previously suffered one from lifting too many logs after cutting down old trees in the garden. Beryl said he should get a lad from the village to help, but such work in solitude was precious in the peace it brought.

Both hands under, he remembered in *Les Misérables* how the escaped convict Jean Valjean had put himself beneath a cart and raised it to save a man's life, though such a feat made him known to a policeman looking on. Aaron couldn't tell whether the frog-croak came from planks at the far end of the beam, or from the ceiling, but the strain at his back and stomach turned into a dread ache, as if his legs would also crack. 'Sweat for England, you bastards.' Lance's voice sounded above the blizzard. 'A rat's staring at me, and I don't like rats.'

Alfred groaned at the load he worked at, sweat dripping onto the rubble. He slid bricks and wood under the beam to get it higher, twigging the stress of the situation as if he had inherited the brain of his engineer father, because should Aaron let go, the beam would only fall an inch or two. 'I wanted to see the explosion,' Wayne complained, 'not have the whole shop fall on top of me.'

Clothes chilled from plastery mud, Aaron raised a weight to last the rest of his life, stomach hardening as wood, a matter of holding on and hoping the body would sustain him: 'I'll count up to fifty, and then let go.'

The effort separated him from the world. Fred and Alfred pulled at bricks to make the gap bigger. Far from book-dealing, or the self-indulgent fits of his sister, or his evil encouragement of her plight, and distant also from his nihilistic streaks of cheating, Aaron knew that everything you did affected someone else and had to be allowed for, no resolution except by pain of spirit and the extreme use of grit and sinew.

'I'll count up to fifty, and then let go,' but when he got there he said, no one to hear because the voice of the blizzard was even louder among the ruins: 'I had better make it a hundred, though it'll be impossible to go on longer. And when they're safe I'll ask Enid if she wants to come away with me. We'll drive to the south coast and stay in a hotel. I don't think she will, because she can hardly bear to look at my raddled grandad face twisted with toothache.'

At the hundred mark he said: 'I'll manage ten more, and try not to brood on my squalid fate for ever.' Then he endured without counting, eyes closed because he couldn't bear to check how the loads were shifting, till it came as almost a shock that no more effort was needed.

Wayne limped to the broken door, gasping, hands pressed against his ribs. Fred helped Lance away: 'I think this young soldier might have broken his leg.'

Aaron stepped aside, and the spike of lath that had gone through his trousers at the calf still waved as he hurried to safety.

'It's lovely. Not a cloud in the sky.' Paul knew those days that started so well: sun on snow which protected and kept warm the little goings-on underneath. Such weather could turn very nasty between dawn and dusk. Visibility was good across moors and hills, scratchmarks of walled hedges in the distance, showing how local the blizzard had been but might not be if it began again. The wind was muzzled of its howl, turned direction and settled from the northwest, God alone knowing what it would do in the next few hours. He lay at full length, checking wires leading to the little black box.

Bill shone the torch. 'Did you ever get a licence for this CB radio?'

'Don't ask, or you'll make me laugh. I might bang my head. The screw's so loose the wire ain't making contact. And the aerial's unplugged. I'm surprised they didn't hear that bang twenty miles away and send a chopper to investigate. My fingers are so dead I can't make the two ends stay together.'

Charlie passed a cigarette. 'They wouldn't know which way to look, would they?'

'The trouble is,' Bill said, 'you need a licence for the CB, and we ain't got one, so the coppers'll nick us when they jump out of the chopper even before they offer a fag and a mug of tea to the injured. It might mean a two-hundred-pound fine. They're bound to ask for our licence.'

Paul rubbed his fingers till they were supple and live enough to knot the wires. Static sounded like chips thrown into a pan of smoking oil and, damping the volume, he pushed buttons to bring voices loud and clear from the outside.

Five gone, and none had stopped on their way to pay what they owed. Well, they wouldn't, would they? Fred mused that just as the dead could tell no tales, neither were they capable of settling their scores, though you could be sure they would be called to account when they got to the other side, if there was such a place which, considering the list of misdemeanours he had built up against himself, he sincerely hoped there was not. In what was left of the kitchen he spent the remaining provisions like a generous sailor. The fridge and deepfreeze had been cut off from the start, and he couldn't imagine any of his guests staying many more hours, in which case they would eat royally of sausages, chops, steak and all manner of vegetables. 'It's no use shoving an emergency stock into the snow, because foxes and wild cats will get their noses at it,' he said in answer to Aaron, as if the time for common sense had long been over.

'What about my father's body, then?'

'Animals roam all over the place in a blizzard,' Fred told him gleefully. 'You always find a few sheep gnawed to the bone.' No longer the manager of a hotel, of which there wasn't much left in any case, it didn't matter who he offended. 'You're not going to bring his body back inside, either.' He was well muffled up, for in spite of a woodstove in the kitchen, half of one wall was down. 'It won't be hygienic, not by this time. It won't be very pretty.'

Wayne turned his steak over. 'Every time I chew, my ribs ache summat rotten. I'll have to wait for a proper blow-out till after Garry's funeral.'

'A mass funeral,' Lance said. 'He would have loved it.'

'You lot just don't care about him, do you?' Enid shouted. 'I hate you. He was all right. But you lot haven't got any sense or feeling to talk like that. You make me sick.'

Wayne stood up unsteadily, holding his knife and fork as if he might make her part of his meal. 'What do you know about feelings?' he wheezed. But with his cracked ribs he wanted to curl up in a darkened room with a bottle of whisky. 'Next time a maniac goes around the country in a blizzard with a van like that we'll arrange for you to get stranded with some nice posh *civilized* people. Then you'll be raped, drawn and quartered before you can wiggle your tight little arse.' He pushed his plate aside, unable to eat. The hotel had fallen in, and the world could do the same as far as he was concerned. 'We'll never forget Garry, so shut your gob.'

She turned to Aaron. 'Are you going to let him insult me like that?'

'Let's get on with our meal,' he said.

Fred came into the kitchen with a tray of soiled pots. Those in the lumber room were belching, farting, or puffing cigarettes and groaning from their injuries. He was sorry about that. The lads were more hurt than they let on, so he would leave them alone and hope the medics got here soon to mend 'em and bandage 'em. Even so, they seemed more harmless under their tribulations than before they had known about the van, and that couldn't be bad. It was amazing how pain and peril turned tearaways into heroes. He would show his appreciation by rustling up something tasty for dessert. What they really needed was a good plate of spotted dick smothered in a rich egg custard, or hot dumplings running with treacle, but neither time nor cooking facilities allowed of that. He kicked at a large rat running across broken glass to safety under the sink. 'Not another one away?'

'She's fainted,' Jenny said. 'Is there a dry bed somewhere?'

He pointed to a mattress. 'I kipped on it myself now and again last night. What happened?'

'She saw the mess.'

'I told her not to go out.'

'Well, now she knows. And so do I.'

He set the tray on the sink. 'We don't even have any water. Everything's frozen, or burst. I hope we'll be out of it soon. It's getting intolerable, even to me.'

She let Eileen gently down, thinking it typical of him not to help. The struggle of getting her in from the storm had been almost too much, as if both might never reach shelter.

He turned doctor again. 'I'll find some brandy.'

Eileen lay on her back, arm over eyes, mouth shaped in the perpetual horror of a half-formed cry. Someone had punched her into a nightmare, and she was running up and down tunnels unable to find a way out. Her forehead was cold, the pale skin unwrinkled, and Jenny hoped that soothing fingers would do some good. Eileen's breathing was even, as if she were asleep, shocked out of herself but into something she had never known about, senseless from the exhaustion of terror and utter loss. Jenny touched her lips, then quickly took the hand away at the thought of being bitten, a melancholy smile at such an unlikely occurrence.

Fred shook the bottle's insides to a froth, snapped out the cork, and put it to her nose. 'This is better than any brandy. A ship's carpenter once gave me the formula. But I wonder where she'll go when she leaves here? Keith picked her up off the road.'

259

Snow had melted into her clothes, but her warm sweet breath came through the odour. 'I'll take her home with me.'

She surprised herself, because what would she do about Lance? Let things happen as they might or might not, she'd see him or she wouldn't, surely no need to worry about wanting her when you had spent a night dying and being born again. She would love who she liked. No, that's not it. I'll never be able to change, nor will she, but if we can't live with each other, at least for a while, who the hell can we live with? 'I'm out of a job as well, but we'll manage.'

'Better you than me,' he said.

'It never could be you, could it?' she responded sharply.

'It's having some effect. She's coming round, but you'd better stay with her.'

'I will.'

'Poor thing needs somebody. And when you get her home, give her this envelope.'

'What is it?'

'How the hell should I know? Keith left it for her. Maybe it's a last will and testament. A Dear Eileen letter, for all I care.'

Alfred dragged a mahogany table from the fireplace and set a box under it where a leg was missing. He stacked jumble around the walls, sorted stuff for burning. A boot through the unhinged door of a wardrobe sent clouds of snuff and splinters towards that part of the ceiling still able to cover them from driving snow. 'We can sit it out here a treat.' He was proud of the order he had made. 'The bikers are asleep, and they deserve to be. I wish I was their age again.'

'You had a good time when you were, I suppose?'

'I worked too hard,' he said to Aaron. 'I never had the guts to be more myself than I dared. With my father in the offing all the time I had to watch my Ps and Qs. He had to know about every little thing. I suppose it did my character some good, by the time I was forty anyway. It seems funny now he's gone. Mother died ten years ago — or was it twelve? — so I'm an orphan! What a bloody silly thing to be, at my age! All I want is to see my daughter married, and get back to business, though the first thing' — he lit a cigar from a burning stick which he threw down before his eyebrows singed — 'will be to get my father decently buried. I have a son, but he cleared off five years ago to live in London, where he's working on computers. He's got two kids of his own, and pays for 'em to go to a private school. He had more guts than I did, and didn't want me breathing down his neck, though I tried not to when he was little. His grandfather was as nice as pie to him, would you believe it? So I hope he'll come up for the funeral, though it wouldn't surprise me if he didn't. I even offered to buy him a car last year, but he said he'd already got one. That's the modern generation for you.'

Enid looked at Aaron as if, he thought, she had never seen him before. 'I'll go home as soon as I can, and let my parents know I'm all right. I don't like them to be worried. When they're worried they get upset.'

'I'm not surprised.'

'I'll write to you about that job.' She didn't think she would, but she might. You never knew how you would feel in the morning, and why should you? If you knew how you would feel from one day to the next you might as well be dead, and who wants to be dead when you can go on enjoying yourself? She patted his folded hands. 'I promise I won't bite my nails any more. My mam and dad will be ever so pleased.'

Fred came in with a tureen of fruit salad. 'I went out to empty the slops, and saw a helicopter over the tor a couple of miles away. I expect it's the police. Or maybe the RAF.'

Wayne yawned, and whispered in his pain. 'Go and wave a white sheet, then.'

'You damned idiot,' Fred said. 'They won't see it in the snow.'

'I've got to go to court next week for speeding,' Wayne grumbled. 'I was doing a ton near Youlgreave. They won't let a biker live these days. I didn't even kill anybody. I hope that was a chopper and there's a doctor on board who can fix my ribs up. They're giving me bloody hell.'

'All I ever hit was a dog,' Lance said, 'and I was only doing thirty. I'll be scarred for life with this bloody gash in my face. The blood's congealed, though, so it's not running any more. The poor bloody dog ran right out of a garden. The little girl who owned it broke her heart, but the farmer admitted it wasn't my fault.'

Fred set down bowls and spoons. He would stay in Nottingham with his old shipmate Tommy Blidworth who had a fuel delivery service, work with him till he could get a job, or until he made up his mind about buying another hotel, unless it paid him to insist that the insurance build up this one to exactly what it was like before. He had done nothing but send Doris insulting letters since she left, but if he wrote nice things and posted some flowers maybe she would come back. We'll start all over again. I'll need a bit of help in a new place. Her cook's bound to be fed up with her by now. The only thing worse than being together is living apart.

'We'll have a concrete motorbike built on Garry's grave,' Lance said. 'A sculptor can do it, set him up in full riding gear, and put some dandelions in an Ogri mug.'

Alfred was ready with money. 'We'll have a subscription list, a whip-round. I'll put fifty quid in, if you like.' He pushed his scraped dish away. 'You lads did wonders last night and this morning. And Keith as well. I feel bad that he had to go. He was one of the best.'

'Shut your stupid gob,' Wayne said. 'Everybody gets what they deserve. We all did what we could, that's all.'

'Now what have I said wrong?'

'Nothing.'

It's no use, Lance said to himself. I've got to get out of this, though I can't say what *this* is, except it's everything and I've been in it all my life. I've only enjoyed being in it because there was nowhere else to be, but it's finished, because I know I don't belong, and ought to find somewhere else. I don't know where that *else* is, either, but I'll get there soon. Garry's dead and gone, and there's no one left at where I am, but I would want to skedaddle in any case, otherwise I'll fly head-on into a juggernaut and die like Garry if I don't escape from this foggy pothole I've been in too long. Now that I can see the future I might write some good songs.

'You look as if you've swallowed a fairing,' Wayne said. 'I feel a bit like that. I just can't believe that maniac killed him, not to mention Keith. The wind's not howling like it was, so maybe we can go out and find him. I'll kick him from here to Tipperary if I get my hands on him.'

'I wouldn't waste my time,' Lance said. 'Let him rot. Anybody who has anything to do with something like that was rotten as soon as he was born, if not sooner.'

'How are we going to pass the time, though? Fred said he's seen a chopper, but we might be here all day. I'm bored to death now I'm not waiting to be blown up. And when I think of Garry I want to cry.'

Lance lay as far away as he could get, also wanted to cry but knew you never could. The mattress was damp and the wind cold, but his face burned at the pain in his leg, and he thought he was going to sleep, or faint.

'We should make an effort to welcome them,' Fred said. 'Stand outside and wave. They've found us, and they're circling to find a landing place.'

No one seemed bothered. He straightened his jacket, brushed dust and cigar ash from his waistcoat, and took a comb out of his lapel pocket like a concert party magician who had proved it to be empty a moment ago. If he could find a better suit he would change into it, though who could be a pretty picture after such a night?

All of them looked wounded, walking wounded thrown into a bombed-out building after a skirmish, sprawled any old how, and dead to the wide, unable or unwilling to care, couldn't even put hands over their ears to stop the roaring of the blades, though it seemed like the best of music to Fred.

The fun was about to begin. Welcome to The White Cavalier Hotel – as was, gentlemen, as was – though having been the host, and still am even over the ruins, I have put a bottle of something very extra old and special on the table for you to partake of on this wintry but nonetheless soon to be beautiful morning.

20 November 1991
St Pargoire-London